THE
GATHERING
STORM

**Center Point
Large Print**

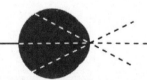

**This Large Print Book carries the
Seal of Approval of N.A.V.H.**

ZION DIARIES

THE GATHERING STORM

BODIE & BROCK THOENE

CENTER POINT PUBLISHING
THORNDIKE, MAINE

This Center Point Large Print edition is published in the year 2011 by arrangement with Riggins International Rights Services, Inc., agents for Summerside Press.

Scripture references are from
The Holy Bible, King James Version (KJV).
"A Nightingale Sang in Berkeley Square," words by Eric Maschwitz, music by Manning Sherwin and Jack Strachey, first performed in 1939, on page 461.
"I Shall Not Live in Vain," by Emily Dickinson
(1830-1886) on page 404.

The text of this Large Print edition is unabridged. In other aspects, this book may vary from the original edition. Printed in the United States of America on permanent paper. Set in 16-point Times New Roman type.

ISBN: 978-1-60285-934-0

Library of Congress Cataloging-in-Publication Data

Thoene, Bodie, 1951–
The gathering storm / Bodie & Brock Thoene. — Center Point large print ed.
p. cm.
ISBN 978-1-60285-934-0 (lib. bdg.: alk. paper)
1. World war, 1939–1945—Germany—Berlin—Fiction. 2. Large type books.
I. Thoene, Brock, 1952– II. Title.
PS3570.H46G38 2011
813′.54—dc22
2010040908

With love for Natan Shalom—
"He gives Peace"

JEREMIAH 1:7

PROLOGUE
DECEMBER 22, 2008
HAMPSTEAD VILLAGE,
LONDON, ENGLAND

The sun set as I rode the Northern Line from central London north to Hampstead Village for the scheduled interview with the woman I had come to know as "Loralei B.G."

Lora had escaped from the Nazi Blitzkrieg as a young woman. Over fifty years had passed when the old woman read my early nonfiction account about the Kindertransport of Jewish children and the evacuees during the Blitz. She contacted me through the publisher.

Her letter read:

I am a Christian Zionist, not Jewish by birth, but by heart and through marriage. I was born in Texas to a missionary family, though I grew up in Europe. My mother was American. My father was an Austrian and among the leaders of the Christian resistance opposing Hitler. He was killed by the Nazis in France during the war. I was very involved with the refugees. Perhaps I could add details to your research.

Over ten years' time I received Lora's story in bits and pieces by post. The true identity of Lora remained a closely guarded secret because her son was a member of the Israeli government. I was faithful to answer her letters at a box in northwest London. Before the era of e-mail we became old-fashioned pen pals.

Though uncertain of Lora's true age, I guessed she was in her late seventies or early eighties. Though I knew many details of the elderly woman's past, I knew surprisingly little about her present life. When the letters began to come less frequently, I wondered if her health was failing. Perhaps the old woman's sense of dignity was one reason she did not want to meet me.

Now, as Lora approached the end of her life, she reached out to me. I received a telephone call from her granddaughter, also named Loralei. It had come one month earlier, summoning me to a home on Church Row in Hampstead Village.

"Will you come for dinner on December twenty-second? Your old friend would like to meet you before Christmas."

I knew the Hampstead street well. My husband and I frequently met friends for supper at the Holly Bush pub around the corner. How strange it seemed to me that I had probably passed Lora's house a hundred times over the years and had never known she lived there.

The aroma of roasting chestnuts greeted me as I emerged from the tube station onto Hampstead's

High Street. It was the stuff Christmas carols were made of. Irresistible.

Shifting a big bouquet of roses, I buttoned my jacket against the sudden chill and fished for the heavy one-pound coins in my jeans' pocket. "One, please."

"American? Done in a minute." The chestnut seller stirred a fresh batch over the coals of his brazier. "The south?"

"Close, Henry Higgins. Arkansas, originally. Then central California."

His eyes brightened. "Arkansas. Y'all?"

"Arkansas may have seceded from the Union since I left. I've lived in London for ten years."

"Then you're almost home."

"Almost."

He scooped the warm chestnuts into a fist-sized, brown paper bag. "Very hot. Take care. Cheers, thanks, and happy Christmas."

Pocketing the paper sack, I used it as a hand warmer. Striding quickly past shops, restaurants, and my favorite creperie, I made my way toward the Georgian townhomes lining Church Row.

Christmas garlands and twinkle lights gave the village a feel like something out of a Dickens' novel. I shelled a hot chestnut and popped it into my mouth. Nothing like it on a cold winter's night.

The directions to the house simply said, *House on the end of the row—right. Corner of Holly Walk and Church Row.*

Eighteenth-century construction had not included street numbers on houses. Instead, fan-shaped windows called *fanlights,* above the front doors, contained a unique pattern used to identify the residence. Like a logo, letterhead on household stationery reproduced the pattern of the residence's fanlight. The image was then copied on all answered correspondence. This assured even an illiterate messenger could look at an envelope, compare the patterns, and deliver mail to the correct residence.

I walked briskly to the imposing brick townhouse. Christmas lights beamed from every window. I could plainly see in the leaded glass of the fanlight the images of a nightingale and a rose.

Beautiful, I thought. It was so much like the Lora I had come to know through correspondence: the rose and the nightingale; a story by Oscar Wilde; or a poem by Keats. Like much of London, coded in the very building was the memory of a distant, more noble, age.

I suddenly wished I had not worn jeans and my usual black ostrich cowboy boots. I had meant to honor Texas, the state of Lora's birth, but I was acutely aware I was underdressed. And, worse yet, I looked like an American tourist. The dignified elegance of the Church Row townhome made me self-conscious.

I rapped the brass lion's-head knocker on the black door and announced my arrival. Holding the roses beneath my chin, I smiled, hoping the flowers would be noticed, rather than my casual attire.

Hinges groaned as the door opened. A beautiful young woman in her midtwenties beamed at me. Her hair was thick blond, shoulder length, and framed her oval face. With blue eyes and straight white teeth, I noticed the clear family resemblance to a photo Lora had sent of herself and her husband from those desperate years before the war.

"You must be Missus Thoene?" The young woman pronounced my name correctly in the accent of an American who had long lived in England. "Tay-nee? Is it? Welcome. I am Loralei Golah." She was wearing jeans and a red wool cardigan like mine.

I resisted the urge to mention our identical red sweaters. So she shopped at the street merchants' stalls in Covent Garden? I laughed. "You pronounced Thoene right. So few do. But call me Bodie. Thoene is for author bios."

Loralei said cheerfully, "Yes. Sunny eyes. Green. Like a forest in this light. Red curls. And the boots! Lora would love them. Her heart is half-Texan, you know. Yes, Bodie suits you."

Relief!

"So good to meet you. Loralei? Lora's granddaughter? You rang me. I recognize the smile in your voice. Happy Christmas."

Loralei inhaled the roses. "Oh, lovely! So beautiful! Who would think? Roses in the dead of winter. Must be grown in greenhouses, don't you suppose?"

Feeling instantly welcome, I stepped into the warm mahogany-paneled foyer. A row of coats was draped on a rack above an umbrella stand. When Loralei hung up my coat, hot chestnuts dribbled out.

I retrieved them, feeling like an idiot. "Kent. You can get everything out of season. Tomatoes, even."

Loralei headed off down a corridor and grinned back over her shoulder as a signal I should come along.

Happy to see me, I thought.

The aroma of basil and oregano in simmering sauce filled the house. Loralei said, "But winter tomatoes don't hold a candle to the ones from the garden in summer."

I followed Loralei into a living room decorated with fine antiques and wreathed in reds and golds for the holidays like an Oxford shop window. An eight-foot Steinway filled one end of the room, overlooking French doors and a garden. The instrument was open and sheet music of J. S. Bach was unfurled above the keyboard. The grand piano was more than mere decoration.

A small, drab bird fluttered in an ornate cage beside the piano.

"A nightingale," Loralei said. "I found her in the garden a month ago with a broken wing, the same day I rang you."

"She seems to be doing well," I marveled. "Nursing wild birds never worked out for me as a kid. I always ended up burying them in the flowerbed in shoeboxes."

"That's why she lives beside the piano. My husband sings to her."

"You're married." I noticed her ring for the first time.

"Enough about me. Look! We're both wearing jeans and red sweaters. I'm so glad. I wondered if I should dress up a bit. I've made pasta for dinner. There's Chianti. Garlic bread. Tri-color salad with balsamic. Hope the tomatoes are all right."

We both laughed, and I decided I liked her immensely and instantly. I followed her into the kitchen where marinara sauce steamed in a saucepan.

The table, antique pine, was set for two.

"Will Lora . . . ?"

"Not tonight. I'm sorry. But she has a Christmas gift for you—and a request for you. Please, sit down. Make yourself comfortable."

I obeyed, trying to conceal my disappointment. "Will she know I'm here?"

"She knows. I'll be right back." Loralei bounded up the stairs to the bedrooms. Doors opened and closed. I heard voices. A man's deep voice. The elderly voice of a woman. Was that Lora? The young Loralei laughed like a bright bell. Moments passed, and she returned with a thick black binder. I knew what it was. For several years I had been encouraging Lora to comb through her diaries and set down her own story.

"I've been typing it all out so you could read it. It's all here. Everything. She's written a book, you see. Her story, like you wanted her to. The full story. Changed the names, but the story . . . all the same. Before the war. And then the Blitz. She said you wrote her once and said you would stay up all night to review a manuscript if only she would write it down." She paused, hesitant for a moment as she searched my face. "Did you mean it? I mean, that you would like to read it?"

"Would I? I've begged her to write it down!"

"Well, then, she asked me if you would . . . would you read it? Tonight?"

I was ecstatic. Of all the interviews I had conducted and all the personal accounts I had gathered, not one person had ever taken me up on the suggestion that the stories should be set down.

Loralei blushed and, suddenly shy, said quietly, "She combed through her diary. Dictated into a recorder. Changed the names, of course. Pseudonyms. She wouldn't write it any other way. Details she wouldn't trust to anyone but you. I've read your books . . . and she . . . well, it would mean so much to her to have you review the manuscript. Offer suggestions. And, maybe someday . . . if you know a publisher perhaps?"

I felt cheered by the prospect of hours spent reviewing a manuscript no one had ever read before. What a gift!

We ate spaghetti while Loralei gleaned the details of my life and work. I answered her questions between bites of pasta. "I'm forty-four. Three kids in college. Family originally from around Fort Smith. University of Hawaii alum. Long story there. Working on my Ph.D. at London University. Married to Brock Thoene, Ph.D. in history, among other things. Researcher, writer, and director of an American study-abroad program in England."

When we finished dinner Loralei led me to an overstuffed chair before the fire. The black-covered journal was open on my lap: *The Book of Hours—L.B.G. Part One. War Years.*

Loralei patted my shoulder. "It's a quick read, I think. Quicker to read than it was to write. Only Part One. I'll wash up and bring coffee . . . coffee or tea?"

"Coffee, please."

"White or black?"

"Black."

"Go on . . . enjoy." Loralei poked at the coals in the fireplace. "I love a good fire and a good read.

She hopes . . . well, it reads like a novel, but she needs the help of an expert. Your help."

"I love a good story. Her letters are the bright spot of my day when they come. Always have been."

I suddenly realized this young woman knew a lot about me, but I knew nothing about her except the color of her eyes, that she cooked great pasta, liked red sweaters and boots, and wore a size six jeans.

Mellow baroque music played over the BBC. The fire crackled and embers glowed as the story of one life unfolded.

PART ONE

A time to get, and a time to lose;
A time to keep, and a time to cast away.

ECCLESIASTES 3:6

1

BRUSSELS, BELGIUM
MAY 8, 1940

The night before everything about my ordinary life changed forever, I dreamed a dream.

It was dark and I sat on a boulder in a garden where the stone of a tomb had been rolled away. A rose tree grew with thirty-six white roses in bloom beside the great stone. A nightingale sang in the branches among blossom and thorn.

I heard a soft voice like wind chimes sing, *"And if I want him to live until I return, what is that to you?"*

Sleeping or half-awake, I saw thirty-five men and women, each dressed in the costume of a different generation. They gathered outside the gaping mouth of the grave. They were discussing something. What was it? The war? The Jewish refugees who slept in the dorms of Alderman Seminary? The conversations seemed familiar to me, but I could not quite make out what they were saying.

The first in line, a pretty woman of middle age, with gentle brown eyes and soft curls, was wrapped in a cerulean blue shawl. She held a torch aloft. Stooping low, she entered the cave, fire first, carrying the flame into the darkness without terror. A golden glow emanated from the hewn

19

interior. Flickering light cast her shadow onto the feet of the tall young man who was second in line. He looked down at her shadow, then at his toes and smiled, before turning his face toward where I observed. He beckoned to me.

I did not move. I wondered how he had seen me dreaming about him. . . .

By and by the woman emerged, smiling, from the tomb and said quietly, "Death is conquered at last. It truly is empty. He is risen indeed."

She passed the torch to the man. He entered as she had and returned, declaring her proclamation to the next in line. And so it went through the hours of the night, from one witness to the next and then the next. One by one, they left the garden, and I could hear their footsteps and their voices. "Don't be afraid," they declared. "The tomb is empty. Death is no more."

Finally, the last of the thirty-five, his face concealed, emerged from the tomb and looked to the right and then the left. The sun was rising. "Who's next?" he called.

I was the only one remaining. I stood, and the light was too bright for me to see clearly. Lifting my hand to shield my eyes, I felt the handle of the torch pressed into my palm.

"It's your turn now. The long night is almost over. It's your turn to stand as witness. You shall be the Watchman on the Walls."

This, then, is my story.

MAY 9, 1940

Light shone through the stained glass flanking the green lacquered door of the stone cottage. Ruby red blossoms and emerald glass leaves made puddles of color on the flagstone steps. I stepped onto a rose-hued pool, shifted my valise, and fumbled for the latch key. Though my mother had died four months earlier, the engraving of my parents' names remained unaltered on the brass lion's-head door knocker: *ROBERT & JANET BITTICK.*

The lock clicked and turned. I wiped my feet and entered the dimly lit foyer. It was almost curfew in Brussels. I closed the blackout curtains. Today, May 9, 1940, was my twenty-second birthday. My first birthday without Mama. The house felt especially lonesome.

"I'm home," I called, hoping my sister, Jessica, and eight-year-old niece, Gina, might have dropped in. No one answered.

For most of seventeen years the stone head-master's cottage bordering the parklike grounds of Aaron Alderman Seminary had been home to our family. But things were changing. Since Easter, every male student in the school of theology had been called up to military duty in Belgium's antiquated army. The news reports were grim. If the Nazis attacked, few expected Belgium could survive.

The classrooms were empty. Those faculty who had connections abroad fled the chaos of Europe for England or America. But Robert Bittick remained. Faithful Papa. The Alderman buildings had been leased and were now managed by the Jewish Agency. The seminary was transformed into a transit hospice for Jewish refugees fleeing Nazi-occupied Poland. The ebb and flow of desperate strangers was constant.

Thirty-six Jewish orphan girls from Poland had been given Aryan names and enrolled in St. Mary's Convent school, where I taught English. Girls were easier to assimilate than circumcised boys. If the Nazis attacked Belgium—if Belgium fell—Jews would be the first to be eliminated. A girls' convent school like St. Mary's would remain a safe haven for the children.

With one finger I parted the blackout curtain and peeked out the window.

A thin sliver of forbidden light gleamed from Papa's office in the chapel. The air-raid warden would soon be knocking on the door to reprimand him. No light allowed. Only stars were permitted to shine brightly over Belgium. Perhaps Papa was immersed in another emergency meeting with the Jewish Agency. His grief over the loss of Mama had been submerged in travel permits and arranging passage for hundreds of Polish Jews to England and South America and the United States.

Perhaps Papa had forgotten my birthday. Without Mama to remind him, he was hopeless about remembering occasions.

I placed my briefcase on the scarred pine kitchen table. Opening a cupboard I mindlessly stared at the blue floral Meissen china Mama had bequeathed to me in a letter left in her top drawer.

And to my precious Loralei I leave my pair of silver candlesticks brought from Texas and also my best dishes. With them, I leave joy and laughter and the memories of all our special times together. . . .

On last year's birthday I had come home to a white linen tablecloth and places set for twelve guests. Since Mama's death, I had not once set the table with her shining legacy.

Not even a cup of hot tea was waiting for my homecoming this evening. The copper teakettle was cold on the unlit back burner of the stove. Without Mama, the kitchen—neat, quiet, and uncluttered—was the loneliest room in the house.

No wonder Papa could not bear to be in the cottage alone.

Papa was Austrian while Mama, Janet, had been born in Texas. They met at a Gipsy Smith revival meeting in 1909 and fell in love. Mama had a Texan's way of talking like no one else. She ended statements with a question, as if to ask if you really understood what she was talking about? Papa said she enchanted him. From their first conversation he knew she had to be his forever. They married two months after they met and Mama never stopped asking questions. Like a pair of eagles, their hearts were bound for life.

They pastored a church in a German-speaking settlement at Creedmore, Texas. My sister, Jessica, was born there, in 1911. I arrived seven years later. The family returned to Europe as missionaries after the "War to End All Wars" concluded. Though I had little memory of Texas, Jessica and I spoke perfect American English and considered ourselves Americans. Janet Bittick had not let her daughters forget their mother's first language. From our childhood, Papa made sure the honor of our U.S. citizenship was prominently noted on our identity papers.

I switched off the lights and retreated down the hall.

The parlor was dark. The keyboard of Mama's upright piano was open, and sheet music spread out on the stand.

Someone had been visiting. The piano was seldom played since Mama passed away. No one could pound out a song like she did. Honky-tonk and Southern Gospel music. *I'll fly away, Oh, Glory! I'll fly away!"* Mama could draw a crowd every time.

Perhaps some seminary student in a shining

new military uniform had stopped in to visit Papa before being called to duty in the Belgian army.

My husband, Varrick, and Jessica's husband of nine years, William, were together at the border. With most of the young men of Belgium they stood guard against possible invasion by the German army. The horror stories of the Nazi invasion of Poland were fresh in everyone's mind.

Entering my bedroom, I kicked the door shut with my foot and closed the curtains before turning on the lamp. I picked up the framed photograph of Varrick and me beside the river Zenne last summer. We were squinting into the sun as Mama grinned around the camera and snapped the shutter. Holding the frame against my heart, I could almost see Mama's face, commanding us to smile and not blink. With a sigh, I turned my back on the memory. What was a birthday, anyway, with so much going on in the world?

"Only another day. Never mind."

Replacing the snapshot, I switched on the tabletop radio. Glenn Miller's band filled the space with "In the Mood." American big band music was becoming more and more popular these days as everyone dreamed of sailing into New York harbor.

I held my arms up as if Varrick had come into the room and asked me to dance. A moment.

Imagination. Then I glimpsed my reflection in the round mirror on the wall. Alone. Same thick blond, unruly mane. Sad blue-gray eyes stared back at me as if I were seeing a stranger within my own reflection. Full red lips curved unconvincingly up at the corners as I tried on a smile. *"I want you to smile? Honey? Okay. Pretty. Pretty. Now don't blink while I just . . . just . . . say cheese?"*

I would not allow myself to think of other birthdays . . . like last year. *Belgian chocolate cake and presents on the table. Varrick and the young men from the seminary gathered 'round to serenade.* Who could have imagined what a difference one year could make? The sudden absence of Mama's cheerful strength had left me so weak.

I turned out the lamp, opened the curtains, and raised the window. Sinking onto the edge of the bed, I lay back on my pillow. The scent of lilacs drifted in. I remembered Mama planting the lilac bush on my tenth birthday. The thick bloom of Texas in her accent had returned. *"My darling girl? You're a big girl now. Ten years old? I can't believe it. Outside my bedroom window at home in Texas? When you were born? There were lilacs. Just beginning to bloom. Happy birthday. Happy, happy birthday, my Loralei. From now on? I'll always give you lilacs for your birthday. Forever. And when I fly away? Whenever you smell the scent of lilacs, you'll remember the sweet times of our life. . . . Can you hold onto that? How much your mama loved you? You'll remember me . . . remember us."*

It was past the dinner hour when I heard the sound of Papa and Jessica outside on the walk.

"But are they all leaving Belgium?" Jessica was incredulous. "Tonight?"

Papa replied somberly, "If they don't make it to France before this begins . . ."

Little Gina reprimanded, "Grandpa, my daddy won't let the Nazis in."

A moment of silence passed. I leapt to my feet and hurried to meet my father, sister, and niece in the foyer. The door swung open, and Jessica, eight months pregnant, threw her arms around me in an awkward embrace. "Oh, Lora, the Wehrmacht is massing at the borders tonight!"

As Papa nudged them into the parlor, Gina piped, "Oh, Auntie Lora! All the Jews in the seminary? Leaving tonight! Going to France. Maybe us too."

"Papa?" I questioned.

"True." Papa's dark brown eyes flashed concern as he glanced toward Jessica.

"But . . . us?" I put my arm around Jessica's shoulders. "How can we?"

Papa ran his fingers through closely cropped salt-and-pepper hair. The last months had wearied him immeasurably. "We can't stay. If they come . . ."

I understood who "they" were. But could it be that the Nazis intended to invade as they had in Poland? "Papa?"

Jessica replied quietly, "The train station. Chaos. Riots. They all want to get away."

Papa looked around the room as though choosing what to take away when we fled. "We're as much in the gunsights now as the people we have helped. It will be over in Belgium in a matter of days."

Jessica, alabaster skin pale and expression weary, spoke the name of her husband tenderly. "William."

Gina, the image of Jessica at that age, tossed blond curls fiercely and began to cry. "But Mommy! Auntie Lora? Will Daddy come with us too?"

I embraced the child. "Gina, if we must leave"—Papa nodded. It was a certainty—"your daddy will come along after us to France. Soon. He'll follow."

Gina clung to my waist and turned her face upward, imploring, "And your Varrick? Him too, Auntie Lora? Will Varrick and Daddy come together?"

"Together." I spoke confidently, but my knees felt suddenly weak. Leave Brussels? Leave the stone cottage at Alderman Seminary? The only real home I had ever known? Oh, why hadn't we left Belgium when the other members of

Alderman staff had fled? "Papa?" I questioned with a glance toward Jessica. "What about . . ."

Jessica's clear pewter eyes became determined. She caressed her belly and drew herself erect. "There are doctors in France. Still a month until I'm due. Gina was ten days late. By then? Surely . . ."

Papa seemed to gather strength in Jessica's courage. "Yes. By then, we'll be in Paris. The French army is the best equipped in the world. Your American passports. Your mama always said, better than gold." Papa instructed us, but his passport was Austrian, a nation now under the control of the Third Reich. "We may just have hours. One suitcase each only. I've saved enough petrol over the months from the rations. Enough for us to reach France in the automobile."

I lay in my bed, acutely aware this might be the last time I slept in my own familiar room for a long time. Maybe forever. The door to my room was ajar.

Jessica and Gina occupied the spare bedroom.

Papa's voice floated down the hallway. "Good night, Jessica. Angels keep you, little Gina!"

Gina's sweet voice replied in an almost perfect American accent, "You too, Grandpa. Big ones."

I heard my father's footsteps approach. He rapped softly and the door swung open. The light shone behind him. His hair was still mussed from his hat.

"Still awake, Daughter?" he asked quietly.

"Yes, Papa," I answered.

"I almost forgot your birthday." His voice was sad. "Happy birthday."

"It's okay. I almost forgot too. I think for next year I'll change the date anyway, or it will forever remind me of this night."

"Things will come right for us again. For the world." He spoke the words but was unconvincing.

"What now, Papa?"

He crossed his arms. "Mobilization full on. North railway station packed with soldiers today. I went to see some of the boys off. So many women and children saying good-bye. I fear our brave boys face an uphill battle."

"What will become of Belgium? King Leopold?"

"I looked at the signs in the station. The train to Waterloo. It's only an hour to the battlefield at Waterloo, where Napoleon was defeated by Wellington. Different tyrant, but a tyrant all the same."

"Will there be another Waterloo?"

"Another battle, yes. Seven years since Hitler destroyed the German democracy. Yes. But whose Waterloo this will be is almost certain. This time the Allies have no Wellington to pull it off."

"How long can we hold out?"

"Days, I think."

"I heard from the nuns at St Mary's. After school. They said Belgian soldiers have been issued wooden bullets. I told them it was only a rumor."

"Not a rumor, I'm afraid. Belgian officers are passing out wooden bullets. The kind they use in practice maneuvers."

We considered this bleak information for a long moment. I sighed. "Pointless against German Panzers. Just like what happened to the Poles."

Papa agreed. "Someone in the government must think it will make the soldiers feel better about things if their rifles make a big bang . . ."

". . . before they die."

"Our fortifications against the Germans are built to be impenetrable. So the Germans simply go around, or fly over."

"It is over, then, Papa? The battle for Belgium? Over before it's started?"

"Oh, Loralei, dear girl. I'm praying for a miracle. Miracles can happen."

"The Red Sea parted."

"We will pray."

I closed my eyes and whispered a prayer for Varrick and William. Would they fight the Blitzkreig with wooden bullets? "The Polish Jews have a saying. God is too high up, and America is too far away."

Papa replied, "We won't give up hope. Maybe the Germans will decide Belgium isn't worth their while. The lowlands of Holland. Maybe the Nazis will turn on Russia instead of us. Yes. We will pray."

"That's all that is left to us for the time being."

Papa was silent for a moment. "God is watching to see what brave men will do. That is everything, my dear. So, happy birthday, my darling girl. I'm sorry I forgot."

"We'll celebrate in Paris."

His voice smiled. "Well, then. There you have it. When we reach Paris, we'll have a lovely celebration. Until then, we'll pretend it's not yet your birthday."

"Night, Papa."

"Night, my darling girl." He turned to go, then paused, head bowed. "And . . . your mother loved you very much, you know."

"I'm sure of it."

"Always said you were the strong one. Stronger than your sister in a lot of ways. Texan at your core."

"Like Mama, I hope."

"Your mother always said God loves a good story. Courage and strength. Impossible battles."

I laughed gently. "Remember the Alamo, huh? These Nazis don't know what they're facing if America comes in."

"America must . . ." Papa's voice faltered. "Ah,

well. Enough of that. You'll need to be strong in the days ahead. For your sister's sake. You'll need to help her through this. If William doesn't . . . I mean, he likely won't be around when the baby is born."

"I will, Papa. Be strong, I mean."

"There's my girl. There's my Loralei."

"You should sleep now, Papa. Thanks for remembering."

He nodded and padded down the corridor toward his bedroom.

2

Morning seeped through the blackout curtains. I was sleeping soundly and did not hear the alarm. Little Gina shook me by the shoulder and cried, "Auntie Loralei, wake up! The Germans are coming!" She left, her little feet racing down the corridor.

I got up quickly and opened the curtains, revealing a red dawn with high, streaked clouds beyond the buildings of the seminary. I stood at the window, thinking how everything looked the same as always, but I whispered, "Red sky at morning . . ."

Before I finished the sentence a high formation of about two dozen planes rumbled overhead. The crimson gold of the sunrise glinted on their bellies. Suddenly, dark specks, like so many eggs, spilled out from the aircraft and began to fall. "Papa!" I cried.

The long, shrill whistle of falling bombs was followed by terrible explosions over the treetops.

Papa shouted, "Loralei! Come on! Come on!"

I ran from my room as Gina and Jessica tumbled out of the house and rushed to the air-raid shelter in the yard. Papa followed, slamming the door closed behind us. We stood in the dark as thunderous booms echoed overhead.

After the fact, the undulating wail of Brussels' air-raid siren began.

Jessica clamped her hands over Gina's ears. "Now they tell us!"

I felt the color drain from my face as I considered how ridiculous our tin shelter was against a hail of bombs. "Like closing the barn door after the horses are gone."

Papa fumbled to light the lantern. "We'll be safe here."

We all knew this was a lie meant to make us feel better. The eerie glow cast long shadows. I saw the dark circles under Papa's eyes. Had he slept at all?

Gina, staring, gaped up at the thin corrugated tin ceiling. "Grandpa?"

I patted Gina's shoulder. "It won't last long." My reassurance was unfortunately punctuated by a series of jolting booms as a stick of bombs found their mark.

Papa said, "The airport."

"The first bombs," Jessica remarked. "Was that the North Station?"

Images came to my mind: *Young Belgian soldiers waiting for the trains. Wives and children. Sweethearts who had come to say farewell.* "Papa?"

Papa closed his eyes and nodded. He swallowed hard. The boom of anti-aircraft guns commenced.

"We should all sit down." Papa motioned toward the benches as if we were waiting for a bus or waiting for a thunderstorm to pass.

I noticed we were all barefooted and in our nightgowns.

After an hour the all-clear signal sounded. Our little family sat silently, looking up for a few moments, as if we did not believe the attack was over.

"I'm hungry," Gina said at last.

"Well, then." Papa stood. "That's that. For now."

Another pause before he swung back the doors. Sunlight streamed in, together with the acrid scent of cordite. Above our heads the sky was marred by puffs of white smoke. Above the trees, the horizon of Brussels bloomed with black smoke.

"Poor things," I said as I stared in disbelief at the thick fumes roiling up from the direction of North Station. The clang of a fire truck's bell sounded some blocks away.

"Yes," Jessica whispered. "Poor, poor things."

• • •

The trains were no longer running. The frontiers were closed, yet an endless stream of refugees poured out of Brussels. The news on my radio was a muddle of confusion mixed with the monotony of American swing music, punctuated by Tchaikovsky's *1812 Overture.*

I did not attempt to go to work. I telephoned St. Mary's. A janitor answered with the information that St. Mary's Convent school was closed today for prayer and quiet contemplation.

With the strange incongruity of the commonplace popping up in the midst of great human drama, the postman arrived. Elderly and gray-haired, he carried his leather mail pouch over stooped shoulders. I saw him coming up the walk and threw back the door before he knocked.

"Good afternoon!" he spoke in French.

"I'm glad to see you." I wondered if I had ever been so happy to see a mailman at my door. "You're delivering the mail. Even with the bombing."

"I'm too old to fight. This is how I fight the Boche. I get on with my work." He passed me a stack of letters—delayed birthday cards, no doubt, some with American stamps.

"I'm glad to see you, all the same." I smiled and pocketed the greetings.

"I don't know if I told you: your mother was a

very fine lady. I suppose she is missed?" He knit his brow and adjusted his cap.

"Yes, very much. Thanks for saying so. She wouldn't think much of all this, though."

"No. I suppose not." He shifted his satchel to the other arm. "I see Alderman Seminary is empty. Those refugees. Where to go now, eh? I never had letters to deliver to them, but always there was mail to pick up. They were writing letters home to villages the Germans destroyed and to people who no longer exist. So, they've gone."

"Everyone at the seminary has gone."

"Poor Jews. Perhaps everyone else will adjust."

"They had to leave."

"Two steps ahead of the executioner, always." The postman looked upward, studying the sky for sign of bombers. "North Station is a burned-out hulk. Everyone who goes now will travel on the roads. Unhappy rumors. Trainloads of refugees who left Holland yesterday were machine-gunned. British tanks on the way here are blocked by refugees. The great fortress of Eben-Emael fallen to some secret weapon. German parachutists falling on the countryside like blossoms in a high wind."

"The radio is no use." I concluded that the postman's rumors were no use either.

"Will you still be here tomorrow?" He cocked his head like a dog listening for a whistle.

"Of course," I lied. I did not want my father's whereabouts to become one of the postman's rumors, repeated to the Gestapo if Brussels fell.

"Well, then, I will see you tomorrow. Good luck." He tipped his hat and trudged off to find some other family on his mail route who had not taken flight.

It was after midnight when air-raid sirens screamed again across Brussels. The howl awakened panic in Belgium before the bombs fell. In the far distance a sound like a kettledrum boomed the news of heroic last stands and brave men falling like dominos along the front. They were dying in order to buy time for some to escape.

"France!" came the cry as the booms grew nearer and louder.

As civilians took cover in basements and inadequate bomb shelters, others, including all the Jews remaining in Belgium, took to the highway.

Aaron Alderman Seminary was dark. Fires were reflected in the window glass. Not one Jew remained on the grounds, and those who could leave were fleeing through the dark countryside. Soon enough the seminary would become quarters for Nazi soldiers.

Papa announced we had waited long enough.

Who will live in the stone cottage? I wondered, as I selected a few small mementos to take away with me. *Who will eat off Mama's china plates?*

. . . Some member of the Nazi party might live here, box up the Meissen china, and ship it home to his heiling *wife.*

The thought struck me like a thunderbolt. Suddenly I was angry—angry at the waste of all this.

Behind me Jessica asked, "What are you thinking?"

"I hate them. I don't want some little SS butcher eating off Mama's dishes."

We two sisters stood before the open cupboard. Place settings for twelve. Oh, the memories in all those dishes.

Jessica said, "They were meant to be yours. She left them for you."

"I'm taking one teacup and a saucer. And here. One for you, and one for Gina too." I stretched out my hand to the neat stacks of plates. "We'll never be back."

"No," Jessica concurred.

"They won't have them. I won't let them have one more thing. They are thieves. Butchers! Jessica, I tell you I won't let them eat off Mama's plates."

Jessica crossed her arms and stepped back, smiling defiantly. "Then do it!"

I slipped a plate from the stack. Holding it to my heart, I kissed the blue lilac in the center. "I won't let them steal you. I won't let them toast their pagan gods above your shining beauty."

"Go ahead," Jessica cried, "do it! Mama would want you to!"

With all my might I hurled the plate against the wall. It shattered with a mighty crash. Again and again I smashed the plates until only the teapot and three sacred teacups and saucers remained. I passed the teapot to my sister. "One for Mama."

Jessica smiled like a bitter, fierce warrior and raised the teapot high. She held it there, then heaved it mightily onto the floor.

We stared at the mess and began to laugh. We laughed until tears rolled down our cheeks. We finished with a single sigh.

"We're done here, then," Jessica said, lifting her chin. "Well done, Texan."

Neither of us looked back as we left the kitchen.

I brought Papa my valise. I knew it was too heavy to carry if we had to walk. But what could I leave behind?

Papa pulled the Fiat halfway out of the garage and began to load it with supplies.

I returned to the house for a last look around. Had we forgotten anything crucial? What if Jessica's baby came while we were on the road?

I gathered a few more towels, a washbasin, and disinfectant. Papa had packed groceries. Tea and sugar. Beans and noodles. I snatched up the teakettle and an armful of tin picnic mugs. Surely there would be a stove along the way—some place to boil water for a cup of tea.

The pitch of the air-raid siren changed. I dashed from the house and peered up into the starlit sky. How brightly the stars shone since the lights of every city and village had been blotted out.

Suddenly Brussels fell silent. It was an expectant silence, like the pause between the movements of a symphony.

And, most incongruously, it was pervaded with the scent of lilacs.

Papa called to me quietly, "Almost ready, Loralei?"

"Yes, Papa." I stowed the practical gear beneath the dashboard within easy reach. In my suitcase was a shoebox filled with Papa's love letters and family photos, along with unopened birthday greetings I would read in Paris. I had allowed myself to pack the Meissen teacups and saucers with Mama's silver candlesticks in my valise. High heels and dresses were left behind. I needed only practical clothes—lederhosen and hiking shoes—in case we had to abandon the car and take off across country on foot.

The nervousness of the unknown that had plagued me was suddenly gone. I was calm.

From the stream of civilians passing by the cottage, someone paused at the foot of the driveway and shouted the news: "Pastor Bittick! The Nazis! Broken through! Our line collapsed in less than an hour! Killed all the men of the First. All!"

Jessica's arms fell limp at her sides. "William." She whispered her husband's name.

My stomach twisted into a knot. Grief closed my throat. I knew if William had fallen at the front, Varrick would be at his side. What was it I had said to Papa? *"Remember the Alamo?"*

Gina's sleepy voice called, "Is Daddy coming with us, Mommy?"

Jessica squared her shoulders and looked beyond the Fiat toward the small churchyard where Mama was buried. Her headstone had not yet been put in place on the grave. "No, Gina. No, baby. Daddy won't be going with us."

I slid my arm around my sister's waist. "Jessica?"

"Don't, Loralei. Don't talk sweet to me right now. I'll break."

So, the Germans had sliced through the lines like a hot knife through butter. The worst fears of what remained of unoccupied Europe were coming true. Hitler had broken his promises to the neutral nations.

The sirens fell silent. The sound of feet and handcarts trudging on the road filled the night. An occasional sniffle could be heard.

Jessica bit her lip, then returned to the task at hand. She arranged a bed in the backseat of Papa's auto for Gina and tucked her in. Baby things and boxes of emergency food and water, and Mama's medical supplies from her years as a nurse were stashed in the trunk, out of reach of the hands of hungry exiles.

Papa's black 1928 Fiat 528 convertible had been an elegant automobile in its day, but years of hauling seminary students on mission trips across Europe had left its once-sleek black finish dull and dinged. Mama had told me more than once as Papa set out on his journeys that the Fiat reminded her of a packed prairie schooner heading west across the Rockies to the Promised Land.

Where was the Promised Land tonight? I wondered, as refugees streamed past Alderman. I plucked two sprigs of lilac blossoms. One, I tucked into my Bible. The other I carried to Papa.

Papa tightened the cords around the suitcases and boxes tied to the running boards. "The tank is full of petrol." He seemed comforted that he had been wise with the rations. Perhaps wise enough to save his family.

"Papa?" I nodded toward the cemetery gate and handed him the lilac sprig.

"Yes . . . yes," he answered, then strode away briskly. The hinges of the gate groaned as he entered. Minutes passed. He returned without the lilac bloom and hurried past us. I heard the jingle of keys as he locked the front door of the stone cottage.

A futile gesture in the face of the Blitzkrieg.

I climbed into the front seat beside Papa.

Jessica sat in the back, cradling Gina's head as the child slept. The engine roared to a start. The Fiat lurched a bit as Papa pulled it from the garage, and it rumbled down the driveway.

I turned my face to look back one last time. Memories flooded my mind, and I relived the days when I first loved Eben Golah, and Varrick first loved me.

PART TWO

A time to embrace,
and a time to refrain from embracing.
ECCLESIASTES 3:5B

3
1936

The summer of the Olympic games, Berlin filled with people from all over the globe. Nazi propaganda against Jews quieted down for a time. Demonstrations of Aryan superiority and the smooth workings of National Socialism in a former democracy took center stage. For a short time the borders to free nations were open for us to travel.

My father obtained tickets for us to see the American track team perform superbly. Then we left the oppressive heat of Germany and crossed the border into Switzerland, where my parents had arranged for us to stay in a cottage at a resort near Geneva.

It was late afternoon when we stepped from the train. Suddenly I noticed a tangible difference in the expressions of the people on the platform. They were smiling. Their eyes seemed clear. They spoke to one another without turning their heads from side-to-side to see who might be listening. Outside the oppression of Germany I felt as if I could breathe freely. The air of Switzerland was pure and the sky more blue than I had ever seen. I felt so happy to be alive. I did not think of what was happening in Germany.

A white-haired woman of about fifty years of age hurried toward us and our heaps of luggage. I knew she recognized my parents, though I had never met her. Her eyes were blue like the Swiss heavens. She greeted my parents cheerfully, "I am Frau Helga Thoenen. You are Pastor and Frau Bittick. Welcome! Where do you want to go?"

Papa answered, "We have come seeking freedom."

Frau Thoenen smiled again. "You have come to the right place. The others will be so happy you have come."

By the time we piled into a large touring car, we were already on a first-name basis. Frau Helga and Papa stowed our bags. Mama's face was suffused with peace. We set off from the station as clouds rolled in, and it began to rain. The wipers barely kept up with the downpour. Frau Helga, undaunted, began to sing in time with the rhythm of the ticking blades: "Joyful, joyful, we adore thee. . . ." We all joined in.

It was a long ride to the hotel. I fell asleep against Mama's shoulder.

When I awoke, it was dark. The rain had stopped, and the full moon was rising above the majestic peaks. A bridge of silver light reflected on the water of a lake.

The car halted at an ornate iron gate. I smelled the fragrance of white roses blooming in profusion on the fence.

Frau Helga turned to us. "Welcome to the White Rose Inn."

We drove down a long gravel driveway to a hotel flanked by expansive gardens and guesthouses. I heard voices as we pulled up and recognized one voice in particular. By the light of the moon I saw my father's friend, Eben Golah, come down the steps. Twenty-six, or so, built like a wrestler, smiling broadly and wearing a light linen jacket . . . was I dreaming? I thought I had never seen any man so handsome.

Eben opened the door. "Welcome home, Frau Helga. Who have you brought?"

Frau Helga replied, "Make them welcome, Eben. They are in search of freedom."

I suddenly realized the repeated phrase was a password of sorts.

Eben gripped Papa's hand and helped Mama out of the car. Then, in a sort of miracle, as I emerged, Eben wrapped his arms around me in a wonderful embrace and kissed my cheek. "Look at you, Lora! All grown up. A white rose in bloom. How beautiful you are."

His attention, though intended as kindness to a somewhat gawky eighteen-year-old girl, made me blush. I was grateful that the moonlight hid my rising color. I was in turmoil. I had left Germany less than twenty-four hours before.

Now Eben held my heart captive.

There were a dozen others at the White Rose Inn

who had gathered with a purpose. As we ate a cold supper, we were joined at the buffet by families of Christian leaders and leaders of the Zionist movement. Over an abundance of food, the adults spoke about evacuations and the logistics of children's transports from Nazi Germany to England, America, and Canada. Boys and girls my age introduced themselves. A tennis match was arranged for us for the next day while our parents discussed Hitler and the American isolationists. I only heard Eben's voice among them all.

We were settled in a beautiful little cottage with two bedrooms and a loft, where I slept. My windows opened to a balcony looking out over flower gardens and a wide, tree-filled lawn that sloped down to the edge of the lake. From my perch I could clearly see the porch of Eben's cottage. While in Switzerland, I often sunned myself while he sat in his lawn chair and read or scribbled notes.

We stayed at the White Rose Inn for six perfect weeks. I lived for Eben that summer. His glance lit a fire in me that I had never felt before. The strength and confidence with which he spoke made me ever more shy and silent. He was amused by my blush when he smiled and called me his white rose.

How could he know what had happened to my heart?

By day a group of young people my age played on the beach, swam, or played tennis or lawn bowling. At night we gathered around a bonfire to sing and tell stories. I dutifully wrote picture postcards of the magnificent Swiss countryside to my friends.

But each day as I posted the cards, I knew that my fickle heart had already relegated everyone else to close acquaintances.

Our cottage was a hotbed of anti-Nazi gatherings. Pastors and leaders of the Jewish Agency met together in Papa's study to discuss how to quietly evacuate Jewish children from the inevitable persecution we all knew was coming.

I hovered in the shadows of my loft like a little bird as they held endless discussions about Hitler. As they speculated about how long Hitler could last, I memorized the tilt of Eben's head and the gestures of his beautiful, square hands as he spoke.

All the guests at the White Rose celebrated the news that the black American sprinter, Jesse Owens, beat out Hitler's Aryan athletes at the games.

The events of the Olympic Games in Germany I relegated to unreality. Nothing mattered but my plan to find some moment alone with Eben so I could tell him I loved him.

I noticed that every morning he strolled a mile into the village to buy a newspaper. As summer drew to a close, I realized I was nearing my last opportunity to confess my feelings for him.

I rose early and, ahead of Eben, hurried up the lane. About halfway to the village, I found a shady spot beside a pasture where Hafflinger mares grazed with their foals. I sat down to wait. After a half hour, when he still did not come, I became entranced by the sight of the colts galloping across the field. I did not hear Eben's step behind me.

He spoke my name. "Lora?"

I blushed. The warmth of desire uncoiled in me. I felt my heart pounding. Everything I wanted to say fled from my mind.

"The horses," I said, gripping the fence rail.

I felt him come near. "Beautiful," he said in a wistful voice.

I turned. My voice caught. "Eben . . ." I faltered. "I love you."

He lifted his hand, as though he would touch my cheek. He smiled down into my eyes as if he had never known an unhappy moment. "White rose. So beautiful. So young."

"Not so young."

"Centuries too young, Lora."

"You aren't yet thirty. I heard Papa say so," I protested.

When he held me in his gaze for a long moment, I knew he had thought about me. "You are a memory, Lora . . . so familiar. Another lifetime. Another place. A different world . . . it might have been."

"Why not now, Eben?" I threw myself at him.

He plucked my arms from around his neck and stepped back. "Go home now, or I shall tell your father." Turning on his heel, he strode off angrily.

I wept in the forest for the rest of the day.

On Friday afternoon, Frau Helga Thoenen made preparations for a Shabbat meal. Her dinner was an elegant affair. Long tables were set up on the lawn of the White Rose Inn. I helped her spread white tablecloths and set her fine china. Sterling silver gleamed in the golden sunlight of the late afternoon.

With a smile she inspected our work and said to me, "Soon it will be the rose hour." She held up an instructive finger. "But where are the roses, my dear?"

I blinked at her. Three vases positioned as centerpieces were empty. "I'll gather them."

She placed a basket and shears in my arms. "Three dozen precisely. Thirty-six white roses. Mind the thorns."

I examined the flowers, choosing only the most beautiful blossoms on the rose tree. Perhaps I took too much time at my task. A string quartet was already setting up their music stands when I arrived back at the tables. Frau Helga wore a beautiful sky blue frock, while I was still in my work clothes. Other guests, elegantly dressed in party clothes, began to emerge from the cottages.

Frau Helga seemed pleased with my selection of blooms. "Well done, Lora. I'll set them out. You'll want to wear your prettiest dress tonight, I think."

Eben drew my attention. He was wearing white linen trousers and a blue pinstriped jacket with a red tie. I was certain his clothing was chosen as a salute to the American and British athletes in the Olympic games. He leaned against the railing of his porch, gazed off at the still water of the lake, and inhaled deeply.

I had never seen any man so handsome.

Frau Helga noticed my wistful look toward Eben. "He will sing for our company tonight."

"Eben sings?"

"Eben is a nightingale, my dear. He sings like an angel. You'll see."

I grinned stupidly. My schoolgirl adoration must have shown like a spotlight. "He does everything well."

"And you are his white rose, it seems."

I did not understand what she meant. "Eben calls me his White Rose."

"You know the legend, the one of the white rose and the nightingale, surely?" she asked, arranging the flowers. "My favorite story. I named the inn *White Rose*, because I love the tale so much."

I shook my head, wishing I knew more. "I'm sorry. No."

"An ancient legend. Would you like to hear it?"

I nodded eagerly and trailed after her, passing her roses one at a time.

"From a high mountaintop in Eden, a Nightingale fell in love with a beautiful White Rose. White Rose called to him each day as the sun set, and he sang to her through every night. Then one day, the serpent came into the garden and decided that he wanted White Rose all to himself. He wound himself around her trellis, threatening to choke her into submission. She called out in terror. Nightingale flew to save her. He battled the serpent, flying at him again and again. At last the serpent struck him, sinking poisonous fangs into his brave heart. Nightingale fell, singing his last song, as his blood dripped onto the White Rose. With every drop of Nightingale's blood, a thorn suddenly grew up to surround and protect the White Rose. When the serpent tried to claim her as his own, he could not penetrate the hedge of thorns. Nightingale fell dead at the foot of the White Rose. And where he lay, next spring, a red rose tree grew up. The white and the red roses grew side by side; two became intertwined."

"A lovely story," I said, gazing at the vases as the quartet warmed up with Mozart. "But sad."

"Sad? No. A happy ending, yes? So the two bloom together for eternity in Eden."

"But what about the nightingale?"

"He sacrificed himself to save the white rose. He gave his life for hers. By the shedding of his blood, the white rose was given life. A picture of Christ, some say."

I was both fascinated and terrified by the thought that Eben might be my nightingale. How would I go on living if anything ever happened to him? I was also mildly disturbed that he might believe I needed saving from something sinister.

As I skipped off to wash and change into my party frock, I watched him out of the corner of my eye. His gaze followed me as I ran to our cottage.

I was the last person to be seated beneath the stars. Candles were lit, and we welcomed the Shabbat.

Eben sang a Jewish blessing over our meal in a clear baritone that I thought must surely call angels from heaven to listen. It was strange, ancient music I had never heard before. It stirred my heart, which for a little time took my mind off myself, and made me turn my eyes toward the stars. Just for a few moments Eben was my Nightingale, and I was his White Rose.

It was to be our last journey as a family before we returned home. Papa and Eben and several others from the White Rose Inn had a meeting in Rome with Jewish Agency leaders. All had a passion to remove Jewish children from Hitler's persecution.

Papa and Mama had a private compartment on the train from Switzerland, but I preferred to ride in the observation car. I carried two volumes, which Frau Helga had loaned me. One was a thin volume of Keats poetry, and the other was the Jane Austen novel, *Pride and Prejudice.* I finished the romance novel early in the journey. Then, reading Keats' verse, I imagined I was Elizabeth Bennet, and that Eben Golah, austere and remote and handsome, embodied the character of Darcy.

We wound slowly southward through the great mountains.

In the dining car, Eben stopped for brief conversation with Papa and Mama. He did not look at me at first, until he noticed my copy of the poems of John Keats.

"Is this yours, Lora?" he asked with a sort of wonder in his voice.

"Frau Helga loaned it to me." I blushed at his attention. How I hated to blush. "I read the poem about the nightingale."

"Ah, did you? And do you enjoy the poetry of John Keats?" Eben thumbed through it. He found a verse he recognized and, to my astonishment, recited it rather than read from the page.

"When I have fears that I may cease to be
Before my pen has glean'd my teeming brain,
Before high piled books, in charactery,
Hold like rich garners the full-ripen'd grain;
When I behold, upon the night's starr'd face,
Huge cloudy symbols of a high romance,
And think that I may never live to trace
Their shadows, with the magic hand of chance;
And when I feel, fair creature of an hour!
That I shall never look upon thee more,
Never have relish in the faery power
Of unreflecting love!—then on the shore
Of the wide world I stand alone, and think
Till Love and Fame to nothingness do sink."

"Bravo," Papa said.

Eben's perfect lips curved slightly upward as he wistfully scanned the page. "I got it right, I see. After all these years." He closed the book.

I said quietly, "I understand the meaning of the words, but not the nuance."

Eben reared back a bit. "Keats' poetry is all nuance. John Keats' grave is in the Protestant Cemetery in Rome. Perhaps you and your mother should visit. It's in the guidebooks. A lonely place. He insisted there be no name carved upon his marker, just an epitaph: *Here lies one whose name is written on water.* He left his life in England and the girl he loved. Not yet thirty, he vanished from his world. Keats did not believe his poems would be ever be read and appreciated by a lovely young woman in a distant generation."

I answered, "I think his name should have been written in stone, not water."

"Perhaps in this generation his name is stone at last." Eben replaced the book beside my water glass and, with his characteristic bow, moved on to his own table at the opposite end of the car.

4
1937

While other Christian pastors ran from trouble, my father faced it head on. Papa accepted a temporary position as the pastor of a church in Berlin. Mama's American citizenship offered us some protection, but all the same, it was a dangerous time to be an outspoken Christian.

It was in the fall of 1937 when I first met Varrick Kepler. We both attended the recently and loftily renamed Reinhard Heydrich Unified Academy in Dahlen, formerly known as the Dahlen School. I'm quite sure Heydrich, a rising star of Hitler's SS, had no knowledge our little school had been named after him, nor would he care. But the new school administration agonized over the renaming for months. They held a formal ceremony at the beginning of the term.

Because of my nationality, I was fortunate to attend this model university prep academy. Most of the nation's schools segregated male from female students in the principal subjects, but ours did not. While young men were being taught their lessons, young women worked silently alone . . . but I was always listening to what the other sex was being taught. I knew the reverse was true for Varrick as well. I was the token American. Varrick was the token Jew.

The papers' insistence that indoctrination was not occurring was for the benefit of non-Germans. The state-controlled media was ordered to allay the fears of a war-weary world. The Germany that was rising again, less than twenty years after the end of the Great War, was an amiable neighbor and not quarrelsome.

Of course, we also recognized the frightening implications of such reports. If newspapers were making claims on behalf of the government, claims we knew to be false from firsthand experience, then it stood to reason their other denials were actually a kind of "reverse inventory" of what the Nazis were, in fact, doing or planning.

The papers proclaimed:

Lebensraum, the supposed intention of Germany to expand beyond the borders established in the Treaty of Versailles, is not being taught in our schools. But an accurate history of geography will not be hidden from our youth. Should we lie to them? Should they be told that Germany was not once. . . .

And,

This government has no intention of wasting money imprisoning individuals who've committed no crime. Law-abiding Jews are free to live their lives and conduct their business in peace, so long as that business does not conflict with. . . .

And,

Chancellor Hitler was very congratulatory of the Negro American Athlete Jesse Owens. Rumors that Hitler remarked on the Negroes' supposed lack of intelligence and sub-human origins are false. . . .

It was after a "science" lecture related to this last event that my newfound admiration for Varrick occurred.

"Without question," Herr Schmidt remarked, "the Negro is an inferior species to the Caucasian. There is near-universal scientific consensus on the point, and those who disagree are considered lunatics by researchers of actual experience. It is their subhuman, animal-like nature that allows them to excel in purely physical endeavors, yes, even above the Aryan. But their brains are no bigger than a dog's, and their incapacity for higher thought is scientifically verified. So, while the Negro may be able to run faster or jump higher, who here would ever trade your place as an Aryan for that of a Negro?"

Herr Schmidt meant the question rhetorically and as a joke, but he paused and looked around the room as if someone might respond affirmatively.

In that moment, Varrick pounced. Slowly raising his hand from his place in the back row, he cleared his throat so Herr Schmidt and the whole class would know.

"A funny man," Herr Schmidt replied, and a few students laughed nervously.

But Varrick did not put his hand down.

Herr Schmidt glared at him. "Do you mean to say, Varrick, that you would prefer to be a mindless, inferior Negro, so long as you could win foot-races?"

Varrick inhaled deeply as he rose from his seat to respond. Before then I had not noticed how tall he was.

"Do *you* mean to say, Herr Schmidt, that there has never been a Negro who contributed anything of intellectual value to the world?" Varrick's eyes flashed defiantly.

"I certainly can think of none, can you?" Herr Schmidt had not finished his question before Varrick began his response.

"Benjamin Banneker, 1731 to 1806, accurately predicted solar and lunar eclipses based on his own calculations, and published them in almanacs. Lewis Latimer, 1848 to 1928, made significant improvements to electric lights. Dr. Daniel Hale Williams, 1856 to 1931, performed the world's first open-heart surgery. Garrett Morgan, born 1877, invented the gas-mask. George Washington Carver. . . ."

The list had been uttered so quickly and so calmly, that at first Herr Schmidt was too stunned to respond. Finally, in sneering reference to Varrick's heritage, he shouted, "And what has a single dirty Jew given us?"

Varrick's face drained of color. He stood, silent and staring, white knuckles on clenched fists. I knew he was fighting an intense battle within himself: whether or not to beat Herr Schmidt to a pulp in front of the class.

Schmidt turned his back on Varrick, picked up a piece of chalk, and began writing on the blackboard. The rest of our classmates remained facing backward in their seats. All eyes were fixed on Varrick as he inhaled raggedly and sank to his seat. His hands, now unclenched, shook slightly as he busied himself tidying a small stack of paper and a pencil at his desk.

As students turned their attention once again to the front, Herr Schmidt resumed his lecture. "Margaret Sanger," he barked, underlining her name on the board, "is perhaps the most notable *scientist* in the field of Malthusian Eugenics. It is her contention that the suffering of the Negro through hunger and poverty could be much reduced by affording them access to birth control and sterilization . . . a position very much in concert with Chancellor Hitler's own views. In fact, she has established, in a primarily Negro population center, an office of her American Birth Control League."

This reference to Margaret Sanger, an American who endorsed Hitler's racial policies, was aimed at me.

I suffered silently through the remainder of the class.

Outside, I couldn't wait to congratulate Varrick.

"The *look*." I laughed, giddy with the memory, as we passed the crumbling complex of an abandoned dairy farm. "Oh Varrick, did you see the look on his face?"

"I lost" came the sullen reply.

I stopped and grabbed his arm, turning him toward me. Only then did I see angry tears hanging beneath both of his eyes. "What do you mean, Varrick? That was wonderful! You gave him all those names, those facts, that *prove* how ridiculous—"

"But I couldn't give him one of my own!" He pulled his arm from my hand. "I could have known he would insult me when he had no answer, but I said nothing. Lora, I dreamed of saying those things when Herr Schmidt first described this lesson at the beginning of term. I knew that when he brought it up again, I would be ready for him. But I wasn't. It was the way he attacked! In that moment I had not even one example in my mind of one of my own people who had contributed anything meaningful to civilized society. And the way he phrased the question, what could I say? Would the salvation of our Lord Jesus be a good example of something 'a dirty Jew' gave the world? But I couldn't even think to say that! I lost."

As he turned from me and wiped his eyes with his forearm, I stepped around to keep in front of him. "Varrick."

He turned away again.

"Varrick."

I stepped again; he turned again, I stepped again, and we shared a little laugh before resuming a slower pace. Varrick walked me home nearly every day, though he lived quite the opposite direction. We continued awhile in silence, but I knew I had to make him understand how brave he'd been, especially in my eyes. "You did *not* lose. Anyway, that was not a *debate;* it was a personal insult. The fact Herr Schmidt had to resort to such a childish response means you *won!*"

"But knowing I'm right is not the same as *showing* I am, in front of people who might otherwise believe such stupidity," he said sternly. He was very earnest then: "Lora, things will only get worse. If I . . . if *we* are not prepared for *everything* to come, this lunacy will continue until . . . I don't know what will happen. I just know that they're very bad people, the ones who make these claims based on *science,* and they will use gullible people to do unspeakable things if we don't all know how to speak up."

It was as if the devil himself wanted to prove Varrick's point to me. Just then four of the boys from our class stepped around a corner as we approached it. It was Webber and Wilmar, the tow-headed Funk twins, and two new boys who'd only just come to Reinhard Heydrich the week before.

" 'Tag," Wilmar said, nodding. Webber repeated the greeting, though quieter, with a nervous chuckle. The other two boys said nothing, but they fanned out to form a semi-circle around Varrick and me.

At first I didn't realize their intention, so I returned their salutation, "Good day."

Varrick stepped forward and guided me behind him with a sweep of his arm. "Come, Lora, your father will be looking for us. We should get back to school before he sets out this way to find us."

"My father?" I repeated dumbly. But as I looked around Varrick's arm and saw the sneering faces of the other boys, I suddenly knew what he had already realized.

"One more lie to tell?" Wilmar said, his voice eerily high and wavering with nervousness . . . or excitement. "Dirty, lying Jew. We know you walk this way every day. There is no one coming for you at school."

Webber mouthed quietly, "Dirty Jew."

"Just like the lies you told in class today," one of the new boys shouted, circling farther to our left. "Trying to make Herr Schmidt look foolish."

"Trying to make Herr *Hitler* look foolish," the other corrected, moving to our right.

"Please," I said, "we don't want a fight."

Wilmar sneered. "Funny thing that those who cannot win a fight are always first to say they don't want one."

Varrick and I had, to this moment, been stepping backward almost in unison, as the boys widened their circle around us. Now Varrick stopped, set his jaw, and squared his shoulders. "I will fight any one of you and win," he said, "but that is not your plan, is it?"

From three sides they rushed at him then, the impact knocking me to the ground as well. I scrambled upright, yelling at them to stop, as Varrick fought a losing battle to free himself from the heap of attackers piled on top of him. The twins got to their feet and kicked him as the other two threw punches from atop his chest and legs.

It was as though I were seeing the whole event from another place. I could hear my own screams and the thuds of their fists and feet against his head and body. I saw the spurt of blood from the flesh of Varrick's forehead as the heel of Wilmar's boot opened a gash.

For his part, Varrick made no sound. The assailants grunted and panted with the effort of the beating, but the only noise that came from Varrick was his hair brushing the dirt and gravel beneath him as he turned his head from side to side in a futile effort to avoid their blows.

A small pebble bounced toward me from the scuffle, and I suddenly knew how I could help. I looked quickly around for a rock big enough to wield as a weapon. At the base of the wall of the dilapidated dairy building a chunk of masonry with jagged edges on one side seemed to glow bone-white atop the brown dirt of the road.

Rushing to retrieve the rock, I began swinging wildly. The first of my flailing efforts missed completely but rustled Webber's hair. The next blow connected with his skull, and he crumpled at my feet.

I repeated the strike at the boy sitting on Varrick's chest, and he yelped like a wounded dog and jumped away, wincing and rubbing his ear. That movement freed Varrick's arms, and he snagged Wilmar's boot in his hands and twisted it violently. Wilmar had to roll away from Varrick and to his knees to avoid having his ankle snapped.

I hit Wilmar next, and he collapsed next to his brother.

Varrick, sitting up now, delivered a single square blow to the boy still atop his legs. With a distinct crack, the adversary's nose disappeared in a torrent of blood, and he screamed and fell backward.

The second boy I'd hit was considering re-entering the fray, but I bared my teeth, growled, and menaced him with the bloody rock. He and his friend ran then, leaving the unconscious Funk twins at our mercy.

Varrick slumped to his elbows, and I ran to him. His face was a mess—lips swollen and cut, eyes puffing shut. A horizontal gash extended from the outside edge of his left eyebrow to the center of his forehead, painting the whole side of his face with a thick sheet of blood. His cheek was swirled brown where it had mixed with the dust and debris from the road.

His starched white shirt had pulled from his waist during the fight, baring his stomach and ribs. His body already showed the first signs of bruising from the punches landed there.

As I helped him to his feet, he still made no

noise, no tears, nor any complaints of pain. That was the moment I realized what an incredible man he was. He had no fear of physical pain, though I knew his must be unbearable. Yet he had cried real tears for being unable to make a better defense of what was right.

He leaned against my shoulder, and I helped him walk to my home for my mama, who was a nurse, to tend. Varrick Kepler was a young man I admired immensely.

It was in the weeks following Varrick's afterschool encounter with the bullies that I began to understand how dangerous life in Germany had become for adults as well.

It was a blustery night in Berlin, about a week before Christmas. A howling wind gleefully flung handfuls of sleet against the upper-story windows of our home. No doubt the furnace in our basement was doing its best, but it could not keep chilling drafts from exploring every hallway and rushing down the back of my neck when I shifted position. I was unconsciously holding my breath, but when I finally gasped for air, what I inhaled was a combination of the crisp scent of pine boughs, the reek of coal smoke, the familiar mustiness of the old parsonage . . . and danger.

I was not supposed to be listening to the conversation taking place in our parlor. I lay out of sight, on a stair landing one floor above. The hour was late, and the gathering supposedly secret to all but my father and mother.

No such secret could ever be kept around our house for long. From early that morning my father and mother had engaged in whispered conferences. There had been hasty knocks on our front door. My father had accepted cryptic notes passed by messengers with pulled-down hat brims and turned-up coat collars. These and other signals combined to involve me in the conspiracy, invited or not.

Besides, I knew all of the participants by their voices. Along with my father's resonant baritone, I recognized the deeper register of my uncle Theo—his sentences punctuated by dry, barking coughs from the cold he couldn't shake, to which he habitually added, "Pardon me."

I also knew Pastor Bonhoeffer's voice. If my father spoke as an ocean liner moves, forging ahead with deliberate, reasoned speed, Pastor Bonhoeffer's inflection was a sailing ship, swooping in graceful lines before tacking abruptly to bring a whole new perspective into a discussion.

"It is only a matter of time before my seminary is closed," Bonhoeffer said. "The Reich will not tolerate our opposition much longer. Reichsbishop Mueller is on the offensive again."

"I have always found him offensive," Papa growled.

Pastor Bonhoeffer spoke as a founding member of the Confessing Church—the organization of Protestant pastors who denounced the official German evangelical church for becoming one more arm of the Nazi party.

"How long do you think you have?" I heard Papa murmur.

"Months rather than years. They will shut our doors next summer if not before; Finkenwalde and elsewhere; me and others. Barth has already left Germany for Switzerland."

"And what will you do then?" my uncle queried, pausing between each scrap of words for a sound like the rasp of coarse sandpaper on rough wood. "Excuse me. Will you leave for America, Dietrich?"

"I have in mind to keep doing what I'm doing," Bonhoeffer returned, "but in a much less sedentary way. A 'seminary on the run,' as it were. If the students cannot come to the instructor, then I'll go to them . . . one village at a time."

Even though the remaining member of the meeting had not spoken before, I knew him instantly as well: Richard Kepler, Varrick's father. "Perhaps when the Nazis are chasing you, they'll leave off chasing Jews for a time?" This was a grim jest, and no one laughed. All present knew the story of Varrick's beating. Like the Keplers, my uncle Theo was ethnically Jewish, even though Christian. As such they were *untermenschen* according to the Nuremburg laws—subhuman in the eyes of the Reich.

"It's you, Richard, and your family, who should leave for America or England," uncle Theo advised somberly. "The same choice I face myself."

Papa said, "Surely we can protect the members of our congregations, Aryan or Jewish."

I shivered at Pastor Bonhoeffer's next words: "You will not even be able to protect yourself, Robert. If they close the Confessing seminaries, they will also suppress resisting churches. They will replace each true Christian shepherd with one more properly wolfish . . . I mean, patriotic." Almost as an afterthought he added, ". . . and the synagogues they will burn."

5

That Christmas everything I had believed about life changed forever.

My cousin, Elisa Lindheim, returned home to Berlin from Vienna, where she played violin in a prominent orchestra. Elisa's mother, Anna, was my father's half-sister.

Though Elisa was older than me by several years, we were closer than just cousins. There was nothing I could not reveal to her. No secret was too sacred that I feared to share it.

Even so, a wide gulf seemed to separate us that holiday.

Elisa had returned to a Germany almost unrecognizable from that of her childhood. The strain was palpable on their family.

Elisa's father, Theo Lindheim, was a decorated war hero who had flown aeroplanes in the Great War. He was also the owner of a much-admired Berlin department store.

But my uncle Theo was also a Jew, and Elisa was half-Jewish. By reason of the Aryan laws about racial purity, my dear cousin was among the second tier of those most hated by the Nazis. Her father, being both wealthy and a Jew, was in the highest category of those slated for arrest. The Lindheim family was watched by the Gestapo. Without changing one bit, without committing any crime, they had become enemies of Hitler's Third Reich.

I had not suspected that Uncle Theo and Aunt Anna had been preparing for the worst for some time. Elisa's passport was Czech, not German. She performed in Vienna under the Aryan stage-name of Elisa Linder.

I never imagined that the worst could actually come to pass in my own family as madness gripped Germany by the throat.

Elisa was distant and very quiet at our family gathering. She played her violin for us as we opened gifts several days early before the

Christmas tree, but I noticed the light of joy was gone from her beautiful face. Blue eyes, so much like those of my aunt Anna, were downcast.

That Christmas Lindheim's Department Store was bursting with holiday cheer. The birch-paneled walls and the mirrored columns of the hall dedicated to scarves and shawls were festooned with greenery. Bright red holly berries and sprays of mistletoe defined the archways.

Only the red-and-black banners of Nazi supremacy, which state ordinance decreed must drape the outside facade of the building, spoke of how things had changed. The shining electric lights of the Christmas star on Lindheim's roof seemed in danger of being swallowed up in a swarm of creeping spiders.

The day she and I went Christmas shopping in her father's store, she was constantly glancing from side to side. I must admit, I was startled when I followed her gaze and spotted a Gestapo agent trailing behind us. He smiled in a tight-lipped, arrogant way when she noticed him.

He wanted her to know she was being watched.

Over lunch in the elegant Tea Room, with its pale blue and silver brocade carpet and its art deco brushed-chrome wall sconces, I confessed to Elisa that I was in love with Eben Golah. Her expression was one of pity for me.

Elisa replied, simply, in a barely audible whisper, "Oh, Lora, but Eben is a Jew . . . as I am,

75

as my father is. Eben must be leaving Germany forever."

I nodded in agreement that this was the plan, never thinking that perhaps Uncle Theo had also made plans for a desperate escape for his family. Elisa knew what was about to transpire, but she never spoke one word to me.

Who among us would live and who would die was something I pondered when I climbed into my bed at night. The pink floral wallpaper and row of stuffed teddy bears on my shelf seemed suddenly too childish for the terror raging around us.

Varrick was still recovering from the beating and did not come to church all through Advent. Many whom we had counted as faithful parishioners stayed away that year. I wrote Christmas cards to my Texas cousins and dreamed of holidays in America.

Papa and Mama and I called on the Keplers at their beautiful three-story home on Christmas Eve. Swastikas and foul epithets were scrawled on the hewn stone exterior.

Servants who had worked for many years in the Kepler home had quit at the "suggestion" of Nazi party members. Mrs. Kepler, a petite, elegant woman in her late thirties, peeked out from behind the lace curtains and then answered the door herself. Her doe-eyes brimmed with tears when my mother stepped into the foyer and embraced her. The aroma of cinnamon and apples filled my senses.

"Happy Christmas," Mama greeted Mrs. Kepler, though we all knew it was not happy, nor could it be.

"Oh, Janet!" Mrs. Kepler cried. "What a chance you take coming here."

Just then, Mr. Kepler, looking very gray and weary, stepped from his study. Papa extended his hand and greeted him with these words, "The Messiah of Israel is born in Bethlehem. We bring good tidings that our Redeemer is near."

Mr. Kepler could not speak for a moment; then what he said startled me. "Herod rules even now. He seeks the lives of the sons of Israel."

Papa replied, "But we who see through the eyes of faith know the end of Herod's story."

I glanced past Mr. Kepler into the study. Handsome and muscular, Eben Golah looked back with brilliant green eyes from the burgundy leather chair opposite the mahogany desk. Dressed in a brown tweed hunting jacket and corduroy trousers, Eben offered a faint smile. His tan boots were scuffed as though he had hiked a long way through the mountains. I did not smile back, but rather stared at him with open curiosity as though I were studying a framed photograph. For the first time it struck me that he looked Jewish, with his strong jaw and curly hair—much like Varrick and Varrick's father—only Eben's hair was a dark red.

Mrs. Kepler kissed my cheek. "And you, Lora, brave girl."

Papa replied, "Lora will not be returning to school after the holidays. I'll instruct her at home."

Mrs. Kepler directed me to the parlor as the adults went into the study. I heard Mr. Kepler say, ". . . Eben is a very old friend."

Varrick was stretched out on the ornate Victorian sofa. Light filtered through leaded-glass windows and streamed over his shoulder. A red, leather-bound copy of *Ivanhoe* with gilt-edged pages was open on his lap. He looked up when we entered and smiled through swollen lips. I had been told some ribs were fractured. His beautiful Sephardic nose was broken. The break would forever be a reminder to me of that terrifying day. I went to him and sat in the highbacked chair near him as our parents and Eben spoke in quiet, urgent voices.

Suddenly shy, I said, "Happy Christmas, Varrick Kepler."

"Happy Christmas, Lora Bittick." He shrugged. "Because of you I'm alive, I think."

"Oh, Varrick." I simply gazed in pity at his poor, wounded face.

He held up the volume. "*Ivanhoe*. Have you read it?"

"No."

"Eben brought it to me from England. A Hanukkah gift. Sir Walter Scott. So I can practice my English."

I admired the volume. "*Ivanhoe.*"

"I must loan it to you when I'm finished. The heroine reminds me of you. Very courageous."

I blushed at the intensity of his eyes on me. "I should like to be the heroine of a novel, but I'm not made of courage."

"You don't look like her. She's dark, and you're fair. But inside, your heart is like her heart. I thought of you when I began to read. I remembered you wading in among them."

"I think of how you spoke the truth."

"Foolish, I suppose."

"We should all remain fools, or truth will perish. What did St. Paul say? The wisdom of the gospel is foolishness to those who perish? Something like that."

"I fear wise fools may perish and the truth with us unless we leave Germany."

I touched his arm and then drew back, startled at my boldness. "Varrick, there's a place in the world where truth still survives. Must be."

"Maybe in America. Not in the Reich, Lora. Fear has made truth unpopular. The world's upside down."

"Christ in us must turn it right again."

"One day, perhaps."

We looked into one another's eyes for a long moment. In the study Mrs. Kepler cried quietly, and we heard Mr. Kepler say to my father and mother, "The leaders of the Youth Corps seek the hearts of the youth. They'll have them, too, unless we can hold firm to the education of our children."

Papa replied, "Lora won't return to state school at the beginning of the term. We must resist the anti-Semitic, anti-biblical teaching, or we'll no longer find Christ in the hearts of our youth."

Eben chose his words carefully. "It is too late for those in the Reich who are Hebrews. They have no choice but to leave the Reich, or they will not survive. This is not a new evil, but it is perhaps the most violent assault against Jews since Jerusalem fell beneath the boots of Rome. I'm doing everything I can to find a way of escape to England for my Hebrew brothers and sisters."

Papa's voice was deep and confident when he answered. "God declared to Israel, in Genesis chapter 12: 'I will bless those who bless you. And those who curse you I will curse.' Neither the church nor the nation will stand if we turn our back on such a promise . . . God's Covenant may not be disregarded. This is how we know National Socialism is the darkest and most ancient evil."

Mr. Kepler answered, "If my son is beaten

nearly to death, and my wife is refused service by the neighborhood baker, the Covenant won't save me. Germany will eventually fall in disgrace for what it has done, but I must seek refuge for my family before we're swept away as well."

Varrick nodded at his father's words and said to me, "So, you see, Lora, we must go away. Not because we're cowards, but because we must live to fight against this on another front. Germany is lost."

"I understand. I'll miss you." I felt very grown up in that moment. The friend I admired with all my heart would be leaving for some distant haven. I did not like growing up so suddenly. I asked God in my heart, *Why must we know so much?*

God answered me with a thought. *Just as a young David faced Goliath, the youth who follow Christ are compelled by the apathy of the world to carry heavy burdens and fight great battles.*

I said to Varrick, "Christ the Savior is born. . . . Greater is He who is in you, than he who is in the world.[1] I'll pray that the Lord will help you find a way of escape."

"And you? Back to Brussels? Or America?"

"I'm not afraid for myself. But I don't want to stay in a nation where children of Abraham are not welcome."

---

[1] See 1 John 4:4.

He took my hand in his and brushed my fingers with his lips. "Then it's indeed a happy Christmas, Lora Bittick."

Eben was polite but cool to me when he met with Papa. His reserve broke my heart. "Why does Eben Golah come here so often?" I asked Papa after one such visit. I knew Papa heard the resentment in my voice. I do not doubt that he understood the true reason I was so angry when Eben came to talk all night: my adolescent infatuation with him, my childish resentment of his indifference.

"History holds the truth. It must not be forgotten. He is a man who brings us gifts from a distant place." Papa passed the bread and then the butter. He looked away from meeting my gaze in such a way that I recognized he knew a secret he would never share.

I assumed Eben was a messenger who delivered some financial support for our family and the ministry.

I said no more about it but ate my supper in sullen silence.

The next morning my studies were laid out on the dining table like a banquet. The volume of John Keats' poetry had been my favorite since our summer in Switzerland. Among all his poems, I most cherished "Ode to a Nightingale," which was strangely linked in my heart to my love for Eben Golah.

Thou wast not born for death, immortal Bird!
No hungry generations tread thee down;
The voice I hear this passing night was heard
In ancient days by emperor and clown:
Perhaps the self-same song that found a path
Through the sad heart of Ruth, when, sick for
* home,*
She stood in tears amid the alien corn;
The same that oft-times hath
Charm'd magic casements, opening on the
* foam*
Of perilous seas, in faery lands forlorn.

Frau Helga had spoken of the nightingale's love for the white rose. I imagined Eben was the nightingale singing the same unchanging song through the ages. Keats' poetry was too beautiful to ever be rendered into the harsh Germanic tongue. I whispered it aloud, pronouncing it as it might have been read by Keats on Hampstead Heath, where he first wrote it.

Papa interrupted my adolescent reverie when he brought me a tattered volume from his library. It was written in Latin and printed in an archaic typeface.

He opened it and said, "I thought perhaps you might like to learn more about our friend Eben."

"He is cold and arrogant and boring." I turned up my nose.

Papa's eyes narrowed in disapproval of my

disrespect. "He is among the thirty-six most eminent scholars of church history who live among us in the world. Apart from Edersheim, there are few who know the links between Israel and the church better than he. Here is a text he knows well. I do not doubt he could dictate it by heart. Written by Eusebius. *The History of the Church.*"

I was aware that Eben was a scholar recognized for his mastery of ancient history and languages. At the White Rose Inn I had often listened, while pretending to be disinterested, as Eben explained ancient heresies reborn in the modern church.

Papa gave me my assignment. "Today you will translate this passage from Latin to German and then into English."

"But I am translating Keats. 'Ode to a Nightingale.'"

"The message is the same . . . so? No mathematics today. This is far more important."

Though I sighed and pretended to be unhappy, the task was not unpleasant to me. It was rather like unraveling a mystery. I loved language and welcomed the chance to delve into its hidden secrets.

I began at 9 a.m. and finished just before dinnertime. The meal was before us. We sat in our places and as Papa led us, we sang the blessing of Father, Son, and Holy Spirit: *"What was in the beginning, is now and ever shall be . . . world without end, Amen, Amen."*

Papa raised his eyes to me. "Well, Lora? You have something to share?"

With a sense of accomplishment and excitement, I unfolded my work for the day. I began with the heading: "Eminent Evangelists of the First Generation."

"Among the shining lights of the period was Quadratus, who, according to the written evidence, was, like Philip's daughters, eminent from a prophetic gift. Besides them, many others were known at the time, belonging to the first stage of apostolic succession. These earnest disciples of great men built on the foundations of churches everywhere laid by the apostles. They spread the message still further, sowing and saving seed of the Kingdom of Heaven far and wide through the entire world."

I looked up to see Papa's eyes shining with pride. "Well done, Loralei." Then to Mama, "Our daughter is set to be a scholar."

"There's more, Papa." I felt such a surge of joy.

"Much more," he agreed. "The most important part."

I continued reading from my translation.

". . . for even at that late date many miraculous powers of the divine Spirit worked

through them, so that at the first hearing, entire crowds in a body embraced the worship of the Lord with wholehearted eagerness."

This small triumph of decoding the past was just the beginning.

Papa questioned me, "What do Keats' nightingale and the stories of Eusebius have in common?"

I smiled. "Both are unchanged by time."

"Well spoken. True." He waved his hand, drawing more from me.

"Beauty and miracles continue. The source of all is Christ our Creator, who is immortal and unchanged."

"True. And therefore?" He urged me to further conclusions.

"I don't know," I said, doubtfully, feeling drained.

"What is your spiritual genealogy?"

I did not understand the question. "You told me how to be a Christian, Papa. And Mama too."

"And who shared the story of Jesus with me and your mother?"

"You said Gipsy Smith."

"And who told him about our Savior?"

"I don't know. Can't say."

Papa lowered his chin and peered at me over the top of his glasses. "From one spiritual parent to another, the same, immutable truth is handed down, generation to generation, right back to the beginning. From the moment Christ emerged from the tomb. From the day of Pentecost when the Holy Spirit filled Peter and the others in Jerusalem. Death is conquered. The power of the Holy Spirit is unchanging, passed down from one to another. Miracles continue and abound even in our own dark time. The nightingale's song . . . eternal, unchanged. Today you have deciphered a true story about the first generation of your spiritual family. They knew Jesus. They spoke and wrote the truth. They met Jesus. Ordinary people like us heard stories from the great ones who knew our Lord and spoke with Him after He was crucified and raised from death to eternal life."

Papa paused, as if conveying a great truth. "Jesus said, if He chooses that some live until He returns as our King, then what is that to us? From the laying on of their hands, the great gifts of the Holy Spirit are passed to each new generation. True witnesses, the righteous, survive in every generation. What was in the beginning is now . . . and ever shall be. . . ."

I did not fully comprehend the mystery Papa revealed, or why he had chosen that moment in my life to open my heart to something so profound. Perhaps he sensed that there would come a time when he could not share these things with me.

Time was running out.

I laid my head on my pillow that night with my thoughts swirling. Outside my window I heard the nightingale sing. Had Ruth heard the same immortal song as she gleaned the stalks of wheat in the field of Boaz? Had Mary heard these same notes on a moonlit night beside the well of Nazareth? And Mary Magdalene, as she waited by the tomb before the dawn?

I recognized some golden refrain ringing in that evening's melody that I heard. Yet I could not identify the meaning. Many years would pass and many tears fall before I would hear that song outside my window again.

Darkling, I listen; and, for many a time
I have been half in love with easeful Death,
Call'd him soft names in many a mused rhyme,
To take into the air my quiet breath;
Now more than ever seems it rich to die,
To cease upon the midnight with no pain,
While thou art pouring forth thy soul abroad
In such an ecstasy!
Still wouldst thou sing, and I have ears in
  vain—
To thy high requiem become a sod.
Thou wast not born for death, immortal Bird!

There were times when Eben Golah did not come to the clandestine meetings in my father's study.

Along with a few others, like Dietrich Bonhoeffer, he was set to the task of traveling and spreading the word of our plight in Germany.

I asked Mama if we would see Eben again.

"I think so. He is hard at work, Papa says."

"Do you know where he is?"

"Back in England, I suppose. He has influential connections with the English writers. C. S. Lewis and J. R. R. Tolkien are among his friends. They are speaking and writing."

And then I asked a question that surprised me even as I spoke. "Who is Eben, Mama? Or . . . *what* is Eben?"

It seemed like minutes passed before she replied with words like a poem. "He is the nightingale. An ancient voice sings at every twilight. His song is heard more clearly in the darkness."

6

It is true that unrequited love can be very close to hate. I loved Eben. I hated Eben. Though Papa was oblivious to my sulky behavior when Eben came to the house for meetings, Mama noticed my pouty looks. She made mental note of the nights when I pretended to be ill so I could retreat to my bed and pine away in the darkness.

It was a Monday night sometime after my aunt Anna, uncle Theo, cousin Elisa, and her

American husband, John Murphy, had escaped to the safety of England. The Jewish Agency and my father's evangelical Christian organization were working hard to arrange Kindertransports for Jewish children. Papa had organized a meeting of Christian pastors and Jewish Agency representatives from Great Britain that had lasted most of the night. Eben was among the group. Though I did not see him, I had listened to Eben speaking through the furnace grate. I longed to tell him again how much he meant to me. I remembered Frau Helga's story of the white rose and the nightingale.

Eben's mellow, confident words were the nightingale's song. Though I thought I had put him out of my mind, I was sick with love for him.

At last I fell asleep, aching for him to come into my room and take me into his arms. I dreamed all night about the White Rose Inn and Hafflinger horses grazing in a field around an enormous Tannenbaum decorated with English volumes of Shakespeare and Dickens and Robert Louis Stevenson, while Eben sang.

My dream made no sense, but it was a pleasant escape from the reality of the Reich.

Mama knocked softly on my door the next morning before I was awake. "Lora?"

I answered with a reluctant groan. The clock said half-six. I opened my eyes as, with a cup of steaming tea, she came in quietly and sat on the edge of my bed. She was beautiful in a soft blue cotton robe and slippers.

Mama did not speak. She merely took a sip of tea, then offered me a pitying smile.

"Mama?" I asked. "What?"

"I want to tell you something about myself. Between us girls."

"All right, Mama. But at half-six?"

"Isn't everyone asleep?" she whispered.

"Not you."

"Lora, darling?"

"Mama?"

"When I was younger than you, there was a music teacher. His name was George Helstrom. A young fellow, a music professor out of Amarillo. Handsome, handsome. Oh! I tell you, he was the love of my life, wasn't he just?"

This was interesting. I propped myself up on my elbow. She offered me a taste of her tea. Suddenly we were more like girlfriends than mother and daughter. I still had not grasped why she was sharing such a deep, intimate secret with me.

"And?"

"He loved another. Terribly. But she didn't love him, poor fellow. I loved him. Wouldn't my heart pound every time he came to the house? Just imagine how poor George and I suffered."

Mama brushed my hair with her fingers. I asked, "What happened to George?"

"He ran off to Hollywood and married a rich girl. Works for his cousin at a film studio. A director of Marx Brothers movies. Can you just imagine?"

"And you?"

"I married your papa and have been happy every day of my life. I should have known all along: how could I have ever loved a man who would move to Hollywood and get hitched for money? So shallow."

"Mama?" I paused, wanting to tell her everything.

"Yes?" She lowered her chin, and I knew she knew.

"Eben is not shallow."

"No."

"I have loved him since the first time I ever saw him."

"I know, dear."

"He is older than I am."

"Yes."

"And I know he doesn't care about me. He thinks I am a child."

She chewed her lower lip. "Poor Varrick."

"Yes. Poor boy."

"I think he loves you very much."

"Perhaps he does. But Mama, how can I fight such a love as I feel for Eben?"

Now her expression grew more serious. "Has Eben told you how he feels?"

"I told him how I felt."

"What did he say?"

"He . . . said he would tell Papa how foolish I am."

Mama sighed with relief. "Well, then. How can you love a man who threatens to tell your father everything?"

"I thought the very same thing. Cruel."

"But young Varrick. Can't you just see how he could be helped through this difficult time by a mature young woman who sees things as they are?"

I considered her suggestion. "I like Varrick. Once I thought I loved him. Perhaps I did in a way."

"Maybe you'll find a reason to love again, Loralei Bittick. Just don't give up hope. Aren't I certain the Lord has some fine young man for you to love?"

"How old is Eben?"

"Perhaps twenty-seven or twenty-eight, I would guess. Thirty?"

"Mature."

Mama looked at her hands a long time before she answered. "You cannot know the life of a man like Eben Golah. Few know him well. Your father knows his history but tells me nothing about him. Perhaps he is too old for you. I do think so. If he is ten years older than you, think of it. When you are my age . . . forty-six . . . wouldn't he be fifty-six?"

A shocking thought. "Oh, dear. So old." I lay back on my pillow. I felt as though my soul was purged. I rubbed her hand. "Thank you, Mama. I have felt very alone until this morning."

Mama winked. She seemed so very young in that instant. I marveled that my own mother did not look even close to her age. "Between us girls, eh? I'd hate for your father to ever *think* I wanted to marry a fellow who lives in Hollywood."

Just as Mama's American citizenship protected my father's interim ministry in Germany, my U.S. citizenship became a cherished treasure that might somehow save lives.

As I completed my studies at the dining room table late one night, men I had first met at the White Rose Inn discussed the saving of even one Jewish life.

Bonhoeffer, Eben Golah, and members of the desperate Jewish community, including Varrick's father, Mr. Kepler, used my mother's citizenship as an example. The Nazis still feared American opinion. As long as America remained neutral, the Third Reich could do whatever they liked. The Nazis were not eager to offend Americans by preventing Jews or German opposition from leaving. The marriage of a Jew to an American might open the way for an entire family to emigrate to the U.S.

I heard Mr. Varrick say, "The only way now for

a German Jew to obtain a visa to the U.S. is by marriage to an American."

Bonhoeffer said, "What we need is a surplus of American men and women willing to marry."

Varrick's father immediately cried, "My son Varrick has great affection for your daughter Lora, Pastor Bittick! Could we not consider—"

Then Eben added, "Robert, the marriage of your daughter to young Varrick could possibly open the door for all the Kepler family to escape. Would your daughter Lora consider such an arrangement?"

I felt the blood drain from my face as I heard my name on Eben's lips, emanating from behind the door panel of Papa's study. *Marriage?*

Mama came out of the kitchen door. She was drying her hands on a dishtowel. Her jaw dropped, and her eyes grew wide. She looked at me, then stared at the door. She lapsed into English and said in her strong Texas accent, "Are those men discussing what I think they are discussing?"

I nodded and closed my book. "Oh, Mama."

"Marry you off like a mail-order bride?" She threw the towel onto the table and untied her apron. "I'll set those fools straight." She started toward the door.

I stood. "Mama, don't. Don't! They're right!"

She turned on her heel and stared at me as the dialogue behind the door continued. My heart pounded.

"What are you saying, Loralei Bittick? Marry a young man you don't love so he can get a visa to America . . ."

"So he can be free? Oh, Mama! Yes! Yes, I'll do it. I'll marry Varrick in a minute, if he wants to. This is the first time I've felt . . . like I can do something. Don't you see? I will!"

Mama's beautiful lips curved in a knowing smile. "But Lora, you don't love him, do you?"

I inhaled deeply and exhaled slowly. Did I? Did I love Varrick? Or was I still hanging on to some shred of hope about the older man in my life? Was I still dreaming of Eben?

"Jesus," I whispered, "help me know what to do."

Mama put her arms around me. I cried a little on her shoulder. "I . . . like Varrick. A lot. Maybe love. I mean, I think I could love him. But that's not the point. The Kepler family . . . all of them. If this is the way—"

She stroked my hair. "You are amazing, Lora. You know you are, honey?"

I nodded. Suddenly I was no longer helpless. I could make a difference in a world gone mad.

"I'll tell them," I volunteered. "If Varrick Kepler will have me for a wife—I mean, if it's okay with Varrick—it's okay with me."

And so, in March 1938, Varrick and I were married by my father in a quiet ceremony witnessed by an American newsman named Shane Dean, who was on assignment in Berlin. My parents knew him well. His report of our wedding was sent by wire to the American newspapers. It was illegal in Germany for a non-Jew to marry a Jew, but my citizenship put the issue outside Nazi jurisdiction. An article was printed in the *New York Times* pronouncing that true love had even overcome the racial laws of National Socialism.

Varrick and I spent our first two nights holding hands on a slow train carrying us to our honeymoon across the German border to Kitzbuhl, Austria. The newsman also rode on the same train as we and in the same carriage, in case there was trouble from the authorities.

His presence and our marriage certificate, combined with my American passport, made the crossing uncomplicated. From Austria, the plan was for Varrick to go on to Switzerland without me. We would meet again later. I would return to Berlin to start arranging papers for his family.

The Nazi border guards who inspected our exit documents sneered at our youth and the fact that we were on a honeymoon.

"Where are your skis?" laughed one fat fellow with a Hitler moustache as he flipped through our papers.

His companion, a florid-faced civil servant,

jibed, "They are not interested in the snow. They are only going to Austria to keep warm."

I felt myself blush. Varrick held my hand tightly. He did not look them in the eye. I spotted Mr. Dean leaning forward, as if to spring into action if there was any trouble. Our identity folders were tossed back in Varrick's face, and I heard the guard mutter the word "Jude" as he left us.

We entered Austria. Shane Dean, en route to Vienna, clasped our hands and wished us well as we disembarked. He warned Varrick: "Get out of Austria as soon as you can. The Anschluss is coming. Soon Austria won't be safe for you either, American wife or not."

Hours later, we were riding in a sleigh on our way to Kitzbuhl. I could not look at Varrick's face. I felt like a child and he looked at me like a man—hungry and filled with desire. Our hotel room was grand, nicer than anywhere I had ever stayed before. The heavy furniture had marble tops. The room had mirrors on three walls: enormous, gilt-framed, glass panels reflecting not only whoever stood before them, but the entirety of the chamber, including the four-poster, canopied bed.

"No, don't open it. Just leave it for now," I heard Varrick say.

While Varrick tipped the bellhop for bringing up our bags, I wandered about the room, touching everything: table, chair, lamp, curtains, as if rehearsing the reality of where I was . . . and how my life had irrevocably changed. I needed to prove this was not a dream, but I also wanted to remember it all. If I was to leave my love, my husband, my Varrick, so desperately, painfully soon, I wanted to carry with me an exact image of our first night together.

When I glanced up from playing with a silver candy dish, I saw Varrick staring at me. On his face was a mixture of wonder and . . . something else. Something that frightened me and thrilled me, both at the same time.

"The manager sent up a bottle of champagne," Varrick said, flourishing the dark green bottle. "Would you like some?"

"My father doesn't approve," I said, then stopped at the absurdity of what I had said. I was a married woman; a woman grown, no matter if the calendar might assert otherwise. "Yes," I said with a toss of my head. "I think I would."

Varrick struggled with the wire cage over the cork and then just as he succeeded in removing it, the cork shot out of the bottle and bounced off the mirror near my head. As Varrick ran to hold the gushing wine over a pair of glasses, we both laughed and laughed.

It was a very good thing to laugh just then—a very good thing indeed.

After passing me a glass of champagne, Varrick

sat on the edge of the bed. He took a swallow, then patted the mattress for me to join him there.

When I did so, he smiled at me, the same shy smile I had seen when I had first met him. "To you," he said, raising his glass.

"To us," I replied, clinking the rims together. "To being together again soon, and to never being parted, ever again."

Several quiet moments passed, with Varrick gulping the champagne and me sipping gingerly. I didn't really like the taste but would not tell him so. He started to say something several times, pausing as if searching for the right words.

At last he said, "Do you, I mean, do you know . . . did your mother tell you—"

"How a married man and his wife behave with each other?" I replied in the best grown-up, matter-of-fact voice I could muster. I still squeaked a little, and color rose in my cheeks. "Yes, of course. I bet I've known longer than you have." I instantly regretted saying that. This was not a school competition to prove which of us was smarter. "What I meant to say is, yes, my mother and father are very much in love. She explained to me what that means . . . in the way you mean it too."

Varrick looked incredibly relieved. "I'm so glad! I mean, well, I had *that* talk with *my* father, but he kept saying how when I married you . . . oh, yes, I've always known this day would come!

How when I married you, I must not be impatient. How I should not scare . . ."

"Varrick," I said, setting the tulip-shaped glass on the nightstand. "Stop talking and kiss me."

He sighed happily, put his arms around me, and pulled me close. After that everything was just as it should be . . . perfect in every way.

Three days into our planned honeymoon Shane Dean unexpectedly reappeared in Kitzbuhl. "The Anschluss is happening . . . now!" he said. "The borders are closed. Varrick needs to get out immediately. I'll set it up for tomorrow morning."

Suddenly our time together was shattered. We said our most intimate, personal good-byes long before the sun came up on departure morning. I promised myself I would not beg to stay with him. I would not make this separation any more difficult for my husband than he was already experiencing.

When dawn came, I was not sleeping, but I could not bring myself to wake him. My arms wrapped around him, hugging him fiercely. I committed to memory every bit of him in the way I had sought to record the room.

All too soon it was time to rise, dress, and pack. We would not leave one moment earlier than necessary. Still, the time flew by, despite every angry glare I gave the clock.

As if there were no Nazis, no possible pursuers,

no danger to our families, we acted like the final act of his escape from Berlin was the beginning of a cruise to the South Seas. Varrick adopted a different air than I had seen in him before. He appeared ready and able to do battle with any threat. In between moments of looking fierce he stared at me, drinking me in and embracing me with his gaze.

I also had a part to play. I made certain luggage tags were securely attached. I contrived for every mission to carry me past Varrick near enough to touch him.

I touched the curl of hair on the back of his neck. When I adjusted the angle of the fedora he wore, I stroked his forehead. When nothing else suggested itself, I plucked imaginary lint from his sleeve, then let my fingers rest on his hand. "I love you," I whispered.

"I love you, and . . . I cherish you," he returned.

The porter came, and we silently followed our luggage to the lobby. My throat, already constricted with emotion, contrived to tighten even further at that. We uttered hopeful little glimpses of what our future life would be like.

"We'll have a place of our own," he said.

"You can finish school," I offered.

"We'll raise our own vegetables on—how do the Americans say it?—'a bit of garden.'"

"Flowers," I insisted. "Flowers too."

All too soon Shane Dean arrived to assist

Varrick in crossing the mountain to safety. There were others assembled who would pass into Switzerland today. Varrick stroked my cheek in one final embrace. "I'll see you soon," he promised.

I could not speak. I did love him, I discovered. I nodded. "Soon."

7

The next time I ever saw Eben Golah was on the eve of great terror and tragedy. It was late afternoon on the ninth of November, 1938. Mama was in the kitchen, so when Eben Golah came to our home, I answered his knock. He asked to speak with my father, alone. I ushered him into Papa's study, but I left the door slightly ajar after presenting him.

Such was the air of mystery around the man I could not help listening in the hallway outside.

What I overheard made me shudder.

"It will happen tonight," Golah said to my father. "It will be the worst flexing of Nazi muscle yet seen."

"How do you know this?" Papa queried.

Golah's reply was dismissive of that issue. "Not important. What you need to know is this: tonight will be organized mayhem and destruction. Tonight the thugs will not be drunken rowdies too deep in their schnapps to stand erect. Storm

Troopers dressed as civilians have lists of Jewish homes and businesses. It will occur all over Germany, tonight! Tomorrow Hitler will give out the word this was a spontaneous uprising against the criminal, subversive Jews, but every torch is allotted a Jewish building; every club a Jewish skull."

"The methodical Aryan setting about his chosen profession," Papa said bitterly. "Is there time to get our friends out of Berlin? Country villages, perhaps . . . no?"

I knew from my father's sorrowful ending groan that Eben Golah had shaken his head. I shivered as he answered: "There is no town or village that is safe." He paused.

I held one hand to my mouth and pressed the other to my stomach as I gasped for breath. I had been working for months, unsuccessfully, to get Varrick's family out of Germany.

Then Golah continued, "There is only this ray of hope."

With difficulty I refrained from shouting, "What is it?" even as Papa voiced the same inquiry.

"Jewish homes and synagogues may be attacked only if there is no danger to Aryan houses and shops," Golah said. "If you pack your friends into the church, lives may be saved."

A muffled thud rattled the walls of our house. Seconds afterward, screams and cries echoed down the street.

Heedless of revealing my eavesdropping, I rushed into my father's office to join the two men at the window. "I'm too late," Golah said, his shoulders drooping.

"Papa, what?" I demanded.

"They've bombed the synagogue," he said, pointing at the flames shooting from the roof of the Jewish house of worship. A column of black, oily smoke ascended over Berlin, joining thousands of sacrificial pyres set ablaze all across Germany.

"I must go," Eben Golah said. "The mob is gathered in front of the synagogue for now, enjoying the spectacle. As soon as the novelty wears off, they will fan out through the Jewish homes clustered nearby. If I use the alleyways behind the synagogue I may help some to escape."

"I'll go with you," Papa offered.

Eben Golah shook his head. "Save your own flock, Pastor Bittick. The others are in the hands of Adonai."

My father clasped Golah's hand, hugged him, then the messenger raced away, pausing only to note my mother's stricken face and the fear in my eyes. "Courage," he said, and he was gone.

My father set me to work telephoning those members of our congregation who were Jewish by heritage. "I'll run to the ones who live nearest," he instructed, giving me their names.

"You call the others." There was no safety in Messianic faith tonight. Even if they were not already marked on Nazi lists, many Aryan neighbors would be happy to denounce Jewish Christians to the Stormtroopers.

Though the list of the telephone exchange was alphabetical, the number I first requested was the Kepler residence.

There was no answer.

The next three homes I contacted were answered by fearful voices. "It's Lora Bittick Kepler. My father says, 'Go to the church. Go to the churchyard door. Take blankets, but go now.'" Then I rang off.

Feeling justified by my trio of successes, I tried the Keplers again.

Still no response.

Two others did not pick up, then I got three more grateful reactions of: "Yes! Yes, right away. Thank you!"

When I asked for the Kepler home yet again, there was no corresponding buzz to show it rang. Clicking the receiver, I asked the operator to check the line. She replied that it was dead, but in any case the switchboard was overwhelmed with emergency calls, and I must now stay off the line.

My father reappeared, and I gave him my report, emphasizing my failure with Varrick's parents. He tried to reassure me: "Richard Kepler and I have spoken of this before. He's a good man. He'll remember what to do." My mother stood in the doorway, balancing a stack of coverlets and family heirloom quilts. To her, Papa said, "Stay here and keep the door locked. I won't be back tonight, but I'll try to get home tomorrow."

At that my mother verbally put her foot down. "We will not be separated," she said firmly. "If you're going, so are we. Mothers will need help with babies, won't they? And with keeping the children entertained and quiet?"

When Papa opened his mouth as if to protest, she said quickly, "We're all going."

Papa insisted on checking first to see if it was safe for us.

Moments later, Papa, flanked by brownshirted Stormtroopers, was forcibly returned. "We're being expelled from Germany," he said glumly to Mama. "Your citizenship saved us. But we must leave."

We returned to Brussels, and Papa took his place again as headmaster of Alderman School. Varrick joined the British as a translator and liaison between British and Belgian forces. Jessica's husband, William, was in the Belgian army.

We lived in blithe, foolish hope there would be some great falling out between Hitler and Stalin that would, in the end, destroy both tyrants.

It was not to be.

And so we lived our ordinary lives, worrying about things that had no significance except to distract us from looking at the stars. I longed for a baby. Whenever his duties did not call him away from Brussels, Varrick was always eager to assist me in fulfilling this ambition.

I continued to work for the hour when we might see his family escape from the Reich. Our hope to win their freedom was the preoccupation of our every waking hour. In those brief visits when Varrick came home on leave, we divided our time between the visa offices of the U.S. Embassy and the British Embassy. Our letters during the long months of separation were filled with disappointing news about denied visas and immigration quotas that had already been filled by needy children.

And when, at last, Poland was invaded in September 1939, word came to my father that Varrick's father and mother and brother had simply vanished one night. Arrested by the Gestapo, they were three Jews among millions.

Our entreaties turned to the constant vigil of prayer for their survival.

With Varrick's military duty and long absences, I turned my heart toward helping the refugee children. Jessica, Mama, and I worked every day among the displaced persons. Their sorrow was so much greater than our own. It put the blessings of our ordinary lives in perspective. Mama's

Texas friends made and shipped new clothes for our refugee children. Hand-me-downs were not accepted by the Texas Christian Missionary Society. New quilts. New clothes. New shoes. Hair ribbons and toy pop guns at Christmas to fight the Nazis. Mama personally oversaw the placement of 613 Jewish orphans in the U.S. A rabbi told her later that 613 was the exact number of laws in Torah.

She replied in her Texan way, "This isn't about the laws. This is about all men's broken lives being healed by God's grace."

I am sure he approved of what she said.

Then tragedy came to our home suddenly and without warning. Mama, the joy of Papa's life and the anchor of mine, died of a burst appendix.

Could it be, we asked ourselves, when we all needed her so much? When the darkness of this world was illuminated by her kind heart and ready smile? Could the merciful Lord take away our rock when there was so much heartache poised to spring on our future?

Jessica and I had believed our mother's strength was so much greater than ours. Suddenly, when we needed that strength to survive, we discovered it had become our own spiritual heritage.

PART THREE

A time of war,
and a time of peace.
ECCLESIASTES 3:8B

8
MAY 10, 1940
BRUSSELS, BELGIUM

The drive across blacked-out Brussels was eerie. The whole city had a sepulchral feel. No street lights illuminated the intersections. No cheery glow escaped from any of the heavily curtained windows. Papa drove hunched forward over the steering wheel, guiding the Fiat as much by moon glow as by the feeble gleam cast from the shrouded headlamps.

Despite the earlier alarms there was very little traffic in the crooked lanes or on the main thoroughfares. It was as if everyone remained huddled at home, hoping by collective disbelief to turn the news of a German assault into a false alarm. The whole city was waiting . . . and watching.

Though no one demanded an explanation of the late-night travel, and no one challenged us, I felt the presence of many eyes observing our every turn. Moonlight-induced shadows on row-house fronts turned windows and doorways into eye sockets and gaping mouths. Who lurked behind these wounds in the soul of Brussels?

The stillness of the seemingly deserted city made me feel like screaming. . . . or telling my father to turn around and drive as fast as possible

113

back home. Only familiar surroundings and comfortable memories could possibly lift the oppression I felt.

Out here in the inky blackness I was convinced Varrick was dead, lying facedown on a canal bank.

But what if that vision was wrong, was false, was wicked? What if he had escaped . . . and Jessica's William too? I hastily added to my prayer. What if they had fled alive from the carnage and were even now arriving at the seminary? What if Varrick came for me, and I was not there to greet him? How would he ever find me again?

I was about to suggest all this reasoning to Papa when the next stick of bombs began to fall.

The sirens had not been wrong—merely premature.

Brilliant orange flashes lit up the sky behind them, in the direction of the factories and the warehouses and the rail yards. I clamped my mouth shut on my doubts. Papa had been right. Whatever fate had already engulfed William and Varrick, it was necessary to get Gina and Jessica and the unborn child out of harm's way.

Suddenly, instead of retreating, I wished Papa would drive faster!

The delayed thunder of distant explosions reached us. Orange light raced across the streets, competing with and then overpowering the moon.

New detonations reverberated among the canyons of homes. Crimson fingers in the sky reached out to seize the Fiat and hold back our escape.

Another stick of bombs stitched a row of destruction across the city. Then, unexpectedly, a final flash and a rumble came to me, almost abreast of the auto. Off to the right, much nearer than the rest, a wayward package of ordnance detonated. For an instant the flare silhouetted a church steeple, a familiar pinnacle.

"Papa," I gasped loudly.

"Shh," he insisted. "We're still safe."

"No, Papa," I protested with barely subdued intensity. "I think . . . that last bomb . . . I think it was near St. Mary's. What about my girls? What about the school?"

"Loralei," Papa returned, jerking his chin toward the precious human cargo in the rear seat, "how can we . . . ?"

"It's not much out of the way," I argued. "I could never forgive myself. Please, Papa."

He was easily swayed. The children at St. Mary's had already suffered from this war. The three dozen Jewish girls were without families and in great danger from the coming of the Nazis. Downshifting, he guided the Fiat around a corner and aimed the angel atop the radiator cap toward the church and school.

Within three blocks it was clear St Mary's had indeed been struck. A pair of fire engines raced past, bells clanging, the firemen shouting, "Clear the way! The girls' school . . ."

The chapel had taken a direct hit. The roof had fallen into the interior, as had one end wall.

Half the other wall remained against the skyline. The jagged, semi-circular outline of a shattered rose window suggested an overflowing bowl of suffering and loss.

Hoses snaking across the courtyard and the lanes nearest the school prevented a nearer approach. "Stay with Jessica," I ordered Papa as I jumped from the Fiat, ignoring his words of protest and warning.

I encountered Sister Mary Marcia at the door to the dormitory. As soon as we reached each other the nun fell into my embrace. Together we sank toward the flagstones, kneeling.

Sister Marcia wept.

"Sister," I said urgently, "are you hurt? Are you wounded?"

"No. No . . . not me! The girls, our girls."

Cold fear gripped my heart. "How many are . . . hurt? Are some—"

The sister's slight frame was racked with sobs. "All of them! *All* of them. When we heard the sirens, we moved them to the chapel. We thought they'd be safer there. We never—"

"All?" I repeated dully. "All dead?"

"All but two. Susan and her older sister, Judith. You know them. Seven and nine."

I knew them well. The older sister had not uttered a sound since their escape from Warsaw. Little Susan seemed somehow to read Judith's mind and interpret terrified thoughts to the adults. For weeks I had been working with Judith, attempting to help her find her voice again. What effect would this new devastation have on the children?

"How did they survive?" I wept with Sister Mary Marcia.

"Judith was afraid . . . nightmares . . . so I let the two of them stay with me, in my cell." A feverish light shone in Sister Marcia's eyes, and she fiercely grasped my arms. "You must take them. Judith and Susan. The Nazis will come. Take them away with you. Now. Tonight. At once."

"But we don't even—"

Sister Marcia shook her head violently. "Anywhere! Anywhere is better than here."

"Then you must come too, Sister," I urged.

"No," the nun returned in a hollow, weary voice. "My place is here. But save them if you can . . . any way you can. Five minutes, only, I need. They have so few belongings. Just give me—" And she disappeared back inside.

Streams of water from the fire hoses played tag with the flames. Jets of steam shot upward. Ashes rained down.

In less than the promised five minutes the two

117

Jewish sisters were in the backseat of the Fiat between Jessica and Gina.

The flight from Brussels began anew.

Throughout the first night on the road toward France, behind us the sky was illuminated with flashes like lightning.

"Brussels is burning," I said.

Papa put a finger to his lips, warning me to guard my tongue for the sake of the little ones.

The detour to St. Mary's had cost us our position at the front of the tide of refugees. This meant our forward progress was slowed to a crawl.

Human misery closed around the Fiat like water lapping the hull of a boat. As the sun rose, we put the canvas top up. By midmorning the interior of the car was stifling from dust and sun. Jessica and Gina, miserable in the backseat, shared bread, a boiled egg, and a bottle of water with Judith and Susan, then all but Judith dozed fitfully. The convertible top prevented sunburn and afforded a slight degree of privacy, shielding the three girls from the human misery all around them.

Handcarts and horse carts laden with belongings were topped by the living cargo of humans grown too feeble or sick or old to walk. I glanced in the backseat at the Polish sisters. Surely these heart-wrenching sights were familiar to them from their escape from Warsaw nine months earlier.

Judith's eyes opened as though she felt my gaze on her. Haunted, they registered recognition of me as her teacher. The girl's expression seemed to say, *You see? You told me I was safe, but I knew they would come for us.*

I answered aloud the unspoken cry: "Judith? I told you the Lord would keep you and Susan safe. Remember? Bombs fell in Brussels, but you and your sister are unharmed. Listen to me now. Judith, darling girl, remember what I said that day in the classroom when Susan told me you were too afraid to speak or make a noise because you thought the Nazis would hear you from Poland and come find you?"

Judith's eyes flickered with the memory. Was I getting through to her?

"You see, Judith? The Angel of the Lord encamps around about those who trust Him. You trust the Lord, don't you, darling?"

Again Judith's expression registered some understanding.

I reached back and stroked her thin, pale forearm. "Well then, even if ten thousand people fall all around you, Judith, you are safe. You are here with us. My father, Pastor Robert, knows how to pray. He has asked the Lord to send angels to protect us. Here in this car. Like a little boat. Like the basket baby Moses floated in downriver. You and Susan are safe, no matter what may come. You can rest now."

Judith sighed deeply and closed her eyes, falling into a sound sleep between her sister and Gina.

The running boards of the Fiat were soon crowded with hitchhikers who leapt aboard without uttering a word. Most rode for a while and then, when forward progress slowed to a near standstill, leapt off and took to the fields on foot. Bicycles and motorcycles fared best of all. Young, single-bike riders with no skin but their own to save pressed on faster than those with families. Toddlers rode on the aching shoulders of their trudging elders. Mountains of luggage, packed so carefully before the journey, were abandoned by the way.

The population of Holland merged with Belgium in the panic to escape until millions of civilians were moving and blocking the Allied armies from reaching the battle.

A group of Belgian soldiers, wounded in the rout, stepped onto the Fiat's running boards, three on each side, like ragged bodyguards.

I noticed how passing refugees stared at the Fiat as if to ask what important Belgian official might be inside. Judith opened her eyes and stared in wonder at the Belgian military belt buckles gleaming at eye level. She glanced her questions at me: Were these soldiers sent to protect us on our journey? Were they angels?

The child drifted back to sleep.

Papa and I remained silent as the soldiers spoke to one another through the windows and past our heads.

"What's happening?" Papa asked the grit-covered fellow whose face peered in at him.

The man seemed to be the leader. His arm was in a sling. "Blitzkrieg. Just like Poland. Paratroopers took Brussels this morning. Got the radio station. You don't have a radio in this old wagon, do you? Well, if you did, you'd hear Nazis broadcasting from Brussels. Flew over our heads." He mimed the parachutes dropping like leaves.

A second soldier, the bandage about his head stained crimson, took up the tale. "Panzers drove around our fixed fortifications. Stukas dropping bombs. Our cavalry—horses—charged their tanks and machine guns."

"Where are you going?" Papa asked the passengers.

"We'll join up with the French and the British. We'll fight the Boche like in the last war. On the fields of Flanders we'll push them back."

A stricken youth, who had already seen enough death in one day to last his lifetime, rubbed the dust from his eyes and spat in the road. "Push them back. They're killing the Jews. Like they did in Poland. Behind us as we run away. They're killing all the Jews they can find."

I snapped, "Watch what you say. We have

children in the car. If you speak fearful things, I will ask you to leave."

He apologized. "Sorry. Sorry. I didn't mean to—"

His companion said, "What he means is, this isn't like the last war."

Even I knew this was nothing like the last war. For the Nazis, this was the battle to cleanse Germany's defeat in 1918. The Nazis would change the outcome of that peace by simply waging war like no one had ever imagined. Total war. A world established without mercy. What had begun in 1933 with the annihilation of its weakest citizens by German state-sponsored euthanasia had now burst forth in the full bloom of brutality. The goal was simply to eliminate or enslave everyone who was not of German blood.

The children stirred. Jessica sat up, shifting in the crowded backseat.

Gina said, "Mommy, are these fellows going to protect us?"

Little Susan took her sister's hand. "Look, Judith. Good Belgian soldiers riding with us. No one can get past them. No one can hurt us."

Jessica replied, "And angels fly above us and go before us and behind."

Judith's eyes widened. I knew she heard and understood.

The soldier escorts smiled in through the windows at the youngsters.

"We haven't surrendered," declared a soldier of about sixteen, determined not to speak fearfully in front of the little girls. "We'll fight them in France. France is strong. Stronger than our homeland. Herr Hitler will not defeat France."

None of the six soldiers had weapons. Papa asked, "Where are your rifles?"

An uncomfortable silence passed between the comrades. The leader shrugged. "We didn't have bullets. None left. Why should we carry rifles when we have no bullets?"

I closed my eyes and thought of Varrick and William trying to fight the German Panzers with no ammunition. The vision was too terrible. Everything changed. Every dream broken in a few days. I had not imagined how unprepared the nations of Europe were. Everyone had been unprepared but the Nazis. Even so, I determined I would not be afraid. I would not show fear to the girls, no matter what lay ahead in their journey.

Jessica divided and distributed a fresh loaf of bread and a sliver of salami to the children and the soldiers.

The conversation of the men rattled like the idling engine of the Fiat. "If we can only get to France!"

"Where in France?"

"It doesn't matter."

"The French *poilus* will hold back the Nazis. Has anyone got a cigarette?"

"And the British Tommies. They're fighting men. We can join up with them. They won the war last time."

"Yes. With the Americans."

"They did it in the last war."

"But I haven't had a smoke in days. Anyone got a . . . American cigarettes. Now that's heaven."

"Have the Americans joined the war yet? That President Roosevelt fellow? Has he declared war on the Nazis?"

"They'll wait until a million of us have been killed and then they'll come in. That's the way they did it last time."

"I had a Turkish cigarette from a sergeant in the hospital tent. He said he got it off a dead German. There was blood on it too. But I think it was the sergeant's blood."

"Did you smoke it?"

"What do you think? Of course."

"I've never seen a dead German. Never been close enough to see if they even bleed when we shoot them."

Fingers of smoke from Belgian towns and villages pointed skyward as the Fiat crept forward no faster than a walk. As far as I could see there was no break in the human tide on the highway, either ahead or to the rear.

"Papa," I said, studying the profile of my father's exhausted face, "let me drive."

He nodded, held the wheel of the idling car,

and switched places with me. I took the wheel and, within seconds, he slumped onto the leather seat and slept. I covered his face with his hat. The wheels idled forward. Pedestrians passed the car.

I spoke to the officer of the Belgian troops. "Where are you from?"

"Bruges," he said.

"You have family there?"

He shrugged and gave a rueful grin. "I sent them to my wife's mother's for safety . . . in Brussels." Unable to wave because of the sling on one arm and his grip on the car with the other, he jerked his chin towards the swarm of refugees. "The house is deserted. So they are out here, somewhere."

The first warning of the new attack came from shouts and cries on the road ahead. With the car still barely creeping forward, climbing a long, slight hill in the Belgian countryside, suddenly people were leaping toward the sides of the road.

The pencil-shaped body of a Dornier bomber crested the summit no more than two miles away. At barely above treetop level, its machine guns strafed the packed roadway. The ratcheting assault of its weapons cleared the pavement like a broom sweeps dry leaves.

Vaulting over stonewalls, fleeing pedestrians collided with each other. A pair of men exchanged blows with their fists when neither would move out of the way.

Three soldiers bailed from the Fiat's running boards.

I clamped a hand over the officer's grip. "Help me," I demanded. "With the children. Jessica," I said. "Get out."

"Can't," my sister returned, thrusting Gina forward. "Too slow. Save her."

Letting the Fiat steer itself, I passed my niece toward the officer, then flung the door wide. "Come on! Come on!" I shouted to Judith and Susan. Then: "Papa, wake up! Papa!"

Anguished cries rose from the road as machine-gun bullets tore into flesh and shattered bone. With Judith clinging to my neck and Susan toted by another Belgian soldier, I jumped into the bottom of a roadside ditch.

An overturning cart spilled a heap of suitcases down on top of us.

Ludicrously, I crouched behind a fabric rampart as the Dornier roared closer.

Burying Judith beneath me, I shut my eyes as bullets pocked the roadway and sliced through the Fiat. The warplane flashed overhead, seemingly close enough to touch. It continued down the highway, lancing the massed humanity and draining out its life.

Then its guns fell silent.

I raised up cautiously.

The Belgian captain stood, still holding Gina in his good arm. "Out of ammo," he said of the plane, and then about Gina, "she's fine."

Judith and Susan were likewise unharmed.

The Fiat continued idling forward down the center of the highway.

Papa! Jessica!

Setting Judith atop a suitcase, I ran toward the car, breathing a sigh of relief when I heard Jessica crying in the backseat. She, at least, was alive.

Flinging wide the door, I stomped on the brake pedal and stopped the auto.

"Are you—?"

"I'm fine," Jessica returned. "Terrified, but fine. The girls?"

"Safe." I shook my father's shoulder. "Papa?"

He roused himself and yawned. "My turn to drive?"

I stared at him in disbelief. "You didn't know? Bullets just missed the car."

"No," Jessica corrected, pointing upward.

In the fabric of the Fiat's cloth top two thumb-sized holes had appeared. The rips matched another set of gouges in the upholstery—one in the driver's seat where I had been and the other in the rear seat, where Judith and her sister had been.

The Fiat's engine continued ticking normally, in faithful unconcern.

When I returned to the ditch to retrieve the children, Judith remained atop the stack of luggage. As I reported that no one had been hurt and even the car was almost unscathed, a shy smile spread across the nine-year-old's face. The angels had been on duty, exactly as required.

By the next morning the stream of refugees swelled like tributaries dumping into one great river. Individuals melded into one mighty teeming mass—bundles tied on weary backs; in rickety carts; employing bicycles and rusty jalopies that were in much worse shape than the old Fiat. Black smoke bubbled from the tailpipe of the vehicle, and the engine emitted an ominous knocking.

Ahead, a military motorcycle corps cut through the crowd. Shouting for civilians to get out of the way, they led a thundering herd of army trucks, like elephants in camouflage. These were followed by rows of small-caliber artillery, mounted on tractors.

Papa pulled to the side of the road. Refugees scattered in the fields to either side.

Papa said, "Scots Guards and the Queen's Own Westminsters." He grimaced. "You can tell where the Germans are by the direction the Allies are traveling."

Jessica, ashen-faced, asked, "But isn't that the same road we were—"

I grasped the situation at once. "The Germans are between us and Paris, then?"

Papa nodded. "So we'll go north. If they're between us and Paris, we'll go around the battle. Ghent. Flanders and then . . ." He frowned as he glanced at Jessica.

"Where?" I breathed the question on the minds of thousands. *Where?*

Papa reached past me and grasped a small red volume of the guidebook *Baedeker's Belgium.*

Opening a map, he studied it as yet another fleet of military lorries rumbled past in a cloud of choking dust. "The BEF and the French are also between us and Paris. Here." His finger stabbed the page. "As long as we stay behind British lines, we're safe."

"Ghent? Flanders?" I peered over Papa's shoulder and traced the threading highway northwest on the map. "There are so many hotels there. Remember when we stayed at the Victoria? Jessica could rest, Papa. Ghent. A doctor if the baby—"

"They're bombing Ghent. And the Victoria. We'll go around."

"Go *where?*"

Papa flipped to the index. "Here. Page 50. Only about thirty-five miles beyond Ghent. The village of Passendale. And look, Tyne Cott."

"The military cemetery?"

"The Wehrmacht won't be interested in bombing people who are already dead."

It made sense. What sort of military target would a vast field of dead men make? I asked Jessica, "What do you think?"

Jessica nodded and stroked the unborn child. "He's kicking. He wants out, Lora. I think I'll need a place to rest soon. Someplace out of the crowd."

Papa refolded the map and passed the red book to me. "It's settled, then. Tyne Cott cemetery. I know the caretaker. A veteran of the Great War. He'll shelter us."

I agreed, never imagining that my father's decision to take us to Tyne Cott, and his friend, Judah Blood, would place us directly in the paths of two armies.

PART FOUR

A time to plant,
And a time to pluck up that which is planted.
ECCLESIASTES 3:2B

9

The once bright poppies were withering.

Warm January days and early February rains, so pleasant across Belgium and northern France that winter of 1940, had encouraged a profusion of wild blooms. A continuous drought since March caused that time of exuberant growth to be no more than a two-month-old memory. The grassy fields around Passendale and Ypres yellowed with unseasonable heat. The poppies' drooping heads were bowed with thirst. The once vibrant banks of color had faded to mere streaks, like threadbare, blood-stained carpet.

Judah Blood straightened up and stretched his aching back and reflected on the weather. There were fewer weeds to pluck this year from around the headstones of Tyne Cott cemetery, and none of the stone monuments were in danger of being engulfed in vines. Just the opposite was true: at this rate the entire hillside, where close to twelve thousand Allied soldiers had slept since the Great War, would be nothing but dust before midsummer.

The sun beating down on the tin roof of the shed Judah called his shop was not unbearable, but it was still too hot for this early in the year. Hooking both thumbs under the painted facemask, he pried it away from his cheekbones for an instant to let air flow beneath.

He took a sip of lukewarm water from a flask and studied the workbench. Beneath Judah's skilled fingers, the figure of Saint George and the Dragon he was fashioning in leaded glass was taking shape nicely. It was destined for a memorial chapel in Brussels before the chapel's dedication in July.

The rumble of trucks passing on the highway distracted him from his work yet again. It was another British convoy heading east; young men heading into yet another war. For eight months, since the Nazis invaded Poland last September, an uneasy quiet had persisted along the western front. When Allies and Nazis glared at each other across fortified positions, but no new hostilities erupted, some had taken to calling this "The Phony War."

But now those eager, fearless young British men passing in lorries on the roads were prepared to plunge into battle. Would English dead from new battlefields be brought here to lie beside their fathers and uncles, or would new hillsides be sown with bodies awaiting the blossoming of Resurrection morn?

Judah returned to his work, pondering its ultimate fate. If the Germans captured Brussels, they would have little interest in a depiction of an English saint honoring English heroes. What would happen to it then?

The saint's hands, gripping the shaft of the

spear about to be plunged into the dragon's heart, were particularly tricky to render believably. Judah closed his eyes and concentrated. Almost against his will, he recalled a bayonet charge from more than twenty years earlier. A terrified young infantryman hefted his rifle just so before stabbing downward into the body of a foe across a barbed wire barricade. The scene of desperate combat, illuminated by a shell burst, was etched in Judah's vision. In indelible memory the soldier's knuckles were clenched white, veins standing out in hands and forearms. The motion was the same as a spear thrust, the very grasp Judah needed to depict.

"'Scuse me, Cap'n Blood, sir." The diffident tone of Sergeant Mickey Walker disrupted Judah's image.

Judah shook his head to clear it. He was not sorry for the intrusion. "What is it, Sergeant?"

The remaining members of the Tin Noses Brigade still addressed each other by their ranks from the Great War. The fatigues worn by Sergeant Walker, late of the Argyll and Sutherland Highlanders, had been innocent of rank or other designation for many years. However, at Tyne Cott cemetery the Irishman remained the ranking non-comm, just as Judah was commanding officer.

"Sorry to interrupt, sir," Walker repeated, "but me and the lieutenant has been having a discussion, like." The Irishman paused to wipe a line of sweat from his forehead before it crept beneath his fake nose.

"What about?" Judah inquired.

"We was scrubbing the markers near the Cross of Sacrifice. . . . the captain knows the ones I mean; them as is for the boys who fell during the fight."

The additional description of the location was not needed. During the Battle of Passendale, which some called the Third Battle of Ypres, the British had used a captured German pillbox as an aid station. Those who did not survive their wounds were summarily buried next to the field hospital.

Later, after the war, the pillbox was surmounted by a giant stone memorial cross. The surrounding slopes displayed rank on orderly rank of headstones, but these first, haphazardly placed graves were left in their original locations. It was a tribute to the heroism of those men, and a reminder this hillside was a battlefield before it was a memorial.

"Is there a problem?" Judah asked.

"The lieutenant, sir, sees as how some of them stones is leanin' after last winter's rains. He think we should shift 'em; straighten 'em up, like."

"And you disagree?"

Walker adjusted the earpieces of the eyeglass frame that supported his artificial nose and plucked at the patch over his missing left eye. "I don't like to contradict an officer, sir, but he suggested I put it to you, like. I thinks them leanin' stones is part of the way they was left, a'purpose."

"But we can't have them falling down, can we?" Judah chided.

"None of them is in danger of that, sir," Walker returned. " 'Specially with the ground gettin' so rock hard, an' all."

"I'll walk over before supper and have a look," Judah said.

"Thank you, sir," Walker said, saluting. He turned on his heel and exited the shed as if departing from an office in a proper headquarters.

That's the way he had always been, Judah reflected. Back in the twenties, just after the last war, when the Tin Noses Brigade was much bigger, Sergeant Walker had always been a stickler for military tradition. The men whose terribly disfigured faces barred them from home and sweethearts and society found peace and acceptance among similarly injured comrades. Without an actual plan, they had coalesced around the Belgian cemetery like raindrops sliding down and collecting at the bottom of a windowpane.

They found meaning in their lives as outcasts by serving their fallen comrades—maintaining the memorials and acting as guides for grieving family members.

In those early days Sergeant Walker had been

the only master stonecutter in the troop. Over the years he had trained a dozen others to chisel names into granite and marble with precision and economy of motion.

Now the combined, long-term effects of poison gas, shrapnel, and depression had taken their toll. After two decades of failing lungs, septic wounds, and suicides, Walker was once again the only trained mason left in the brigade.

Judah watched Sergeant Walker rejoin his lieutenant. The latter was Frank Howard. In 1917 he had been a pink-cheeked junior officer. His first taste of combat had been at Polygon Wood, not far from this very spot. There, as the young and inexperienced Howard raised up on his toes to peer across no-man's-land, a burst from a German machine gun had sliced off his nose and one of his pink cheeks.

Sergeant Walker had been wounded in almost the same manner while rescuing his lieutenant. Both were scarred forever. Both received treatment at the Tin Noses Shop in Paris. The two men had been inseparable ever since.

As far as Frank Howard's family knew, he died at Passendale in 1917.

Such confusion was neither rare nor surprising: a million men killed from just the forces of the British Empire alone. Some scholars said as many as ten million soldiers died. The sum was nearly incomprehensible.

In Lieutenant Howard's case it was his purpose to keep his family in ignorance of his true fate. The bullet that had struck him had shattered more than his face. It had shattered his life. Even with the prosthesis hiding the gaping horror of his features, he would have ended his own existence if Sergeant Walker had not rescued him a second time by returning him here to Passendale.

Offspring of a noble house, and well-educated, Howard was the architect and engineer for the troop. There was nothing he could not design and few things he could not repair. Judah's workshop and the stone cottages that housed the brigade had been of Howard's conception.

Now there were only four members of the brigade left, and they stayed in one cottage together.

Yet another convoy bumped past on the road heading east.

Judah strained his ears. Was he really hearing the crump of distant artillery fire, was it his imagination, or simply a memory he already regretted reliving?

How much longer would the Tin Noses Brigade be able to serve their fallen brothers at Tyne Cott? And if not here, then where?

The aroma of cabbage soup pervaded the stone cottage just outside the cemetery grounds. Judah was the last to enter the squat, four-room structure. He had worked longer on Saint George than he expected. By the time he completed his promised inspection of the graves beside the cross, the sun was setting.

Walker, Howard, and the American, Jim Kadle, were gathered around the table. A steaming tureen of soup and their empty bowls demonstrated they had waited for Judah's arrival before eating.

"My apologies," Judah said. "I lost track of time."

"Know you're anxious to get finished, sir," Walker said. "Anyway, we've been having a bit of a chat."

"More like an argument, you mean," Kadle corrected.

Judah shushed the debate long enough to ask Howard to pronounce a blessing and begin ladling out the meal. Once everyone had been served, the captain inquired, "What was this discussion about?"

With that invitation, as usually happened over meals, military protocol was relaxed. All the Tin Noses Brigade were free to state their opinions without regard to rank.

Howard had removed the prosthetic portion of his face. One cheekbone and his mouth were perfectly normal. His nose and the other cheek, of painted, galvanized copper, lay on the bench behind him. Half his features he covered with a black scarf from just below the level of his eyes. With a practiced gesture he plucked the corner of the cloth away from his mouth with one hand and tossed in a spoonful of soup with the other. "Private Kadle maintains that if the Germans cross the Meuse, they'll be here before the week is out. The sergeant and I feel differently. With our boys in the fight, the Boche will be tossed right back to the Siegfried Line in short order."

Judah, who never removed the tin mask covering his nose, eyes, and forehead, swallowed a mouthful of soup before responding. "Why so pessimistic, Private?"

Kadle held his head at an angle while eating his soup, the better to accommodate the fact he was missing part of his jaw on one side. "It's this way, sir. The Germans have better tanks. They have better artillery. You know about their 88s? They have better aircraft. They are better equipped, better trained. Now I don't say your boys won't slow 'em down some, but I'm afraid it'll be 'too little, too late.'"

Kadle, like all the Tin Noses Brigade, had paid dearly for his right to express an opinion about military matters, especially when the topic was German armament and weaponry. The American private was with the U.S. 91st Infantry Regiment on the banks of the River Scheldt when his company was strafed by German bi-planes. With nowhere to escape, Kadle was lucky to emerge with only the loss of an ear and half his jaw; ten others all around him had not even been as fortunate.

That was east of Passendale, at the Battle of Spittals Bosschen, November 4, 1918.

One week before the Armistice.

One week before safety and home and family.

Just as the United States had been a late arrival to the Great War, Kadle had also been a latecomer to the ranks of the servants at Tyne Cott. Before that he had been single-handedly tending four hundred of his countrymen's graves at Flanders Field American Cemetery. Then, quite unexpectedly, in 1928, he had run headlong into his mother and father . . . who believed him to be dead. They had come to Flanders to lay a wreath in honor of their missing son at the Tomb of the Unknown Soldier.

Terrified they might see and recognize him, Kadle had fled to join the Tyne Cott band of brothers and had remained ever since.

"I don't mean to be a pessimist," he said now. "But I'm a realist. The Germans have more tanks and better tanks."

Agreeing in part with Kadle's assessment, Judah said, "The French generals were wrong in thinking this would be 1917 all over again. The Germans can move, and move quickly. This will not be a war of trenches and gains measured in yards."

"So you agree with me, then?" Kadle asked.

Judah shrugged. "But the Germans may still get overextended, just like at the Marne . . . remember? If they outrun their supply lines they can be hit from both sides in a coordinated counterattack: British and Belgians from the north, French from the south."

Lieutenant Howard slapped his palm on the table, jostling the tureen and causing a cup of soup to slop onto the table. "Sorry, but that's just what I said. Overextended. Outflanked from both sides at once."

When the soup was exhausted, the men pushed back their chairs. "I think that's enough about the war for tonight," Judah decreed. He gestured toward where half of Howard's face lay staring upward at the cottage ceiling. "Lieutenant, I see the paint is chipped around your nose. Pump up that lantern, and I'll tend to it for you."

"Thank you, sir," Howard said as Judah opened a box of paints and delicate brushes. As the gas lantern hissed and visibly brightened, Judah mixed flesh tones on his palette and turned to work.

Later, he wandered out into the night without mentioning his destination.

"S'pose he's off again, then?" Walker queried. "Last time it was two weeks. Before that, six. Never says where."

"The captain is entitled to keep his personal

business to himself," Howard returned. "Anyway, I don't think so. It's just this war business has us all jumpy."

"You're right about that, sire. You're right about that."

It was early morning at Tyne Cott, just past daybreak. The Tin Noses Brigade gathered together around a stand of poplars screening the squat concrete form of a derelict German pillbox.

Later in the day the four comrades would disperse to their individual duties, but Judah had summoned them for this special task while the air was still cool from the night. "If we don't get rain soon," he said, "the grass will die. But we can, and we must, keep the trees and the hedges alive by hauling water for them."

This morning's chore involved digging a channel around each of the tall, flame-shaped trees. Once filled with gravel, each ring would trap moisture and direct it toward the poplars' roots.

"Should have done this two months ago," Kadle groused. The American had been wounded in the right hand and arm by the same attack that injured his face. Now he wielded a turf spade with his left hand alone.

No one bothered to respond to this observation. No one could have foreseen the drought that made this effort necessary. Still, it was a soldier's right to complain.

Judah's corded arms and brawny shoulders drove the point of a pick deep into the earth with each blow. As if mining for gold or diamonds, he attacked the resistant ground.

Kadle, coming immediately behind the captain, removed the layer of loosened clods. The broken pieces came out in shards and fractured clumps, more like stone than soil.

Walker and Howard, wielding shovels, deepened the ring until the depth passed the hard-packed upper layer and exposed earth that still retained some moisture. As each of the poplars was served in this way, its encircling ring would be lined with rock fragments.

Judah studied his men as they worked. Already Howard showed signs of tiring. Walker would never admit it, but even his sturdy, bandy-legged form did not possess the strength it once had.

Kadle would bear the most watching, Judah thought. The American would dig until he dropped without a word of warning to his friends.

Judah had already adjusted his estimate of how long this chore would take. There were just eight poplars in all—four flanking each side of Tyne Cott's entry gate. At first Judah had hoped to do one stand today and the other tomorrow.

Later he amended that estimate to just two drainage channels per day.

Now, watching the tremble in Howard's neck and legs, the captain adjusted his plan yet again. They would try to complete one tree this morning and then begin again tomorrow.

Kadle's lift-and-toss action propelled a spadeful of earth farther than he intended. Gravel bounced off Walker's head and something rang metallically against his shovel.

"Hey!" he chided. "Watch what you're about, then."

"Sorry," Kadle responded.

Walker bent to see what had made the strange sound. From the loose soil he plucked a tarnished silver cigarette case. "Look here," he said, holding it aloft. "Too nice for the likes of me."

"Must be mine, Sergeant," Howard teased.

Peering closer at the ground with his remaining eye, Walker adjusted his facemask. Probing in the dirt with his fingers, he said, "I don't think so. The former owner's still present." Brushing aside clods of dirt, Walker exposed a human skull.

"Hold up, then," Judah ordered.

Early records of the burials at Tyne Cott were confused, incomplete, and conflicting. Judah's study revealed that the gravesites of more than eighty soldiers known to be interred within the confines of the memorial had been lost over time.

Apparently one of them had just been rediscovered.

"All right," Judah ordered. "Sergeant Walker,

you're in charge of locating as much of this soldier as you can. The rest of us will go to work on our other tasks. We rebury this man tomorrow morning and then get back to work on the trees."

Walker saluted. "Yes, sir," he said, passing the cigarette case to Judah, who tucked it into his shirtfront. "Initials D.M. May help identify him." The sergeant pointed behind Judah and toward the gate. "Now, what about them?"

A group of civilians, apparently a family group of mother, father, grandmother, and four children, were gathered there, hesitating beside the entry. "I'll see to them. The rest of you go about your duties."

"How can I help you?" Judah addressed the gray-haired man who stood two paces in front of the others.

The man shook his head. His looks went everywhere except at Judah's face. "No English," he said. "Parlez-vous francais?"

"Oui," Judah responded, switching to French. "What do you require?"

One of the children stared openly at Judah's painted nose and motionless eyebrows and forehead.

Another buried her face into her mother's skirts in apparent terror.

"May we rest here? My children are tired."

Judah agreed readily. "You don't need my permission, but of course. Do you need water?

Food? How comes it that you are on the road this way?"

"We are from Namur," the man replied, naming a Belgian town to the east, on the Meuse river. "The Boche . . . they are coming. We have fled."

"The Germans have overrun Namur?"

"No, Monsieur, but we heard they are not far. We heard their cannons three mornings since."

"And where are you going?"

The father gave a Gallic shrug. "Who can say? Away from the Boches. To the sea, perhaps?"

Judah gestured toward the aged grandmere and the small children. "So far? On foot?"

"We had an automobile, but it ran out of fuel," the father explained.

"But surely this is far enough," Judah countered. "Why not go into the village here and find lodging?"

The patriarch of the refugee family pointed toward a trickle of civilians trudging along the highway, traveling the opposite direction to the flow of British trucks. "The Nazis are swallowing great chunks of France and Belgium without even chewing." Leaning closer to Judah, he whispered, "My mother-in-law, my wife—they are Jewish."

"Ah," Judah returned, comprehending at last. "Then at least let us feed you before you set out again."

10

It was nearly midnight. The other three members of the Tin Noses Brigade were asleep in the cottage, but Judah could not rest. As often happened on such occasions, he wandered up the hill toward the Cross of Sacrifice and seated himself between its outstretched arms.

While many would have been uncomfortable to be alone, surrounded by thousands of graves, in the middle of a dark night, such apprehension never bothered Judah. In the first place, all of those buried here were fallen comrades, men to fight alongside and, if necessary, to die with, but never to be afraid of.

Even more important than that consideration was Judah's belief that the spiritual portion of his vanished friends was much more real than their bones. Their frames were real enough, waiting to be rejoined bone-to-bone and sinew-to-sinew, as the prophet Ezekiel wrote. But their present reality was as the crowd of witnesses described in Hebrews: those whose races were already completed; who were in the grandstands cheering for Judah's success.

The tiny flock of which he was the shepherd had dwindled to the point of almost disappearing. Once they were all gone, would he have the strength to find a new set of charges? Another band who would look to him for leadership?

Judah was tired with a soul-deep weariness. Frank, Mickey, Jim—the final few of the fractured bodies and tormented souls left in his charge from the last war—had nearly run their courses.

And even now a new conflict was raging.

Venus hovered just above the tree line in the west. A waxing gibbous moon bowed its head respectfully between the figures of the Virgin and the Lion of Judah.

In the east the Snake-Handler rose—his uplifted heel even now poised to crush the scorpion's head.

"Would it could be true tonight," Judah murmured aloud. "I hear the fear: old demons in new bodies, coming after Your people yet again."

He crossed himself and with the gesture tapped something inside his shirt. It was the cigarette case that had rested there unremembered all day.

The catch was stiff from a score of years buried in the dirt, but the latch worked and the lid still turned on its hinge. Pivoting so that the moonlight fell across his shoulder, Judah raised the case to the glow. A beam falling directly on the upright surface was redirected precisely, as if from a mirror, into the lower portion.

The silver box did not contain ancient cigarettes. Instead Judah saw a photograph and a lock of pale hair bound with a satin ribbon. The photo was of a mother and baby. Both had faces framed with light-colored curls . . . just like the keepsake.

Judah turned the picture over. By squinting he could just make out the sentiment inscribed there: *Love you and miss you, Dan,* it read. *Come home soon.*

Twenty years waiting for a familiar step and an embrace that would never come. How long had this young wife grieved before moving on with her life? Did the little girl even remember her father? Had she been raised to know anything of him, or did she not ever think of him at all?

They should know he had this with him, next to his heart, Judah reflected. *The child would be what—twenty-five—now? No more than that, surely. It's a certainty his last thought was of them. If there's any way to locate her, I'll tell her so.*

Judah sat and pondered what another round of war and shattered lives and vanished fathers would mean to the aching world. He thought and thought until the Great Bear completed a quarter turn around the Pole Star, then took himself down the hill to the cottage and his bed.

One day after the first refugees passed Tyne Cott heading west, the trickle of fleeing civilians became a steady stream.

Three days later it was a torrent.

The road was clogged with as many people seeking to escape the Nazi onslaught as there were soldiers moving up to oppose it. Lorries packed with infantrymen or towing anti-tank weapons or loaded with ammunition and spare parts were mired in humanity as thoroughly as if the roads were impassably muddy instead of perfectly dry.

Gesturing officers and cursing sergeants tried to clear the civilians out of the way but failed. The combination of language barriers and human obstinacy prevented any of their efforts from having effect. The British army was not prepared to run over or shoot down the civilians they were supposed to be protecting from the advancing Germans, so traffic in both directions slowed to a crawl.

Judah stood beside Lieutenant Howard at the gate. "Their strategy is working," Judah observed.

"Sir?"

"The German plan. By bombing and shelling towns in the line of their advance they know they can jam the roads." Judah waved toward the melee of creaking handcarts, screeching drovers flogging their horses, and impotently wailing ambulance sirens. "The Allies might have counterattacked at Sedan, but the necessary forces were still stuck in Vervins, forty miles away. If the high command planned a counterattack for Vervins, the needed troops were no nearer than Cambrai, still—"

"Forty miles away," Howard completed the thought. "So you think it's hopeless?"

"I never said that," Judah corrected. "But it seems clear to me the Germans are driving toward the Channel. If they succeed, they will cut the Allies in two, trapping our boys and the Belgians against the sea."

Reflexively Howard adjusted the tin mask over his face.

He always did that when he was worried, Judah recognized. To divert Howard's attention the captain said, "It always surprises me to see what families decide they must save from their homes. When they had to leave on five minutes' notice, how did they choose what to rescue?"

Howard's painted features could not flex into a grin, but Judah heard the smile in his reply. "I know what you mean, sir! Yesterday I saw the headboard of a bed so big it took three men to lug it. Not even something as practical as a mattress. Just the headboard."

Judah laughed. "Don't try to challenge them on it," he warned. "Family heirlooms are not to be mocked."

"No, sir," Howard agreed. "Mocking not permitted. Still . . ."

"Yes?"

"I also saw a man pushing a baby carriage while his wife carried the baby."

"And?"

Howard shrugged. "The pram was loaded with phonograph records. Family heirlooms again?"

Private Kadle approached the gate. "I was over on the east side. One of the civilians got up his nerve to ask me a question. Wanted to know if they could camp here tonight."

"Camp? Inside the cemetery?"

"Yes, sir. If we want to keep them out, we'll have to stay up all night, one of us at each gate. I figure our looks will manage it for us, but otherwise we'll be overrun."

Judah thought for a moment. "In the dark there are bound to be accidents on the road if it's not cleared. Besides, we're helping our boys at the front if we clear the way for replacements and supplies. All right, tell them they can come in. But we will show them where they can camp. Keep them orderly, yes?"

"Orderly it is, sir."

That night the rows of headstones were illuminated by campfires. Family groups huddled near the flames more from apprehension at the surroundings than from any need for warmth. At least they were free from the dangers of the highway.

The platform supporting the Cross of Sacrifice was the highest point of land anywhere in the vicinity of Tyne Cott. From its summit the next morning Judah surveyed the villages of Passendale and Ypres and the nearby roads. Primarily his attention was focused on the southeast. It was difficult to be certain, but it appeared pillars of black smoke propped up the pale blue sky in that direction.

"How far do you make that, Lieutenant?" Judah said to Howard.

"Fifteen miles," the officer ventured. "Perhaps twenty. Toward Menin, I make it. The Germans could not be that close already, surely?"

Judah reviewed a mental map of the area. "If they were across the river Lys, we would have heard about it. But they could be close enough to be shelling towns on this side."

The civilians encamped among the graves stirred and rose, gathering their few belongings. Judah could not escape the vision of the dead coming to life as families emerged from cocoons of blankets and improvised shelters. Though they had been grateful for the seeming shelter within the walls of Tyne Cott, the temporary guests now appeared eager to renew their flight.

The flow of traffic along the highway was still at a crawling pace. It occurred to Judah that fewer British and Belgian troops were moving up. For the first time since the crisis began, the majority of those on the road were heading away from the fighting. The refugee horde was supplemented by knots of soldiers fleeing as well.

Weary uniformed men, some without weapons, trudged past the cemetery, away from the battle line.

Looking for more current news, Judah summoned a young man whose insignia announced he was part of the field artillery. "Corporal," Judah called, "a word, please. Are you wounded?"

A negative gesture.

"How did you get separated from your unit?" Judah passed the man a bottle of water, from which he drank gratefully.

"How did I? What day's today?" the non-comm replied, glancing over his shoulder.

When Judah answered the question, the soldier replied, "Is that all? I thought I'd been walking for weeks! We were on the Meuse when the Germans broke through. Our captain ordered us out; said we were about to be surrounded." After taking a mouthful of water he continued, "We fell back across another river and set up. Fired a few shells. Never saw a target; never knew what we were shooting at. Loaded up; moved again. Bombed from the air. The captain got killed in that one. Crossed another river . . . the Scheldt? I don't know."

"Take your time."

"That night, they jumped us." The artilleryman looked over first one shoulder and then the other. "Came from three sides at once. I ran. Been looking for my unit ever since. Still haven't found anyone else I know. What's that noise?" the corporal said abruptly, his head spinning around.

A high-pitched buzz, like a mosquito's warning, overcame the rumble of trucks and the ceaseless hum of human activity. A single small, fragile-seeming aircraft droned into view, climbing up from the south.

"Where's a rifle? Get me a rifle," the corporal demanded, his head pivoting back and forth. His wild eyes roved frantically over the concrete platform and the cross and the sky. "Down there," he said. "Can we get inside?"

"Calm down," Judah urged. "That's a Storch, not a warplane."

Gunfire erupted from the direction of the road. Rifles popped and popped again as the German scout craft spiraled lazily overhead.

"You don't understand," the artillery corporal shrieked, throwing himself behind the plinth on which the cross stood. "It's when the spotter plane leaves!"

Even as the young man spoke, the Storch made a dainty wing-over and drifted away toward the east with the seeming indifference and unconcern of a feather carried by the breeze.

"He's gone," Judah observed. "You can get up now."

"No," the corporal protested. "Now is when it's most dangerous!"

Judah could not comprehend the corporal's ravings until he noticed a line of black dots swooping in out of the sun.

"Stukas!" the artilleryman screamed, attempting to bury his face in the granite.

The string of dive-bombers peeled from the sky in a looping, single-file turn, like swooping pelicans darting into a school of hapless fish. Lined up with the highway, the bombers fell toward earth, whistles screaming shrilly to compound the terror.

As if invisible hands swept down the center of the highway, soldiers and civilians alike bolted for the ditches on either side. Their terrified leaps into hedges and furrows gave the appearance of lunatics deceived into believing the fields were made of water into which they could plunge.

Lorries emptied themselves of people as if by magic. Trucks, no longer guided by human hands and with doors left akimbo like flapping ears, lumbered forward like circus elephants.

Black crosses clearly visible, the gull-winged predators closed for the kill.

So densely packed was the roadway it was impossible for the German aviators to miss hitting something. The first bomb exploded in a mass of civilians. The explosion was deafening. The ground shook and rattled beneath Judah's feet. Bodies were tossed end-over-end into the air.

"Get down!" he screamed, waving to the refugees still within Tyne Cott's embrace. "Take cover!"

The second bomber overshot the road, but not by much. Its explosives fell just inside the entry gate of the cemetery. Judah had only an instant to take in the image of families huddling beside headstones and war memorials before heeding his own advice and diving behind the sheltering cross.

The third parcel of high-explosive ordnance made a direct hit on a fuel truck. A massive fireball plunged skyward; hellish heat radiated up the slope. Judah felt the scorching on the back of his neck as it roared past.

Unwittingly, the hit scored on the fuel proved the salvation of many. The flames, billowing cloud of oil, and the black smoke made the fourth bomber sheer off. He deposited his bomb load in the field beyond where the refugees cowered. Once again the ground shook, and windows were shattered in the cottages all around Tyne Cott.

The fifth and final Stuka misjudged his release completely, overshooting the cemetery. He dropped his bomb on the reverse slope of the hillside, where it did not explode at all.

When the reverberations ceased, the noise was replaced by a swelling chorus of cries and moans; of grief and pain.

"They're gone," Judah observed to the corporal. "You can get up now."

"Not yet," the soldier argued. "They'll come back and strafe! You'll see."

At last Judah understood the reason the corporal's head had seemed to be on a swivel. Attacks from the air could come from any direction, at any time. He was terrified of being caught by surprise, out in the open . . . and with good reason.

But this time, at least, the Stukas did not return. Whether they sought higher value targets elsewhere or merely wanted to spread panic over a wider area, they bounced out of sight over the horizon.

Grimly Judah said, "Lots of people will need assistance. Come down and help as soon as you can."

All of the Tin Noses Brigade survived multiple aerial assaults unscathed.

The atmosphere reeked of cordite and diesel smoke and burning rubber and blood. The peace of Tyne Cott had been shattered and remained fragmented. Those who did not moan, or cry with grief or pain, walked around mute, with haunted, staring eyes.

The fresh bomb crater inside the main gate was proposed as a ready-made mass grave for the victims of the Stuka attack. "Them Huns is the most inventive barbarians," Sergeant Walker noted bitterly. "Bomb a cemetery! Killin' and buryin' in the most orderly fashion possible. Next thing you know they'll have a killin' machine as makes their victims line up and ask for it."

"Enough, Sergeant," Judah ordered. "Unlock all the old German pillboxes. Make certain the lanterns have oil. If the bombers come back, we need better shelter than crouching behind headstones. Spread the word. Lieutenant Howard?"

"Sir?"

"Organize rescue parties. Take the wounded into the emplacement beneath the cross. There must be doctors and medical orderlies in the mob. Send them along with as many supplies as they can carry."

"Yes, sir!"

"Kadle," Judah continued, "you and I will organize the burial detail. This corporal will help us."

Lance Corporal Sackett had finally emerged from his fetal position beside the memorial. Like a frightened stray dog with no home in sight, he gravitated toward Judah with desperation on his face.

The remainder of the day was spent clearing up the aftermath of the bombing. Twenty-two people had been killed and another twenty-seven wounded badly enough to require treatment at the impromptu aid station. "Surprisingly modest butcher's bill, considering how jammed the road was," Howard noted.

"Miracle," Judah said. Even though it was amazing scores more had not been killed, there were two scenes Judah knew would haunt him forever.

When the smoke cleared, families gathered around their dead and wounded. Stunned by the sudden ferocity of the attack, the shell-shocked survivors wandered over the cemetery, looking for assistance. The refugees could not avoid stepping over and around headstones, but there was one place that was universally shunned. Judah went to see why.

One grave had been ripped open as thoroughly as if a giant spade had scooped out the earth. The coffin was tilted upright and the cover was askew, revealing skeletal remains. The occupant appeared to be sitting upright, surveying the carnage.

Nor was that the strangest part of the tale.

One of those killed by the blast, a middle-aged civilian, came to rest on top of the exposed coffin, as if desiring the occupant to move over and give him room.

The other haunting death was even more tragic.

Outside the gate were blast victims and burn victims and bleeding wounded, perforated by shrapnel.

And a little girl, about seven years old.

She was lying in the ditch. Her mother knelt beside her. "Please, Meena, wake up. Won't you wake up for Mommy? Please, darling, stop teasing me. You're scaring me, Meena. Wake up."

There was not a mark on the child—no wounds, no burns, no obvious fractures.

But she was dead.

"I don't understand why she won't wake up," her mother argued. "We were walking together. She was holding my hand. And then . . . you know, I saw people starting to run, but I didn't know why. I held her tighter. I really did! I didn't let go!"

A nun, a streak of blood staining her wimple, knelt beside the dazed mother and put an arm around her. "I know, dear. I saw you."

"You did?" the mother asked, her features lighting up. "I'm so very glad. But why won't she wake up? She's just sleeping, isn't she? Isn't she?" The mother's voice gained a note of hysteria.

"Sister," Judah said, "would you like to take her into our quarters? Private Kadle will show you the way. We'll . . . we'll do what needs to be done here."

Throughout the day the quartet of the Tin Noses Brigade were looked upon as heroes. They dispensed comfort and instruction and reassurance to the confused and frightened and grief-stricken.

Then came sunset.

Judah first noticed the change in the eyes of Lance Corporal Sackett. As they continued toting supplies and helping the wounded with food and water by lamplight, Judah saw the corporal sneaking furtive glances at him, specifically at the mask over his nose and forehead.

Nor was the captain the only one to experience the difference. "Captain," Sergeant Walker said, "you know what? No one's asked me for anything for the past half hour. Before that I was mobbed with folks wanting to know: 'Where's the water? Where's the toilets?' But now, nothing." He straightened his eye patch. "I don't mind for myself so much, but the lieutenant . . . it's hit him hard. All day everybody needin' his help and not even noticing our masks, like. Now, he says, he walks by, and a mother covers her child's eyes, like we're the worst thing they've seen today."

"We're the living reminder of the horror of which today was just a sample," Judah said. "War has forcibly come to people who yesterday or last week had simple, ordinary lives. Today they're trying to make the best of hiding in a graveyard . . . and here we are, the keepers of the place."

Walker snorted. "Still don't seem fair. We're the same as we was before it got dark. They all wanted our help then."

"Just need to adjust their thinking," Judah said.

"Tonight everything frightens them, including us. Tomorrow'll be better, eh, Corporal. Corporal?"

But Lance Corporal Sackett had fled, nor was he alone in his decision. More than half of those who had sheltered in Tyne Cott left before the next sunrise. Only those with wounds or wounded family members greeted Judah and his men the next day . . . and they shuddered as they did so.

PART FIVE

*A time to be born,
and a time to die.*
ECCLESIASTES 3:2A

11

Papa? How do we get from here to Tyne Cott?" I smoothed the map out on my knees as Papa and I sat together on the running board and studied by the light of a cigarette lighter. Jessica and the girls slept in the back of the Fiat.

The surrounding fields were sown with sleeping exiles—all too weary to press on in the dark. Behind them the horizon flashed and boomed from the encroaching battle.

"This way." Papa traced the line with his finger.

I looked up into the star-filled sky as lightning flashed. We had come so far from Brussels. Only thirty or so miles to go until the safety of Tyne Cott! Such a distance was nothing; nothing at all for me to walk. Even with three little girls in tow, the distance on foot might be manageable. But as I considered Jessica's swollen ankles, heavy abdomen, and spreading hips, the distance to Judah Blood and the cemetery sounded like the other side of the planet. Paris was the far side of the moon.

"Papa? I don't know if Jessica can."

"She must. She will."

"But the baby . . ."

"We can't stay here until it's born."

"Only five miles back to Ghent. Perhaps we were wrong. Perhaps we should go back."

"You see those flashes of light?" Papa demanded, forcing me to examine reality. "Look. Look over there." He swept his hand toward the glow on the horizon. "That's Ghent. Can't you smell the smoke?"

I rested my head in my hands. "Oh, Papa, there must be someplace. Someplace closer."

"Everyone who can walk is out here. Tonight. On the road. Sleeping in the fields. With us."

There was a stirring in the car. Jessica's exhausted voice called, "Thirty miles? Is that all?"

I whispered, "You awake?"

Jessica coughed. "Go back to Ghent? You crazy?"

I stood and peered in through the open window. For an instant a distant explosion illuminated my sister's face. "Can you walk thirty miles?"

Jessica's arms were around the girls. "As long as I'm going forward."

"I just thought . . . a bed for you. You know?"

"What are you talking about? Go back? Loralei Bittick! I've got to have this baby someplace safe."

"I miss Mama," I blurted. "She'd know what to do."

Jessica lay back, stroking Gina's hair. "I miss her too. And you know what Mama'd say? She'd say, 'Girls? Remember! Never look back!

Somebody might be gaining on you.'" She laughed. Her laugh sounded so much like Mama's. "Loralei, there's just one thing. We've got to save the teacups. Wrap up Mama's teacups. I can carry them."

Tears stung my eyes. I wiped her cheek quickly as the moisture spilled over. "All right then, Jessica. You're older than me."

"And wiser."

"But I'm taller."

"My feet are bigger." Jessica chuckled. "So I can walk farther. You just make sure Mama's china is wrapped good."

"All right. We'll save Mama's teacups."

Papa folded the map. "It's settled, then. You'll save your mother's teacups from the Blitzkrieg. And we won't look back. Go to sleep. Get some rest. Tomorrow we start walking."

Before the sun rose the rolling thunder of tanks and artillery jolted me awake. Papa was already up, standing in his stocking feet, staring at the ensuing panic of civilians returning to the road.

I called, "Theirs? Or ours?"

He licked his lips and shook his head. "Ours, I think. In that wood, a few miles away." As he spoke the *whoosh* and freight train rumble of a shell passing overhead obscured his words. A moment afterward something like a Fourth of July fireworks display erupted in the woods.

"That was theirs," he said regretfully. "The Panzers have found the range."

People screamed and began to run, pushing and jostling to escape.

"Papa!" Jessica's face was ashen as she peered out from the Fiat. "Which way will we go?"

Hands on his hips, Papa scanned the fleecy white clouds for some sign of enemy aircraft. His eyes narrowed as he calmly observed the frantic fight of thousands to escape. He shouted to us over the noise: "They're all going that way."

"Where?" I covered my ears. "Where are they going?"

The roar of explosions drowned out his reply. He shook his head in disbelief. He pointed toward the woods and, beyond the forest, to hedgerows dividing pastures. He yelled above the tumult, "We're going that way . . . off the roads . . . enough food and water in the pack. Tyne Cott!" His face turned away from the chaos. "Never look back."

Despite this warning, it was impossible to avoid looking back as we reached a still-too-close hill. Breathless from our awkward sprint, we collapsed onto our knees behind a row of trees. Lifting our faces in horrified supplication, we watched and knew who was gaining on us.

Flashes from the French artillery emplacement winked like fireflies against the dark green backdrop of the woods.

My count reached five before the pop of the guns reached me.

"French 75s," Papa observed.

In the debate between weapons the German artillery offered an overwhelming response. Much too far away to be heard as they launched, a fearsome rain of shells fell on the French positions.

Instead of the gentle blink of fireflies, the Nazi return fire was lightning falling from heaven, obliterating trees, brush, and French cannons.

"German 88s," Papa said sadly.

One by one the French guns fell silent. The rolling barrage of the German weapons lifted to trample the field that had lately sheltered scores of families.

"It's good everyone left when . . . ," I began.

Then the German shells tracked onto the highway, jammed with fleeing civilians gripped by the traffic and unable to move. Like giant fists slamming against an ant trail, the road jumped and buckled. A direct hit on a car left a smoking crater behind it. Bodies were flung aloft, spinning crazily before plunging back into the midst of the flames.

Jessica was very brave, I decided.

Very, very brave.

Sometimes my extremely expectant sister trudged along with both hands under her belly, as if supporting an inconveniently placed and awkwardly loaded cannon ball.

Sometimes Jessica walked bent forward, one hand pressed to the small of her back, as if the baby were carrying her instead of the other way around. I also saw that she was stepping pigeon-toed, trying to shift the weight to the outside of the soles of her feet.

But she never complained; not once.

"Papa," I urged, "we need to stop. We need to rest. The girls are tired."

The truth of the matter was that the three young females were managing better than we adults. With barely any weight in the knapsacks on their backs, they still found energy enough to dart ahead of the group. Gina and Susan carried on animated conversations, long after Papa and Jessica and I had lapsed into the silence of misery.

Papa was puffing, and his complexion was a sallow gray. He squinted at the sun, now dropping below the trees. "I agree. I think we've come far enough for one day. We're in the valley of the Lys. If I haven't led us too far astray since we started this cross-country jaunt, we should reach the village of Nazareth by tomorrow. We can cross the river there."

"Nazareth?" Gina chirped. "Is that where Jesus lives? Can we see Him?"

Judith frowned and waved to get her sister's

attention. "Judith says He won't welcome us," Susan replied. "We're not Christians."

Papa smiled at his granddaughter and his wards. "First of all, Judith and Susan, He most certainly would welcome you. You are children of Abraham and so was He. And He loved children and loved telling stories to children best of all. He was a famous rabbi, you know."

Judith continued to frown, but Susan's eyes grew big and round. "Then why do the Hitler-men shout at us and call us Christ-killers?" the younger sister asked. "If your Jesus was a Jew, wouldn't the Nazis have hated Him too, and tried to kill Him too?"

"Yes," Papa agreed. "They do hate Him and every time they hurt His people they are trying to kill Him all over again. But enough of this serious talk of hating and killing," he said brightly. "Gina, you know Jesus lived in Nazareth a long, long time ago. And anyway, this is a village named for Jesus' home, but not the same one He lived in."

"Seriously, Papa," I asked, "can we find a place to stay in the village for tonight?" I inclined my head slightly toward Jessica, who was using both hands to rub her belly in alternating circles.

"I wish we could. But Nazareth is where several roads come together to cross the Lys . . . do you understand me?"

No more than a week earlier I would have needed further explanation as to why roads and bridges were places to avoid. Now, after getting close to war, I had begun to know how the Germans thought: locate a spot where traffic backed up and refugees crowded against army trucks. Such a location was an irresistible target for bombing and strafing.

"I understand," I said.

Tucked within the band of trees was an ancient charcoal-burner's hut. The roof was sway-backed and the floor dirt, but it was vacant and secluded. "I think we may borrow its use for one night," Papa said. "And since we've seen no one else all day, I think we may have a fire to toast some bread and heat water for tea . . . a very small fire," he cautioned.

I made my sister sit down. Jessica had to do so in stages, like the mechanical folding of a carpenter's rule. She leaned her back against the wall of the cabin. "Remember: stopping now was your idea," she scolded me. "I won't be able to get up again until tomorrow."

"Never mind," I agreed. "Just let me see your feet."

As soon as I removed my sister's shoes, I gasped. The soles of Jessica's stockings were outlined with blood. "Jessica! What?"

"Don't tell Papa," Jessica cautioned. "He'll just fuss. I know you packed Mama's nursing kit. Just let me rest them tonight, and tomorrow we'll bandage them before we set out again. I can do this, Lor. I have to."

The next morning the trees and the charcoal-burner's hut were shrouded in mist. It clung to the branches and dripped onto the turf with a soft patter like rain. I woke before the others with a sense of peace. Perhaps today we would reach Tyne Cott and relative safety. Perhaps today we would find a doctor for Jessica and her baby, who must surely be arriving soon.

At the moment the need was fresh water. "Papa," I whispered, "I'm going to refill our water bottles."

"I think there's a meadow just west of here," he returned, "where the valley slopes toward the river. You may find a creek there. Just don't take any chances and don't be gone more than a couple minutes. And don't . . . ," he added, peering out at the dense fog, "don't get lost."

The thick vapor covering the copse of trees was even more dense than I first thought. By the time I had gone a handful of steps from the cottage the shelter's humble form had completely vanished.

The pines and spruce, laid out in orderly rows, were not native to the area. They had been planted after the Great War to hide the hideous moonscape scars of shell craters and trenches and earth works. The original beech trees were only just now struggling back to life in the isolated clumps where they had survived the conflagration.

The replanting had been done in such a methodical manner that whichever way I faced I peered down an avenue of conifers. Papa was right, I thought. Better pick just one such vaulted row and follow it out and back. If I adopted any other course, I would never get back to the shack before the sun burned away the mist.

Because I could not see more than a handful of steps before or behind, I began counting the trees I passed. At least I would have some record of how far I had come and how long the return should take.

I had just reached seventy when the fog ahead began to lighten. The curtain of vapor parted enough for me to see I had reached the edge of the wood.

As I reached out to touch the branch tips of the last spruce before the meadow, I had a sudden appreciation for the friendly corridor of trees. The fog was still dense up ahead, but there were no well-defined passages, just a great, gray void. All the openings back into the rows of trees looked the same. How could I mark the one out of which I had come so as to find it again?

There was a handkerchief in my jacket. I tied it around the outstretched arm of the spruce. Even if

I wandered a bit on my return, eventually I would find this marker again.

Besides, I told myself, if I went straight out and straight back, how lost could I get? I would have to attempt it. If I turned back now, Jessica would tease me.

I marched resolutely forward. Papa had been right again. The meadow sloped gently westward. There must be water somewhere nearby.

A few paces ahead the grass was cropped very short. Cows or something must have been here recently. A farm would be a good thing to find. Perhaps we could get fresh milk for the children and some bread and jam.

My stomach growled.

Three more steps forward and I stopped in my tracks and dropped abruptly to my knees.

Looming up from the mist were large, ungainly shapes. They had long snouts, like elephants, only they crouched near the ground.

Tanks!

But whose? French, Belgian, English . . . or German?

I had heard that tank crews slept in their machines. If I appeared suddenly out of the fog, might I not be shot, even if these mechanical beasts belonged to friendly forces?

On my stomach, I began creeping backward toward the sheltering trees.

Then I heard voices! Behind me and just a few

meters to the right of my position, I could hear but not see them. There were at least two men speaking in quiet conversation.

"Ein, zwei, drei, vier. . . ."

They were counting . . . in German!

I turned my head back and forth until I fixed the direction of the conversation. In the mist there was no way to tell how far away, but they sounded close, coming from within the stand of trees and not from the meadow.

"Take no chances," Papa had said.

Now what?

German tanks in the meadow and German soldiers in the trees? Was I surrounded? Was there no way to escape back to the cottage to warn the others?

Now I prayed for the vapor to stay dense; heavier and thicker would be better still. Creeping, creeping, scooting backward, angling away from the voices, I was no longer concerned with retracing my path. Just let me get beneath the arms of the trees, and I would scamper away from the meadow.

My foot hung up on something. A dead branch? When I tried to shake it loose it flipped up in the air and landed with a clang against the water bottle tied to my waist.

"Was ist?!" a German shouted. *"Schnell, Hans!"*

The chatter of machine gun fire spattered

wildly, and an engine roared to life. A motorcycle zipped past where I lay, the sidecar-mounted weapon firing wildly into the fog. It shredded the limbs of the trees. Bark splinters and pine needles flew into the air to shower down on me.

I hugged the ground, certain I would be killed or captured any second. The motorcycle, after bounding over some hummocks of earth, disappeared out of sight and earshot.

If the tanks were German, why had the motorcycle team fled?

But if the tanks belonged to the Allies, why had they not fired back?

Cautiously, slowly, I raised my head.

"Loralei! Loralei," I heard my father calling.

"Stay back, Papa," I warned. "Don't come any closer!"

As if ripped asunder by the rapid-fire bullets, the fog began to lighten and lift from the ground.

Still prone, I peered ahead as once more the domed shapes reappeared, sunlight transforming them into . . . haystacks. Each cabin-sized mound of hay still had the ladder by which it had been stacked lying across its top.

Papa emerged from the trees and ran to me. "Are you hurt? We heard gunshots!"

"They must have been German scouts, Papa. They were fooled the same as me . . . counting the tanks!" I felt relieved and embarrassed at the same moment. "It's all right now," I concluded.

"Yes, thanks be to God," Papa agreed. "But the Germans don't send scouts unless they are planning an advance . . . through here. We must go at once!"

12

At Tyne Cott it was as if the endless current of misery on the road from Brussels had settled into a pool. Hundreds of bicycles leaned against the outer fence. Carts and wagons and baby carriages cluttered the open space that might have been a parking area. The parade ground outside the cemetery, about the size of a soccer field, was crowded with makeshift camps. There was no more room, so the travelers' campsites spilled onto the cemetery. They sheltered from the harsh sun beneath blankets draped from tombstones. They sat on their bundles or crouched on the ground.

The lawns surrounding the chapel were also packed with hundreds of refugees who had climbed the stone fence and broken through the gates.

I instructed the children, "Put your hands in my pockets, so you don't get lost." Gina, Judith, and Susan, eyes wide at the sight of such confusion, slid fingers into my pockets and held tight.

Jessica waddled after us, avoiding knapsacks and heads and arms with difficulty.

To our right was a long line snaking toward the public latrine.

Men, women, and children had staked out territories, leaving barely enough room for us to follow Papa toward the arched entry doors of the stone structure and the office of Captain Judah Blood. A man with a tin mask on his face stood guard at the entry. He held his arm across the door.

With a soft Irish accent he remarked to Papa, "Far enough, mister. Chapel's reserved. Captain figures military'll need it soon enough. They haven't found us yet, but they will. Last war we was the center of the battle. Only a matter of time, and we'll be in the thick of it again. Basement's for medical. Triage. Special cases only." His glance grazed Jessica's pregnant belly. "Wounded soldiers only, ma'am."

Papa replied, "Please tell Captain Judah that Robert Bittick of Alderman's Seminary is here. He will remember. Robert Bittick of the White Rose."

Startled, the guard drew himself erect and saluted. "Bittick. White Rose? Yes, sir." He unlocked the door and stepped aside, allowing the little band to enter the foyer of the chapel. He locked it behind them.

The heat, noise, and chaos of the mob fell away.

Cool serenity settled on us. Color and light from stained glass windows filled the chapel with rainbows. The tin-faced man explained, "Can't let the mob in. The BEF and the Belgian army will arrive soon. There'll be a last stand. This little chapel. A fortress soon enough to hold the jerries back. Cap'n says so."

What would become of this beautiful place, I wondered. How many years to build a house of worship? How many hours to destroy it?

Tears began to stream silently down Jessica's cheeks. "Oh!" she said, staring up as a sunbeam shone through a window depicting Jesus calling His friend Lazarus forth from the tomb. This was a chapel where mothers and fathers of fallen sons could come and remember the resurrection and the life.

Had Lazarus suffered death and decay in a second tomb? Or had the voice of Jesus called him to live on and on in a world choked by the brambles of death?

"Oh, Loralei, look!" Jessica waved her hand as a gallery of beautiful faces depicting the gospel stories gazed down on us. "Look where we are!"

"The steps leading to Eden." I felt it too. There was a holiness in this place; as though we had stepped from the hell of our journey into another dimension.

"There will be fighting here too?" Jessica

seemed to drink in the jewel box beauty of the place.

The Irishman replied, "History repeats itself. And in these fields many men have died. Men I know well." The tin man dipped his fingers into a basin of water and quickly crossed himself.

Motioning for us to take a seat, he hurried away to find Captain Judah.

Long minutes slid by. Our little group huddled together in the pews beneath the life-sized crucifix. Windows in side chapels depicted soldiers in shining armor flanked by the banners of army companies and the names of the fallen.

The trio of girls leaned heavily against my arms and almost instantly fell into deep sleep.

The Irishman stepped out from the vestry door and motioned to Papa. Patting Jessica on her shoulder, Papa strode up the steps, vanishing behind the door with the Irishman.

"Who is this Judah fellow?" Jessica asked.

"I'm not sure. I remember some fellow from the Tin Noses Shop Papa mentioned while we were at the White Rose Inn, but we didn't meet him. That was years ago. In the summer. The Olympics. If he's the same fellow. A kind of prophet, Papa said. I didn't pay attention." I frowned, remembering how I had thrown myself at Eben Golah.

Jessica stretched her aching back. In a hushed whisper she said, "I hope the baby is a girl."

"William would want a boy."

"William is gone."

"He would want a boy. He told me so."

"Loralei"—Jessica's voice quavered—"William is dead. There. I said it."

"Jessica, you mustn't speak such a thing. He could be . . ."

"Plain truth. You know it. And Varrick. You heard the reports. The newspapers. You haven't shed a tear."

I raised my chin defensively. "I won't. I can't let myself believe it."

"They were the first. Our men. On the front lines and there are none left alive in their unit."

"A rumor. A bad, horribly cruel rumor."

"Plain truth. I know it. I dreamed it, and I know."

"We're going to keep praying for them until we have proof."

"All the same, I hope I never have a son. Did you see the faces of the women out there? The mothers. No boys at all above the age of sixteen. I've been watching. They're all gone. You can tell the women who have sons. Haunted faces. Like the Virgin Mary must've looked at the crucifixion, I'll bet. Raise a boy for twenty years, and cruelty ends their lives before they have begun. I never want a son. Never."

I fell silent after that. I closed my eyes and pretended to sleep, but visions of William and

Varrick, dead in a ditch, reared up in my mind. German shells would rend the earth as they had done to Passendale twenty years ago. The earth would heal, and trees would grow again; the poppies of Flanders would bloom. But the boys who had fallen would not stir and rise like the poppies. They would not awaken until Christ came down from heaven and called out their names, "Lazarus! Come forth!"

Jessica and the girls and I remained in the cool shelter of the chapel while Papa met with Captain Judah Blood behind closed doors in the vestry.

The trio of children played a game of Go Fish with the pack of worn, unmatched playing cards.

Jessica stretched out on the pew and dozed with her head on a wadded-up sweater.

I wandered from window to sundrenched window, each portraying in one glance a familiar, well-loved Bible story. The tourist pamphlet in a rack at the back of the church described the famous windows as containing one hundred faces of courage and hope.

There was no artist's signature on the glass. Classic features of the characters glowed like the illuminated paintings of Pre-Raphaelite masters. The deep, soft folds of the cloak of Jesus lay neatly folded on a stone near the foot of the cross as harsh, cruel-faced Roman soldiers gambled to win it as a prize. The twisted feet of Jesus, pierced with an iron spike driven through His heels, bled within an arm's length of a jeering executioner who tossed the dice.

Opposite that window was another battle: the image of a British officer leading his men out of the trenches and over the barricade into machine gun fire.

Carved in the stone block beneath the scene were the names of those who had fallen and these words:

Now storming fury rose,
And clamour such as heard in Heav'n till now
Was never, arms on armor clashing brayed,
Horrible discord, and the madding wheels
Of brazen chariots rag'd: dire was the noise
Of conflict; overhead the dismal hiss
Of firey darts in flaming vollies flew
And, flying, vaulted either host with fire . . .
Deeds of eternal fame
Were done, but infinite; for wide was spread
That was, and various: sometimes on firm
  ground
A standing fight; then soaring on main wing,
Tormented all the air; all air seemed
  conflicting fire.[2]

---

2 John Milton, *Paradise Lost.*

One hundred faces locked in battles upon which all the souls in all the world depended.

Beautiful and terrible faces. I wondered what artist had created the beauty that now lay directly in the path of approaching battle. I mused at the lack of care demonstrated that such works of art were neither boarded up or taped against the certainty of shell fire.

Selecting a prayer book from the rack beside the door, I opened it randomly. My eyes fell on the prayer service for the fallen soldiers of Flanders. The words of Ecclesiastes, chapter 3, leapt up. The ink seemed to be black fire on white fire.

There is a time for everything,
and a season for every activity under heaven:
a time to be born and a time to die.

So many had died, and so many more would die before the sun set on this day. The vigil hours had chimed for them even as Jessica's innocent baby prepared to enter a world so cruel the mind could scarcely take it in.

The innocent suffered while cruel men gambled for possessions and power.

After two hours the vestry door opened. Judah Blood, faceless behind the tin face, emerged first into the chapel. So this was the one who warned of what would come upon the world unless brave men stood up and spoke out against tyranny.

Today, even behind an unchangeable expression, Judah's demeanor spoke of the gravity of the situation.

Little Gina asked quietly, "What's wrong with his face, Auntie Loralei? Why does he wear a mask?"

Jessica sat up and answered. "He was injured in the war, dear. He wears a mask because his face was hurt."

The explanation seemed to satisfy the child, who turned her attention back to the cards.

Papa emerged and raised his hand toward us in a gesture that implied the war was going much worse than they had speculated. Only the details remained to be elaborated upon.

I wondered, could a man age ten years in ten days? Papa looked ten years older than when we had left Brussels. Judah Blood's painted features would never age. He raised his chin in a kind of salute to me. Did he remember me? Had he met me as a child? I attempted a smile of acknowledgment. He nodded and returned into the vestry, closing the heavy door behind him.

Standing up from the pew, I waited for Papa.

He approached and stood silently for a long moment with his hand on the smooth polished mahogany of the pew.

"That fellow, Judah Blood?" My whisper seemed loud.

"Yes." Papa nodded.

"Why is he here?"

"He has lived here since the last war. Would not leave his men. I met him at the White Rose. It was our first meeting, many years ago."

I thought, *Who could forget the face? A mannequin's face. Painted. Tiny hairs set in the tin for eyebrows. His eyes, though, were alive. A lonely man. Fierce and gentle by turns.*

"Judah is a gentleman. In the truest sense of the word."

Jessica rubbed her belly as the baby kicked. "The German Resistance. Clearly that's at an end."

Papa glanced up at the crucifix. "Judah knew it would come to this, if the European church failed to speak out. Like Eben Golah, he warned the committee of what would happen."

I said, "I guess no one believed him."

Papa tried to smile an encouraging smile. "Judah is the authority at Passendale. He says we six may rest inside the church. Jessica. The baby. He says there are cots in the basement prepared for the field hospital." He paused. "Jessica, take the girls downstairs, will you?"

There was a hint of resentment in Jessica's gaze as Papa dismissed her to tend the children.

Papa did not speak again until Jessica and the children had vanished and their footsteps retreated down the stairwell. "Very dangerous, Lora. Very dangerous. All these refugees.

Everyone camped here. Like babies laid down on the tracks in front of a locomotive."

"Who could have imagined?"

Papa took my arm and led me to the side door. He cracked it slightly, allowing me a peek to the west as the sun sank low on the horizon.

Clearly Judah had not only imagined this chaos but warned about it. I spotted him again. He had slipped out another way. His long stride carried him quickly through the campsites toward the caretaker's house nestled behind a high wrought-iron fence. He looked neither to the right nor the left as he picked his way through heaps of belongings. From the back I noted that Judah Blood was a strong, broad-shouldered man with a thick thatch of dark red hair. What sort of man had he been before shrapnel had ripped away his face? Perhaps his features had matched the image of his mask and the strength of his body. Perhaps he had been handsome once?

Papa followed my gaze. "A good man, Judah is."

"The others. The tin men. How long have they lived here caring for the dead?"

"From the last war, until now. He was—Judah is—the artist. The glass in the chapel."

I gasped. My eyes widened as I watched the man without a face of his own who had seen and recreated beauty in the faces gazing down from the window frames.

Papa directed my attention away from Judah. He lifted my chin with one finger. His eyes were deep and sad.

"What is it, Papa?"A sense of dread filled me.

"It will be only a matter of days before the Panzers break through Allied lines."

"But all these people? Papa?"

"The Germans will come here. Are on the way. To Flanders. Like they did in the last war. You heard the stories out of Poland. Holland has already surrendered. Then the Germans bombed Rotterdam *after* the surrender. The lesson is not lost on the other Allies. Belgium and King Leopold hold on by a thread. They are praying the French will come. They won't."

"But the girls! Jessica! The baby! Where can we run to?"

"Judah believes the sea is our means of escape."

"The sea? How?"

"I don't know. Somehow, England."

I looked around as a group of ragged children played soccer between the rows of white crosses. "England? But Papa, there are so many thousands running away. The Jews. How can they all . . . ?"

"They won't."

"I want to press on. To Paris. The Nazis surely won't make it into Paris. The Allies won't let them take Paris."

"Judah says this time—"

"Judah! Who is he? Who is this man anyway to speak such doom?"

Papa's face clouded at my burst of anger. He closed the door and bolted it as a woman in the yard glanced up and noticed them. "Loralei, Judah Blood has warned us all from the first. He has never been wrong."

"But what about Jessica? The baby! Jessica can't travel until the baby is born. And some time after. How will she . . . ? I mean, if only we had a car." The memory of the comfortable old Fiat seemed like a distant dream. "But where can we go?"

"The coast. Dunkirk. We'll rest here as long as we're able. For Jessica."

As if on cue, Gina darted up the stairs. "Grandpa!" she shouted. Her voice echoed in the rafters, disturbing the sacred hush. "Auntie Loralei! Come quickly! Mama says for me to fetch you back, Auntie Loralei. She says the water broke. The pains have started. The baby!"

For the next sixteen hours Jessica lay on a cot in the dimly lit crypt of the chapel. It seemed there was little progress in her labor.

The space was cool and quiet. Papa had long ago sent the trio of girls upstairs. He hung back on the landing—an errand boy following my instructions.

Mama's medical bag was at my feet, but I did

not know what was needed to deliver a baby. Disinfectant and cotton gauze and bandages? Everything seemed useless in this situation.

I regretted now I hadn't taken the Red Cross instruction when Mama had done it two years ago. But who could have known?

A kettle of thin broth had been sent over from the caretaker's cottage. A bit of bread. Hot tea and honey. I spoon-fed my sister, changed the towels, and kept the bedding dry, but I did not know what else to do; how to help.

At first we chatted between contractions, but as the hours dragged on, our conversation became terse and focused on strength and enduring the pain.

How pale Jessica was, I thought, as I held her hand. Alabaster skin seemed almost the color of the linens.

Jessica closed her eyes. "Another one." She panted through the rising agony.

How far apart were the contractions now? I squinted at my wristwatch and timed the viselike grip of the muscles by the sweep of the second hand. Placing my hand on Jessica's abdomen, I felt it tighten and then slowly release.

Jessica exhaled as the pain lessened. "Close now. But not like with Gina. Two minutes maybe. Minute and a half. Really close, Lora. And now so hard. Oh! I'm going to need . . ."

"What, darling girl?"

"Help."

"Yes." I called to my father. "Papa, go outside, into the camp. A doctor."

"I've done that," he replied miserably. "There's no one. All medics at the front."

I snapped, "Then someone . . . a nurse. Midwife. Papa, hurry." As I spoke the next contraction slammed down so fiercely it knocked the breath from Jessica.

Papa's footsteps clattered up the steps and out. The door swung closed behind him.

"Oh!" Jessica cried. "Oh, Lora!" Gritting her teeth, she softly called, "William . . . where is William?"

"Breathe. Take a breath."

"Need a doctor. Not easy like . . . with Gina!" Her brow furrowed, and her lips parted.

"Jesus!" I prayed and dabbed perspiration from Jessica's brow.

Four more sets followed—each more violent and closer together.

"Where is Papa?" I stood and looked about.

Jessica groaned. "Don't leave me."

"I've got to see what's keeping him."

"No! Lora, it's . . . okay. There. A minute to rest. Just don't . . . leave me."

I changed the towel beneath Jessica's hips. It was bright red. Was this normal? Or was my sister slowly bleeding to death?

I knelt down beside Jessica and kissed her

fingertips and prayed, *Lord, I don't know what to do. How to help. Just me and You, Jesus. Help me.*

At that instant the clamor of footsteps sounded on the steps. Men's voices, Papa's and someone else's, echoed in the stairwell.

"How far apart?"

"I don't know. Maybe two minutes," Papa answered.

"We're here," I called, knowing I sounded foolish. "Papa? Did you find—"

Papa answered, "Captain Judah. He's trained as a medic. Delivered babies. He can help!"

Judah rolled up his sleeves and washed his hands—artist's hands. He finished up with disinfectant and blotted them dry. He said to Papa, "Better if you're not here, friend."

"I'll be praying." Papa nodded and quickly retreated up the stairs.

I stepped aside as the man with the green eyes looking out from a tin face came close. He placed one hand on Jessica's belly and the other on her forehead as the next contraction began.

Closing his eyes, Judah counted, wordlessly moving his lips.

Jessica made a soft sound, the humming of a suppressed scream.

"Feel the urge to push?" Judah asked.

Jessica nodded rapidly. "So much."

He said gently, "I think I know what's happened

here. There now. It will be all right. Everything. You'll see." He directed his attention to me. "You're going to be the midwife. I'll talk you through it. How long has she been like this?"

"About an hour," I guessed.

"How long now, total? The labor?"

"Sixteen hours," I replied, wiping tears away with the back of my hand.

Judah leaned close to Jessica and asked gently, "All right. Lots of pain in your back?"

"Terrible." Jessica's glazed eyes looked up at him with gratitude. "You know?"

His head moved in a small gesture of assurance. "I know. Your baby is posterior. Face up. Sunny side up, you see. Instead of shooting down the sled hill facedown as is proper, he's going to come out on his back and looking up into my . . . face."

No sooner had he spoken those words than another contraction seized Jessica. Desperate, she grasped my forearms.

Judah whispered to me, "Hold on to her . . . tight. The cervix is engorged with blood. Normally would be effaced, but . . . all right, then. Good contraction." He ordered me, "Wash your hands." I did so. He continued, "Your hands are small, but strong. You're going to try to open the cervix, force it open with your fingers, over the baby's head . . . like an elastic band."

I followed every command, finding the tight

circle of the opening of the womb and between contractions spreading it open with my fingers.

I wept silently as a low growl of agony, like that of a wounded animal, erupted from Jessica. Her fingers, claw-like, dug into the cot. She cried out, "Don't, please! No more!"

Judah's voice was compassionate but unrelenting. "There . . . I know it's painful. But Lora must. Must!" His eyes radiated deep concern from behind his mask.

Jessica gasped, "I'm sorry . . . sorry. I—I—"

"Go ahead," Judah instructed. "I know it hurts! Yell if you want."

Though he had given her permission, she did not scream. Her eyes locked on my face. The look bonded us. I felt the baby's head descend into the birth canal.

I spoke in a whisper, "So sorry . . . hold on. We've got to open the way so we can move him down!" The contraction eased. The rapid breath of my sister was the only sound in the crypt.

Judah asked me, "Is it open? Is his head through?"

"I think so."

"All right, then. Jessica, I will tell you when to push. Lora, be ready. When I give the word, I'll lift her up and support her back. Jessica's going to sit up and bear down. Push, Jessica!"

Jessica cried, "Here! Another one . . ."

Judah's eyes narrowed. His chin was up as he

gauged the moments and the strength of Jessica's contraction. "Now! Push now! That's it. Push. Push. Push! Good girl. He's on the move."

I saw the baby crown and then emerge into the light. His face was indeed facing upward. I sobbed as Jessica gritted her teeth and bore down with every fiber of her being. Breath exploded from her. With a long groan she fell back into Judah's arms.

Jessica managed to say, "Oh, the lights. Turn on . . . so dark."

I searched Judah's placid face for some sign of emotion. His full lips were pressed tight together. Eyes blinked rapidly. He said, "Stay with us, now. Jessica, stay with me!" Like a lifeguard bearing up a drowning person, his voice seemed to pull her back to consciousness. "Once more . . ."

"Oh! No!"

"You can . . ."

"Please, God! Jesus!"

"Come on, here it is." His tone was urgent. "Loralei, ready? Now, Jessica, give it everything. Push! That's it! There. Loralei, help her. I see his head, his shoulders. All right. Push. Push. Push!"

Jessica threw her head back. Her face turned bright red. "Oh, Jesus, help me!" Tendons in the side of her neck stood out.

I choked, "Help her, Jesus!"

Jessica cried loudly, "I'm . . . breaking!"

Then Judah, at her head, shouted, "Yes! Here he is. Hello, little one!"

I cried, "It's a boy, Jessica. You have a baby boy!" I stroked the baby.

Judah gathered him up and began to work on him, willing him to live. "Sometimes it takes awhile for these little ones to breathe. Come on. Come on, there. It's not all that bad. Breathe for me, now. Handsome boy, take a breath!"

Suddenly the arches of the crypt reverberated with the thin mewling cry of a newborn. Judah tied off the cord and handed me scissors. "Lora, it is for you to do. You and all the ancient matriarchs who stand beside you. Cut the cord."

Trembling violently, Jessica lay back as I cut the umbilical cord. She looked to Judah for help.

"She's in shock." Judah's voice registered new concern. "Take your nephew. There you go." He placed the angry infant in my arms and went to work on Jessica.

I wrapped the baby in a towel and held him close, rocking him gently as I sang the song Mama had made up for me when she rocked me to sleep. "Sugar cookie moon's way up in the sky . . ." It was nonsense, but somehow the song made me feel like my mother was very near.

Judah's words echoed in the vaulted ceiling of the chamber where, tonight, life had overcome death. "That's it, Jessica. You're going to be fine. What a brave girl you are. Walk all this way through a battle line and have a baby too. Strong. Most women couldn't do what you've just done. Brave girl."

He turned to me. "The great cloud of witnesses watches over you."

Through chattering teeth Jessica managed to speak. "We're . . . from . . . Texas."

From the platform of the cross I surveyed the wriggling knots of refugees. Families clustered around headstones, like the Hebrew children in their wilderness wanderings gathered beside tribal standards. It struck me that many of these fleeing the Nazi onslaught were Jews—once again forced to escape oppression; once again on a desperate search for a Promised Land of peace and safety.

Papa stood beside me, studying the crowds. "How many do you think?" he asked. Now that Jessica's baby had been safely brought into an unsafe world, there was time for other considerations.

Perhaps it helped Papa's emotions to review what could be done when facing so many things that were out of his control. "How many refugees?"

I had already been considering that very question. "More than a thousand, I think. Twelve thousand headstones." I paused to allow a shudder to exit my neck and fingertips. "Those are easily numbered. I'm glad the living are harder to count. So many women and children and older men, who should be home with their grandchildren. Oh, Papa, I don't like this picture!"

He put his arm around me. "Focus on the needs of the living. That's our duty, and our freedom from anxiety." Squaring his own shoulders he said, "Nearer two thousand, I should think. And what is their greatest need?"

"Food?" I ventured. "Blankets?"

"Organization," Papa said firmly. "See that family guarding the hundred-pound sack of rice? They have no pot to cook it in. And over there, those folks? A prosperous burgher and his family, from Brussels, perhaps. They seem to have brought an entire kitchen's cookware but have no stove on which to use it." He rubbed his hands together with anticipation. "Loaves and fishes," he said, pleased at his own metaphor. "Now, where can we build outdoor ovens?"

"Beg pardon, sir," interjected the Tin Nose member named Sergeant Mickey Walker. "Captain Blood said I was to help you. Lieutenant Howard and Private Kadle is already setting up cookpits on the far side of our cottage. What help was you needin' from me, sir?"

"Excellent, Sergeant, excellent," Papa said. "Loralei, you circulate through the families. Locate all the largest kettles you can. Explain where they are wanted. Sergeant, you and I will round up supplies for soup. Along the way we'll detail able-bodied men and young women to bring buckets of fresh water. Clear enough?"

"Right you are, sir," Walker returned.

I noted, "But Papa, won't some of them try to hoard their supplies just for their own families?"

The Irish sergeant aimed his painted mask in my direction. Walker's remaining eye twinkled as he said, "Just you leave that to me. When it's me as makes a request, very few has the boldness to disagree, if you take my meanin'."

Within an hour large cauldrons of stewing rice and beans were simmering. Chunks of bread, torn from loaves toted from Brussels and Maastricht and Namur and Waterloo, were being shared from hand to hand down the waiting rows of refugees.

13

So Papa had done it; he had pulled it off. Robert Bittick, the miracle worker! He had created order out of the chaos of Tyne Cott.

The four Tin Men cooked rice soup in giant washpots over an open fire.

The long line of hungry, hopeless exiles formed.

Gina, Judith, Susan, and I stood behind narrow tables made from sawhorses and boards. We wielded ladles, sloshing soup into tin cups and bowls held in trembling hands. Eager half smiles of wonder peered into the depths of plain grub and saw visions of the future, the possibility of life.

Susan, the smallest, handed out thin white wheat wafers.

Papa cajoled the snaking line, "Enough for everyone. That's it, plenty to eat. Plenty!"

It was a miracle of a kind. A cheerful wake, held in a graveyard, for the corpse of life as it used to be. Dead. Nothing of the old ordinary life endured. Toss the handful of earth into the deep grave heaped with things and stuff and worries. It all came down to this, didn't it? Really?

I sang a silent song as I watched Judah and Frank Howard lift a simmering kettle from the open fire and carry it toward the soup line. My heart hummed, *Nothing is the same. Fling away what you were holding onto so tightly yesterday. Smashed china on the kitchen floor. Does it matter now? Springtime was waiting for you to notice it had come. You only read the paper and worried about what you would lose.*

A glimmer of the red poppies remained. I could see the crimson color, once so bright. Tonight in the sky there would be stars I had forgotten to look at. Tonight I would remember to see them.

Behind me in the camp, young women laughed together. Spoons clanked on metal bowls and someone played a gypsy tune on the violin. It was as though someone had arranged it all. But who? Who arranged a giant picnic for strangers living among the dead?

Papa looked at Judah as he drew near and then at me. He said to neither but to both of us: "The oldest suffering has met the newest, and finally the tree bears fruit."

I understood what he meant. Judah's suffering was a lone pain. His loneliness was born of other men's fears that the face behind the mask could be their own.

Judah's green eyes were alive, happy, behind the fixed apparition that concealed his true self. Judah's living vision drank me in. In his long savoring of me, I saw him smile.

"We don't know what to do with ourselves," Judah said, "we Tin Men. We've been talking to the headstones so long. To hear real voices talking back, we don't know what to do with ourselves."

Mickey Walker called across to Frank Howard, "Bring me a bowl, will you, Frank? I think this might be edible the way they're all after eatin' it."

A single light illuminated the crypt, casting my shadow against the ceiling. There was a work table and a large pattern laid out with a jigsaw puzzle of a half-completed stained-glass window. A man's navy blue sweater was on the back of a wooden chair. The name, Judah Blood, was written in indelible ink on the laundry mark.

"He's the artist. He created the windows," I remarked.

"Judah?" Jessica breathed. With my nursing and the captain's watchful care, my sister was slowly recovering her strength.

"Yes. Papa told me. And I saw a glass-cutting tool in his vest pocket. It's him."

"He's a miracle worker. I don't think I could've made it if he hadn't . . ."

"Don't say such a thing." I squeezed my eyes tight. The image of Judah's eyes, burning with emotion behind an emotionless mask, made me ashamed.

But ashamed of what? That I had not seen his soul when first we met? That I had only looked at the outward appearance? That I had never quite understood that a real human being lived inside the painted shell?

I exhaled slowly as the image of Jessica's agony replayed in my mind. Who was Judah Blood—that he knew how to design and create windows worthy of the Vatican or the great cathedrals of the world? What sort of fellow worked alone on fragile glass in the bowels of a war memorial chapel in the heart of a battlefield? Who was he before? What had he done in his life before the war that made him able to help a woman deliver her baby?

I did not mention these questions aloud, but they gleamed in the front of my brain like a searchlight seeking a secret road home.

Jessica ran her thumb over the baby's downy hair. "I can tell you this, Loralei. The man knew what he was doing. More even than Doctor Coffel in Brussels. He knew. And I think he saved my life and the baby's life too."

"You would have been okay," I argued, though the reality of what might have happened was a powerful what-if. "I don't want to think about it, okay?"

"Sure." Jessica searched my expression, knowing my heart.

I sat cross-legged on the cold stone floor beside her and watched as she cradled the baby in her arms. The infant snuffled and turned his face instinctively toward her breast. We grinned in delight as he latched on with a sudden tug.

"Whoa!" Jessica laughed as the baby slurped noisily.

"Impeccable table manners. He's not going to let even one drop escape." I tenderly observed the infant's perfection. "What are you going to name him?"

"I've been giving that lots of thought," Jessica said. "You know I didn't think I wanted a boy . . . a boy who would be sent off to war someday like his father. So I've decided to call him Nathan Shalom."

"I like it: 'God gives peace.' "

"Yes, it's a prayer. Every time I say his name, it's a prayer."

"Mama would like it, Jessica."

"Hmm." Her smile wavered, and I knew she was thinking of William. Jessica stroked the velvet cheek. "If only William could have . . ."

"Don't you think he did see him? You know, the great cloud of witnesses?"

Jessica kissed the baby. "Your daddy is so proud."

"He's beautiful. And you're amazing. Hike as long as a soldier. Carry weight like a fieldpack in your belly. Then give birth in a crypt and . . ." I wagged my head. "You oughta have your name in some sort of record book."

"That Judah." Jessica frowned. "Papa didn't tell us he was a doctor."

"I don't know if Papa knew. I never knew. Even from what I heard, he was just some sort of anonymous fellow behind a mask. I almost didn't much think of him as being a . . . real person, if you know what I mean."

"His eyes," Jessica said softly. "I only saw his eyes. It was as if he somehow felt . . . and understands, at least . . . pain."

Both of us considered Judah's own pain. What had he experienced when his face had been blown away? "He knows what it means, all right."

Baby Shalom continued to nurse. We sisters sat

silently for a long time. I said at last, "Want a cup of tea? I've got the hot plate. See, look. Judah set it up over there."

"Can we have it in Mama's teacups?"

"They're all wrapped up. I wanted them to be safe even if I fell on them."

"Mama would like it, wouldn't she? You and me sharing hot tea served up in her teacups in the crypt of an old church with the entire German army booming toward us. A sort of occasion. Don't you think?"

"If you put it that way, how can I resist?" I set the kettle to boil on the hot plate, then carefully unwrapped two delicate china cups, leaving the saucers in their nest.

It was true, I thought, as I steeped the Darjeeling and sweetened Jessica's with a single lump of sugar. When I carried the steaming brew to Jessica, the baby was sleeping. Lips parted, a single drop of milk trickled from his rosebud mouth.

Jessica smiled misty-eyed into the cup. "Mama's watching us from heaven, you know, Lora. I heard her cheering when I made it that last mile."

I turned my gaze upward and lifted the cup in salute. "Hey, Mama."

Jessica repeated the motion. "Hey, Mama!"

We each raised the gold rims to our lips at once. "In honor of the boy in the family!"

· · ·

Their stomachs were filled, and the atmosphere was like Regent's Park on a warm Sunday afternoon. The occupants of Tyne Cott sunned themselves and dozed on blankets spread on the lawn.

From the shade of a sycamore tree, I watched as Gina, Susan, and Judith ventured out from the camp to gather flowers among the silent, other residents of the vast field of dead.

Wilted poppies and nodding lupines filled their arms as they scampered back to me. "We found these for Mommy and the new baby." Gina buried her nose in blossoms.

The younger of the sisters proclaimed, "And this for the doctor, Captain Judah, for saving Gina's mother and the baby too."

Their gesture filled me with a sense of contentment. For a moment I almost forgot the distant rumble of the approaching enemy. "Precious girls. Gina, your mommy will be so pleased. Go on. Take them to your mommy and Captain Judah."

Eyes wide in sudden terror, the girls looked at one another and shook their heads in unison. I asked, "Why? What's wrong?"

Gina pursed her lips. "Well, we can take the bouquet to Mommy, but not to *him*."

The sisters wagged their heads in solemn agreement.

I asked, "Gina? Why ever not?"

She hesitated, as though her thoughts made her ashamed. "You know, Auntie Lora. You know."

I did know. They were afraid of his face. Afraid of the mask and his beautiful eyes that observed everything from behind the painted tin.

Gina squinted as she often did before asking me for something beyond her reach. "Auntie Lora, will you? Will you take our flowers to him? Just say we like him. Tell him I said thanks."

"A messenger, am I?" I dried my hands, winked, and gathered the floral offering into both arms. "All right then." The trio followed on my heels as I entered the chapel and knocked on the vestry door that Judah used as his office. "Captain Judah, it's Lora Bittick . . . Kepler." I announced my married name, which I seldom used because of my American passport.

His deep, resonant voice replied, "Missus Kepler, come in."

I opened the door and with a backward glance tried to entice the girls to come in with me. They would not but linked arms and peered around me, like three lambs looking into the lion's den.

I left them outside and entered alone, not wanting to draw Judah's attention to their revulsion. He occupied a chair at a massive carved oak desk cluttered with papers. A distinctive cigarette case was open on the green desk blotter before him.

His eyes smiled at me and then beyond me at the girls. I knew he had seen their terror. "Come in, please, and shut the door."

"I've brought a thank offering." I looked around for a vase. "The girls gathered these for you. By way of gratitude for Jessica's life. And for the baby."

He stood and rummaged through a box, producing the empty shell casing of an artillery round. "Will this do?"

I laughed. "I suppose that's a man's vase."

His green eyes leveled on my face from behind his rigid mask. His voice was surprisingly gentle. "I am a man."

A charge of embarrassment went through me. I stammered, "I—I—I hope it's okay they picked so many."

Pouring a pitcher of drinking water into the shell, he said, "Those who sleep at Tyne Cott won't miss them. And those who are coming to Tyne Cott would have only trampled them. They're fading fast now, anyway."

"Those who are . . . coming?" I arranged the bouquet.

Judah sat down and extended a hand, inviting me to join him. "You hear the artillery?"

I nodded and sank onto the chair opposite him. "Yes."

"Most of what you hear is not from our guns."

"Yes. My father said that might be the case."

Judah picked up the cigarette case and stared at the inscription inside. "We found this: a memento from the last war. We're still finding little treasures on the grounds. Some artifacts from other wars as well. I lived in Harfleur for a while. A battlefield of Henry the Fifth."

I knew it from Shakespeare's play. "How many centuries ago was that?"

"Every battlefield is riddled with little things the living cherish and carry into battle. A locket with a lock of hair. A silver cross. A lucky coin. And this." He held up the case and passed it to me.

I read the inscription. Personal. Filled with hope for a future that ended too soon. "Makes me feel as if I'm eavesdropping somehow." I nudged it back to him.

"I thought maybe I could find the woman who gave this to him. Some clue. Maybe she never knew where he fell. So many were unidentified. She would not be old. Forty, maybe. It's worth a try." He sighed and placed the artifact in an envelope that he labeled in red ink. Grasping a poppy, he tucked it inside. "But now, I don't know if there will be time. We finish up planting one graveyard, and then there's a new crop of young men to be sown."

"I am sorry it has happened again."

"Peace only lasts as long as the memory of war."

I changed the subject. "So you were a medical doctor in civilian life?"

"And many things since. I love the peace of this place. We are all waiting for the trumpet. Waiting for the earth to crack open and our friends to rise." He raised his face to me. "Your husband, Missus Kepler? Jewish name, isn't it?"

"My husband, Varrick Kepler. On the front with the BEF, last I heard. A translator for the BEF. He escaped from Germany."

"Ah, yes. You are an American. The marriage. Was it a help to save him?"

"I wish I could have married ten Jews and—"

He laughed. "If you save the life of one Jew, you have saved the universe."

"Varrick is my universe."

He nodded and considered my words. "I am glad to hear it. A happy ending, Missus Kepler."

I breathed no word of my anxiety that Varrick was dead. "Please. Lora. Just call me Lora."

"Yes. Loralei? It seems to me I remember . . ."

I warmed to Judah. "Papa calls me one thing and another."

"Your father is a good man." Judah's words seemed wistful, almost familiar.

"Yes."

"And your mother?"

"She died of a burst appendix. Very suddenly. Very . . . terrible for us all."

Judah steepled his fingers. "You must look like

215

her. Very beautiful. She must have been very proud of you. You know, I could use your face for the Madonna. And baby Shalom as the Christ-child. If there was time to create more windows."

His words were so frank, yet so matter-of fact that I did not blush or feel that he was looking at me like a man looks at a woman. I might have been a poppy plunked into an empty artillery shell to brighten a windowless room.

"Both Jessica and I resemble her. I'm glad." I stood and touched the dead man's cigarette case with my index finger. "I hope you find the woman who gave this to him. I mean, I hope she's gone on without him and found a new love. A new life."

"Yes."

"Anyway, thank you. I don't think Jessica or the baby would have made it without you."

"No." His statement was blunt—a reaffirmation of fact, not boasting.

"Then I thank you again for both their lives. I hope all goes well for you."

I took my leave, pleased to see that the girls had scampered down to visit Jessica and the baby. When I hurried downstairs, she was sitting up nursing Shalom as the trio of girls watched her in wonder. Faded poppies and drooping lupines still made a magnificent bouquet in a tin bucket.

14

W hen Jessica's baby boy was only days old a grim-faced British officer entered the foyer of Tyne Cott's chapel at the head of a muddy file of soldiers. The man looked weary to the point of exhaustion. Despite the deeply etched lines of pain on his face, in my judgment there was no mistaking his air of authority.

"Colonel Gilmore," he said, introducing himself. His eyes swept past Judah and the others to survey the chapel. "And this is now my headquarters. Who's in charge here?"

Judah Blood stepped forward. "I am. I'm caretaker of Tyne Cott." He saluted the British officer.

Colonel Gilmore's right arm was bound in a bloody sling. He acknowledged Judah with a nod. "As of this moment the entire facility is under my command. All civilians"—Gilmore's gaze seemed to rest particularly on me—"all civilians are to be evacuated immediately. The entire cemetery."

"Colonel," Judah returned, "these"—with one hand he pointed out the doorway to the huddled throngs camped among the headstones—"these have already been bombed out of homes and villages. They have come here seeking a place of refuge. Where do you suggest they go?" Though the implacable mask of Judah's enameled forehead registered no tension, I heard it in his voice.

Gilmore stepped closer to Judah and lowered his voice. I still overheard him as he tersely replied: "This is no refuge, man! This is front line country, or will be soon. Reports say German Army Group B is no more than a day away. Not only are the lines collapsing westward, but there is a thrust aimed directly at this spot."

Judah nodded his understanding. "The River Lys runs here from Armentieres to Ghent. The line of hills on our side of the river valley guards all the approaches from the east. Cassel is key to the south. Ypres in the center, and then Passendale and Tyne Cott."

Gilmore's eyes widened at Judah's succinct analysis.

"I was here in the last war," Judah explained simply. "We rebuilt this chapel like a fortress."

"Just so," Gilmore agreed. "This spot is the highest ground in the vicinity. Nothing has changed from twenty years ago. This is still the hinge of the entire line. We must, and we will hold here, and the civilians will have to leave."

"And go where?" Judah said softly.

Gilmore rubbed the stubble on his cheeks. "Where we're all going, I suppose. To the sea."

"And France? Are there any roads still open?" Judah queried.

Gilmore shook his head. "The Wehrmacht are about to reach the sea at Abbeville, splitting the Allied forces. If we can hold here, perhaps we can mount a counterattack; us from the north and the French from the south." He spoke with an air of resignation; as one committed to an action he already knows will be futile.

"When?" I blurted. "We have wounded here and mothers with infants."

Gilmore's expression softened. "Soon," he said. Abruptly the tenderness vanished as quickly as it had arrived, and the tensile steel of military necessity returned. "Mister Blood—"

"Captain," I interjected, surprising myself at my forwardness.

"Very well," Gilmore said, "Captain. Do you have maps of this place?"

"I've kept military charts from the last war," Judah explained.

"I understand the German pillboxes are still serviceable?"

"The four at the corners of the grounds," Judah agreed. "They serve as potting sheds and storage rooms for the cemetery, but the concrete walls are still stout and the gunports easily cleared."

"And here?" Gilmore inquired.

My eyes wandered over the chapel, especially the beautiful windows. *Here? Surely not! This place of reflection and sorrow and the hope of meeting vanished loved ones again?*

"There are a handful of us, besides Winston Churchill, who saw this day would come. We have kept the chapel unoccupied. As you see. Cleared for action." Judah turned to the girls and instructed them gently, "Go to my cottage. Fetch your father, if you can find him."

"Stout walls," the colonel echoed Judah's words. "Open field of fire on three sides. I'm sorry, Captain, but your days as caretaker are at an end."

At another nod from the colonel his aide directed a squad of British infantrymen, who jumped into action. The young girls were herded toward the door, but I refused to leave just yet.

Piling benches beneath the windows the soldiers formed makeshift firing steps. . . . then broke out the lower courses of glass with their rifle butts. I stared at the devastation until it reached the depiction of the crucified Lord in the eastern vault. Only when Christ's wounded feet vanished into shards of shattered crystal, and bent and twisted lead, did I stifle a sob and retreat with the rest.

The flare of a night bombardment lit the southeastern rim of the world like the view of a distant thunderstorm. That the explosions posed no immediate threat to the refugees camped at Tyne Cott was apparent. But, come morning, the German army rolling this direction would be as unstoppable as the tornados of the Texas plains.

Cookfires had been extinguished at dusk, to provide no targets for German gunners. The darkened expanse of the cemetery below my perch near the cross offered little clue that a couple thousand people slept . . . or at least rested there. Their bellies full of rice and beans, and their fears temporarily assuaged, most of the camp was quiet.

In the middle distance a child sniffled and complained about being afraid of the graves. The mother's hushed tones spoke reassurance and calm.

Farther off, a baby cried.

For a moment I wondered if it was my sister and newborn nephew. Then I dismissed the thought. Jessica and the baby, as well as Gina and the Jewish sisters, were tucked safely beneath the chapel.

There was a continual rustling in the night as if a herd of sheep grazed amid Tyne Cott's memorials. Come morning these human sheep would be looking for a reliable shepherd to give them direction.

Rumors heard over supper placed the Germans everywhere, as if Tyne Cott were the center of a collapsing steel ring. Colonel Gilmore told them otherwise. The Wehrmacht was advancing from the south, southeast, and east, but routes toward the northwest were open.

Northwest was the English Channel. What would happen when this throng reached the sea no one ventured to discuss. Perhaps they refused to think about it. Somewhere they believed they would find a wall of French, British, and Belgian soldiers to tuck themselves behind.

The sea, though no more than thirty miles away, was only a distant consideration.

Low on the western horizon, above the unseen Channel, hovered the bright beacon of Venus. Though the time was nearing midnight, the brightest of planets hung like a lantern pointing toward escape. I wondered if we would need its guidance in the nights ahead.

I scented Papa's bay rum cologne before I saw him. "You performed a wonder here," I said. "They are fed and peaceful, like after a camp meeting on the Brazos."

"For the moment," he agreed. "Tomorrow will be another matter. *Sufficient unto the day is the evil thereof,* eh?"[3]

"I have always thought of you like the Good Shepherd in David's psalm, Papa." I quoted back at him: *"I will fear no evil: for thou art with me."*[4]

Papa did not comment on this observation. After a long pause he said, "Did you know? A great many wounded soldiers came in just at

---

[3] Matthew 6:34
[4] Psalm 23:4

dusk. In the days ahead there won't be stretcher-bearers enough to carry them, I think. Many will have to remain here and make the best of whatever comes."

I felt a lump of ice form in my chest. "You . . . you aren't coming with us, are you, Papa?"

He sighed heavily. "I'm needed here."

I was resentful and hurt. "But what about us? Jessica and baby Shalom? Gina and the girls? What about our needs, Papa? Who will take care of us?"

"I am counting on you, Loralei. So like your mother. So strong. So capable. You will be the leader now."

"But why, Papa?" I protested still. "There will be wounded soldiers wherever we go. Needy people, anyplace we are. Why must you stay behind here?"

When he spoke again, it was clear Papa had anticipated the question; had marshaled his reasons ahead of time. He delivered his settled opinion in quiet, sensible words, against which there was no argument. "Because," he said, patting his jacket pockets for his pipe, then saying, "ah, mustn't light any matches, of course." He stopped to look me right in the eye. "Because," he resumed, "the more desperate the fight becomes between here and safety, the tougher it will be at each bridge, each intersection."

"What are you talking about?"

"Colonel Gilmore discussed it with me. It's my accent, you see. Austrian. Not like you or Jessica . . . American. Even Texas-American. I will only hold you up; might even endanger you."

I bristled with anger at the very thought of my good, kind, generous father being taken for a Nazi . . . and a Nazi spy, at that. "Then you must have Colonel Gilmore write you a pass," I demanded.

I heard Papa's gently mocking smile, even if I couldn't see it. "What would it say? 'Please excuse this German-sounding man? He's really harmless'? Really, Loralei, now is not the time and this is not the place to take chances with your sister or the children. No, my place is here. We'll meet up again in England when I can get away, eh?"

My heart was breaking. Bits of my life were being violently torn from me. There was never time to recover before the next gash exposed already gaping wounds—Mama, our home, Varrick . . . now Papa too? How could I stand it?

"I miss your mother so much." Papa's voice floated wistfully in the dark like a secret whispered on the breeze. "I'm not afraid. I want to be with her, if . . . if it's time."

"Papa, Papa." I clung to him.

"Shhh, shhh," he said, as if I were five years old again. "Remember your mother's favorite story?

The Alamo, she always said, was the highest form of bravery. It's not heroic to fight if you have no choice. But to stay and face the enemy when there is a choice to go or to stay? That is true heroism. Maybe no one will remember this place or make up songs about it. But you, my Lora-liebling, you will remember. And someday, to your children you will speak of it."

The morning chores on the day we departed from Tyne Cott cemetery began well before sunup. I did not sleep but busied myself in repacking our few belongings, especially the precious teacups.

Dear Lord, I thought. *I don't care how few of our belongings make it to England, so long as we're all safe . . . and these three teacups!*

The more I found to do, however inconsequential, the less time I thought about Papa staying behind. If Mama were here, what would she have really said about Papa's choice? She could have swayed his decision, I knew.

But what course would Mama have demanded of herself?

I not only grieved for my mother, but I desperately missed having her around for advice and comfort.

Gently nudging her awake, Papa spent time with Jessica, explaining to her his determination to remain at Tyne Cott and help with the wounded. I overheard part of the discussion. There was no chaplain with these British soldiers. Papa spoke English. English boys, wounded and perhaps dying away from home, would need his solace. It was a duty not to be shirked, as binding as if Papa was a medical doctor. "And I'll have company," he said. "Private Kadle is remaining with me. Says he's ashamed America is not yet in this fight. He wants to represent her until she 'gets her head on straight,' he says. Your mama would approve, eh?"

Papa was not as direct with Jessica as he had been with me. With his older daughter he emphasized this separation was only temporary, promising to catch up with us "as soon as he could."

"And you may rely completely on Captain Blood," he said. "The Tin Noses are fine men; fine and sturdy. They'll see you get across the Channel safely. You like the captain, don't you, Jessica?"

"Yes, Papa," Jessica replied. "Shalom and I are both grateful he was here."

I heard the members of the Tin Noses Brigade as they roused the rest of the camp. "Let's be up and moving now," I heard Sergeant Walker urging. "Pack up! With a good foot under you, you can make Langemarck by breakfast. Look alive there. Langemarck," I heard him reply in answer to a question. "Why, it's not but seven or eight miles off. Just a good stretch of the legs."

Judah returned to the basement sanctuary with Papa just as I made the girls ready for travel. Jessica, holding Shalom, still looked pale but resolute.

"We've a garden cart for you and the baby," Judah told Jessica. "It's not an elegant carriage, but it does have rubber tires and won't bounce too much."

"Let the girls ride," Jessica protested. "I can walk. And I can carry Shalom, too."

I exchanged a look with Judah. "No, you can't and no, you won't," I said firmly. "And you won't start off arguing with the captain, either."

"It's all right, Mama," Gina piped. "We don't mind walking."

"That's what Judith says too," Susan reported for her sibling.

"To begin with, we're going cross-country," Judah said. "It'll be rougher, but safer than being caught on the roads."

I remembered the aerial attacks on the refugees. "I know," I agreed with a shudder. "The deeper the woods, the better."

"And it won't be for long," he added. "There are good roads beyond Langemarck."

"How do we know where to go?" Gina asked.

Taking the girl by the hand, Judah led the small band of travelers up the steps and faced them toward the west. "See that band of clouds, just there? That's called the marine layer. That's where we'll find the sea."

"And England?"

Judah nodded. "Just beyond that bit of cloud."

Papa leaned against the doorframe, biting his lip. Gina hugged him around the waist. "Come soon, Grandpa," she said.

"Take good care of your baby brother," he said, before kissing Jessica and Shalom each on the forehead and helping Jessica get seated in the cart.

He held the baby close for a moment, putting his nose against the top of his head, as if he would inhale Baby Shalom. Then he surrendered the baby to Jessica.

I saw Papa dab at his eye. Perhaps a bit of dust had lodged there.

"Form them up, Sergeant," Judah said softly to Mickey Walker. "Short good-byes are best." Then louder, he directed, "Lieutenant, I'd like you to be the rear guard. Sergeant, you are the advance scout. We'll take turns pushing the cart."

I ran back to my father's side. "I—I love you, Papa. And I'll pray for you . . . pray for you lots."

"And I you," he said, squeezing me tightly. "Do whatever Judah says. You'll be fine."

I lost sight of Papa as the procession exited the back of Tyne Cott and dropped into the swale beyond. When we started up the next slope, I couldn't help myself: I looked back. Papa was there, dark suit outlined against the light backdrop of the platform of the stone cross. He was waving and waving.

By the time the entourage reached the edge of the woods and I looked again, he had gone.

15

Despite Judah's assurances, the garden cart rumbled and jolted its way down from Tyne Cott's plateau and into the farmland. I saw Jessica bite her lip and flinch when the wheels struck unyielding stone ledges or banged down hard over stones, but she made no complaint.

Sometimes we encountered a pit too deep or narrow to cross easily. Then Sergeant Walker and Judah picked up the entire contraption—mother, child and all—and carried it across.

Baby Shalom slept serenely throughout.

As we emerged from a stand of trees, I saw a large number of other fugitives from the Nazi onslaught trailing after us. No matter how intimidated by the painted masks they might be, the refugees instinctively sensed in Judah a man of leadership.

As I walked, Gina held one of my hands, while Susan held the other with Judith attached on the far side of her. The morning progressed into a fine, blue-skied day. With hundreds of people tramping across the meadows, it was as if an entire village had turned out for a spring festival or picnic.

Why were we leaving Tyne Cott? It seemed so unreal, so against my senses, to imagine that we fled from the horrors of war, even though I had recently seen its reality.

The country ramble vaguely reminded me of something, but I couldn't place it exactly. I said as much to Jessica.

Her brow furrowed for a moment and then she exclaimed: "Of course! Tonkawa Park. But you can't remember that. You were too little."

"Tell us, Mama," Gina demanded.

"When your aunt Lora was very young—tiny, even—Papa took us to Waco to a big meeting."

"That's in Texas, U.S.A.," Gina explained with authority.

Susan and Judith nodded.

Jessica had stopped speaking. I knew she was thinking about leaving Papa behind, back at Tyne Cott.

I was too. When would we see him again?

"Go on," Gina insisted.

When Jessica resumed there was an unfamiliar huskiness in her voice. "There's a park outside of town where a camp meeting was held. It had a grove of trees and a stream and a big rock. People would leap from that rock into a swimming hole."

The girls giggled when Jessica unconsciously lapsed into talking Texan: "swimmin' haul."

"Anyway," she continued, "today reminds me of that. The whole crowd from the camp meeting traipsed across the countryside to the creek."

More giggles when she pronounced "crick."

"But you were so little," she said to me. "You can't possibly remember it."

I shrugged. "Something locked in my head all these years."

Leading the advance, Lieutenant Howard held up his hand for a halt. A thin plume of black smoke rose into the still morning air right in our line of march.

Cocking his head, Judah listened carefully.

I did the same but heard nothing except a low chuffing sound, like the heavy panting of a St. Bernard.

Motioning us to move on cautiously, Judah led the way up a small knoll.

On the other side the ground sloped away sharply. In a black line at the bottom of the slope a passenger train lay on a siding. It was motionless, its idling engine causing the resonant rhythm.

The engine pointed north, toward the sea.

As the throng of refugees topped the rise beside us, excitement swept over them. "A train," one shouted.

"No more walking!"

"We'll ride to the coast!"

"Wait!" Judah warned.

No one heeded his alert. Like a pent-up wave, the tide of civilians swept down from the crest. Many waved and hallooed, as if afraid the train might suddenly depart, leaving them behind.

"Why not?" I asked.

The answer came, not from Judah, but from an insistent buzzing that began behind my right shoulder and grew louder with each moment.

Judah's next words were: "Get down!" He lifted Jessica and the baby out of the cart and into a ditch.

The diving German warbirds were already in their attack. Heedless of his own safety, Judah waved and shouted to the crowds. "Get back! Get down!"

But it was already too late. A train stalled on a siding was raw meat to hungry carnivores. The Stukas pounced from out of the sun.

Lieutenant Howard gathered in the girls and shoved them inside a culvert and put his body across the entrance.

Jessica cradled Shalom at the bottom of a pile that had me lying across her, and Sergeant Walker and Judah atop both of us.

The high-pitched shriek of the falling bombs and the shrill, terrifying noise of the swooping bombers fell from the sky. The noises collided with the screams of the people caught on the train and in the field beside it. I wished I could plug my ears from the screeches.

A startlingly loud explosion told of a direct hit, and the ground rose and bucked beneath us. A second later another detonation was only slightly muffled. I felt the shudder in the earth even greater than from the first.

Instead of subsiding, the noises grew louder as something on the engine exploded. Waves of concussion rolled across the landscape.

The planes roared past overheard, heading east.

"Keep down!" Judah warned. "It's not over."

The shrieking of human voices was louder than ever, coupled with a guttural moan that rose in intensity with the agonies of grief and pain.

For once, Judah was wrong. The Stukas did not return.

At length we unpiled from the ditch, and Lieutenant Howard retrieved the girls from the storm drain.

Sergeant Walker's mask had slipped in the tumbling. Hurriedly he straightened it.

Seeing his embarrassment, Jessica hugged him around the neck. "Thank you," she said.

A blush crept out from under the tin faceplate like a spreading pink stain.

"We can follow this channel around," Judah said to me as he helped me to my feet. "There's a railroad bridge no more than a quarter mile away. The sergeant will lead you. Once on the other side, there is a good place to hole up."

"While you see what you can do for the wounded?"

"We won't be long," Judah promised. "Just . . . don't let the girls look back."

The image of a carefree throng heading toward a picnic was gone forever. Shattered lives; shattered memories. Once across the tracks I checked: Mama's teacups were all still intact.

It seemed absurdly important to me.

The journey toward the English Channel had lost any resemblance to a pleasurable country outing. Now the small bands of travelers had a furtive air. When two family groups had an encounter, they treated each other with suspicion and sometimes hostility.

Beyond Langemarck a spine of low hills curved around until it was aimed northward. Since the crest and sides were tree covered, Judah elected to use it as our path.

"We must have come at least ten miles," I said. "Can't we get back on a road of some kind?"

Calling a halt to the procession, Judah led me to the crest of the ridge. Before the summit he made me crouch down and creep up the slope beside him. The view down the other side included a road about a mile distant.

It was packed with British military vehicles . . . all heading toward the coast.

"Not only is that convoy a bull's-eye for the

Luftwaffe," Judah said. "It also means something has gone terribly, terribly wrong. For this many British units to pull back this far means the Germans have broken through in strength. No, we'll keep off the roads."

I did not ask again.

The rough terrain made frequent rest stops necessary. The young girls were exhausted. Sergeant Walker had taken over scouting duty, and Howard was now assisting with the cart, but no one had relieved Judah.

Looking at the strain in his neck and shoulders, I realized the captain was likewise exhausted. I also knew he would never call a halt for himself, so I pretended to need the break for myself.

We had not eaten since early morning. It was now late afternoon.

Lieutenant Howard rummaged in the knapsacks and under the blankets with which the cart was lined. "Sergeant," he asked, "where's the kit with the grub?"

"Tied to the back of the—"

The canvas duffel bag containing our food supplies was no longer on the wagon. "I'll go back and find it," Walker volunteered. "It might have bounced loose when we crossed that last culvert."

"All right," Judah approved. "But no more than fifteen out; fifteen back. That's all we can wait."

It was actually no more than twelve minutes

total before the curly-haired Irishman returned. He was sporting a goose-egg at his hairline, and he did not have the duffel bag.

"What happened?" Howard demanded.

"Somebody took a shot at me," Walker said.

"Are you hit, man?" Howard said with alarm. "Sit down and let me see."

Walker waved off his friend's attention. "Not a wound," he argued, touching his forehead and wincing. "Least, not from a bullet. Hit it on a tree limb while ducking."

"Germans?"

"Trigger happy Belgians," Walker corrected. "But I didn't stick around and try to explain. Sorry, Captain."

"We may have lost the pack clear back at the rail line," Judah suggested. "Anyway, never mind. We'll get by." A box of crackers was located amongst the other sacks, and this was shared by the girls. "The rest of us will tighten our belts until tonight. We'll come across something by then. Sergeant, take the point again."

"Let me help with the cart," I suggested. "You've been pushing and dragging it all day."

Judah protested. I insisted.

In the end he allowed me to share the duty, trundling one of the wheels while he propelled the other and Howard hefted the handles.

Judah smiled at me, and I returned it.

"This line of hills ends at Dixmude," he said. "We'll make for there; try and find food and lodging for tonight."

"Do you do a lot of hiking?" I teased. "How do you know this country so well?"

"I fought across it in 1917," he said. "And I saw it . . . other times as well."

The day, which had begun with such pleasant weather, had turned increasingly sultry. By sunset it was clear a thunderstorm was brewing out over the Channel.

Since we had been walking all day, Gina and her friends were now genuinely tired. Despite Judah's desire to have us push ahead as rapidly as possible, we just weren't able to move any faster.

"Don't worry," he said, eyeing the sky. "We'll still make Dixmude by dark."

Judah kept us entertained by stories about the area. "Dixmude has a wonderful old parish church. Has a three-hundred-year-old painting: *The Adoration of the Magi*, by Jordaens."

"You sound like a *Baedecker's Guide*," I teased.

"Studied the painting for a window I was building," he said.

I was struck again by what an amazingly complex man Judah was. An artist and a warrior.

So was King David, I recalled.

It was about this time we encountered the supply convoy. Our path intersected a road on which ten English lorries were parked. As we emerged from the brush, the guards fingered their rifles nervously. They only relaxed when they saw that women and children outnumbered the men, and that we had no weapons.

Judah approached the sergeant in charge and explained who we were.

The sergeant peered in the gathering gloom at Judah's artificial features, then at Walker and Howard. "Didn't get those in this war, did you?"

"No, and we don't want any new artificial parts, either."

"Not likely! You done your bit. Get back home and keep out of this. 'Course," he added confidentially, "we may be headed home right behind of you, I shouldn't wonder."

Judah asked the sergeant to confirm the distance to Dixmude.

"Blimey," the sergeant in charge responded. "Is this the road to Dixmude? We're s'posed to be headed for Ichteghem; however you might pronounce it. All these names like to strangle me, they do."

"Back the other way, I'm afraid," Judah corrected.

"Crikey!"

The sergeant confided, "This is all a proper foul-up, this is! Three days ago we was in Surrey on a trainin' exercise. Two days ago we shipped over, with these spare parts. Yesterday we drove halfway to Germany, like. Today it's all busted up. Go here, wait, go back, go again."

"Sergeant," Judah said with a tone of authority, "you seem to be way too free with giving information to strangers."

The sergeant grimaced. "You're right! But we've not even seen a Jerry since we come here. Bein' chased by phantoms for all I know."

The wind pushed the storm clouds toward us. There was the smell of rain on the air.

"The Boche are real enough," Judah said. "And they're not far away."

The racing of engines alerted us to the arrival of more vehicles.

"Hope that's an officer what has the straight of it," the sergeant said. "Best get your troop off the road," he added to Judah. "We seen some folks get run over, like, so we have."

"Good advice," Judah returned, and he directed us out of harm's way through a gap in a hedgerow flanking the road.

"We'll wait here until the convoy moves off," Judah said. "Then I think we can safely use the road. Be easier from here to Dixmude."

Jessica nursed Shalom. Lieutenant Howard took up a position at one end of our line and Sergeant Walker at the other, their backs to us six in the center, as if they were our personal guards.

Judah continued watching the road.

A motorcycle purred up to the head of the line

of trucks and stopped. Just behind it was a staff car, followed by another motorcycle.

In the gloom we heard the sergeant say, "Is that Captain Moody? What sort of helmet are you wearing?"

There was no reply except for a sudden ratcheting sound.

The next thing I knew Judah was pushing me down, hard, for the second time that day.

Machine guns split the night, tearing apart the quiet and the darkness. Screams and cries of alarm echoed from the trucks. Shouted commands in German said to "Kill them all."

In moments that seemed like hours the carnage was over.

We were all unhurt, flattened in the ditch, but barely yards away from the Nazi patrol that had just slaughtered twenty men.

I heard boots crunch on gravel and saw the flash of an electric torch playing in and out of the line of lorries.

Then Shalom squawked.

It was a soft, newborn infant protest at being squished, but it sounded as loud as a train whistle in the malevolence-laden darkness. I felt Jessica cuddle him close, trying to comfort him; difficult when her own breath was coming in short, scared sips and she was shaking.

So was I.

Gravel crunched underfoot again . . . closer.

A bolt of lightning split the night, followed immediately by a peal of thunder that sounded as if it broke right on top of us.

And then came the rain.

I heard disgust in the German officer's voice when he told his group to mount up. He added that they would find other convoys on which to pounce, and they moved off.

But we did not dare move yet.

By flipping the cart upside-down, Judah contrived a shelter for Jessica and the baby that also accommodated the girls by squeezing them under.

The three men and I huddled miserably out in the rain.

"Can't we at least get inside the trucks?" I asked.

"And if the Germans return and decide to take them along this time?"

We remained in our hiding place. The rain finally stopped around eleven, but we were too stiff to move any further that night.

16

We never did reach Dixmude.

The morning after the German attack on the British supply convoy Judah made us backtrack through the fields. We remained in the shadows of the hedgerows and away from the roads entirely. "We will stay safe as long as we can," he said. "We'll have to come out in the open to cross the bridge at Dixmude, but if we can remain under cover until then, we will."

I no longer questioned any of Judah's decisions when it came to keeping us out of harm's way. I did say: "You've never said where we're going. I mean, how you plan to get us to England."

"Ostende," he said, naming a Channel port about twenty miles away. "I have a friend who has a fishing smack there."

After the terrors of the night, Gina, Judith, and Susan traveled in a tight-knit band, seldom further than arm's length from each other. When Susan swooped on something lying in the dirt, the object was passed from hand-to-hand before any of the adults got a look.

Gina, who had it last, passed a military cap to Judah. Pointing to the skull and crossbones on the badge, she asked worriedly, looking around, "Did this belong to the Hitler men?"

Judah took it. "No," he said, reading the motto underneath the chilling emblem: *Death or Glory.* It belongs to a British soldier—a Lancer. My old unit."

This was new information to me. I knew Walker and Howard had been in the same outfit in the Great War: the Highlanders. I had just assumed Judah had been part of the same force.

What else did I not know about this enigmatic man?

When we approached Dixmude we came upon a mob of refugees huddled together a quarter mile short of the bridge. "Why have you stopped here?" Judah asked.

"The Britishers," a portly Belgian replied. "They say the bridge is mined, and we're too late to cross."

"No!" Judah exclaimed. Then, "Wait here!" and he ran forward.

A series of dull thuds erupted from the crossing of the Yser River before he had covered half the distance. With typical British efficiency each span of the bridge collapsed inward on itself with a minimum of fuss.

The girls watched the demolition with great interest and no trace of fear.

In thirty seconds, where there had been a river crossing, there was now a heap of twisted girders and a trail of smoke.

Judah stood on the bank and shouted across, "Oy! Hey, Lancers."

Someone bellowed back: "What d'ya want, chum? Miss your ride?"

"We've got to get across."

"You and the whole German army. Why do you think we blew the bridge?"

"I know. But how can we get to Ostende?"

There was a silence and then: "Can't help you there. Nazis are already in Ostende. We're falling back on Dunkirk."

The Yser, though not a mighty current, was still too much for the children and Jessica and the baby to cross safely.

"Is there another way?"

Another consultation, then: "Follow the tracks of the trolley line. If you run, you can cross by their bridge. Best hurry, though. Good luck."

"Thanks," Judah bellowed back. He urged our aching limbs into the fastest motion of the journey thus far. No obstacle was allowed to impede the progress of the cart for more than an instant before the combined strength of the three men hoisted it clear.

It was one of the ironies of the spring of 1940 that the trolley tracks we now followed connected the interior of Belgium at Ypres with the seaside pleasure resorts of Ostende. We had started our escape near the one but could not return there. Judah thought we were headed for the other end of that excursion line, only to learn it was in enemy hands.

"What now?" I asked. Oddly I felt no anxiety at the imposed changes. I was confident Judah would work out alternatives.

"Just cross the river," he said. "Figure out the rest after that."

The gorge spanned by the trolley line bridge was neither deep nor terribly wide, but it was completely exposed. We would have to pick our way over for about a hundred yards.

Given what we had experienced with the German air assault on the train and the slaughter of the British troops on the road, none of us were eager to go.

"No choice," Judah said. "Lieutenant, Sergeant: we'll carry the cart all the way. Too bumpy otherwise, and we can't risk it getting stuck between the ties."

"Yes, sir," both men returned.

"I have a better idea," Jessica challenged. "I can walk. Carry the cart with our supplies, but you'll not carry me this time. And I can manage Shalom."

Lieutenant Howard crossed first, checking to see if any explosives were attached to the frame of the span. "They haven't made it here yet," he reported as he trotted back. "Come on!"

There was planking along one side of the bridge for a narrow footpath, but it was scarcely broad enough for one person. The spacing of the ties was too great for the girls to cross without leaping.

"Here's what we do," Judah said. "Jessica, you go across first. Now, Gina, you line up behind your aunt Lora, with your hands on her waist. Judith, you behind her, and Susan, you last. You four are pretending to be the last trolley for the seacoast. Ready? Go."

And that is how we shuffled across the bridge.

Even without the weight of mother and child,

the three Tin Nose troopers had to set the cart down midspan to change and get better grips. That was when the first mortar round landed in the river about a hundred paces away. Falling without warning, the first news of the shell's arrival was its detonation and the eruption of a geyser of water.

Jessica was already across. I was only a few paces behind with my parade of ducklings when the second shellburst struck the far bank where we had stood just moments earlier.

The cart, in an exhibition of just what Judah feared, wedged a wheel between ties and refused to move. "Leave it," he ordered, as the sergeant wrenched at the handle. "Run!"

When all of us were across, we did not stop to look back but pushed on into the thickest brush we could find. We never did know if the shelling came from Germans or the British.

What we did know was that all of our supplies were lost with the cart. What remained was in the knapsack on my back: my precious teacups, and very little else.

With Ostende no longer an option, Judah directed our steps further along the coast toward Dunkirk, until we reached the Belgian seaside bathing spa of Nieuport. We were inside the British lines, but only just.

Over its long and storied past, Nieuport had

been ruled by Flemish counts, Norman lordlings, and Knights Templar. It had been fought over by the Dutch, the French, and even the Spaniards.

Now the unfortunate Nieuporters might have to learn German as well.

When we reached the town square we might have walked into a dream. Belgian soldiers sat at tables in the plaza, swilling glasses of wine. Most had tied napkins to their gun barrels.

"What has happened?" Judah demanded. "Has the war magically ended? Have the Boche surrendered to the might of the Belgian forces?"

"Ah, no," returned an artillery captain. "Our great and wise king, Leopold, has ordered us," the officer waved expansively at his table of friends, who raised their glasses, "to cease fighting. He says to prevent unnecessary loss of life."

"And leave your Allies holding the bag," I heard Sergeant Walker growl. "I'll be showin' you loss of life, me boy-o."

"Easy, Sergeant," Judah cautioned. "They do still have guns."

"To carry their flowers in, more like," Walker added before subsiding.

We held a hasty conference beside the town hall. "If our boys are falling back on Dunkirk, shall we push on for there?" Lieutenant Howard asked.

Judah squinted at the sinking sun. "Not tonight.

We need rest and food. I'll scout for supplies. Sergeant, lead the way into the basement of the post office."

The building mentioned was a squat, ugly, one-story structure. "Can't we stay in a hotel? Or at least in the church?" I queried.

"The soldiers are already drinking," Judah said, looking at me with significance. "When the taverns on the plaza run out, they will ransack the hotels."

"I—I understand," I returned weakly. I had considered that the only danger to us was from Germans. "Why not the church, then?"

Judah pointed to the bell tower. "The Nazis tend to view towers as observation posts to be shelled or bombed," he said. "They don't stop to inquire what sort of tower it is. No, the post office is best for our purposes. The Germans, in their Teutonic way, pride themselves on making anything they capture work more efficiently than it did before. If they can take the post office intact, they will."

I felt even weaker and more discouraged than before. "Do you think they will? Capture Nieuport, I mean?"

The lines of Judah's grim face visible below the corners of his mask relaxed slightly. "Not tonight. And tomorrow we sail for England."

The girls applauded.

"Lead the way, Sergeant. I have some foraging to do."

"Want me to accompany you, sir?" Howard asked.

"No, you best stay together." Judah headed off toward the far end of the street.

We scoured the basement of the post office from one end to the other. The girls turned up three tins of sardines and a wedge of moldy cheese. When we opened one cupboard, we thought our luck had changed because the bottom shelf contained a large pottery crock of pickles.

Unfortunately the rest of the contents of the armoire was postal supplies.

The girls turned up their noses at the fare. "Sardines and pickles? Really, Aunt Lora, nobody can just eat that."

Within an hour Judah returned. He carried four roasted chickens and a pillowcase full of fresh baked bread.

"How? Where?" I marveled.

"Natural-born scrounger," he reported. "Turned up a case of champagne the Belgians missed. Traded the wine for a crate of cigarettes someone had taken from a looted supply truck. Traded the cigarettes for all this."

"Well done," I praised. "Kept none of the champagne or tobacco for yourself?"

"Now's no time to be drinking," he said. "And I don't smoke."

After supper, when everyone was tucked in, Judah said, "Sergeant, I'll leave you on guard here. Lieutenant, I've a mind to reconnoiter over toward Dunkirk. Are you with me?"

"Count me in, sir," Howard said.

"Must you leave again?" I blurted, feeling myself color immediately after I spoke.

"Thought we'd find our transport here," he said, "but all the boats are gone from Nieuport. We won't be away long."

Fed and exhausted, the girls went immediately to sleep. Sergeant Walker posted himself at the head of stairs to keep watch.

By the light of an oil lamp Jessica nursed baby Shalom. The flickering flames streaked her hair in light and dark. It cast shadows across her profile as she smiled tenderly down at him, and illuminated her bare shoulder and the top of his downy head. She saw me watching and smiled. "You never know," she said.

"What?"

"How much God loves you until you have one of these of your own. Then you begin to understand."

Judah did not return until very late. Though his mask registered no expression, his voice reflected worry. "You won't believe the scene on the beach. This isn't a retreat. It's a rout. There must be a hundred thousand men—British and French—camping there, waiting to be rescued."

I tried to picture it and failed. "What's it mean for us?"

"Nothing good, I'm afraid. I quizzed a beachmaster. They're not taking any civilians. Every boat, every ship, every ferry and tug, is being pressed into service rescuing soldiers. They're coming from as far away as Scotland and the Isle of Wight."

"But no room for us?"

He squared his shoulders. "Something will work out. It has to."

I slept then. Later, when I groaned myself awake while trying to find a softer spot on the stone floor, he was still up, thinking or praying. I studied him.

It was impossible to not see the mask first. I admit that.

But now that I knew him—the man and not the wave of pity or revulsion or apprehension that the mask inspired—I saw much more. Now I saw Judah's strong jaw, his broad shoulders, his strong hands, and sensitive artist's fingers. I saw his courage, his compassion, his leadership.

In a half-waking, half-dreaming vision, I saw him cup my face in his hands and kiss me as I fell into the embrace of his eyes. The mask played no part in the image at all.

After no more than an hour's sleep, Judah went out again before dawn seeking transport for us, but without success. When day approached, I insisted on going with him. Perhaps I thought I could plead with the British officers to save the lives of the children and my sister and nephew.

Even though Judah tried to describe for me the scene on the beaches of Dunkirk, nothing he explained prepared me for the reality. He had said a hundred thousand men awaited rescue from Blitzkrieg, but the number had no physical counterpart for me until I saw it for myself.

Up and down the dunes, as far as could be seen—all the way to the billowing clouds of dense black smoke that marked the port of Dunkirk—the sand was covered with the figures of men.

Immense spirals of soldiers, like coils of living rope slowly unspooling toward the waves, awaited deliverance. Hundreds, perhaps thousands, of British troops were in each curling figure. "And this is no more than half of them," Judah said. "The rest are embarking through the fires of Dunkirk."

Just as the dunes were alive with men, the Channel was bustling with ships. Every sort, every kind, from coal carriers to twenty-foot runabouts, plied the waves off the coast. The shallower draft vessels came up until their keels touched. Forty men scrambled aboard, and the craft pushed off again to ferry the fortunate few to larger vessels waiting beyond the breakers.

On this shore the tide receded immensely far out, exposing an expanse of wet sand that seemed to stretch halfway to England. Each ampersand of soldiers was crowned with an exclamation point formed by a makeshift pier: trucks, jeeps, passenger cars, all these had been driven onto the beach and muscled into place to form arms binding the land to the sea.

"When the tide returns," Judah explained, "the men leap from car roof to truck bonnet. Then bigger ships come in further and more soldiers can get off the beach more quickly."

It was the blueprint of a fantastic machine cobbled together by a mad scientist.

A plane flew overhead. Judah pushed me down, but I contrived to watch just the same. All the men fell to the ground and burrowed into the sand, as if they could cram their entire bodies under their helmets.

Though a few men remained upright, futilely firing their rifles at the intruder, this time the plane neither dropped bombs nor strafed. It winged its way out to sea and out of sight.

"A spotter, looking for bigger targets," Judah said. He gestured toward the Channel.

Far out on the horizon cruised the biggest vessels in the rescue flotilla: British war ships. "Those would make the biggest prizes for the Germans," Judah said.

"And in all this there's no place for us?" I know I whined as I asked it. It seemed impossible to me that amid the hundreds of boats I saw bobbing on the waves there was no room for the nine of us.

"Rescuing the army so it can fight again is the first priority," Judah said with resignation.

"Not for me," I returned.

Another plane arrived overhead, and this one had attack in mind. We ducked again as the bomb whistled down.

It struck in the damp sand halfway between two coils of men and exploded with a sodden thump.

No one was killed or even injured. The British soldiers, jumping to their feet, shook their fists and jeered at the pilot. "How'd y'manage to miss us all, you near-sighted Nazi?"

"They should all be saved," I admitted, acknowledging the heroism and bravado. "But so should we."

"Let's get back," Judah said.

We tucked in and out of sight among the hillocks of sand and beach grass. In this game of hide-and-seek with the buzzing planes we almost missed our salvation.

A curl of rocks forming a tiny cove presented a question mark amid the chaos. And floating upside down in the pool, so far unnoticed, was a lifeboat.

I spotted it before Judah. "Could we use that?" I asked, pointing.

"Brilliant," he said, hugging me.

We ran toward it. "It's intact," he said. "We'll row out."

"Stay here," I urged. "I don't know how you'll do it, but don't let anyone else take it. I'll get the others." I shouted these words over my shoulder as I sprinted inland. I gave him no chance to argue.

"Come on!" I shouted to the seven in the basement. "We've got a boat," and, "Where's my knapsack?"

Without stopping to explain, I led the way up the stairs and out of Nieuport. Gina was on my back, Susan on Lieutenant Howard's, and Judith on Sergeant Walker's. Jessica carried Shalom.

Halfway to the edge of town a string of explosions sounded behind us. "Good timing," Howard asserted. "Germans are shelling Nieuport."

The last detonation, the closest of the set, drove me to my knees. As Sergeant Walker helped me to my feet, I looked back: the post office had taken a direct hit. It had tumbled in on itself, forming a crater of bricks and mortar.

"Lousy aim," the sergeant noted.

It took all of the adults to heave the boat upright, then we bailed it out and loaded the children. There were only two oars that remained whole, and these were wielded by Judah and Lieutenant Howard. The rest of us seized broken fragments of boards with which to paddle.

We had been rowing for about an hour. It seemed as if we might have to row all the way to

England. If true, that necessity was fine with me. The more space we put between us and the Nazi-dominated continent, the better I felt.

At last we entered the shipping lanes. The crews of a pair of fishing trawlers, inbound for Dunkirk, waved and shouted to us, but Judah waved them off. "Pick us up on the way back," he yelled.

A mile farther out in the Channel was a cruising British destroyer. As we watched in horror, a squadron of German planes pounced on the ship.

Lightning bolts of anti-aircraft fire streaked upward from the warship.

Lethal eggs tumbled out of the bombers.

One of them at least must have struck the destroyer amidships. There was a mighty crash, a whole series of additional explosions that made us duck our heads, and then the British vessel folded up on both ends. It settled into the waves, sirens screaming. A fireball rose from the hulk, then a torrent of oily fumes oozed across the water.

The breeze pushed the strangling vapors toward us.

But not fast enough.

A circling bomber, satisfied with the destruction of the ship, spotted us. It dove toward our fragile ark, guns blazing.

We burrowed into every makeshift cavity, girls

and baby beneath, Jessica and me next, men atop the heap.

A line of splashes marched directly toward us as the bullets ripped into the sea. One shattered the sternpost of the lifeboat, another splintered the gunnel near my head, and the third struck Sergeant Walker.

Throwing up his hands toward his head, his body jerked upward and toppled sideways into the water.

Without hesitating an instant, Judah dove in after him.

A fist of smoke wrapped greasy fingers around us, shutting out vision.

"Captain!" Howard called urgently. "Sergeant!"

"Judah," I yelled. "Where are you?"

We paddled in circles, heedless of whether the plane would renew the attack or not.

No trace of either man did we locate.

We drifted for a long time after that, unable to find the heart to row.

Eventually Lieutenant Howard roused himself. "Let's pull ourselves together," he said with difficulty. "There's a boat. Let's make for her."

The rescue craft coming to our aid was a French canal boat. Already crammed to the rails and rigging with scores of the rescued, including many children, a broad-faced woman shouted to us, "Just a moment. I'll toss you a line."

And that was how we reached port in England:

in a rowboat towed from the stern of an aging canal barge.

But I thought little of this at the time. It seemed incredibly unjust that Judah and the good sergeant, who had accomplished so much and brought us so far, should have died so near to safety.

One small tragedy among thousands during those grim days, it still left me feeling bitter and angry.

PART SIX

A time to weep, and a time to laugh;
A time to mourn, and a time to dance.
ECCLESIASTES 3:4

17
LONDON
JUNE 1940

It was nearly time for the evening service at Westminster Abbey—the hour when we gathered in the deep gloom of that ancient house to sing prayers for all the brave boys fighting the Nazis in France.

Like many other refugees in London, Jessica and I had not missed attending a service since we arrived from the miracle of Dunkirk.

We were about to be late. Thunderclouds gathered above Regent's Park, and I had misplaced my umbrella. Jessica was impatient as I searched the flat we shared with another young refugee named Eva Weitzman. I was irritated. Had I left it on the bus? Was someone walking around London protected from the impending rain by my umbrella?

Jessica stood, impatient to leave our flat in the tall Georgian house at the foot of Primrose Hill. The three girls and baby Shalom were already in the below-ground flat where our landlady, Arlice, baby-sat for us.

The BBC radio news blared the reports of the Nazi Blitzkrieg sweeping through France. Our prayers seemed more important than ever.

And so was our need for comfort. Tyne Cott had

been overrun. We heard Papa was killed in the last bombardment just before the final Nazi onslaught. I was numb with grief.

Where was my umbrella?

Those of us who had escaped from Europe and made our way to freedom knew that the great, unnumbered mass of human suffering was made up of individual stories. Even one single refugee child strafed and killed by a Luftwaffe fighter along the road from Belgium to France was too many. I could not think of one child left dead along the highway. The story of one was too painful, too real. Better to hear the estimates of the numbers of dead and dying and forget that each one had a story. There were too many innocent victims to memorialize in one BBC broadcast.

Where had I put my umbrella?

The world as we knew it was coming to an end, yet I could only think of myself. It was as though there was no tragedy—no story but my own. There was me, selfish and self-absorbed . . . and then were those hundreds of thousands of refugees all lumped together into one tragedy. I knew, because Eva had told me, entire populations of Jewish villages in Poland were machine-gunned and dumped into mass graves.

I could only think of my husband, Varrick, out there . . . somewhere. There was no story but him and me. Holding onto the belief that he still lived and would join me in London was my one prop. Our love was the hub around which the universe revolved.

"It's going to rain. I'll have to buy another umbrella." I sighed.

The knock at the door and the sad-eyed messenger boy with the telegram signaled the end of my hopes and dreams.

"Missus Kepler?" He did not look into my face.

Jessica stood at my shoulder. I felt her firm hand on my arm as I took the wire and closed the door. "Steady," she said.

My own voice, distant, as if it belonged to someone else, panted Varrick's name, praying: "Oh! Not Varrick! Please God, not Varrick."

Eva, silent and pale, stood in the doorway of the sitting room as I tore open the telegram. Her bright blue eyes brimmed with tears. Her beloved Mac McGrath, a news photographer with the Trump European News Service (TENS), had sailed off with the flotilla of little ships to rescue the desperate British Army at Dunkirk. She knew Mac might not return. We all knew. Yet in this moment, Eva's fears were all focused on me and the dreaded envelope in my trembling hands.

The typewritten words on the yellow slip of paper blurred for a moment, then came into sharp focus. The air around me became heavy, too thick to breathe, as I stammered aloud the curt, matter-of-fact message about my husband . . .

"Deep regrets STOP your husband Varrick Kepler killed STOP Heroic action near Cambrai STOP Deepest condolences."

Jessica groaned. Eva gasped and rushed to my side.

The telegram fluttered like a dry leaf from my fingers. The world spun and darkened as my knees buckled. I collapsed slowly to the floor.

I do not know how long I was unconscious. A cool damp cloth dabbed my face. I did not want to awaken to the nightmare of reality. Squeezing my eyes tight, tears escaped and trickled down my face.

"No. No. Can't be."

Jessica's voice said, "Lora? Maybe it's a mistake. This is all they sent? No explanation?"

Eva whispered, her words tinged with a Polish accent, "The world collapses. Chaos in France. How can we know what is certain?"

Jessica said, unconvincingly, "We'll pray. They could have got it wrong."

Eva said, "I will ask at the news office. Surely TENS reporters will have some way to check the list of casualties."

I opened my eyes. Jessica's worried face hovered above me. Eva stooped and held a glass of water to my lips. "Drink, Lora. Drink."

The cool liquid on my tongue pulled me back toward consciousness, but I did not attempt to sit up. "Jessica, am I . . . is it a dream? Varrick?"

She did not answer at first. The telegram lay beside us on the black-and-white-checkered foyer tiles. The handle of my umbrella stuck out from behind the coat rack. I fixed my gaze on it and thought, if only I had found it earlier, we would have been gone and missed the telegram.

Jessica held me in her arms, as Mama would have done. "Poor darling. Loralei. Dear Lora."

So, it was true. How many months had it been since I saw him last? Six? Eight? More? I couldn't remember. But always I had thought of him as being somewhere . . . alive. Yet even as the Nazis rolled over Europe, Varrick, my beloved, had been killed.

Twenty-two years old and already a widow, my life seemed finished before it had begun.

Jessica brushed back my blond hair from my eyes. I lay with my head in her lap. Yet we were now more than sisters. We were two women, widows, united by grief at the loss of our husbands.

"So," Jessica said, as our tears mingled, "it has come to this. Papa warned them all. It seems so long ago now, yet it has come, just as Papa said."

I wondered how many other women would receive the confirmation this week that missing sons and husbands would never come home again. The large tragedy—the imminent fall of

France—suddenly fragmented into hundreds of thousands of shards that tore my soul.

"No more!" I cried, covering my ears.

With a nod, Jessica asked Eva to switch off our radio.

Eva turned her eyes away from our grief. I heard the front door close behind her. She was going to the Abbey—one soul among thousands of Londoners, praying a miracle for the fighting men and the women who waited for them. Then she would return to the TENS news office where all the news from France would be grim.

Jessica and I did not attempt to rise. I closed my eyes as she gently stroked my cheek.

Jessica did not move or attempt to rouse me as I slept where I had fallen. The tile was cold and hard. I opened my eyes. Jessica's head leaned against the wall as she dozed. Lightning flashed through the still open blackout curtains. She started and awakened. The sitting room was like a photograph, washed in monochrome silver.

Thunder followed like cannons. The downpour pounded on the roof, cascaded down the windows.

"The rain," Jessica said.

"I knew it was coming." I wondered about the men fighting in France. Were they cold? Was it raining there?

I regretted I had not gone to the Abbey to pray with Eva.

"What time is it, Jessica?" I croaked.

Just then the clock chimed nine times.

"Nine o'clock." She shifted her position.

I sat up slowly but did not rise. We sat together on the tiles, resting our backs against the wall of the entry.

The house was dark. The city was dark. But London did not sleep. Anti-aircraft gun emplacements crowned the brow of Primrose Hill Park. Members of the Home Guard kept watch over the great city. Air-raid wardens prowled the streets in search of even a glimmer of light escaping from behind blackout curtains.

The clock, like Jessica's steady heartbeat, measured my life in time before and after the telegram. How many seconds, minutes, hours, since Varrick died? All the time I had been living, I had imagined him alive too. He had not died when the first rumor of his death reached me. I had been right not to believe that.

During the long months of our separation, I thought of him thinking of me, desiring me in the night, and I had been content in a restless sort of way. I could not imagine my beloved's blood spilled out on a field. Hadn't Papa taught us that righteousness and truth are stronger than evil? I had been certain happiness would win out in the end. It had to be. Life for me was still the stuff of fairy tales before the message.

I had been happy not knowing the truth, hadn't

I? My ignorance had left me with reason to carry on.

False hope had, in the end, laid me out flat. He had not died when first I heard it, but he had still died!

What hope remained to give me purpose?

Every twilight we had gathered in the great echoing stone hall of Westminster. How many times had I looked up and thought I heard the agonized prayers of generations now beyond their earthly grief? The ancient ones who had whispered heartache before I lived were now reunited in heaven with the men they had prayed for and lost. When the harmony of the Psalms died away, had I not heard their voices echo in the vaulting? Someday, I thought, another generation would sit in the Abbey and hear my prayers emerging from the stones. What truth would a generation yet unborn hear in the echoes of my life?

For me, Varrick's death had not taken place in France. My husband had perished this very night before my eyes.

How many others would die before this night ended? Evening prayers were no longer about me and Varrick. I had crossed over the line of demarcation . . . into another life.

"They are coming to England," I whispered to Jessica. "All the boys who escaped."

"I was praying for them. For their wives and mothers. Just now."

"What was it the BBC was reporting before the telegram? Food and blankets. Clean clothes? The trains from Dover crammed with wounded. Rail station platforms overflowing with survivors." I struggled to stand. "Poor fellows. I must go there, Jessica. Help them. So many. But every one of them—any one of those boys—could have been my Varrick. Perhaps on his journey some woman brought him food. Perhaps—"

Jessica looked up at me. Lightning flashed again, and I saw her expression, beauty cast in pewter light. She smiled. "There's my girl."

Clouds burst. Rain roared like a river from the eaves.

"Varrick would want me to go. Expect me to go."

"Yes." Jessica grasped my fallen umbrella and stood up. "We'll go together."

The pendulum of the tall clock in the foyer swung. The hour struck. *Too late . . . too late . . . too late . . . too late . . .*

The unthinkable was now our reality.

Before we managed to get out the door, the phone rang. "I—I don't think I can talk just now," I said.

Jessica went down the hall to answer it. When she returned she said, "It's Eva. Says she's met an American missionary and orphans. They're in London. Lora, they need translators at St. Mark's Church."

I knew the church on North Audley Street well. St. Mark's was a block from the American Embassy near Grosvenor Square. Known as the American Church in London, it was a gathering place for important evangelical church leaders from the U.S.

"Eva says St. Mark's has been made into a temporary shelter. And will we come?"

"Call her back and tell her we'll be there soon." As if to hurry us along, the downpour slowed to a drizzle and stopped altogether.

Into a hamper Jessica and I gathered tins of tea, bread, scones, and pots of jam, along with our kettle and teacups. (But not Mama's precious teacups, which were secured in a cupboard.)

Arlice would watch the girls for the night. Shalom was coming with us.

Switching off the light, we emerged from the house into the utter darkness of London. The air was rain-washed, fresh and cool. A breeze swept over us from Regent's Park.

I might have been happy to experience the sweet scent of the plane trees. *If only . . .*

I steeled myself. I would not think of Varrick tonight. Perhaps tomorrow, when the sun rose, I would have time to mourn, but not now. Tonight the world no longer revolved around me.

There was a slight reflected glow on the street from the slit headlamps of automobiles. The curbs were painted white, which helped a bit.

Without stars or moon shining down on us, we felt our way along the sidewalk.

Jessica asked, "Shall we try for a bus? Or walk a bit?"

"Bus." We linked arms as we made our way across the road to the usual bus stop at the park. Fifteen long minutes passed. I wondered if the buses were still running. Then a taxi rattled to the curb. Pinpoints of light shone from the headlights. How had he seen us? I wondered. I could not make out his face as he spoke.

"Evenin', ladies."

"Will you please take us to St. Mark's Church in North Audley?"

"Americans, eh? Righty-o."

The taxi driver said little as he drove us from Primrose Hill toward Mayfair. I did not know where we were as he drove, nor could I say what route he took to get us to the church. Suddenly his brakes squealed, and we were in front of the pillared portico of St. Mark's.

Stepping out, I pressed coins into the cabbie's palm. Already I could hear a babble of voices from within the shadowed maw of St. Mark's. The great stained-glass window above the entry was cloaked in black drapes. In former days light from within the building radiated out. It had displayed a stunning portrait of Christ the King in his majesty, standing among the seven candlesticks of the seven churches of His revelation.

So, I thought, as we entered the packed and bustling building, the long arm of the Nazis has reached in to hide God's glory even in the American Church of London.

Within the sanctuary every window was painted over or boarded up. A dim glow illuminating the human misery in the crowded hall reached upward to the hammer-beams supporting the ceiling. I saw the outline of the now obscured clerestory windows just below the roofline. In each the leaded glass pattern of the Star of David was barely visible. The colors of God's Covenant with Israel were concealed. On every wall, the stained-glass visions of our Savior were painted over, lest German bombers flying high above London see Christ's light and bomb St. Mark's.

It had come to this: Nazi oppression cast a shadow over the whole of the terrified earth, and a friendly gleam of light could produce death.

18

In search of Eva I scanned the restless refugees who packed St. Mark's Church. Built for the orderly worship needs of 1,500 Victorian parishioners, the Greek-revival structure was never meant to house five hundred homeless hungry people who had lost everything but their clothes.

Against my will I remembered the fires of

Kristallnacht in Berlin. The ashes of Jewish homes had filled my nostrils. We had left everything behind that night . . . everything. Surely the strong presence of my mother would be with me tonight, as comforting to many as she was for me.

I had so little strength to offer. I walked between two worlds: the world where Varrick peopled my memories and the hollow, accepting emptiness of my loss.

Where was Eva?

She was nowhere to be seen.

Confusion reigned in St. Mark's. The dark cherrywood pews on the floor of the church were being transformed into beds by a mix of quarreling French, Dutch, and Belgian refugees. They had somehow managed as we had, amid the chaos of war, to sail across the Channel in small vessels. Women and children dominated the population. A handful of American expatriates were among them. The cacophony of foreign languages and the cries of hungry, exhausted children were deafening.

Jessica, who had mastered five languages in our family's travels, scanned the crowd and spotted a harried, dowdy British matron serving tea near the altar rail. It was clear she spoke only English and a smattering of unintelligible French. Every nuance of communication was lost to her.

A Belgian woman with two small boys whining at her side asked in clear Flemish where the lavatory was located. The Brit grimaced at the rafters and tried to comprehend, then replied in fractured French, "No. No, thank you. Patient her prevail. Tomorrow he bathe."

The refugee blinked in horror at the butchered verbiage. "Tomorrow?"

"*Oui.*" The British matron seemed pleased to have communicated successfully.

The Belgian spread her hands in exasperation. She gestured emphatically at her squirming little boys, then firmly complained, "Tomorrow, too late!"

The tea-server tried another approach. In very loud and carefully pronounced English she said, "PLEASE TAKE YOUR TEA AND BE SEATED. WE WILL FIND A PLACE FOR YOU TO SLEEP SOON." She sighed and muttered to herself, "Somewhere." The matron continued to dole out weak tea in mismatched cups to a line of weary and anxious exiles.

Shalom tucked into the crook of one arm, Jessica grasped the Belgian lady's and marched her to a narrow passageway flanking the narthex. Together they discovered two lavatories. Jessica bid the grateful mother *adieu* and made her way back to a queue of other dejected supplicants yammering in French at the hapless matron. In precise language Jessica stepped up and directed the women and their young ones to the toilets. The troop evaporated.

"What did you say to them?" the tea attendant asked in wonder.

With a smile, Jessica introduced herself. "I'm Jessica. This is my sister, Lora. Both our husbands and our father were killed fighting the Nazis." Jessica's matter-of-fact pronouncement dissolved any suspicion.

The matron managed, "I'm dreadfully sorry for you both. And I am extremely pleased to meet you, as you might imagine. Hermione's my name."

Jessica asked, "How can we serve?"

Beads of perspiration clung to the woman's round, flushed face. "No one here seems to speak English except myself." Then she added in what pretended to be a confidential whisper, "One cannot count the Americans as English speakers."

Jessica did not take advantage of Hermione's gaffe. "We received a call that there was a need for interpreters? My sister and I—"

Hermione pressed her palms together in a prayerful gesture of gratitude to God. Grasping my sister's hands with relief she cried, "An angel, you say? Two angels? I am Missus Hermione Smythe-Jones, also widowed, but my late husband was a bigamist and a drunkard, and thus not as noble as your own. By the grace of God I am secretary to the pastor of St. Mark's.

Reverend Hill and his wife are quite ill with bronchitis, so this disaster has fallen upon my head. A judgment of the Almighty for my slackness in school in the study of languages. Every foreign tongue is Greek to me."

Jessica replied, "May I call you Hermione? It seems we have come to the right place."

Setting the hamper on the table, Jessica went to work with confidence, issuing orders as if we were back home. Somehow the throngs previously milling in disarray between the horseshoe-shaped arches and the ranks of immigrants acquired a newfound orderliness.

It was like watching Mama and Papa rolled into one. I was so glad to have Jessica take charge.

"Lora, find paper. Look in the church office for supplies. Paint signs in every language you can think of, directing to the lavatories. Also post signs for male and female." As I hurried off, I heard her say firmly, "We must divide the hall into sections. Sleeping arrangements by nationality. War has made too strange the bedfellows here in St. Mark's. Belgians do not like the French. Dutch do not like the Belgians. The French do not like anyone."

Jessica was suddenly at her best: taking charge and organizing the chaos of misery into method. Everyone she met exclaimed about what a beautiful child Shalom was. The baby and his winning smile were the only credentials required for women of all nations to trust Jessica and obey.

As for me? I did not have a moment to think of my loss. No time to grieve. I saw grief on the faces of nearly every wife and mother in the church that night. I walked among them, understanding in part their sorrow. We women of the war were divided by language and nationality, but loss united our hearts.

What had they endured to bring their children to this island haven? What scenes of death had they seen on the highways as they fled for their lives?

Hollow, vacant eyes identified those who had suffered the worst. Those who sat alone, unseeing, were the most wretched. They carried the image of Luftwaffe dive-bombers etched into their faces. Bombs and machine-gun bullets had scored their souls, even if their bodies were undamaged.

"Stay busy, Lora," Jessica warned. "Keep your thoughts focused. There's so much to do. Better for you too."

The gallery and choir loft overlooking the auditorium was reserved for single women and girls over the age of ten, as well as women who were pregnant or nursing infants. Did they find comfort and security beneath the image of Jesus as the coming King? Or had desperation and weariness left them desolate and without consolation?

There were less than seventy-five men in the

number. For the sake of modesty, men and boys above the age of ten were assigned the crypt as their quarters.

A chapel at the front of the left aisle was commandeered as a place to offer clothing, blankets, and hot tea to all, regardless of nationality. The walls were lined with memorials to the fallen British dead of the Great War. Bronzes and marbles honoring brave young men who had lived and died before I was born offered cold comfort to present hurts.

French and Belgian women with children outnumbered the Dutch and were assigned the back three-quarters of the auditorium. They were closest to the toilets. The Dutch occupied the front quadrant of the left aisle, nearest the tea trolley and the supplies.

It was some time after midnight when the hubbub in the church began to settle down. The women bedded on the gallery pews spoke very softly to one another. Children slept propped upon their mother's shoulders.

Hermione lumbered toward Jessica and me with cups of tea on a tray. "Well done," she said, and we three sat down near the back of the hall.

I sipped my tea, conscious of my exhaustion, grateful to be weary. Perhaps I would sleep tonight and not dream of where I had come from. Perhaps I would not wonder where I was going.

Jessica and Hermione, now fast friends, discussed what must be done tomorrow: food and clean clothes. Organize transport into the countryside for women and children.

I inhaled the steaming brew and peered around the sanctuary. One window, boarded up on the outside, drew my attention. Even in the darkness I could see another stained-glass image of young Mary holding the Christ child in her arms. At that moment in her life did she know what sorrow awaited her? Had she really understood the words of the man who warned her that a sword would pierce her heart? Somehow that image and the picture of Judah Blood saying he would use me as a model for a Madonna were entangled in my mind.

Love was so dangerous, I thought, as I looked out over the human driftwood that had washed onto England's shores. Once they had been teachers and housewives and women waiting for their men to come home from work. They had cared about shoes and silverware and school reports. They had mirrored beauty, anger, affection, and expectation. They had identified themselves by where they lived, and who their neighborhood greengrocer was, and how many family members were coming to supper on Christmas Eve.

All that was gone. What were they now? Who were they without all the things they had believed made up their lives?

I heard the door of the sanctuary open and close. Eva and her Mac, now safely returned from Dunkirk, entered. They were surrounded by a little flock of ragged children. I stood. Jessica stood with me. Eva waved with some amazement at the tranquility of the sleeping refugees. Hermione saw her duty and hurried off to fetch more tea.

And then I spotted him . . . just behind Mac's right shoulder. It was Eben Golah. He seemed like a ghost who had stepped from the past to remind me of a time when there might have been a way to stop this . . . all this.

My heart beat the message. *"Too late . . . too late . . . too late . . ."*

Eben was unchanged. His resolute expression was unmistakable. His gaze fixed on the baby in Jessica's arms. And then he looked at me, full on, taking me in, just as he had when we were in Switzerland.

His look seemed to say to me, *"So, Lora. We have come to this moment at last. The German church shrugged and accepted the socialist plans of Hitler as though it was the will of God. The German nation has shut out the light of Christ. And now the churches of England and the world must shut in the light."*

It came to me that Eben was not surprised to see me standing erect among the wreckage. It had all come to pass, just as Eben predicted.

. . .

As I helped a mother and two children settle in the side chapel, I felt Eben's gaze upon me. I remembered our encounter beside the pasture in Switzerland when I foolishly proclaimed my love for him. What a child I had been. It had ended with Eben threatening to tell my father.

Now I was not a schoolgirl but a woman, and a widow.

I did not want to speak to him—not now. The deaths of Varrick and my father were too fresh to try to make small talk. The reality of what had befallen the world since that blissful summer was too painful. My infatuation for Eben was long over, leaving behind only a residue of embarrassment.

He did not approach me but waited at the top of the aisle until I finished my task.

I glanced up, hoping to appear uninterested in his presence. His gaze was strong and full, taking me in like an embrace. I raised my hand in a slight acknowledgment as I scanned the dimly lit auditorium for Jessica and the others. Jessica was in the back of the church. I walked toward her. It was enough for Eben.

He lowered his chin and met me, blocking my path. He took my arm and guided me into an alcove. "Lora, my White Rose." Handsome. Confident. Unchanged. Arrogant?

"Just Lora."

"Never . . . just."

"Too much has happened for us to have this conversation as if I am a child you can tease and flatter."

He bowed slightly. "Of course you are right, Missus Kepler."

"You heard about Varrick?"

"Eva told me, yes. I'm sorry. And for the loss of your father. A great man."

"It doesn't seem to matter how great or good, does it, Eben?" I felt angry. Bitter. "My father dead in his prime. My husband killed before we could have a life together. It's all too late."

"Yes." His intense green eyes seemed to see into my soul. "I am sorry for you, Lora."

"Thanks. I suppose your sympathy should make me feel better, but it's too fresh, Eben. And all that talk—all those meetings—what good did it do?"

"You're here. You and thousands of others made it out."

"A drop in the bucket, and you know it."

"Every drop matters, Lora."

Ashamed, I answered, "Of course. Every . . . what I meant was . . ."

"Yes, I know what you meant. You were listening to us. A white rose clinging to the banister. You bloomed above us in your little loft while we talked about saving millions."

I remembered that summer. I had not cared

when they spoke of saving lives. Selfish and vain, I had thought only of how much I loved Eben. At the memory, the blush climbed to my cheek once again.

"What is it?" Eben asked.

"We were all young and innocent then, weren't we? White roses reaching for the light?" An angry tear escaped, coursing down my cheek.

He was silent for a time, as if he heard a distant voice. Raising his index finger to my face, he caught my tear and raised it to his mouth, tasting my sorrow. Eben whispered, "Lora. White Rose." Then his hand caressed my cheek so tenderly I could not draw back. A moment more he held me with his eyes before he left.

19

Besides Eben Golah, there was another familiar face among the volunteers at St. Mark's: Madame Rose, the incomparably competent manager of children and canal boats, who had rescued our lifeboat off the beach at Dunkirk. Madame Rose was a missionary who had spent a lifetime after the Great War caring for the orphans in Paris.

Madame Rose's broad face and bowed mouth gave her the appearance of a smiling bullfrog. I liked her immediately. The light of her faith shone on her face.

She said in a gravelly whisper to my Jessica, "All glory to God. Not one of them is lost. Not one."

Madame Rose held an infant in her arms. The flock of children who leaned against her was asleep on their feet. Hermione led them away to a quiet corner beneath the towering pipes of the great organ and helped to bed them down.

Eben continued, "But now, because they are aliens, Madame Rose's children have been brought here with the others. All will be sheltered here until there is determination of their status." He raised his eyes and suddenly at all the exits of the building we saw uniformed and armed members of the Home Guard appear.

Jessica and I exchanged unhappy glances. Jessica asked, "All who are here at St. Mark's?" I peered around at little knots of mothers and children. One group especially drew my attention. There was a heap of toddlers, tumbled together like puppies, who were sound asleep beneath the altar window depicting the outstretched arms of Jesus on the cross. The words *Suffer the little children to come unto me and forbid them not* echoed in my mind.

Mac nodded somberly, confirming: "All."

We had known from our arrival in England that aliens were placed into three categories. Class A was openly pro-Nazi. Those had been arrested and interned when the war broke out the previous

September. Class B involved refugees without papers. They were restricted in their movements and required to report their activities. Class C, which included Jessica and Eva and me, listed a category of refugees who had lived in England for at least six years, or who were vouched for as being from Allied nations.

Over the past few weeks, after the Nazis broke through the lines in France, innocent victims of Nazi tyranny had been rounded up by the British government. The classification system had broken down. Interned in substandard camps, Jews were imprisoned all together with Nazis, Jew-haters, anti-Nazis.

Now this.

"What can this mean?" Jessica's eyes reflected the horror of memories from our days in the Reich. I knew her thoughts replayed the horrors of the secret police knocking in the middle of the night, of neighbors who had disappeared, never to be heard from again . . . like Varrick's family.

Mac explained, "Everyone here must endure the classification process. Evaluation, you see." He gestured toward the black squares and white squares of the checkered floor in mute definition of what he meant.

Eben's tone was meant to be oil on troubled water. "The British government must make certain. Must *be* certain that everyone here is . . . friendly."

The youthful features of a Great War soldier frozen in marble gazed across the throng. Was he to be the depiction of their protector . . . or their jailor?

Jessica's eyes brimmed as she looked over the sleeping women and children, then shook her head in disbelief at the guards standing at every door. "Friendly?"

Eben took Jessica's hands. "Your father was a great man. He sacrificed everything. And you are Americans."

Jessica nodded. "You are saying that I, and my family, will not be interrogated again?"

Mac replied, "You are free to go home if you wish."

Such a declaration of our freedom after a night among the suffering was unacceptable to Jessica. "Lora?" Her gaze was steady into my eyes.

I thought of the mothers with their exhausted children who had witnessed the brutality of war and somehow survived. I reviewed again how abandoned I had felt at the loss of my former life. It had been so hard to grasp my new identity. How impossible was it for all these so recently torn away from everything familiar? "No, Jessica. Let's stay with them," I answered. "They will need someone who understands the language of suffering to speak for them."

Jessica thanked Mac and Eben. "You knew before you asked us."

I said, "We must speak for those who have no voice."

Eben fixed his eyes upon mine. "You are truly your father's daughter." And then he bowed slightly and took my hand. "I am sorry for your loss. The Lord, Yeshua, once said, 'If you do it unto the least of these . . . you have done the kindness to Me.'"

I replied, "Where else could I go in my brokenness but to my suffering Lord?"

Eben Golah appeared deeply touched at hearing those words. He bowed and kissed my fingertips in a gesture of profound respect. With that he turned and wordlessly went to speak to the British officer in charge of the incarceration. I watched him closely as he gestured toward me and Jessica. No doubt he was explaining who we were and demanding utmost respect for our position.

We spoke only of practicalities: food and clothing and bedding. How long would these unfortunate souls be held prisoner? Where would they go if they were released? Where would they be imprisoned if they were not?

I slept on a pew in the St. Mark's choir loft and remembered Varrick. It made me sad and then angry that I couldn't see his face more clearly in my memory.

I mourned what might have been for our lives. More separation than time together. I regretted the loss of our future much more than what was in our past.

Only when the great hall of St. Mark's lapsed into the quiet stirring of exhausted women and children did I allow myself to think about these things. I considered what all these dear people around me had lost. My own loss was put into perspective. The past was irretrievable. The world as we had known it had vanished. The future was uncertain. We who had survived to see this moment only had *this moment* in which survival was a certainty. The refuge of England's green shores, to which a merciful God had surely brought us, was only a temporary haven.

I was awakened by the tramp of English boots as a military guard entered the church vestibule. The sorting out of alien sheep and goats had begun.

Male refugees who slept in the crypt at St. Mark's were rousted out, rounded up, and escorted under guard to an undisclosed location just after dawn. Most were French who had escaped through Dunkirk. Some were fishermen from the coast who had sailed their vessels with a few family members and friends. I pitied them all. Wives and children cried out as their husbands were led away.

Madame Rose consoled Jessica and me. Her thick American twang was tinged with a hint of Gallic accent. "Perhaps those who are young enough to serve in the military will be drafted into a Free French fighting force and trained to drive the Hun from the soil of France. We shall pray it happens thus." She embraced a young Frenchman in the line and called him by name. She instructed him that he must keep his eyes on God. I understood her admonition. "Maurice, from the time I saw you as a child, I knew the Lord has His hands on your shoulders."

The young fellow replied, "Madame Rose, I was an orphan, alone with my brother in the streets of Paris. It was you who raised me and my brother to trust in God. But now I tell you this, in the crypt beneath this church lies entombed General Hudson Lowe. He was the very man who guarded the Emperor Napoleon in exile on St. Helena after Waterloo. It is not a good omen for those of us who are French to sleep in the tomb of Napoleon's jailor."

Like a French grandmother, Madame Rose kissed him farewell upon each cheek and said, "Even in exile the Angel of the Lord encamps around those who revere Him. Only trust God, Maurice. You will not be in exile long."

There were tears in the gruff old woman's eyes as she hugged the weeping women and bade the Frenchmen farewell. I prayed the Lord would hear her petitions for them and that they would soon find their life's purpose in battle, lifting up their trodden nation from beneath the Nazi jackboots.

More news came by messenger midmorning. Madame Rose, because of her American citizenship, could return to America, but without her orphans. She read the message and angrily strode out of the church. She appealed to the American ambassador face-to-face. Within an hour she and the children of her Paris orphanage received the papers that allowed them to find haven in the tiny Welsh community where my cousin Elisa and her mother and several other children lived. This was good news.

Jessica rocked Shalom as the documents arrived. Madame Rose opened the thick brown envelope and smiled broadly. "Well, well." She leveled her gaze on my sister. "I received the permissions. Jessica, you and Shalom and Gina and the girls must come along to Wales as well. And Lora too. When the invasion begins, things will be difficult here in London. Come with me and the children, back to Wales. I will need your help."

Sizing up the sun-bronzed old woman, I had the sense that beneath her wings, all would be well. Her spirit exuded safety, and unseen angels stood guard over those she loved.

"We'll be safe in Wales," Madame Rose said. "I saw that road blocks have been set up everywhere in the south. Overturned carts and automobiles. Across the roads. Manned by civilians." We all knew that such things would not stop the Nazis.

"For the children's sake, you must come to Wales and help me. We can do what my sister Betsy and I did in Paris after the last war. So many little ones will need our care."

Jessica agreed immediately, but I did not. Feeling the hands of the Lord upon my shoulders, I knew some other destiny awaited me in London. The fleeting thought came into my head that perhaps I would stay in London and die. I was not unhappy at the possibility of death.

I said quietly, "I can't go to safety when so many here face peril. Jessica, you know that."

Jessica replied, "So like our father. But you should come with us."

"If the Nazis invade, every hand will be needed here in London. I can better fight those who killed Varrick and William and Papa if I remain on the front lines."

Jessica looked up at the great window above the entrance of the church: Christ the King, returning in glory to redeem His own. With the blackout curtains drawn back, the light beamed through his face. The flames of the seven candlesticks that represented the churches of Revelation chapter 2 seemed especially radiant.

"Perhaps before this war ends we will meet Christ Jesus in the air," Madame Rose remarked, following Jessica's eyes. "And then it will not matter that one is here and the other there. We will all rise together to meet Him."

Such an argument transcended time and space, life and death. Jessica nodded in agreement that I should remain in London. She promised if the island fortress of England held out she would come back to visit me from time to time and bring the baby with her for visits.

So it was settled. I went home to our flat to bathe and change as Jessica packed up her meager belongings for the journey north to the safety of Wales. I confess that I did not care for my own life or my safety. Whatever was to come upon London and England, I hoped that I could die fighting. I expected to die. My heart only longed to go home to heaven and see Mama and Varrick and Papa very soon.

Civilian refugees from Holland, Belgium, and France continued to trickle in throughout the next week. Those who claimed some link with America were escorted to St. Mark's for shelter.

No matter how tenuous a connection, anyone with a distant relative in the U.S. was among the blessed. I could hear the chattering throughout the hall:

"My father's aunt lives in Chi-ca-go."

"My great uncle moved to America after the great war. A musician. I think he works in Hollywood."

"My brother-in-law's brother . . ."

"Philadelphia!"

"Pittsburg."

"Texas."

"Atlanta."

Without documentation the authorities could not be certain about any story, and all U.S. visas were marked *Pending*. This meant pending a work permit, or pending a guarantee of sponsorship, or pending proof of familial relationship.

With Eva's help, we set up tables for processing applications that would be submitted to the American Embassy. Eva, who spoke several languages, would check the pitiful attempts at written English and conjugate verbs properly in order to add some air of worthiness to the documents.

Were the applicants worthy to go to America? Are they worthy? Will they be worthy?

We knew the answer to these questions would lie in the hands of some junior clerk in the basement of the American enclave. The power invested in someone we had never seen, nor would likely ever meet, made us aware of how a whim or a hangover could change the course of a life irrevocably. If the answer was no, then the refugee might face long-term internment in England.

It was Eva who began the practice of laying hands on the documents and praying over each. We prayed with her and soon we looked up to see the haunted faces of the hopeful survivors all around us.

Within days Eva had begun a Scripture study for women in the hall. She stuck to the Old Testament because there were so many Jews among our group. There were not enough Bibles to go around, and the women shared with one another.

It was rare that a visa was granted. When travel papers did arrive, this was cause for great celebration.

Hope and sorrow had made sisters out of these who were the flotsam and jetsam of war. Like the beams of a dozen ships broken on the shoals, these shattered lives joined together to be built into a new ship. The women of St. Mark's carried one another's burdens and cared for one another's children. They had come to England not knowing one another, but they became a family in those first days.

I cannot think of any other shelter in London in which there was such camaraderie and hope.

20

It was past mid-June 1940 when the certainty of what we were facing came home to every soul in Britain.

Eben rapped twice on the frame of my open office door. I glanced up from the stack of refugee documents I was translating.

I smiled, but he did not return my greeting. "France is lost," he said. "The Nazis are marching into Paris."

I closed the file containing the account of three Jewish sisters who had escaped from Calais. "We knew it was coming."

"Come on, then. Churchill is speaking on BBC." Eben waited for me in the hall as I cleared my desk. We hurried from the church into the Star and Garter public house. The radio behind the bar was turned up full volume. The pub was packed with men and women who neither spoke nor moved nor lifted pint glasses to sip.

Churchill's droning voice penetrated a haze of cigarette smoke:

". . . The battle of France is over. I expect that the battle of Britain is about to begin. . . . The whole fury and might of the enemy must very soon be turned on us. Hitler knows he will have to break this island or lose the war. . . ."

Beads of perspiration glistened on Eben's forehead. His gaze was riveted on the radio. He unconsciously clasped my hand in his and raised my fingers to his lips. It was not a kiss but a protective gesture, as one might reassure a child that all would be well in the end. Still, I felt the intimate warmth of his tenderness uncoil in me. I longed to have strong arms around me. My feelings for him at such a desperate moment startled me. I gently pulled my hand away, and only then did he look down at me in surprise and embarrassment.

Churchill's dire warning continued:

"If we can stand up to him, all Europe may be free and the life of the world may move forward into broad sunlit uplands. But if we fail, then the whole world, including the United States, including all that we have known and cared for, will sink into the abyss of a new Dark Age made more sinister, and perhaps more protracted, by the lights of perverted science. . . ."

The ominous truth of the prime minister's warning could only be fully believed by those who had already seen and survived the perverted, eugenic, pseudo-science of the National Socialists in Germany. Abortion, sterilization, euthanasia, socialized medicine, which selected who should live and who must die: these were only the tip of the iceberg in Germany.

Matters of life and death had gone far beyond who was physically acceptable to the state.

Now the state granted the right to live *only* to those citizens who *agreed* with the right of the state to kill those who disagreed.

Eben took my hand again, and this time I did not pull away from him. Churchill, who had for years been warning the world of what was to come, had finally been proven correct.

"... *Let us therefore brace ourselves to our duties, and so bear ourselves that, if the British Commonwealth last for a thousand years, men will still say, 'This was their finest hour.'*"

So the broadcast ended, and everyone in the pub stood and with tears began to sing "God Save the King."

From across the room I spotted Mac and Eva. I could tell his lips moved, as mine did, with the words of America's version of the song, "My Country 'tis of Thee, Sweet Land of Liberty . . ."

Our spontaneous hymn ended with three cheers as strangers embraced one another in a show of solidarity and grim determination in the face of death.

Eben enfolded me in his arms. I laid my cheek against his chest as the crowd roared. The room reeled around me. He kissed the top of my head. His left arm encircled me as he shook hands with the men in the room. My eyes closed, I leaned against him for what seemed like a very long time.

The voice of Mac McGrath brought me round.

"Eben!" he hailed.

Eva chimed in. "Lora! Lora! What do you think?"

I hugged her, and she held my face in both her hands. There were tears in her eyes. "So, it has come to this at last," she said to me in French.

Mac corrected her, "English, Eva. You're going to be an American."

We made our way to an empty table littered with empty pint glasses. Eva remarked, "I will be an American. Like you. I promised Mac I will speak only American. The French will soon be speaking German, I think."

Eben said, "If only the world had listened to Churchill eight years ago, this could have been stopped."

Eva raised a finger. "Poor fellow. He has been beating his head against a dead horse, I fear."

Mac interjected, "Something like that . . . oh well." He pushed back an overflowing ashtray. "The Brits will have to give up American cigarettes."

Eben agreed. "There will be rationing of everything in England. Not just luxuries."

I asked, "Do you think Hitler will invade soon?"

Eben scanned the blue tobacco-smoke haze. "I believe our future is recorded in history. A siege will come now—an ancient military tactic. Isolate, blockade, and starve your enemy. Unless

America enters the war, England will be broken by siege."

Mac ordered cider all round. "Churchill made a clear call to President Roosevelt today. The isolationists are still in control back home. England is the last fortress against Hitler in Europe. Got a letter from my mother from the States yesterday. She says U.S. sentiment to keep out of this is strong."

As the men discussed the collapse of France and the desperate plight of our island fortress, Eva rested her chin on her hand, smiled strangely at me, and addressed me in French. "You? And Eben?"

I protested, even as I felt my face redden. Had the electric charge I felt at his embrace been so obvious? I feigned insult and replied in English, "I don't know what you are talking about."

"Time. That is what I am speaking of. Time to love. If this is the end of the world, then I want to have lived my last moments loving and being loved. Only one time, and that is now." She smiled sweetly, batting her long black lashes over wide, bright blue eyes.

"I had my time."

"So brief. You can count it in only a few months."

"I loved, and I cannot love again."

"Cannot? The vow was: till death part you." Eva stroked my arm and lapsed into French again.

"Lora? Don't you see the way Eben looks at you?"

Mac raised his head in protest. "Eva! Speak English please. Translate. . . ."

She shrugged. "Sorry. Yes, English. I was saying, the English are between a rock and a fireplace now. No more ladies' stockings. No French perfume."

Eben lowered his chin as he considered Eva's interpretation. "Is that so?"

Eva raised her eyebrows comically, defending herself as she leaned close to Mac. "Stockings. Perfume. All feminine luxuries must be rationed. But love will survive, eh?"

Mac sipped his cider and winked at Eva. "There'll always be an England. I'll drink to that. Yes, indeed." Desire glinted in Mac's eyes. Eva returned the look.

Eben and I glanced away, both of us embarrassed by the unconcealed eagerness of our friends.

We knew without being told more details what trauma the young woman had suffered at the hands of the Nazi soldiers. Her battered face and haunted eyes spoke more eloquently than words.

Hermione leaned close to me. "I rang Women's Hospital. They are swamped. Not room for even one more. A doctor, I told them. Poor thing. Something. What's to be done?"

I somehow knew that I must be the one to help her. Perhaps I hoped that ministering to her would also help my grief.

"She has not spoken," Hermione whispered. "Nor has she eaten."

"Do you know her name?" I asked, reticent to approach the young woman as she lay curled up on the pew.

"Inga. That is the only name she gave when she arrived. Everyone in her traveling party was killed. She is the only survivor." Hermione looked upward at the dark rafters. "If you can call this survival." Hermione took my arm. "Lora, she is near your age. Perhaps a year or two younger. Surely you can find a way. Break through to her."

Was she French? Belgian? Dutch? I did not know if I spoke her language.

Something inside nudged me gently. I prayed as I went to the girl and sat down at her head. She seemed oblivious to my nearness. It was as though her soul had died somewhere along the road. What vision was playing out again and again in her mind? Her gaze was fixed on the red hymnal in the rack on the pew in front of her.

"Inga?" I spoke her name quietly, hoping she would acknowledge me in her mother tongue. But she did not reply.

I plucked the hymnal from its holder and pretended to study its pages. Inga's eyes did not shift or follow my movement.

I silently asked God what I could do. How could I help this pitiful young woman who would rather be dead than alive? The answer came clearly that she and I were alike.

Retrieving the crumpled telegram I always carried in my pocket, I smoothed the yellow paper on my thigh. Slowly I read aloud the message. "My husband," I said.

Glancing down, I saw a single tear trickle from the corner of her eye and roll down her cheek.

Her gaze turned toward my face then. She said in the clear, sweet Flemish of her native Belgium: "My mother. My brothers. All dead. Brussels. The first shellings. Papa went to fight. The Ardennes. I do not know what became of him."

I replied in French, "My father. A pastor. Killed by the Nazis."

Her delicate hand lifted as though she was letting a sparrow free. "What is your name?"

"Lora. Bittick was my father's name. My husband was Varrick Kepler."

"You are not French."

"No. American."

"You speak French very well."

"English better."

"Where are you from?"

"Mostly Brussels. We lived for a time in Berlin."

"Did you ever see Hitler?"

"Yes."

That horrible reality drove her to a moment of thoughtful silence. "I told myself I will always hate everything German."

"We too are refugees. My sister and I. Like you."

"You were married, then."

"Yes. He was a Jew."

"You were very young."

"Yes. We were. Young." My answer implied that I was no longer young. Nor was she. We had both lost our innocence. Or rather, innocence had been torn from us by force and ravaged by death.

She raised her head and rested her cheek upon her hand as she considered me. "So was I. Very young. I will always remember that I was very young on the day war came."

"Inga?" I said her name and then forgot what it was I had wanted to say.

"Where am I?" she asked, as though she had just awakened.

"Safe," I replied. "England. London. St. Mark's Church."

"I do not know how I came here." She eyed me curiously.

This was a mercy, I thought. Perhaps God had blotted the horror of her experience out of her memory. Perhaps it was like a nightmare only vaguely remembered in the dawn. "We crossed the English Channel in boats. All of us who are here."

Her eyes clouded. "Ah, yes. That part of it, I remember now. The planes. The bombs. The water spouts. So many dead men in the water."

"You are alive for a purpose, Inga."

"You are very young to say such a lofty thing."

"How old are you?" I asked.

"Eighteen. Soon nineteen."

"I'm twenty-two."

She nodded slowly, then considered me. "Tell me, Lora. Tell me about your husband. What was he like? Tell me how you escaped here to London."

21

The sun had only barely risen. I accompanied Madame Rose and another covey of refugee children to Paddington Station for their journey north to the farm in Bettws-y-Coed, Wales. As they boarded, I saw painted on the side of the train a message from Dunkirk's returning soldiers: *Look out, Hitler; we haven't started on you yet!*

"A brave sentiment," Madame Rose said, but we all knew the truth. What led to the rescue at Dunkirk was still a crashing defeat.

Madame Rose's bullfrog mouth was turned downward slightly at the corners. In her gravelly voice, she said, "Still no word from my sister, Betsy. I have left my address with the Red Cross.

Who can say how long it will be before we shall see Paris again?"

I linked arms with her for a moment. "Perhaps a very long time. It may be that our American countrymen must come again to Europe to fight Hitler."

Madame Rose herded her little brood onto the train. "Wales is lovely this summer. Perhaps by autumn we will have beaten back the Hun."

"I'll pray this comes to pass."

I embraced her as the final call for boarding sounded. I knew the train was a slow one with many stops and at least one change. I missed Mama. I missed Jessica. Grief for Varrick struck me like a physical blow once again.

I was trying to be brave.

Paddington was a whirlpool of emotions. Whether because of the joy of greeting or the grief of farewell, all present looked stunned. It was as if the station swallowed human reactions, leaving the previous owners pale and drawn.

Determined not to cry, I remained on the crowded platform and watched as the train slowly pulled away. Why had I volunteered to stay behind in the city? What use could I be here? Even before the last car had left the shelter I regretted my decision. What was I doing here? Me, a widow, as clearly as if I had seen Varrick fall and die before my eyes.

Just at the moment exhaustion and the events of

the last few days seemed overwhelming, I heard a man's voice behind me.

"Lora?"

"Eben." I knew who it was before I turned to face him.

He was smiling down into my eyes. His straight, white teeth were so perfect, so friendly and welcoming. "I just saw two professors off. A man and wife. Mathematicians. Refugees from France."

"Of course." I ran my hand through my hair, aware of how exhausted and disheveled I must look.

"French Jews. From the Sorbonne. They'll adapt well at Oxford, I think. And you?"

"Madame Rose and more children. All going to Wales."

"Wales." He said the name like it was a far-off dream.

"I could have said Camelot."

"All the same these days. But we both have work to do in London." After a moment of awkward silence he asked, "Would you like a cup of tea?" I knew he could see right through my deception.

"Oh. Tea. It's been awhile. Yes."

"Breakfast?"

"My stomach has forgotten the meaning of the word."

"Well, then. I've come at the right moment."

I followed him to the station tearoom like a lost puppy, happy to be found and eager to be fed.

I do not know how many hours Eben sat with me in the Paddington tearoom as I recounted the story of my escape from Brussels, then Tyne Cott, and finally, Dunkirk. His eyes, tender, were fixed on me, drawing me out of myself. I talked more than I had intended. I wept without embarrassment. At the same time his gentle questions drew me into his soul. He wiped my tears like an old familiar friend.

"I am inside-out now, Eben."

"Yes," he agreed, paying the tab.

I sipped my tepid tea as an announcement came over the PA system that blackout would begin in fifteen minutes.

"Well?" My tone meant to intimate that our time together was at an end.

"Would you like dinner? My hotel serves full-course meals. As if there is no war on. No rationing."

"I'm not dressed for it." I stared down at my drab brown skirt, wrinkled blouse, and low-heeled shoes.

"If you'd like to go home and change? I'll wait."

We rode the Bakerloo Line as far as Baker Street station. On every corner workmen were taking down the street signs in anticipation of the coming German invasion. Everywhere across the

English countryside road signs had been decapitated, and travelers were left to a medieval form of navigation by landmarks and memory. It seemed surreal and desperate to me, however. In the heart of London could anyone in government believe the Nazis would find themselves unable to locate the Houses of Parliament because a road sign was missing?

Eben and I walked across Regent's Park to my flat at the foot of Primrose Hill. In the long twilight of early summer, slit trenches marred the gardens. Anti-aircraft guns pointed skyward to sun-bright clouds, where the great flocks of enemy bombers would surely fly. The boys and girls who manned the guns perched on sandbags and shared sandwiches.

I asked, "England is still not ready, is it?"

"Let's hope the German High Command does not realize how unready we are."

When we reached my flat, the blackout curtains were already drawn. Eva was home. Mac McGrath sat beside the radio listening to a BBC broadcast. He glanced up as we entered. His strong jaw was clenched at the news that no part of France would any longer resist the Nazis.

"Evening." Mac's hands were clasped. "England's all alone, now."

Eben nodded. "But three hundred thousand rescued, Mac. That's the number I heard."

"Yes. A miracle, I guess."

I heard the bathwater running upstairs. "Where's Eva?"

"We're getting married tonight." Mac brightened a bit. "She'll be glad to see you. We've been looking over half of London for you. St. Mark's. No one knew where to locate you."

"Married?"

"I found a fellow, a Methodist preacher, who'll do it. Lives in Hampstead. You two will come along, won't you? Stand up with us?"

"Sudden, isn't it?" I gaped at Mac and then looked up to the landing as I heard a door shut. Eva appeared at the top of the stairs. Her face was gloriously happy.

"Lora! Come up! You must help me. We're getting married, Mac and I. Tonight. A Protestant fellow. An American friend of Mac's, I think. He'll marry us, and we'll sort out the details later."

I ran up the stairs and embraced her. She clung to me tightly and laughed. "Where were you? I've looked all over. No one but you could be the witness. Where have you been? They said you left this morning, and now, here it is, dark already. We'll have the devil of a time getting a cab to Hampstead. Maybe a bus?"

Eva's delirious happiness could not be dampened. I helped her choose a pale blue dress. She eyed it and slipped it on, admiring herself in the mirror. "Not white as for a proper bride, but I suppose I'll be married all the same."

"Deliciously beautiful," I said brightly, though my heart was heavy, remembering my wedding night with Varrick.

I had so few dresses suitable for attending even a very small wedding. I chose a little suit of navy blue background with white roses on the collar and stitched around each button. My dress was several years old. I had found it in the used clothing barrel at the church. I had washed it and mended a tear, replaced missing buttons, and embroidered roses. It looked brand new.

Our shoes were also out of style, but as we descended the steps, Mac stood slowly to his feet and whistled.

I told Eva this was the greatest of compliments from an American male.

Eben stood and switched off the radio. He busied himself by examining the cover of an open book. He did not look at Eva or at me.

Mac kissed Eva at the foot of the stairs. It was clear they were deeply in love.

I thought to myself as the bus labored up the road to the top of Hampstead Heath: *What does it matter if the bombs fall tomorrow? Tonight they will be happy. Tonight they will love one another as though it is the last night of the world.*

As Eben and I stood witness, Eva and Mac were married. I felt Eva's breathlessness as Mac gazed down into her face. Her cheeks, as smooth and white as porcelain, blushed a little when the pastor said Mac could kiss his bride. Mac's lips hovered above hers. There was a delicious moment of hesitation. It was the sort of pause that comes when a thing of beauty is first embraced by the eye, or the scent of a rose is inhaled, or wind like the hand of an angel bends the tree tops. All this was in Mac's faint smile as he touched his lips to Eva's mouth. Her head back and eyes closed, she savored his kiss. I watched them seal their covenant of love as though I was seeing my memory play out before me.

Only this was their life, not mine. My life seemed finished before it had begun. Was my expression wistful? I felt tears burn my eyes.

The kiss lingered. I turned my gaze away from them, knowing what was to come beyond their kiss. A dance. The tango, slow and smooth. The man leading each step and the woman yielding, following, reaching, moving to his will and to his rhythm.

I knew the dance. I heard the music far away. My body longed for the music and the dance.

When I looked up, Eben was staring at me in the same way I stared at them.

I smiled back at him and raised my eyebrows as if their lingering kiss amused me.

Eva and Mac surfaced and looked around dreamily. I embraced Eva. Her heart was racing. Her happy tears dampened my shoulder.

"Well," Mac said, "I guess I'm hooked for good."

Eben shook his hand heartily. I kissed Mac's cheek. Congratulations were spread all around as we witnessed and signed the document declaring the marriage was official.

And then we were all out in the cool night air of wartime London.

Mac said awkwardly, "Thanks so much. Very much. We'll be heading back to the flat now."

Eva took my arm. "Oh, Lora! If it's all right. I mean, you weren't around to ask, and I . . . we . . . I mean, I knew you were staying at the church. Helping out with the—"

I had not seen it coming, but I wished I had thought of their honeymoon and offered them the use of the flat. "Of course. Not a problem. I'll swing by and pick up a few things."

We rode together on the bus back to Primrose Hill. Eben sat stiffly beside me as Mac and Eva kissed in the seat at the very back.

I heard Mac say, "I have a surprise for you, my darling Eva. Have you ever heard of Rudy Vallee?"

Neither Eben nor I commented on Mac's choice of music as we walked from the bus stop to the door of our flat.

Mac lifted Eva into his arms and carried her across the threshold.

Eben waited for me outside on the steps as I

dashed in and threw a few things into a satchel. I spoke to Eva and Mac as I passed them in the foyer, but they did not seem to notice me.

The door slammed closed, and I felt as though I had escaped a room where the heat had been turned up too high.

Eben was barely visible in the darkness. I could hear the grin in his voice. "I keep looking at the chimney for sparks. Scorch your dress as you passed?"

I laughed. "Incendiary bombs have nothing on them. I'm afraid the house will ignite when he plays her the Rudy Vallee recording."

From behind the blackout curtain we heard the phonograph belch out the first notes of the Rudy Vallee song, "Orchids in the Moonlight."

"When orchids bloom in the moonlight,
And lovers vow to be true,
I can still dream in the moonlight
Of one sweet night that we knew . . ."

"Well," Eben said, "I guess that's it."

"Must be," I said too loudly. I felt my eyes widen, and I clamped my hand over my mouth.

Eben mused, "You think a man like Mac McGrath is a fan of Rudy Vallee?"

"Hmmm. Must be. I don't know about Eva. I mean, she's Polish."

There was a long pause as we imagined the

rugged bachelor alone in his room playing Rudy Vallee phonograph records as he dreamed of love.

I whispered in astonishment, "Mac MacGrath? Could it be?"

Then Eben snorted, and I began to laugh. We laughed until our stomachs hurt. Leaning against the pillar we howled until tears flowed from our eyes.

Gasping for breath, Eben grabbed my arm and led me quickly down the walk. "We are quite thoughtless."

"Insensitive."

"Crass." More gales of laughter as we shuffled along the sidewalk with no destination or purpose in mind.

"Where shall we go?" Eben said cheerfully.

"I don't know. I suppose back to St. Mark's." For the first time in days I was happy. "I can sleep in the choir loft."

Instead of returning immediately to St. Mark's, Eben and I climbed to the top of Primrose Hill Park. The details of the city were lost beneath a blanket of darkness. He spread his jacket out on the grass beneath a plane tree, and we sat down. I tried very hard not to imagine the romance of Mac and Eva in my little flat at the foot of the hill.

I asked, "How long do you think I will be banished from my own bed?"

"You should give them a few days alone, I should think," Eben answered.

"A honeymoon. It may be their only chance."

"The Germans have moved their planes to new bases in France—much closer to us. Soon it will become very difficult indeed for this little island, I think."

"Then I'll let Eva and Mac stay in the flat as long as they can. To be alone."

"Yes. Kind of you. We can't know how bad it will become. How much time we may have? Kind of you, that is, if you have a place to sleep."

"The church first. And then I was thinking the Young Women's Christian Association."

"The one on Great Russell Street?"

"That's it."

"Overflowing, I'm afraid. They've double-bunked all the women in one wing and returning BEF soldiers have taken over the rest."

"Oh well, then. I'll stay at the church. After all, I have experience with difficult living arrangements. You should have seen us camping in Papa's Fiat."

"Ah, yes. I forgot you are a seasoned pro at this sort of thing." He laughed. After that he was silent, thoughtful for a time. I did not interrupt his reflection.

Eben said at last, "Again, I am sorry about your husband."

"Thank you."

"You were not married long."

"You knew our fathers in Berlin. We were friends, and then . . . I knew I loved him. We were together in Brussels for a short time, but then the war came and he had to go. Not much time to get to know each other, I suppose—hardly any—but I loved him. With all the passion of a first love."

"You were so young. Are," he corrected himself, "are so young."

"I was young. All of us were young. But then we grew up when Hitler drove through the streets and the crowd of his old friends followed him. Or when the first Gestapo agent knocked on the door. You know, young in years is not young at heart. I sometimes feel as though I have lived ten lifetimes."

His head bowed slightly as I spoke. "I understand."

Something in the tenor of his voice told me again that this was a man well acquainted with suffering. What did I know about Eben Golah really? He had come to my father's study to speak of the exodus of Jews from Germany. He had given us the warning of impending attack on the day of Kristallnacht.

Somehow he had escaped the onslaught. But what did I know about his own suffering?

I asked, "Tell me about yourself. I know my father thought well of you. And Bonhoeffer too. The others."

"But they did not heed my warning. They only half-believed it would come to this." He spread his hands over the city. "This night. This moment." He groaned softly. "I see the fires yet to come. I feel the heat."

"When?"

"Soon. Weeks at most, and then it will begin. Here."

"How can you know?"

He did not reply, but I understood he had no doubts. "So, you have a job. A purpose." He had changed the subject.

"I suppose I'll continue on at the church."

"You are an excellent linguist. Translation. Your father taught you well."

"He believed language was the most important. . . ."

"How would you like an official position with us?"

"Us?"

"The Jewish Agency. Immigration. Working together with the U.S. and the British governments. We need a skilled translator. An English language teacher. Someone to help refugees learn English. To help them tell their stories in a common tongue. For more placements, you understand? They cannot work if they can't speak English."

I brightened, suddenly feeling I had some purpose in the midst of this chaos. I could see past my own personal loss and help others like myself to find solid ground upon which to stand. "Yes. I have already been . . ."

"We know how you have been working. We have been watching."

"Where?"

"At St. Mark's. I'll arrange for you to have a salary. I will be your liaison. You'll bridge the gap between the wide world and those who are lost in it. You'll speak for those who have no voice."

"When?"

"Tomorrow? You'll need a good night's sleep. I'll walk you back to the church now. Tomorrow morning we'll begin."

22

The casualty lists grew longer every day. So many brave men had died in France. So many women, mothers, sisters, and wives grieved. I was only one young widow among thousands in England. With these, my sisters of the heart, I put my suffering behind me for the sake of the living.

As the bombing of England increased I fingered the telegram and prayed I might remember the greater need. The heart of my father called me to press on. I was consumed by the desire to do what I could for those whose suffering and loss were beyond my own.

The Nazi invasion of the Channel Islands of Jersey, Guernsey, Alderney, and Sark sent another wave of desperate refugees to the shores of England. French Jews who had fled to the islands, hoping to escape battles in their homeland, arrived with the departing British. They escaped across the stormy Channel waters in tiny sailboats, fishing boats, and skiffs. British patrol boats rescued some while others washed onto British beaches planted with tank traps and land mines strung with concertina wire.

The suspicions of the British government about every new arrival were heightened as the Nazi air assault along the coast increased, and news of casualties poured over the wires. The German invasion of England seemed certain . . . and imminent.

Eben came to my office with a long list of Jewish Channel Island refugees. He was all business, scarcely looking at my face. "The Jewish Agency needs your help placing 163 Jews from the four islands. Many among them do not have documentation. Most are secular Jews. Women with children sent from France, Holland, and Belgium by their husbands to wait for the end of the war. With the fall of France, no French Jew will be going home any time soon."

I scanned the list of new arrivals. French and Belgian women were not difficult to place as servants. The Dutch were at a disadvantage because of their Germanic-sounding accents. "More Dutch Jews than French," I said, very businesslike. "And so many youngsters."

"Do your best, Lora. I know . . . we know, you will do your best." He thanked me and turned to go. Then, as if he had a second thought, he turned round and took an envelope from his pocket. "I wrote this some time ago. For you." He placed it on the corner of my desk and hurried from the room.

My heart was pounding. I waited until his footfall receded down the corridor. The door to the street slammed. I rose and closed my door, shutting out the clamor of children's voices as they practiced English in an adjacent class-room.

Lifting my chin and drawing a breath, I picked up Eben's letter and slowly opened the envelope. An old black-and-white photograph fluttered to the ground. Retrieving it I saw it was a picture of me between Mama and Papa beside the white rose tree that embraced the iron fence outside the White Rose Inn in Switzerland. I did not remember Eben had snapped it.

It was the only photograph of my father that survived.

"Papa." I smiled and propped it up on the base of my desk lamp.

Looking into the envelope I found a folded paper, containing a closeup of myself, so young and innocent, standing alone among the blooming roses.

Eben's message to me was thirty-six lines inscribed in a beautiful Victorian hand. The words were arranged vertically on a hand-drawn trellis of thirty-six roses.

For Lora—The White Rose.

Sweet
familiar
scent
gentle
hands
embrace me
before
I see
you
rosetree
white
roses
seeking
light
you
climb
joy
spilling
over
impossible
walls

tenacious
promise
full
bloom
lavish
expectant
you
raise
your
face
shine
beautiful
epitome
revealed
fulfilled

I read each word again and again, grouping them in different combinations, like bouquets of roses. Each time I read his poem I found a new and different meaning.

My heart heard the breathless rhythm of love and hope.

The London heat was oppressive. Citizens lounged in the parks and slept on roofs and balconies. My little office doubled as my sleeping quarters since Mac and Eva had taken over the flat. It had only one tiny window that would not open more than a few inches.

It was almost teatime. Eben, visiting the shelter

with members of the Jewish Agency, poked his head in the door and called me to come join them. I stood up from my desk and suddenly the room began to spin. The air turned pale yellow. Suddenly everything went black.

I awakened on the floor. Eben fanned me with a magazine as worried faces of strangers peered down at me. One of the contingent was a physician. He checked my pulse and listened to my heart, and with a disapproving look at my cot in the corner, asked me if I had a home and if I ever left St. Mark's.

Hermione in her high-pitched, public school accent declared I had given up my own flat for newlyweds. "She has barely seen the outside of St. Mark's since Eva's wedding! She stays in here all day and all night, too."

I simply lay on the floor, too hot and weak to stand. I did not have to answer even one question.

The doctor declared, "Young woman, sleeping and bathing and eating among the ebb and flow of strangers for weeks on end is wearing on anyone. You must return to your own flat for a few days' rest."

Hermione clucked her tongue in sympathetic agreement. "My dear, Eva and Mac have had your house to themselves quite long enough, I should say. You've given them a decent interval alone. Go home tonight. Sleep in your own bed."

The memory of my Primrose Hill bedroom seemed like a distant dream. The thought of a good long soak in a cool tub sounded like heaven. Eva and I had shared a room for months. I imagined she and Mac had pushed our twin beds together and made one big bed. I could sleep in Jessica's old room. A private bedroom and a WC, a kitchen, and a sitting room with a piano sounded like a mansion after sharing a lavatory with a hundred women and children.

Eben drove me home to my little Primrose Hill flat and helped me to the door. I heard the phonograph playing. I went no further than the front steps. "I'm not bursting in. I won't go in there alone unless I know I'm not interrupting anything."

"I'll have to put my foot down. No Rudy Vallee, eh? No tango in the middle of the night. You need your rest. Yes. I can see it here in the light. You have lost the bloom on your cheeks."

He knocked loudly, then rang the buzzer. After a time Eva answered, peering cautiously through the crack in the door. Her eyes were red and puffy. She had been crying, and when she saw me on the step, rushed to embrace me.

It seems I had returned home just in time for the newlyweds' first spat.

Eben observed me holding Eva in my arms. He gave me an admonition, "If it gets too difficult, I will share my little garret room in Hampstead with you. Everyone in London is sleeping around."

I looked at him with indignation. "I will not, and no, you most certainly will not."

He saluted and grinned. "My apologies. Of course. What I mean is, you may have the use of my place, and I will go . . . somewhere else. The tube stations are all converted into sleeping quarters in the event of air raids. Very democratic. Rich and poor alike. I will take my pillow to the High Street tube station and no one will think the worse for me if I sleep on the platform."

Eva was sobbing and muttering in incoherent English. There was something about the prime minister's wife and Mac being humiliated. She would not tell me more. Eva ran into the house.

My shoulder was damp from Eva's tears.

Eben asked, "Are you certain about staying? Mac would say, 'Out of the frying pan and into the fire.'"

I thanked Eben for his offer. "Very gallant of you. But I think we will manage well enough."

"We shall see. And now, my dear Lora, I wish you good luck and bid you good sleep."

I entered the flat and saw the program for the government press reception on the entry table. The importance of the day for Eva came flooding back.

Today had been the foreign press meeting with Prime Minister Churchill at Number 10, Downing Street. Mac had arranged for Eva to attend with him and meet Mr. Churchill. For days, Mac had coached her in protocol. Eva had practiced exactly what she would say to the eminent leader of wartime Britain.

Something had gone terribly wrong. Eva sat alone at our dining table. Her head was cradled in her hands. She glanced up at me through red, swollen eyes.

"Why are you crying?" I asked, hanging my umbrella on the hook beside the door.

She shook her head like a small child trying to deny the obvious. "This marriage! I am out of the frying pan and into the tea kettle!"

"I see," I said.

She dabbed her eyes, wanting me to see that she had indeed been crying and would continue to do so. She asked through plugged sinuses, "How was your day?" The question was followed by loud sniffing, and then honking, as she blew her nose on a kerchief.

I started to tell her everything but thought better of it. Eva was making it clear that the conversation would be about her, no matter where we began.

She attempted to smile through her tears. "Oh, Lora. Me and Mac are not okie-dokie."

"Where's Mac?" I asked, suddenly alarmed.

"Off to the public house, I suppose. Dowsing his unhappinesses while I am sobbing over split milk."

I mentally translated. Mac was drowning his sorrows, and Eva was crying over spilt milk. "Eva, why don't you tell me in French what has happened."

Her head wagged broader than before. "I promised Mac only English. How will I ever be a real American if I can't get it right?"

"I understand," I said, comprehending the importance of mastering the language of her new life. "But whatever has happened?"

Her shoulders shook. She could barely speak. "I have hit my head upon a stony wall." More sobs followed.

I made a pot of weak tea, fetched two mismatched china cups, and sat opposite her. "Here. A cuppa, as the natives say."

"I do not care what they call it," she muttered in perfectly correct French. Then back to American, "Absolution I am a failure. I did not get it right."

"What didn't you get right?"

"Mac told me what I must say when meeting Mister Churchill at the foreign press meeting. I practiced. You heard me. Night after night. I am bird in a fool's gilded lily."

"I won't make you explain it."

"Please, don't. I got it right with the Prime Minister, Lora. But no one told me she would be there too."

"She?"

"Churchill's wife. Clemmie."

"Oh."

"I had to speak to her, didn't I?"

"Unavoidable, I suppose."

"I did my best. First I addressed Mister Churchill. All very proper. 'And how do you do, Mister Prime Minister.' But then there SHE was. And so I said, 'I am very also pleased to meet you, dear Prime Mistress.'" Poor Eva's shoulders shook as she confessed. "Prime Mistress! Oh, dear me! I am not okie-dokie!"

I patted her back. "Poor Eva. Perhaps she didn't notice."

"Notice! The whole room fell silent. Mac turned as red as that." She pointed to the red book cover of her copy of *Proper Etiquette in British Diplomatic Society.*

The key turned in the latch. Mac was home. Eva covered her face with her hands. Mac, disheveled and remorseful, appeared in the kitchen door. His sorrowful eyes, well drowned in good English beer and split milk, were riveted on Eva.

"Good evening, Mac," I said.

He did not appear to hear me but rushed past me to the empty chair beside Eva. He grasped her hands and kissed her fingers. She began to weep and threw herself into his arms. The two embraced and kissed as I cleared the table and padded upstairs to my room. Behind me I could hear Eva as she apologized in a gush of unstoppable Polish for whatever verbal gaffe she had made when addressing the prime minister.

"It's okay, my darling. My darling Eva. No. No. Please. It doesn't matter to me. My fault. My fault entirely. Please, my darling . . ."

I climbed into bed as the sound of the Rudy Vallee tango pursued me. Muffled voices seeped under my door. Covering my head with the pillow, I must have slept a little.

I wasn't sorry when the air-raid siren sounded some hours later, and I bumbled out of the house and into the shelter.

23

The air-raid siren sounded again as I crossed Regent's Park on foot the next evening. I did not believe the danger could be real. How many times had pilots from the German Luftwaffe flown harmlessly above London on their way to industrial targets in the Midlands?

The lovely parklands had been dug up— subdivided into allotments for vegetable gardens among the ack-ack guns. A small portion of the rose garden near the Open Air Theatre remained intact.

As the warning siren screamed, irritated Londoners hurried to shelter. I found a park bench and sat beside a glorious plot of white roses. Fragrant red roses bloomed nearby.

I thought that soon the shrill warning would fall

silent, and I would be alone above ground in a deserted world. If a bomb tumbled on my head, I thought, then I would be in heaven with Papa and Mama and Varrick. So much the better. I was not afraid of anything.

Sighing with contentment, I looked up at the ripening colors of twilight. Silence dropped like a curtain. I could not see the enemy planes, but after some minutes I heard a distant drone of aircraft engines. By and by the crack of fighter plane machine guns popped above the clouds.

I prayed for the brave British pilots, so outnumbered and outgunned. I knew they were sure to be victorious because they were fighting against the most profound evil in all of history. Surely God was paying attention. No doubt there were angels soaring above England.

Then my thoughts went to the German boys I had known before Hitler stole their minds and ravaged their hearts. Were any of my neighbors or schoolmates dropping bombs on England now? I prayed for dying Nazi pilots who, spiraling to earth in burning planes, would feel the fires of hell even before they reached their final eternal destination.

Could young men be fighting for their lives? It seemed impossible. The sky above me was so beautiful. Such beauty made me hate the war more fiercely. Young men should not have been dueling and dying on such a night as this.

I rummaged in my handbag, removing Eben's photographs and the white rose poem. On my knee I balanced the image of me smiling beside Papa. Once again I scanned the words inscribed on the thirty-six roses: *Sweet . . . familiar . . . scent . . . embrace . . . me . . . before . . . I . . . see . . . you. . . .*

In the quiet of a city waiting breathlessly for destruction, I heard the plaintive call of a nightingale perched on the limb of an elm tree. Glancing up I saw a middle-aged woman with a pleasant, close-lipped smile observing me from a park bench across the path. She was dressed in a shabby blue dress, at least two decades out of fashion. Her gray-streaked, tawny hair was tied back and tucked beneath a straw boater-style hat. Her shoes were low-heeled and scuffed. Her hands were folded in her lap.

"Good evening," I said when she did not look away from me.

"Good evening." She looked up at the pink-tinged thunderheads. "Such a beautiful sunset tonight."

Far off, perhaps up the river in Richmond, the anti-aircraft cannons boomed. "Are those bombs, do you suppose?" I asked.

"I couldn't say," she answered, standing and coming to sit very close beside me. She leaned in to examine my photograph. "This is you. And your father and mother, is it?" she asked me.

"A long time ago. In Switzerland."

"You look most like your mother here. The lips. But I see your father in your eyes. Much alike."

"I never thought I looked like him. He's dead now. Nazis."

"The resolve in his expression. Yes. Very similar."

"Thank you. I hope I may be as wise. He saw all this. What was coming."

"What is the saying? *A sach mentshen zehen, nor vainik fun farshtai'en.*"

"Yiddish. You are a Jew?"

"Many people see things, but few understand them." She translated the proverb as she picked up Eben's poem and scanned it.

I was neither offended nor surprised. "What is your name?" I asked her.

She did not answer. "A lovely poem. For you, my dear?"

"From a friend."

"White roses. Like the photograph."

"Are you from London?" I asked, suddenly curious.

She continued to study the paper. "Thirty-six roses. See here. Hebrew words embedded with the pattern of each rose."

Startled by the revelation, I leaned in close, following her finger as she traced the pattern of Hebrew writing that rimmed the edges of the petals of the blossoms.

"I didn't see them. What does it mean?"

"Have you not heard? Everything means something. Thirty-six. Twice the number of Life. The number of *Lamed Vav*. There are thirty-six ancient righteous ones who live among mortals in this world." She raised her gaze to meet mine. The intensity held me riveted. Deep blue eyes were clear like water flecked and rimmed with gold. In the soft light her face glowed like the page of an illuminated manuscript.

I meant to ask her name again, but instead I whispered, "Who are you?"

She reached out and plucked a rose, placing it on my lap. "White roses behind you." The nightingale sang again. She seemed very pleased. "Dusk. There and here. Then and now."

My rose tumbled onto the paving stones beneath the park bench. I bent to retrieve it. "Where are you from?" I spoke as the all-clear siren suddenly erupted behind me. Turning away for a moment I regretted that my chance meeting with the Jewish stranger had been interrupted.

When I turned back, the woman had vanished.

Leaping to my feet, I spun around. The gravel paths wound away into shadows. I could not see her anywhere. For a moment I doubted my encounter. Then, straining my eyes, I glimpsed a flash of pale blue hurrying into the shadow of the plane trees. As Londoners emerged from the slit-trenches and shelters, a chill coursed through me.

Was my encounter real? Had I been dreaming? I stared at the distinct Hebrew writing encoded in the petals of Eben's roses. The hidden words rimming the petals were not my imagination.

Gathering photograph, poem, and white rose, I made my way toward Primrose Hill.

Seven Sephardic Jewish schoolboys from Holland were brought to St. Mark's in the middle of the night. Twelve years old, of bar mitzvah age, they had sailed across the stormy English Channel in a tiny fifteen-foot sailboat.

Lieutenant Howard of the Tin Noses Brigade escorted them. Since his return to England he had been helping with wounded, shell-shocked soldiers. When the refugee boys were presented to him, he remembered hearing of my work at St. Mark's and brought them to me.

Hermione's shrill voice had an edge of panic when she rang the flat and woke me up out of a sound sleep. It was almost dawn.

"I don't know why they were brought to us here. They do not seem to speak any known language. No language any of us can understand. Little Jew boys. Bare feet and terribly sunburned. I cooked scrambled eggs and bacon. Bread and butter. They won't eat anything I set before them."

I dressed quickly and caught a taxi to St. Mark's.

I greeted Lieutenant Howard with a hug and a questioning look, but then Hermione took over the explanations. Hermione, bleary-eyed and wrapped in a tattered bathrobe, led me to the offending tribe of Israel, where they had been sequestered in a classroom.

Tin plates heaped with Hermione's non-kosher rations were untouched on a study table.

"The waste! The waste!" she cried.

I suggested she take the food away and reheat it for others as the sun was coming up. She did so under the surly stares of the boys.

I greeted them in Dutch. "Are you hungry?"

They looked at me with interest. They spoke Ladino and Yiddish well, but the most mature-looking boy answered me in Dutch: "We can't eat that."

"Would you eat plain bread?" I asked. "Until we can get this sorted?"

"We keep kosher. Plain bread. A little butter would be good."

"You are Sephardim?" I asked, unsure if I had pronounced the word correctly.

Dark, curly heads bobbed in the affirmative.

"I will call Rabbi Brown at Bevis Marks synagogue. Sephardic. East London. You will be right at home."

"That's the ticket," Lieutenant Howard said enthusiastically. "I knew you'd know what to do."

"How are you keeping, Lieutenant?"

Even the tin mask could not hide the pleasure coursing through my Tyne Cott friend. "I was dead wrong about my family. I screwed up my courage and went to see them. Once they got over the shock that I was alive they can't stop loving on me! I was wrong to stay away. So wrong! Love should never be avoided, should it?"

By nine o'clock that morning, Rabbi Brown arrived. He was a jolly, imposing, rotund rabbi with a grizzled beard and thick spectacles. His pleasant, mild-featured wife was at his side. By 9:05 the future of the happy boys was all arranged.

"Of course they will live with us!" declared the rabbi's wife. "Seven sons of Israel. A blessing!"

Rabbi Brown instructed, "These are good boys. Intelligent fellows. Sailed the little boat through twenty-foot-high waves to escape. HaShem was surely with them!"

Hermione's expression of relief was too obvious. They were "too Jewish" for her comfort, an expression she used often.

As the boys prepared to leave, Rabbi Brown said to me, "Any more like this, you must remember us. Better our children are with our own kind. You know."

So we were too Gentile for Rabbi Brown.

At the last moment before their departure, the

puzzling words on Eben's poem flashed in my mind. Perhaps Rabbi Brown could shed some light on their meaning.

"Rabbi Brown!" I fumbled in my handbag for the paper. "Please! Can you help me decipher a bit of Hebrew?"

He smiled at me curiously as I extended the paper. Adjusting his glasses, he did not seem to read the English writing at all but instantly saw the Hebrew words that gilded the petals of the roses. Eyebrows instantly went up with astonishment, then furrowed into a deep frown.

"A copy . . . clearly. Young woman," he spoke in a barely audible voice, "where did you get this?"

"A friend gave it to me."

"A Jew? Someone who escaped the Nazis?"

"One who helped others escape."

"I cannot—this is . . . extraordinary." He pressed his lips together in a way that let me know he would say no more.

I had to take the chance. I blurted, "Thirty-six . . . The Lamed Vav."

"If you know of the Thirty-six Righteous ones, you need not ask me."

"Who are they? These Lamed Vav?"

He stared at the paper. "Their names . . . They are righteous ones who live among us. They, the presence of the Thirty-six, hold back the judgment of HaShem against the earth." He

337

paused. "This is, well, a legend. There are among them . . . Guardians of Israel. They witnessed the fall of Jerusalem two thousand years ago. Their names, upon the roses, as you see."

"Eben?" I asked as he placed the sheet in my hands.

He pointed to the Hebrew letters. "Eben. 'Stone.' He was a cantor in days of old. And his name read in reverse means 'prophesy.' So it is written the stones will cry out and proclaim the coming of Messiah."

"Thank you." I refolded the treasure.

"I suppose such copies will surface as our people take flight in these last days. We will know the truth of the end if Israel, by some miracle, is again a nation. As this says . . . White Rose."

My legs were weak as the rabbi gathered his flock and drove away.

I read Eben's poem, word-by-word, gathering phrases into bouquets, like the thirty-six roses I had chosen so long ago for Frau Helga at the White Rose Inn. Closing my eyes I remembered the haunting song of Eben as he sang the ancient blessing at the moment of Shabbat.

The Cantor.

Who was Eben Golah?

". . . *tenacious promise full bloom lavish expectant you raise your face shine beautiful epitome revealed fulfilled . . .*"

• • •

As the Germans bombed the southeast coast of Britain, ranks of new evacuees swelled our numbers. In all of London rumors of imminent German invasion grew, and the ripple of terror moved through our congregation of refugees.

Eva, her ivory skin flushed with the heat of the London tube, hurried into the schoolroom where Hermione and I were assembling bunks. A small crowd followed her, packing the stuffy chamber. An official government leaflet fluttered in her fingers.

"Lora!" Eva was breathless. "Look! Here it is!" She thrust the paper into my hands. The heading was ominous.

Hermione leaned over my shoulder and read, *"If the Invader Comes."*

The faces of our charges gathered around me, anxiously staring down. As I read in English, the message was translated into various languages: *"If the Germans come, by parachute, aeroplane, or ship, you must remain where you are. The order is, 'Stay Put.' . . ."*

Eva interjected, "This is because of what happened in France. The refugees so clogged the highways that the army could not move."

Nods all around from those who had witnessed the chaos of Nazi strategy using civilians as weapons against the Allies.

I read on:

*"Do not believe rumors, and do not
spread them. When you receive an order,
make quite sure it is a true order and not a
faked one. Most of you know your
policemen and your ARP warden by sight.
You can trust them. If you keep your heads,
you can tell whether a military officer is
really British or only pretending to be. If
in doubt ask the policeman or ARP
warden. Do not give the Germans
anything. Do not tell him anything. Hide
your food and your bicycles. Hide your
maps. See that the enemy gets no petrol.
Remember that transport and petrol will
be the invaders' main difficulties. Make
sure no invader will get your car, petrol,
maps, or bicycles. . . ."*

Every face was riveted upon me. Eva said to a
small group of girls, "Of course we have no cars,
petrol, maps, or bicycles. That is not the point.
The point is that the British believe the Germans
are coming."

One teenaged Polish girl with her young
siblings gathered around her began to weep.
"Stay put? We have seen what the Nazis will do
to us Jews. Our parents! The village," she
exclaimed. Others in the group were flooded with
the despair of shared memories.

I held my hands up for silence as I continued.

"Be ready to help the army in any way. Do not block roads until ordered to do so by the military or LDV authorities. In factories and shops, all managers and workmen should organize some system by which a sudden attack can be resisted. Think before you act. But think always of your country before you think of yourself."

Silence fell over us. I considered this instruction. Though we were neither a factory or a shop, I was a sort of manager. We must organize and train our people to help defeat the enemy as best they could.

I looked up from the muddled and confusing government document. Puzzled expressions ringed me.

Denise asked, "What does it mean?"

"What can we do?" Irene asked.

"How shall we prepare to stay put?" Cheryl queried.

There was also the issue of discerning whether a soldier was British or only pretending to be. The Allied soldiers rescued from the beaches of France were French, Polish, Dutch, Norwegian, Danish, and Belgian. Among us were a few from tiny Luxembourg.

Hermione cleared her throat. "My dears, it is clear that this was written by someone in the government who has two heads."

Eva sighed with relief. "Well, at least the cat is out of the hen coop. They want us to stay put, and do nothing, because they do not know what to do."

"But that is what we shall never do." Hermione held up a regal and instructive finger. She looked at me. "What shall we do?"

I thought a moment before I spoke. "Perhaps something is coming which may break our hearts, but they will not break our will. We will stand firm, as Mister Churchill has said."

My admonition to stand firm sounded very noble even as the daily reports of Nazi coastal bombings poured in. In London, British civilian women put away silk stockings and lipstick and donned fashionable uniforms. Our refugees of St. Mark's, as eager to defeat Hitler as any beings on earth, lived under a cloud of suspicion. They wore cast-off clothing and were left to wonder how they might help England to persevere.

We continued to arrange evacuations to the countryside for women and children. British and German dogfights raged high above our heads, yet London remained relatively calm and unscathed. The Nazi assault heated up against English convoys, ports, and manufacturing. We wondered if anywhere in our island haven was safe.

I received a heavily redacted letter from Jessica

in Wales, telling how she and Madame Rose and Cousin Elisa could hear the crump of bombs falling on an unnamed target. They watched the fires set by German incendiary bombs burn a village through a long, long night.

Did we dare send any more orphans to Wales since the attacks seemed to be everywhere?

I took a night off, looking forward to discussing some possibilities over supper in our flat. Eben, bringing his own daily ration of butter and meat, joined Eva, Mac, and me.

We ate by candlelight as the long day drew to a close. Mac played his phonograph records. Glenn Miller and Benny Goodman made the meager meal more enjoyable. I looked up more than once to see Eben's eyes fastened on my face. After a dessert of wild berries Mac and Eva had picked on Hampstead Heath, I read Jessica's letter and the news from Wales aloud.

"A Nazi pilot was shot down and managed to parachute to safety. Madame Rose and her own little Jerome helped capture the fellow. Madame Rose held him facedown on the ground in our field with the farmer's shotgun until Jerome could run for help and the farmer and constable arrived. They beat the fellow senseless when he attempted to resist. This after Madame Rose had held him captive on her

own for nearly an hour. She attributes this to an angel who accompanies her everywhere, and though I cannot claim I see him, I certainly do believe her account."

Eben, Mac, and Eva applauded Jerome and Madame Rose. Mac declared that a story must be written about this American shotgun-toting missionary and her flock of orphans now capturing downed Huns in Wales.

They were the lucky ones, we concluded. How could we equip our people for the fire that would soon fall upon London?

Eben, who had witnessed the bombing of Madrid in Spain, said, "When they begin to hit London, it will not be hundreds of casualties, but thousands. While they remain here, your women should be trained by the Red Cross. I will speak to the Jewish Agency, and we will make an official request."

No sooner had he finished speaking than the air-raid siren sounded. The anti-aircraft gun on the top of Primrose Hill began to bang away as Nazi aircraft droned toward some target in the Midlands. We carefully gathered the remainder of our pudding and tea and made our way to the tin Anderson shelter in the garden.

It was almost dawn before the all-clear sounded. News came to us in the morning that the Germans had begun firing cannons from France and hitting Britain's shore from across the Channel.

Eben said quietly, this was surely a signal that more difficult days were ahead.

24

Early on in my service to the Community Undertaking, Placing Children (CUP-C) I learned to hate Sundays at St. Mark's. The mornings were somewhat uncomfortable, as the regular parishioners arrived to hold their Sunday morning service. The unplaced refugees gathered pitiful bundles of belongings and stood around the walls. Knots of children, each with a chaperone who was in some sense a guard, likewise huddled together.

Many of the refugees did not understand the words of the preaching. Many of the parishioners were caught between feeling imposed on and feeling guilty about not doing enough.

Pastor Swanson did his best to alleviate the disquiet. He kept his messages short and encouraged those who were bi-lingual to translate for their countrymen. He also increased the number of hymns that were sung, correctly reasoning that voices lifted in praise to God crossed all national and ethnic boundaries.

The pastor lavished praise on the efforts of the committee and on the community for its involvement in placing the refugees in homes. As he said, "It is entirely right and proper that our organization is known as CUP, because as our Lord and Master said, 'Whoever gives a cup of cold water to the needy, it is the same as doing it for Him.' We may not be able to do much; we may not be able to do all we wish we could, or as quickly as we might wish, but nevertheless, we persist. Each child given shelter, each family given hope, is yet another cup of refreshment. And as the Lord adds, so I also say to you, 'You shall not lose your reward.'"

But if Sunday mornings were awkward, the Lord's Day afternoons were downright agonizing. It was around teatime on Sundays that families arrived en masse to look for children to foster.

Despite all CUP's good intentions and Pastor Swanson's kind words, the process shared many of the qualities of a cattle market. Or, as Eben Golah whispered to me, "A slave auction."

All too often the young and cute children were placed in homes right away, leaving their older siblings to languish unwanted against the pillars—the human debris of war. After any blue-eyed, blond-haired urchins had been carted away by families looking for living dolls, next came a cadre of hard-eyed, keen-witted bargainers, who almost had to be prevented from checking teeth and arm strength. These folks were searching for unpaid servants, particularly docile maids, and to some extent, broad-shouldered, young males for service on farms, to replace men absent in the military.

No matter how alarming the motives, we could not turn down those willing to accept refugee children. If our interviews determined the offered living conditions were acceptable and the family's ability to provide food and clothing adequate, then we had little choice but to agree.

When the immediate sorting had been completed and those interviews accomplished, I looked around the room at the ones who had not been selected. Some offered sheepish grins, as if still hoping to find favor. Some glared sullenly, defying anyone to reduce their worth to insignificance because of their hair color or their lack of ability to be beasts of burden.

And then there were those who turned inward, suffering from God only knew what grief and loss.

Yosef Helmann was a perfect example of how imperfect was this system. Born into a middle-class Polish-Jewish family in 1925, he grew up in a German village of less than two thousand souls near the Polish border, where his father kept a textile shop. At first everyone got along: Jews and Gentiles, Poles and Germans.

Then the Nazis came to power.

In 1934 Yosef saw his father beaten and left for

dead by SA thugs. In 1936 Yosef himself was thrown out of a second-story window by exuberant Hitler Youth eager to prove themselves equal to their elders in their capacity for evil and senseless violence.

Now, at age fourteen, with his scarred face, crooked right arm, and thick glasses, Yosef was alone in an alien land, desired by no one. On his face I read resignation and the desire to end it all. Had I ever been that despairing? After less than a decade and a half of life, was there no hope left for him?

I called him over and tried to console him. This I knew I could not accomplish by false promises that next Sunday would be better or different, so I recounted my own story about escaping from Brussels to England via Dunkirk. How even then I had not known my father and my husband were both dead.

Yosef nodded solemnly. "Two years ago next October the Nazis told us we had to leave our home. Poles, but especially Polish-Jews, were not wanted in Germany. We were given one day to gather our belongings and leave for Poland.

"But do you know what happened then? The Poles didn't want us either! We were put in a camp between the Polish and German frontiers— a place called Zbaszyn."

I acknowledged that I had heard of that horrid place.

"The lucky ones slept twenty to a small tent. The rest of us shared smelly blankets on wet ground all winter long." He paused, then shuddered. "I hate cabbage soup. That's all we ate for six months, I think."

"How did you get here?" I encouraged him to continue speaking, trying to establish a connection with him.

Yosef removed his glasses and wiped them on his sleeve. After he replaced them, he resumed, "Three trainloads of us were packed up and sent to the sea coast. Only children, you see. None of the rest of my family." His voice trailed away as we both contemplated what that separation had cost him and what it probably meant. He resumed, "We didn't even know where we were going. Some said Russia; others, Palestine. It wasn't until we were crammed onto a ship that we learned we were coming to England. They assigned me to the grounds of a summer youth camp. It was better than Zbaszyn," he said, offering me a sly sideways glance and a wry smile. "Do the British really think the rest of the world eats smoked fish for breakfast and sausages for supper?"

I smiled in return. "I do not understand kippers either."

"Anyway," Yosef said with a shrug, "when it rained, the camp flooded, so we all had to move again. The next camp over was already full to bursting, so they sent me here instead, where I'm likely to remain until I'm sixteen and forced out on the street."

"That's not going to happen," I vowed, somewhat foolishly. *Oh, Lord,* I prayed. *How much is enough? When do You show Yourself to be all-loving and all-merciful?*

"Pardon me, miss," said a voice at my elbow.

I looked up to find a tastefully dressed man, of medium height and build, holding a bowler hat as he bowed to me. I almost snickered at the seeming caricature but restrained myself just in time as I recognized what the English call a "gentleman's gentleman," or man-servant.

"May I help you?" I said.

Yosef started to edge away from me but something prompted me to seize his arm and hold on.

"That gentleman over there," the valet said, pointing to Eben Golah, who smiled and waved, "said to speak with you about placing some boys with our establishment."

"Your establishment?"

"I'm sorry if I'm not making myself clear. My name is Flornoy, miss, valet to his Lordship, Baron de Rothschild."

"His . . . lordship?" Realizing I sounded near to babbling, I swallowed carefully and observed, "Of course. How many can you accommodate?"

"His lordship specified boys," Flornoy said. "I

should think, twenty or twenty-five, if you have that many."

Without stopping to take a breath I said in a rush, "This is Yosef. He is my assistant and will be in charge of gathering . . . twenty-five, you said? It should take . . . fifteen minutes."

A few days went by, and then I received a letter from Yosef Helmann:

Dear Missus Kepler,

We are at the Baron's country home. As the English say: "We have fallen into a tub of butter!" There is a lake here on which we may canoe, and tennis courts! We have a regular school. We sleep only three to a room. And best of all, the village lads came to play football with us and when they left said, "Let's do this again soon." Can you imagine? And all of us Jews! Thank you for your prayers, Miss Lora. May the Almighty reward you.

The flush-faced, broad-hipped young woman who stood before me in St. Mark's Church spoke English with a thick Irish brogue. "Please, yoor ladyship," she said. "Meghan O'Toole's me name. From near Warwick." She pronounced it "Wahr-wick," instead of the way the English say "Wor-ick."

I liked her immediately.

"My name is Lora Kepler, Meghan," I corrected. "And I'm not a ladyship. How can I assist you?"

"Well, yoor lay—Missus Kepler, that is—it's like this: I'm maid-of-all-work to the Tunstall family; them as has gone to America. So they left me in charge, don'tcha see? To mind after the big house in their absence. There's just me and Liam, but we does what's needed."

"Yes, I see," I encouraged.

"So, me and Liam," she continued, "we wuz talkin'. 'Bout bringin' in a coupla them foreign kids, like. Them as has nowhere's else to go."

"I'm not sure we can do that," I said with reluctance. It was difficult to pass up any willing volunteers. "Without the consent of the Tunstalls we couldn't billet children—"

Meghan's plump hands flew to her rosy cheeks. "Oh, I wasn't meanin' that! Not atall, atall! Never in the big house! I've me own cottage, don'tcha see, as does Liam. Well, mine's good and snug, with a fine thatched roof. And I've got room and to spare . . . now." She paused, seeming to need a moment to come to grips with some inner turmoil, before continuing.

"Anyways," she resumed, "Liam allows as how he could use the help, what with him gettin' on in years, and there still bein' the livestock and the gardens to tend and all. So if you'd be havin' a pair of strapping girls not afraid of a bit o' work,

I promise to see 'em cared for and fed and all."

My thoughts instantly leapt to the Cohen sisters. Ages ten and fourteen, they were raven-haired Jewish beauties from Hamburg. With their heavy, dark eyebrows and prominent noses the girls were the total antithesis of Aryan perfection and well off to be out of Germany. They had left father and mother and one older brother behind, not knowing if they would ever see them again.

Strong and bright, you would think their placement would be simple, but it had not proved so. They spoke Yiddish and German, but their English was limited to a few simple phrases. This had already been cause enough for them to be considered and rejected a few times; that, and the fact they were desperate to not be separated from each other.

I had tried to reassure them that any parting would be only temporary, but the younger, Leah, clung to her sister, Naomi, and sobbed. I made up my mind to keep them together at all costs.

"Meghan, I think that's a wonderful idea. And I think I know just the girls for you."

I summoned Leah and Naomi from where the sisters were helping mothers tend their babies. I had them stand beside me and instructed them, in German, to introduce themselves, which they did.

Meghan's face broke into a brilliant, gap-toothed smile, but before she could speak, the woman behind her in the queue interrupted: "I can't imagine what you must be thinking."

It took me a moment to realize she was addressing me.

My chastiser was an angular English woman, thin of face, body, and legs. She was clearly agitated, and her right thumbnail picked incessantly at the other fingers of that hand as she spoke. "These young women are Germans, are they not? They are already suspect as enemy foreigners, wouldn't you say?"

Leah did not understand the words, but the hostility came through loud and clear. She buried her face in her sister's sweater, while Naomi glared at the woman.

"What are you trying to say?" I demanded.

"Are you foreign too?" The woman sniffed. "Even so, you can't be unaware of how things stand in this country. Everyone knows that Ireland is a hotbed of German spies. Why, even now the Irish are in league with Hitler, planning to invade us. Are you trying to plant an entire Fifth Column in the heart of England? Aren't there camps for such as these?"

Her expression implied she thought Meghan should likewise be interned.

Meghan's head bobbed in a slantwise motion. "I didn't think. Wasn't meanin' to cause no trouble, I'm sure." With a last sorrowful look, mirrored in Leah's pleading eyes, Meghan turned to go.

At that moment something whispered a question in my mind and I called out, "Meghan, wait. What did you mean when you said you had room to spare . . . now?"

Wiping her eyes on her sleeve Meghan faced me again. "It's this way. Me man, Sean . . . four years wed, we wuz, and him a soldier. I just got word from his mates as come home from Dunkirk. Sean was . . . killed on the beach, so he won't be comin' home, you see."

"I lost my husband too," I said, and before I knew it Meghan and I and the Cohen sisters were tangled in a fierce embrace of shared loss.

I like to think my formidable stare would have shriveled the English woman like an overdone joint of stringy beef. But when I searched for her again, she was nowhere to be seen.

There was joy in Inga's expression as we organized the sleeping quarters for mothers and children refugees who remained at St. Mark's. We set up bunk beds in schoolrooms in the annex, freeing up the pews in the main auditorium for lectures and music concerts and children's activities.

I believe Inga might have regained her desire to live if it had not been for one woman who had been a long-time member of the congregation of the church. The woman's name was Mrs. Reese. She had been the president of the Women's Auxiliary at St. Mark's for many years.

Hermione warned me, "When Mrs. Reese is in the building, something very dark indeed seems to sit whispering upon her shoulder. She has told the rector that our church has no business taking in enemy aliens who have never been given a classification. She hates Germans. But she hates Jews even more. We may have some trouble from that quarter."

Hermione's prediction was not long in coming true. Mrs. Reese's resentment of strangers and foreigners invading her territory was clear to those of us who worked day to day among the refugees.

As the temperatures climbed, rationed bathing gave St. Mark's the permanent and offensive aroma of strong onions. Inga was changing the soiled nappies of a tiny baby when Mrs. Reese stopped to reprimand her. How dare she wash a baby's behind beneath the stained-glass images of Peter, James, and John? It was, she proclaimed, the desecration of a holy place.

Inga attempted to explain in broken English that the toilets always had long lines and that the baby needed his nappies now or risk a rash.

"This is the last straw!" Mrs. Reese roared. "I never thought I would live to see such a thing. Look at you! Jew! You have no respect for our church. None. Desecration! Last straw! We'll see about this." Mrs. Reese proclaimed that "her" beloved church had been overrun by filthy, illiterate foreigners and that she intended to put an end to it. As Inga dissolved into tears, the woman stormed from the building.

That evening Mrs. Reese returned, looking very smug as she led the head of the local branch of the Home Guard to Hermione in the office. Colonel Taylor was an elderly gentleman who had fought in the Great War. His time in the trenches in France had left him with a bitter hatred of all things German. No matter that our residents were German-Jewish women and children who had miraculously escaped from the Nazis. He could not tell the difference between Yiddish and German. To him it all sounded alike. "Besides," he declared, "there were plenty of German Yids who fought against us in the last war."

Mrs. Reese added, "Once a German, always a German. Why are these people not in internment camps like the others?"

Colonel Taylor waved his swagger stick and with great authority cried, "I demand to see the documents of every enemy alien now housed in St. Mark's."

We had no official documents for these who had most recently crossed the English Channel.

Hermione squared her shoulders and pointed

out that most of the children did not even have shoes to wear. "Nor do the mothers have ration books, let alone the official British immigration documents."

The confrontation went downhill fast. The Mayfair magistrate was called in. He agreed with Mrs. Reese and Colonel Taylor that St. Mark's must be cleared of dangerous foreign influence immediately. By morning, he promised, the human debris of the war in France would be swept away. Mayfair would be Mayfair once again.

It was late when I heard Inga crying softly in the choir loft. "It is my fault, Lora," she sobbed. "I'm so sorry! I should not have argued with her. It was wrong of me to change the baby's nappies. I did not think of it. I am so sorry. My fault. I've brought trouble upon everyone."

I wrapped my arms around her and pulled her against my chest. I stroked her hair and my thoughts flew to everything she had survived to come to this beloved haven of freedom. How could it be that Inga, who had endured so much brutality, could now blame herself for Mrs. Reese's fury? Could Inga believe they were being punished because she had changed a baby's nappies in the sanctuary?

I had witnessed such madness in Berlin. I had heard of a Jew beaten to death because he had dared to sit on a park bench beside an Aryan woman. The act of violence had no context to any reasonable person. It was cruelty for its own sake—perverted demonic pleasure. And now there were those who ruled nations and made laws that granted mindless brutality a right to exist in society. The world of Europe was upside down.

But here? In London? This was the place we had all dreamed of coming! I thought of the death of Inga's family. Her brutal rape by a gang of Nazi men along the highway to the sea. Did this dear young woman believe she had caused the evil men had committed against her?

After a time, Inga's trembling ceased. I said softly, "You must not blame yourself, Inga. Not ever, ever again. It is not your fault when evil people do brutal things. They choose to punish simply because they have the power to do so. Inga! You must never blame yourself for the evil others have committed against you."

She did not reply. I saw that once again she had lapsed into silence. Her expression was stunned, her eyes unseeing. When I said her name, she did not acknowledge my voice.

"So, you are gone again," I whispered.

I slept on the pew with Inga in my arms through the night. In the morning when trucks came to collect their precious cargo and carry them away, Inga was first to climb onto the transport. She did not look back or answer me when I called to her. Her eyes were empty as she stared through the slats.

As suddenly as St. Mark's Church had filled with the destitute and desperate refugees, it had been emptied out.

I had taken my freedom for granted. My American documents were ready to be presented if any petty bureaucrat demanded to know what I was doing in England.

The order by which the refugees of St. Mark's were arrested demanded that every unclassified person between the ages of sixteen and sixty be incarcerated until a determination of status could be made. Mothers with small children would not leave them with us. The misery was palpable.

Had they fled the Nazis only for this?

Children whimpered. The heat radiated off the cobbled streets. Here and there I saw self-satisfied expressions on the faces of our Mayfair neighbors. It was no secret that many viewed the transportation of enemy aliens out of London as a precaution. No matter that the "enemy mob" was actually Jews about to be imprisoned by the very Nazis they had fled from.

Madame Rose, back again from Wales for yet another cargo of refugees, warned the commander in her gruff American accent there would be a great outcry in America.

But he paid no attention.

Midmorning, more livestock trucks pulled up

at the front doors of the church. A collective groan rose through the ranks of those who waited.

Stricken, Hermione buried her face in her hands. "Not here! Not in England!"

I watched in horror as nearly everyone who had come to us for help and refuge was loaded and driven away. "Where will they be taken?" I cried in anguish.

A young Home Guard soldier remarked cruelly, "Straight to hell, for all I care. They're Jerries, ain't they?"

Madame Rose stepped between me and the youth. She was a fortress he could not get past. "What is your name?" she demanded.

"Ted Walker, if it's any of your business."

"I'll make it my business."

"A Yank."

"And a well-connected Yank." She pulled out the front page photograph of her and her orphans arriving with the Dunkirk ships in Dover.

"Ah," he said, studying the newspaper. "I thought I recognized you." His face reddened. He tried to laugh off his rudeness.

She would not have it. "Young man, this is Lora Kepler. Also American. Daughter of the brave and famous Christian theologian Robert Bittick, lately murdered by the Nazis. Her father fought the Nazis before you were out of knee britches. Stand down, or you shall think the bricks of this hallowed building have fallen upon your head."

She was too much like the head mistress of a school for the fellow not to obey. "Yes, ma'am," he said, tucking his chin.

"Now," Madame Rose insisted. "Apologize."

He tipped his hat. "Pardon me."

Madame Rose continued. "And you will treat every man, woman, and child in this sorrowful exodus with respect, or I will personally see to it you are set to work cleaning latrines . . . for the duration of the war."

My imagination worked overtime. I remembered the stories of Nazi concentration camps. Would there be food for the little ones? Beds? Clothing?

I raised my eyes to see Eben hurrying up North Audley Street as the last truck rumbled past him. He raised both arms as if in an embrace. His expression was as angry and troubled as my own.

"What's this? What's this?" Eben cried as he reached us.

Madame Rose replied with disgust, "You know very well what this is. Not content to intern the men, someone has ordered all the shelters be emptied. And so everyone . . ."

Eben's head wagged in disbelief as the cattle truck rounded the corner. "Not here. Not England."

I felt ill.

Hermione wrung her hands. "What to do? What to do?"

Madame Rose wagged the folded newspaper in the air like a club. "We fight. We speak out. For those who have no voice."

25

It was hot that afternoon as Eben and I made our way to the TENS offices near teatime. I wondered what the temperatures must be in the Bermondsey warehouse, where our people were interned.

We hurried past the Coal Hole pub near the Savoy Hotel. From within I clearly heard the latest anti-refugee drinking song.

"As I go rolling down the Strand,
I see them strolling hand in hand.
And I really don't,
I just don't understand
Why there are so many Jews
Around, in London . . ."

Eben's lips pressed together in an angry line as the chorus followed us.

"Why can't the Jews simply disappear?
Hitler's got them on the run in Germany,
Why can't we do the same thing over here?"

I halted midstride as Inga's face came to my mind. Eben stopped after a few paces and turned as if to ask me what I was waiting for.

Pressing my fingers to my temples to counter a pounding headache, I asked, "Why do they hate so much?"

Empty palms up, Eben looked at the sign above the Coal Hole entrance. "If only we could see the demons who stand behind these fellows and whisper in their ears."

I argued from the center of the sidewalk: "Not here. Not in England."

"Everywhere, Lora. And in every generation."

"That still doesn't explain why."

There was no time to waste, yet Eben pulled me from the crowds on the Strand into the cool portico of the Savoy Hotel. I was aware that only the elite of society could afford this place. With a nudge, Eben guided me through the revolving door, past the uniformed doorman, and into the lobby.

"Where are we going?" I asked, uncomfortable among the wealthy hotel guests who sipped tea and ate delicate sandwiches from silver trays. My pocketbook was empty. I could not afford even a cup of tea.

In spite of this, Eben spotted a vacant camel-backed sofa and we sat down in the midst of London's opulent society. I smoothed my working class skirt, my back ramrod straight. The clatter of fine china teacups and sterling silver cutlery accented the murmur of conversation.

"I want you to remember this." Eben's glance swept the room.

"Remember this?"

"It is an illusion. This world is as unreal as a stage set in a Noel Coward play. The real world is the refugees who swelter inside a warehouse across the river in Bermondsey."

I watched as a waiter poured Darjeeling tea from a polished tea service for four matrons in elegant hats. I thought of the faces of mothers and children in the cattle trucks being driven away to internment.

Eben put his hand on mine. "Do you understand what I am saying?"

I nodded "yes," then shook my head "no."

He replied, "For these, the suffering of others is an intrusion. How can one enjoy scones and strawberry jam when London is suddenly crowded with people who have lost everything? So these"—he swept his hand across the picture of ease—"they hate the Jews who remind them of the dark storm gathering force thirty miles across the Channel. Even in Buckingham Palace the royals tell themselves and one another that the Jews really had it coming. The Jews brought trouble on themselves in Germany, they say."

As if to confirm Eben's words, a woman's shrill, aristocratic voice remarked, "What is it about? Why should we fight a war because Hitler invaded Poland?"

Eben arched an eyebrow. "There. The thoughts of a lady who no doubt is welcome at the Chelsea Flower Show, or in the gardens of the Palace. How can Jews fight against the Nazis and high society as well? I say this woman will terribly miss the Paris fashions. She will lay down at night knowing her lack of haute couture is the fault of Poland, and she'll blame the Jews, who disturbed the ambitions of Hitler."

Once again the misery of Inga came strongly to my mind. She and the others had been herded into a brick warehouse on the South Bank.

Eben asked, "Who comes to your mind when you hear such a thing? Or when you hear a song such as the one we heard on the street?"

I replied honestly, "Inga. A Belgian Jewish girl a bit younger than me. Family killed. She . . . was . . . beaten. Beaten and raped by a Nazi gang. Somehow made it to the coast of France. Made it here. Interned now."

Eben raised his chin as if to sniff the wind. "Bring it down to one soul. Inga, orphaned and raped, sipping tea in the lobby of the Savoy. Can you imagine? Eh? She brought it on herself, didn't she?"

I understood. "So they sing, 'Why can't the Jews simply disappear?' And they will make them disappear."

"All right. That's the way it is. And then here *we* are, reminding the tea and crumpets crowd of unpleasant realities." He paused a long moment. "I read the words of the prophet. Oh, it was centuries ago. Ezekiel 33. 'I have set you on the wall as a watchman to warn my people. Whether they heed you or not, the warning you give will be imputed to you as righteousness. But if you hear the trumpet of the enemy and do not sound the warning, then the blood of my people will be upon you. . . .'"

Suddenly the pleasantries and complacent detachment of the crowd in the hotel lobby were more than I could take. "I am afraid for them."

"Yes. Oblivious, they have made *this* their Paradise. Hitler has another goal for England: oblivion and living hell."

"I am more afraid for Inga. No hope left for her."

I followed Eben's gaze to the black tuxedoed maitre d' who eyed us with concern. I had no gloves. I did not wear a hat. Our incongruous appearance had made an unpleasant ripple in the lobby. The maitre d' walked toward us with an official demeanor.

"We are about to be cast out of Paradise." Eben smiled bitterly.

"May we help you, sir?" The maitre d' bowed ever so slightly.

Eben ignored him and said to me, "There is

always a reason when God brings someone into your thoughts. You must not delay. Go to the internment center. Tell Inga what we are doing. Tell her and the others that I've gone to the news office and the press will assail Parliament and the Palace. We will not find the help we need among the residents of the Savoy. Tell her, with God's help, we intend to turn this around."

"May we help you?" the unsmiling maitre d' asked a second time.

Eben said, "We are in search of Eden."

"Sir?"

"Well then, is this Parliament?"

"Parliament? I beg your pardon?"

"Is this the Palace, then?"

"No, sir, this is the Savoy."

"Then, no, thank you, you cannot help."

Cool and focused, Eben and I determined to meet back at St. Mark's Church in two hours. We parted and went separate directions under the glaring eyes of the hotel guests: I, across the river to the Bermondsey warehouse, and Eben to the TENS news office.

Crossing the river by the footbridge below the Savoy, there was just time enough for one last glimpse of St. Paul's Cathedral.

Then I plunged into the squalor of warehouses with bricked-up windows. In walking rapidly through the crooked South Bank lanes and sweltering alleyways en route to Bermondsey, it was easy for me to imagine I had entered the world of Charles Dickens.

In point of fact, Dickens would have recognized it all as well. This was the world of the cut-purse and the debtor's prison. This was where press gangs swooped up unwary drunken sailors and shipped them off for lengthy and dangerous sea voyages. This was the world of rag-pickers and beggars; of Fagan and the Artful Dodger.

But those images, however grim, were too romantic. I recalled Papa explaining that Dickens' own father had been imprisoned for debt. To keep from starving, the young boy, who would later become the master Victorian storyteller, worked twelve-hour days, labeling bottles of boot polish.

So things in London had always had a grim side. But this was the twentieth century. It was an age of learning and achievement; of philanthropy and enlightenment; of the brotherhood of man.

Try telling that to the refugees who lost everything in Germany and Poland and Czechoslovakia. Try explaining the wonders of the modern age to the evacuees who had barely escaped from the Continent with their lives.

Try explaining to Inga why she was locked up in a warehouse on the South Bank of the Thames.

I squared my shoulders and took a deep but cautious breath. The Thames was tidal much farther upriver than here. Just now the tide was out, exposing acres and centuries of muck. And the breeze, it seemed, always blew from north to south. It spared London but asserted the abiding presence of the river to Southwark, and Bankside, and Bermondsey, at least half of every day.

A pair of wharf rats quarreled over a rotten head of cabbage. I hurried on.

The abandoned warehouse that had been requisitioned for refugee "housing" was far enough from the river that its walls did not drip slime or grow mold. In a curious contrast to the surrounding air, it had a sharp, pungent scent that I had trouble placing at first.

"Tannery," explained the guard when I presented my credentials and asked for admittance. "No more bales of hides, but the caustic soaked into the walls, like. Cowhides in one door, shoe leather out t'other. Hotter it gets, the stronger the smell."

The interior still had three floors, pierced at intervals with wooden ramps and staircases. The men occupied the uppermost floor, orphans and mothers with children the bottom, single women and older children the middle level.

I found Inga in the midst of a chicken wire jungle. The entire second story had been subdivided by wooden frames and tacked-up farm fencing into twenty inmate dormitories. Bunks, four high, occupied the outer walls of each pen. The center of the enclosure was left bare and sported a couple wobbly tables and a handful of unmatched wooden chairs.

A game of checkers moved with all the flash of a snail race, closely observed by women for whom observing the rats fighting for the cabbage would have been an exciting spectacle.

Inga sat alone on the bottom bunk in the darkest corner of the room. She barely glanced up when I entered and sat beside her on the thin mattress.

In a word, Inga looked limp. Her hair hung in unwashed strands, concealing her forehead but exposing one shell-like ear. The girl's shoulders drooped, and her chin almost touched her chest.

"Inga," I said softly, taking the young woman's hand in mine.

"Hello, Lora," Inga acknowledged at last. "Have they put you in here too?"

I felt guilty when I shook my head. "This is not how it's going to be. We are working on it, Eben and me. Others, too. We have friends with the American news agency. You'll see."

"Did you know there are Nazis here?" Inga asked without seeming to hear my words of hope. "They say Hitler's coming here; will be here within weeks. They whisper it, but with pride. They still hate Jews, but they are afraid of the rest of us, so they keep to themselves." The girl turned hopeless, empty eyes on me. "Can you imagine anyone being afraid of me?"

"You just have to be strong a little while longer," I encouraged. What could I say that would make any difference? What did I have to offer that was not empty words? "I know—at least I think I know—how you feel; what you're going through. But war is just starting to become real to the people of England. I remember when I didn't believe what was happening; how I could wake up one day and find everything as it was before Hitler. You'll see. The Brits are confused, but their hearts are right. They want to do the right thing, and they will. Just wait a little longer."

Looking toward the blank wall, Inga said, "There's just nothing left of me. I'm hollow inside, Lora. I have no strength left."

In an instant I remembered what Eben had said to me in the lobby of the Savoy. God had a reason when someone came strongly to mind. Perhaps this moment of need in Inga's life was the reason I was here.

"Inga." I reached out to her and drew her into my arms as I had in the choir loft of St. Mark's. "God loves you and has a wonderful plan for your life."

She answered dully, "What life? Look at me. Where I am. And it's my fault this happened."

"It isn't your fault. And I promise you it will all be set right. If you hold on, Inga!" I remembered the promises of Psalm 91, which Papa had prayed over us every night. "I will say to the Lord, 'My refuge and my fortress. My God in whom I trust.' For he will deliver you from the snare of the fowler and from the deadly pestilence . . . under his wings you will trust."

For a moment I believed Inga heard me with her heart. She sighed and raised her face to look into my eyes. "But God has not delivered me from the snare. He has not been my fortress."

"Oh, Inga! But you are alive! Still you are alive after everything that has happened. Can you not see the hand of the Lord on your shoulder?"

She drew back, suddenly resistant. "No. No, I feel nothing. I don't want to live anymore. I want to sleep the long sleep and be finished. The world is too cruel for me to live in it."

I clasped her hands, not willing to give up. Had I not felt the same when news of Varrick's death had reached me? But now I could see some reason to go on; some purpose for living as I helped bind the wounds of those who were more wounded than I. "I promise, Inga! This is not the end."

"No," she said, her fingers limp in my grip. "I fear you are right. This is only the beginning. My father tried to get us visas to go home to Eretz-Israel, even though England governs there. That was our hope, but England would not let us enter our ancient homeland. So my father and my mother . . . my family is dead. How many millions more will die before we Jews are allowed to live in our own homeland? I can't go on, Lora. I don't want to live without the ones I love. If England hates us as the Germans do, then there is no place we Jews will ever be safe."

I could not deny anything Inga said. Hundreds of thousands of desperate Jews fleeing the Nazis had attempted to return to British-controlled Eretz-Israel. They had been rejected, so now would surely die. The cruelty of England's actions would go down in history as a crime born of apathy. It allowed the Nazis to do as they wished to everyone of Jewish heritage. Still, England was on the right side of this war, and the only European nation still standing. I was convinced that, in the end, they would do the right thing.

I sighed as Inga pulled her hands away and balled her fists. "We will work to get you out of here, Inga. Soon. Soon. And then, when this war is over, we will work hard to tell the whole world what happened here. Someday there will be a Jewish homeland in Israel. And the Bible says when that happens, we will see our Messiah return to reign in glory in Jerusalem."

Inga, so very young, looked at me with the eyes of someone who had seen too much tragedy to believe me. Or perhaps she had not lived long enough to believe that in the end all things work together for the good. I hugged her farewell and said, "If only you will hang on, I promise things will turn around for you. It is written: 'Tears last for the night, but joy will come in the morning.' "[5]

Inga did not emerge from her shadowed nest as I greeted mothers and children, offering them hope that this travesty could not, would not, be allowed to stand.

One thin, gaunt woman with a baby on her hip said quietly to me, "They sweep our heartbreak under the rug so they will neither see nor hear. Speak for those who have no voice."

My heart was heavy when I left that black, stinking hole. Thunderheads loomed in the twilight sky. I rode the top deck of the bus, welcoming the rain on my face. With a sense of dread, I prayed for Inga as I made my way back to St. Mark's. Surely the Lord could not allow this heartbreak to continue.

26

Morning dawned hot and muggy, the kind of humidity that made me certain the day would end in a thunderstorm. Munching our ration of bread spread with a paper-thin layer of butter, Eva and I strolled across Regent's Park. Sunlight glistened through the broad leaves of the

---

[5] Psalm 30:5

ancient plane trees and dappled the anti-aircraft emplacements with light.

Reaching Baker Street, we decided to ride the bus rather than descending into the heat of the Baker Street tube station. Eva and I climbed the stairs of the red double-decker to enjoy the sunshine.

We passed Madame Tussaud's famous waxworks, where the wax replica of Adolf Hitler had recently been placed in the Hall of Tyrants between Genghis Khan and Emperor Nero. Eva remarked, "It will be hot enough today to melt Madame Tussaud's tyrants."

"It's going to rain." I peered up at the blue sky. "I forgot my umbrella."

"I will welcome the rain."

"I wonder how our people will fare with the heat in the warehouse," I mumbled.

Eva glanced upward. "I am praying the rain will come early today."

We stepped off the bus in Grosvenor Square. When we reached St. Mark's, Hermione had organized an efficient cleaning crew. Pews were being polished, marble floors mopped, and stained-glass windows shone from behind the criss-cross pattern of masking tape.

Above the high altar a team of workmen labored in the organ loft under the supervision of a master pipe organ builder. They were dismantling the great instrument, which had been built to perform the music of Fredrick Handel.

The German composer had once lived nearby in Mayfair, where he composed his most famous pieces, *Zadok the Priest* and *The Messiah*. More than any other venue in London, Handel's *Messiah* was most often performed on St. Mark's magnificent instrument. Now, as I watched the famous organ being dismantled and packed in wooden crates for storage in the crypt, I thought of Inga and the precious human lives packed into a tanner's warehouse. I bitterly wondered what Handel's enemy alien classification would have been.

My job for the next few days was to translate and prepare for the tribunal, the stories of the St. Mark's refugees who were being held as prisoners.

Hermione, at the altar, mop in hand, spotted Eva and me as we observed from the entrance to the auditorium. She waved broadly but did not smile as she hurried toward us.

"Good morning, Eva. Lora." There was something ominous in her eyes as she greeted us. Without taking a breath, she said to me, "Lora, Eben Golah is in the office. He asked me to send you to him the minute you arrived. He wishes a word with you."

Her tone gave me the same uneasy feeling in my stomach as the messenger boy at the door of our flat when I learned that Varrick had been killed. "What is it?" Eva asked.

"Come with me, Eva." Hermione led Eva away and whispered quietly.

I made my way to the church office, where Eben sat with a uniformed police officer. All three looked up at once as I stood framed in the doorway.

"Good morning?" My greeting was a question.

Eben stood and offered me his chair. "Lora. Sit down. This is Inspector Watts."

The policeman was a tall, bespectacled fellow with frayed cuffs and rundown shoes. He observed me through thick lenses as though he suspected me of something. But what?

"What is it, Eben?" I asked, my heart pounding.

He put a hand on my shoulder. "Inga."

"Inga? But what—"

"Steady, Lora," Eben whispered.

"Eben?"

"Inga is dead." Eben pronounced the words with such finality.

The room spun around me. If Eben's hand had not been on my shoulder, I would have fallen.

"But . . . how can she be dead? Inga!" I gasped for breath as I asked the question.

The inspector sniffed and in a matter-of-fact tone said the word I most feared. "Suicide." He paused. "At least we think it is a suicide."

Eben added, "There are confirmed anti-Semites—virulent Nazis—interned in the warehouse with our people. With Inga. There is no note. So the inspector must ask you a few questions."

I was trembling as if it were the coldest day of the year. "How? What happened?"

The inspector offered me a cigarette to calm my nerves. I did not smoke. He lit one for himself and answered through the first puff, "Found hanging, she was, behind a bale of hides. Rawhide rope thrown over a beam. Seems she climbed onto the bale and threw herself off. Hung herself. Or so it seems. We just don't know why she would have done it. No motive. To come so far. Survive so much. Escape the Nazis. Why would such a young girl hang herself after all that?"

I had no doubt that Inga had killed herself. Our conversation flooded my mind. I told them everything she had said: her fear that the Germans would invade; the threat by the Nazis that the end of England was very near.

"I should have known," I cried. "I should have seen it coming."

The account of my last meeting with Inga satisfied the policeman. He closed his notebook. "Clear case of suicide, then. Not homicide." His interest was without emotion or compassion.

I don't remember how we parted. Eben walked into the corridor with the officer. Their voices seemed very distant as I leaned my head upon my hand and tried to rewrite my time with Inga so the ending would be different. What could I have done that would have changed everything for her?

Hermione entered the room. She towered over me and said sorrowfully, "Death is so final. Why? Why would she do such a thing when there is a light at the end of the tunnel?"

I did not reply. The burden of my failure weighed heavily on my heart. "I should have known. Should have done something. Warned someone. Stayed with her."

"You did all you could, dear," Hermione said as she left me alone.

I felt Eben enter the room. He simply stood silently behind me for a long time.

"Come with me, Lora," he said gently. "We must get out for a while. You have been working nonstop." He pulled me to my feet. I fell against him, barely able to stand. Strong arms held me. Gentle hands stroked my hair as I wept for a time. He gave me his kerchief to wipe my eyes.

"I must get back to work," I managed. "Their stories. The tribunal."

"Not today. Come with me, Lora. A cup of tea. Selfridges, eh?" He led me out of the church the back way. We emerged into the chaotic wartime traffic of Oxford Street.

The tearoom at Selfridges was crowded with women shopping to fill their rations for the week.

Eben sat across from me at a small table mercifully tucked in the corner. The tea came without sugar or cream. He produced a small jar containing his personal sugar ration and spooned some into my cup. I took a tiny sip, determined to make this cup last. The taste of Eben's shared ration in the warm brew calmed me.

He was silent, waiting for me to speak. His eyes were on my fingers as I caressed the cup. I held the liquid in on my tongue as if to savor the sweet memory of days before the war. The tea was tepid before I allowed myself a second taste.

At last I asked, "Do you suppose life will ever be the same as it was?"

He answered, "No. Never."

"Well, then."

"But that doesn't mean life can't be good."

Long minutes passed before I spoke again. He waited patiently.

"What I mean is, Eben, will it ever be easy again?" I inhaled the aroma rising from my cup as if it were a garden and this were the last rose of summer.

"The season will come when sugar is no longer rationed and sweetness is taken for granted again. A poor metaphor for life, maybe, but the secret to getting through difficulty is knowing that both good times and bad are only seasons. You live through the night, knowing dawn is coming."

"I promised Inga joy would come in the morning. Now this."

"You told her the truth. She didn't believe you. Didn't believe dawn would come. I am sorry for her. She gave up too soon. She has missed out on the joy meant to be hers and which she would have given to others. Joy would have risen in her heart like the dawn."

"It's been so long since I have believed it myself. I have forgotten how to hope."

Eben placed his hand over mine. "Do not give up now, Lora. I need you to promise me you won't give up. There is yet so much joy ahead for us." He searched my face as if to ask if I understood what he was saying.

I could not form my thoughts into questions. *Us?* What was he saying? Did I dare to hope that my future joy might somehow be bound to Eben?

He said, "Your life is a jigsaw puzzle, the pieces all jumbled together in a box. It will take a lifetime to put the picture together, but I know it will be a beautiful picture when it is complete."

I asked, "What is it? What do you see?"

"I stood on the edge of a clear sea one morning. Water so clear I could see the boulders seventy feet down. Your eyes, Lora, remind me of . . . that. Beautiful. Deep. Clear. I see into your soul."

"I look up into a clear blue sky, then I carry my umbrella because I think it might storm."

"It will. Thunder and lightning. A downpour, Lora. Bucketing down. Someday."

"We are speaking in metaphors again, aren't we?"

Eben's smile was as gentle as if he was calming the fears of a small child. "Yes, Lora. The trick is not to fear the storm when it comes. Knowing it will pass."

That day, as we sat together for hours in the noisy tearoom, something happened in my heart and was confirmed in Eben's gaze. Time seemed like nothing when I was with Eben. We walked for many hours in the park. At sunset he took me home and ordered me to sleep, leaving me with these words: "Joy will come in the morning."

27

The meeting place of the Select Committee for the Consideration of Refugee Affairs was in an Army Stores Depot in Deptford. Located east of London and south of the Thames, the area was dank, dirty, smelly, and subject to miasmic fogs.

Eben told me that part of the lingering acrid aroma was due to the fact that the area had been a cattle market until the British army took it over in 1914. "Before that it was a British navy chandler's yard clear back to King Henry the Eighth," he added. "Amazing how the effect of combining manure and tar survives long after the visible evidence is gone."

The Select Committee consisted of a lean, pinch-faced magistrate, with the peering eyes and hunched shoulders of Ebenezer Scrooge. Flanking Magistrate Hawley on his right was a larger-than-life-sized woman, Mrs. Somersett, from the British Home Secretary's office. On Hawley's left was Major John Vincent, who had lost his right leg in 1918, but who now represented the Local Defense Volunteers detailed to guard the "dangerous" refugees.

Despite the benign-sounding name of the committee, I could not help but think of them as a tribunal, like in Dickens' *Tale of Two Cities*. These three judges had the power to round up and commit to imprisonment, without trial and without appeal, all foreign refugees within the environs of London.

It was terrifying.

I was glad my part in preparing for today's proceedings had been that of arranging for the participation of Madame Rose and Mac McGrath. That Eben Golah came with me was a given. Since most of the detained evacuees were Jews, Eben's position as representative of the Jewish Refugee Placement Agency was expected.

None of the detainees were present. None of the evacuees were allowed to speak on their own behalf. That weight fell squarely on the shoulders of Eben and Madame Rose.

"Come, come," Hawley intoned. "Let's begin. We haven't got all day."

"With respect, mi'lawd," Eben said, "since we are considering what may be the lengthy incarceration of innocent people, let us proceed with all . . . deliberate . . . speed."

"Innocent," I heard Major Vincent mutter. "Fifth columnists, more like."

"Who will speak first?" Hawley demanded.

Madame Rose, who had returned at my request, specifically for this meeting, stood and cleared her throat. In the enclosed space with the high ceiling the effect was akin to firing off a small cannon. "I am Madame Rose, lately of La Huchette orphanage in Paris. I am an American, so you would not dare to detain me! But since many of the children imprisoned by your orders were brought to this country by me, it is for me to present their case." Madame Rose turned her withering gaze on the lone woman member of the committee. Mrs. Somersett quailed and dropped her eyes.

"You have perhaps heard," Madame Rose continued, "of how we, my children and I, escaped from the chaos of Paris and survived a Channel crossing in a canal barge at the height of the Dunkirk miracle. We even"—here Madame Rose fixed her sights on Major Vincent—

"managed to cram some British soldiers on to our decks, so my children actually participated in the rescue efforts. In proof of which, I have pictures."

Mac and Eva stood and between them unfolded and displayed the *Times* front-page photograph of the *Stinking Garlic* being towed into port, its deck jammed with waving children and cheering Tommies. "And I am a witness," Mac sang out. "I'm the one who took the pictures."

"And who might you be?" Hawley demanded.

"Nobody, really," Mac said with a wicked grin. "Mac McGrath. American too. I work for TENS. Maybe you've heard of them? American news agency with—oh, I dunno—maybe forty million readers. America, while officially neutral, has a keen interest in watching how England treats immigrants."

When Madame Rose, Mac, and Eva sat again on the wobbly wooden bench, it was Eben's turn to rise. He introduced himself, then said, "Here is how I see it: quite apart from what could be considered ingratitude." He nodded toward Madame Rose. "And without regard to possible damage done to Anglo-American relations, there are still two more points to consider. The first is that these fathers, mothers, boys, and girls have no countries to which they can return. Jews cannot go back to Germany without being interned . . . or worse. France has fallen, Holland has fallen, Belgium has fallen, Poland has fallen. You may not want them here, but where would you suggest they go?"

"We're in a war," Vincent argued. "Can't have unknown foreigners traipsing across the countryside, now can we?"

"Not our problem, is it?" Hawley rumbled.

"But that is where you're wrong!" Eben thundered.

I shivered at his rebuke. It reminded me of the story of how the prophet Nathan confronted King David, shaking a finger in the king's face and shouting, "Thou art the man!"

"What do you mean by that?" Hawley demanded.

"These people are Jews. My kinsmen. If they were allowed to choose, many of them would go to Palestine. But they are not permitted that choice. The British government has refused—categorically denied—the right of Jews leaving Nazi-occupied Europe to have entry into the British Mandate of Palestine. Very well. They cannot go home. They cannot go where they wish. Will you, then, keep them imprisoned for the duration of the war? Keep in mind they have escaped the very tyranny your brave soldiers and sailors are trying so desperately to keep from reaching these shores. They know how the Nazis operate, how they think, how they strike. If you crush the spirits of those who fled to you for refuge, what a denial of your own glorious heritage."

It was impressive, but not enough. The woman, Mrs. Somersett, might be convinced, but not the two men. Hawley was obstinate; Vincent, belligerent.

It was with some surprise I found myself on my feet. "Sirs," I said, "may I say a word?"

"And you are?"

"Lora Bittick Kepler. My father is . . . was . . . Robert Bittick of Brussels. The Nazis killed him. He was aiding the wounded at the defense of Passendale."

Mrs. Somersett nodded vigorously and leaned over to whisper in Hawley's ear.

"Though I am also a refugee," I continued, "I am American, and my own status is not in question. I have been vouched for by members of the British government."

More whispering.

"You may speak," Hawley allowed.

"I had not intended to, but feel I must," I said. "I want to tell you the story of a young woman, almost the same age as myself. Her name was Inga. She was one of a million refugees running ahead of the Blitzkrieg. She could not run fast enough, and during the panic"—I drew a deep breath and squared my shoulders. Eben squeezed my hand in encouragement—"in the escape she was caught . . . and raped." Fixing my eyes on Mrs. Somersett, I continued, "Brutalized. You may say such things happen in war, and that is easy to say when you do not know the names and faces of the victims. But I met Inga . . . after she managed to arrive in England. I heard her story. I saw how the flame of her life was barely flickering. She could not speak; could barely breathe. Life was not precious to her; she barely still lived at all. Then, just in the smallest way, she came to have hope. She began to talk to me; to recognize that she might once more feel safe . . . feel protected."

I shook my head sadly and could not keep the tears from coursing down my face. "Inga began to speak of helping others; reaching those who daily lived with recurring nightmares. Then she was rounded up, transported by cattle truck—*by cattle truck*—to a prison camp. She had come so far, endured so much . . . for what?"

During the last sentence the volume of my voice had dropped so low that the three members of the committee were leaning forward to hear the conclusion. "Inga," I said, "killed herself. She gave up hope for rescue and protection. She gave up wanting to live."

I sank to my seat. Eben embraced me. Madame Rose patted my arm. Mac scowled, and Eva cried softly.

The committee deliberated fifteen minutes in

private, then returned. "We find," Magistrate Hawley intoned, "that we must enforce the provisions of the Alien Registration Act . . . in regard to adult males, who are going to be interned on the Isle of Man. However, all females and all children under the age of sixteen will be released and returned to the responsibility of the appropriate agencies. We are adjourned."

At nine in the morning the trucks bearing our freed exiles began arriving at St. Mark's. The auditorium was filled with laughter and the babble of a half dozen languages as territory was reclaimed by former occupants.

There was only one who was missing among the crowd. I felt the loss of Inga acutely. I could not help but think how different her story might have been if only she had waited.

Along with the hundreds of familiar faces, suddenly there were also mother-and-child refugees who had been arrested in a dozen locations around London. They were released to our care through the decision of the tribunal.

By midday our ranks had swelled to more than double the number of those who had first come to us. It was to be my task to find homes around Great Britain for them all.

Eva joined me to help as we personally took charge of reregistering women with children under sixteen. We divided the queue into two groups: one for refugees from Eastern Europe, and the other for Dutch and French languages. I was grateful for Eva's mastery of Polish and Czech and her smattering of Russian. In between long, animated conversations with refugees she would speak to me or Hermione, demonstrating her mastery of English as learned from Mac.

"You could have knocked me over with a fender. Polish, she is. That woman has five children, and she left when the Nazis came. Leaving her husband where he lies under the affluence of alcohol, she takes it on the sheep to England."

"I understood nearly everything except the sheep," Hermione droned.

Eva blinked at the ceiling. "On the sheep. Takes it on the sheep."

I got it. "On the lam."

Eva squinted her eyes. "What does it mean?"

Hermione sighed and shook her head. "Must be American. One cannot understand anything they say."

My task was easier than translating Eva's faulty American slang. I worked mostly with families speaking Germanic languages, French, Italian, and a smattering of Spanish.

Hermione, her voice shrill like a London Bobby's whistle, spoke only English to everyone. With a series of gestures and grimaces she managed to get her message across clearly.

In one magnificent day the refuge that was St. Mark's became a cross between Noah's Ark and the confusion of the Tower of Babel.

So many refugees to feed and clothe and house. How could we begin to manage them all?

"Our responsibility is great," Hermione admonished us as she brought us tea. The sun sank low, and there were still so many waiting in the line.

Eva nodded solemnly and tapped her pencil on the stack of applications. "As Mac says, 'The butt stops here.'"

Hermione sniffed and raised her chin regally. "Hmm, Americans. My dear. In the vernacular, we British might say, rather, 'The bum stops here.'"

PART SEVEN

A time to love.
ECCLESIASTES 3:8A

28

In mid-August we heard the news on the BBC. Nazi Deputy Rudolf Hess promised impending military action against Britain.

The Blitzkrieg against London was on.

We spent days and nights descending into deep tube stations for shelter, and climbing up the stairs some hours later to find whole blocks of London shattered.

I was sheltered in the crowded Oxford tube station one afternoon when I pulled out Eben's "White Rose" poem to read it once again. Scanning the roses, I studied the beautiful calligraphy inscribed within the Thirty-six. On the back of the page I had written the words of the Rabbi from Bevis Marks Synagogue: *Thirty-six Lamed Vav.*

Behind me two elderly men remarked, "The most peaceful place in London is the basement of the British Museum Reading Room. I spent four hours yesterday in the vaults reading an early copy of *Treasure Island*. The air-raid siren sounded and we barely heard the bombs."

The next day I made my way to the British Museum Reading Room and was directed to the basement, which now contained long reading tables. I presented a slip of paper to the balding, bespectacled research assistant. Only two phrases that I had gleaned from the Bevis Marks' rabbi were written there:

Legend of the Lamed Vav—Hebrew tradition
36 Righteous men—Christian tradition

I did not write down the question I had asked Mama so many years ago in Germany: "Who is Eben? Or rather, *what* is Eben?"

Mama had answered me like a poet on the Texas prairie might: "Eben is a nightingale. His ancient voice sings to the world in the darkness."

I had not thought of Mama's words for years, but now the memory ignited a question that burned in my heart. I had no expectation that this visit to the library would yield any helpful material in my quest. I took my seat among a dozen silent scholars who were surrounded by mounds of books and papers. The only sounds were an occasional clearing of a throat and the rustle of turning pages. In such a peaceful place, who could guess that there was a war going on?

After nearly thirty minutes the research assistant emerged from the vaults. He was pushing a trolley heaped with antique volumes and bound documents, each of which contained some reference to my question. A printed list of page numbers and passages was placed before me like the main dish of a banquet.

In a whisper that seemed loud in the absolute

silence he said, "These are the most recent volumes. Nineteenth-century copies and commentary mostly. The originals are stored away safely in the vaults. There are many ancient manuscripts in the Vatican Library, of course, but the war, you know. Mussolini's Italy now in the Axis . . . Rome may be difficult to reach."

I thanked him, too loudly. My voice echoed in the dome. An aged scholar looked up from his book and glared at me in disapproval.

Top of the stack was a Talmudic commentary dating from the nineteenth century. I opened my lined notebook and began to write as I scanned the pages of one book after another.

Lamedvavniks:

The source of the legend is the Talmud. The Lamed Vav Tzadikim (Hebrew: מיקידצ ו"ל), "36 Righteous Ones." Abbreviated to Lamed Vav, this name refers to 36 righteous people. This concept is rooted within mystical Judaism.

The source is the Talmud itself:

As a mystical ideal the number 36 is intriguing. It is said that at all times there are 36 special people in the world, and that were it not for them, all of them, if even one of them was missing, the world would come to an end. The two Hebrew letters for 36 are the lamed, which is 30, and the vav, which is six. Therefore, these 36 are referred to as the Lamed Vav Tzadikim; the Thirty-six Righteous. This widely held belief, this most unusual Jewish concept, is based on an ancient Hebrew text that in every generation 36 righteous "greet the Divine Presence." The number 36 is twice 18. In gematria (a form of Jewish numerology), the number 18 stands for "life," because the Hebrew letters that spell chai, meaning "living," add up to 18. Because 36 = 2×18, it represents "two lives."

As I pondered the idea of eighteen pairs of lives . . . two lives, two witnesses . . . something my father had taught us when we studied the book of Revelation came suddenly into sharp focus.

And I will give power unto my two witnesses, and they shall prophesy a thousand two hundred and threescore days, clothed in sackcloth. . . . And when they shall have finished their testimony, the beast that ascendeth out of the bottomless pit shall make war against them, and shall overcome them, and kill them. . . . And after three days and an half the Spirit of life from God entered into them, and they stood upon their feet; and great fear fell upon them which saw them.

And they heard a great voice from heaven saying unto them, Come up hither. And they ascended up to heaven in a cloud; and their enemies beheld them.[6]

With Papa we had puzzled over who the two witnesses could be. Were they prophets like Moses and Elijah at the Mount of Transfiguration, returning again to deliver God's final messages to the defiant earth? The account in Revelation certainly pictured "two lives" as holding forth for righteousness and judgment, prophesying against rebellion and sin. Clearly a Jew would define them as Lamedvavniks.

I returned to my study.

The purpose of Lamedvavniks:

Mystical Judaism, as well as other segments of Jewish faith, believe there are, at all times, 36 righteous people whose role in life is to justify the purpose of mankind in the eyes of God.

In folk tales the Lamedvavniks appear at critical times and by their spiritual powers succeed in averting the impending dangers to a people from the enemies that surround them. They return to concealment as soon as their task is accomplished. The Lamed-

---

[6] Revelation 11:3, 7, 11-12

vavniks, dispersed throughout the world, do not even know each other. Rarely, one is accidentally "revealed," but the secret of their identity must not be disclosed. Some believe the concept to have originated in the Book of Beginnings (Genesis), chapter 18, where it is recorded:

"And the Lord said, 'If I find in Sodom fifty righteous within the city, then I will spare all the place for them.' "

After hours of study, my search had only begun. One reference to the legend led to another and another. After four hours I leapt to Christian traditions. The medieval tales of Prester John made up one tall stack of books. Reportedly a descendant of the Magi, the Prester John legends were exaggerated and filled with fantasy. I laid these accounts aside. Then an old, familiar volume of Eusebius caught my eye. I remembered the day Papa had made me put down the poetry of Keats and had set me to the task of translating a passage from Eusebius.

I set to work again. I found that even here, in the writings of the early church fathers, there were references to those who had been healed by Jesus still living two hundred years later. The writings of Irenaeus, Polycarp, and Eusebius spoke of those who had reached a great age among the first generation of Christ followers.

The lights blinked and from behind his desk the librarian announced that the library would soon be closing. The precious volumes must be returned to the bombproof vaults. London was burning down around us all through the first weeks of that hot and terrible August. Only thoughts of seeing Eben again illuminated my heart through the long, dark nights.

After evening prayers, I walked to my now usual meeting with Eben, preferring daylight to the mole tunnel of London's Underground system. Silver-skinned barrage balloons floated like giant fish above the city.

In the daytime London's scars were as visible as the painted faces hiding the disfigured features of the Tin Noses Brigade.

I reached the top of Primrose Hill and stood beside an anti-aircraft gun. From my high vantage point I looked out across the villages of London. She was a grand old lady, built upon the swales and gentle rises of the terrain. A low, horizontal city, London had grown up around lush green parks and genteel squares. Her buildings were topped by a forest of clay chimneypots. Structures of red brick or white stone were tarnished by centuries of coal smoke and streaked by time.

Despite the soot, London had aged gently. She resembled a dignified grandmother who had suffered a fall, leaving her unable to get her hair done, or put on a dress, or find her lipstick.

Like the ladies who now inhabited her, London was a city without makeup. There was no hiding her scars in the daylight. Beyond Regent's Park I saw whole blocks of shops and houses damaged or destroyed. Wedding cake spires of churches, rebuilt after the Great Fire of 1666, were collapsed, charred, and roofless.

Yet what London lost in beauty, she gained in character. For the proudest of reasons, she remained proud. There was grandeur in London's poverty. She wore stoicism like a medal earned in battle. Nearby, a row of five houses bordering the park had been hit. Walls still standing, they were windowless, gutted, and boarded up.

I watched as three women picked through the bricks, salvaging what they could of a lifetime's possessions. Uncommon courage was common these days.

Behind me I heard Eben's familiar voice. "They say a robin's nest ravaged by a hawk will be rebuilt beneath the eaves by the next generation of robins. But perhaps we are the last."

I turned to him, somehow not surprised he knew what I was thinking. He smiled, stooped, and kissed my mouth. "You're late," he said.

"I'm early," I protested.

"I've been waiting for you . . . centuries." He pulled me against him and kissed me again. His broad back was strong and hard. I was vaguely aware the soldiers who manned the gun were watching us. Pushing him away, I turned and crossed my arms over my chest—a gesture that warned there would be no more public kisses this afternoon.

He laughed at my petulance and placed his hands on my arms. I was stirred by his warmth against my back. Leaning my head against him, we stood observing the city in silence for a time.

After long moments, he spoke. "I have always loved her."

"London?"

"Her strength. No, her *dignity* is a better word."

"Wounded, but still standing."

"Beautiful still. Beauty with that sad, tortured look, like the faces of those who have suffered terribly and who are capable of enduring terrible suffering."

For a fleeting moment I thought of Varrick, then my father and mother. So many others, gone. My soul mirrored the trio who picked through the bricks of their broken house in search of something familiar. Small treasures plucked from the midst of cataclysmic destruction were reason to rejoice. *The miracle of an unbroken teacup. A photograph. A book. A pair of gloves. First one shoe and then the other . . .*

Eben whispered, his breath soft in my ear, "I was reading last night. Emily Dickinson. I found you in the pages. You, Lora. I see you. I hear your heart. In you, Christ's love sings.

> *"If I can stop one heart from breaking,*
> *I shall not live in vain.*
> *If I can ease one life the aching,*
> *Or cool one pain,*
> *Or help one fainting robin,*
> *Unto her nest again,*
> *I shall not live in vain."*

I inhaled slowly. Had I ever felt such love from anyone? His eyes perceived in my soul a beauty I could not perceive in myself. "Eben? This is what you see in me?"

"Lora, I have not dared to speak of love to any woman—not since, well, not for a very long time. But now . . ."

"Why now, Eben?" I did not dare look at him.

"I think, perhaps, time grows short for the world. For me, at last. I have seen so much—too much. But never anything like this. Surely the hour glass has run, and in these final moments, I am permitted to love again."

"Permitted? You speak in riddles."

"Love . . . you . . . Lora. No riddle in that." He did not turn me but stepped around to block my view of the broken city. He held me in his gaze. "Open your eyes. Look at me. Eye to eye. We meet now, in this time and place. I am a man like other men. Do you understand? There is no time. I am in love with you."

I saw my reflection shining in his haunting green eyes and knew he was speaking the truth. He lifted my chin and kissed me gently.

Warm coils unleashed within me. Breathless in his embrace, I could not answer. My knees weakened. I nodded, loving him as I had never loved anyone. Did Eben believe, like so many others, that the world had reached the breaking point?

How many soldiers had proposed with these words: "We must live and love through every remaining hour." Was all the suffering of centuries summed up in this war?

Eben's next words were a statement of fact, not a question. "You love me."

"Yes." I rested my cheek against his chest. "Yes, Eben. I do."

I had never heard a story so horrific or sad or courageous as the story of the four Kopeck children who stood before me. But there was a problem.

The line of waiting refugee children was long. The babble of European languages echoed in the hallway outside my Sunday school room office.

The last transports of evacuee children to the United States were being arranged. Only those children with American relatives or sponsors would receive visas. The clamor and confusion were deafening as I attempted to sort out personal details like some petty government bureaucrat.

"My name is Yehudit Kopeck. My uncle Shmuel, lives in Chicago," insisted a mop-headed Polish teenage girl. Her arms encircled three younger siblings, all boys. They were thin and malnourished. Blue eyes had dark circles beneath them. "Uncle was called Shmuel Kopeck when he left for America, but he changed his name when he became a citizen."

I studied her paperwork. Brief words told of their escape through the woods as the slaughter of their entire village took place within their hearing. Mother and father were machine-gunned and buried in a mass grave. The siblings hid for weeks in the forest before finally making their way on foot to a refugee center at a Sacred Hearts seminary in Belgium.

Then the Nazis broke through the West's defenses and the Kopecks' terror began again.

Their story was so dreadful that surely these four children deserved a place on the evacuee ship to America. But there were too many blank sections on the forms for four children from Poland to be granted visas to America. I asked, "Do you have your uncle's contact information?"

"We lost his address when we lost . . . our parents. How many Jews could there be in

Chicago from Poland, who used to be named Shmuel Kopeck?"

I did not tell her how large the Jewish community in Chicago was, nor that her particular Shmuel, who now had an unknown last name, might be difficult to locate.

Eben had heard the miraculous tale of the four children's survival. He peered above the mob of heads. Pushing through the crowd he made his way upstream to my desk. Anxious, resentful glares followed him. He apologized in at least five languages.

Smiling down at me, Eben took me by the arm and led me to the cloakroom, out of hearing of the children. He remarked quietly in English, "Uncle Shmuel, Chicago? It can be arranged." He winked.

I stuttered an incomplete protest. "But . . . but . . . but . . ."

His lips against my ear, he said, "What these kids have been through, Lora. You know the Jewish Agency in America knows many American Jews in Chicago named Shmuel. Does it matter if it's the right Uncle Shmuel? No. They're going to America. We'll work out the fine print later."

"Tell me how?"

"I'll send a wire. I promise there will be a Jew named Shmuel in Chicago who always dreamed of being uncle to four Jewish orphans."

His warm eyes were luminous. He was so certain of God's mercy and leading. I simply smiled in awe of this man.

"All right then," I said, feeling giddy.

"All right."

"Thanks. Thanks, Eben. You are sort of miraculous sometimes."

He tipped an invisible hat and bowed slightly. "At your service."

I started to return to my desk, but he clasped my arm and spun me around. His eyes drank me in, and I felt the flutter of yearning deep inside. "Eben?" I managed to whisper.

"Lora? And I would like to ask you . . . do you enjoy cinema? American cinema?"

I had seen so very few films since we had come to England. Our budget often put groceries beyond our reach. Going to the cinema was a luxury I had not allowed myself. "I suppose I would. If I could . . ."

He reached into his pocket and pulled out two tickets to the Odeon in Leicester Square. "I show you a miracle. Two tickets to *Gone with the Wind*."

I gasped. "Who did you kill to get them?"

Eben wagged his finger. "No, no, no. You know how many months this has been sold out?"

"Clark Gable." I sighed.

Eben laughed. "A true miracle. Lora Bittick Kepler, you have not had a break in weeks. These were given to me by a colleague from Oxford who was suddenly called away to Dover. He could have sold them, but I had a better plan." The priceless tickets lay in his open palm. "Tonight I am taking you to see *Gone with the Wind*."

In my office after work I changed into a short-sleeved blue frock that was too long and several years out of fashion, but I thought the color would be nice with my eyes. Eben seemed pleased when he rapped on the door and I answered it eagerly.

"You look like a summer sky." He bowed slightly.

"In London that is a very uncertain compliment."

"Well then, beautiful. You are . . . beautiful. I should take you to Simpson's for roast beef."

"Perhaps after the war, Eben."

I did not expect Eben to take me to a restaurant. Instead, I had prepared a meager picnic of our rationed food to share before the cinema. After all, there was rationing in effect, and prices were high. The hotels bought their food in enormous lots and tourists could eat pre-war amounts for five days before their ration coupons were required. With enough cash you could eat as if you lived in America, except . . . no one had cash but Americans. Dinner at Simpson's-in-the-Strand with soup and dessert was a costly two dollars. Though the price of all food items had risen, wages remained low and fixed. Margarine fortified with vitamins was a poor substitute for butter. Eggs were eighty p. a dozen, but we were only allowed four per week. Four ounces a week of bacon and ham per person. Eight ounces of sugar per week and only two ounces of tea. We could only purchase one shilling, tenpence—about 37 cents—per week of meat of any kind.

England's solution was to plant victory gardens in every spare inch of soil. As Eben and I tramped toward the river that evening, every flower box bloomed with purple cabbages and dripped with ripe red tomatoes.

I reasoned that a meal at Simpson's would have been far too elegant for my plain blue frock. And what if the maitre d' asked for our ration coupons? We would have starved afterwards for a week.

So . . . on a bench beside the River Thames, Eben produced a packet of his ration of butter. We shared a plowman's supper of thin cheese sandwiches with chutney, washed down with weak, slightly sweetened tea from a jar. "The most lovely picnic I have had in years," Eben said with a sigh of contentment.

Above us, in the last golden rays of twilight, the great silver barrage balloons swam in the summer sky. Though the German air raids were doubtless closing in again on London, I did not fear the Nazis. I had almost forgotten Eben's words of warning. On such an evening it was hard to imagine the German air force making the short hop across the Channel to drop bombs on our heads.

Behind us the stately Savoy Hotel towered. I was aware that the elite of London could see us as they ordered their meals in the posh Savoy dining room. Perhaps they pitied us our poor meal, but as I munched my slice of bread, I felt as though I was the wealthiest woman in London.

Eben sat back and crossed his muscular arms across his chest. He gazed into the purpling sky. "The moon will shine full tonight. Not a perfect night to go to the cinema. But perhaps the German Luftwaffe will not interrupt us."

Nazi pilots navigated by the silver light of the moon. Moonlight reflecting on the river formed a road map leading to their targets.

"I think it will be a perfect night," I argued, not willing to believe that planes and bombs could interrupt as we watched Clark Gable and Vivien Leigh make love at Tara.

Eben studied me intently. I pretended I did not feel his eyes upon me as I gazed at the barrage balloons. "Look. The wind has picked up. They are trying to break free and sail away."

Eben murmured, *"The moon shines bright. In*

such a night as this, when the sweet wind did gently kiss the trees, And they did make no noise, in such a night. . . ."

I recognized the quote. "Shakespeare? Lorenzo to Jessica, I think. *Merchant of Venice.*"

"The play first performed just there, on a summer night—across the river from where we sit now . . . on such a night as this." He raised his arm and gestured over the brown current. "The Globe Theatre was there. You could shout from here and be heard by the actors."

"You tell it as if it was your own memory."

"Perhaps it is my memory. Of a kind. I see it in my mind from across a gulf of time. What was. What is. What will be. Written in Scripture. Your father knew this."

"You're an Oxford professor through and through, aren't you?"

"I've played many parts."

"Papa kept us in touch with English by reading Shakespeare aloud."

He laughed. "How long was it before you learned Elizabethan English was no longer current?"

"Awhile." I smiled. "Once in Brussels, when I spoke to an American tourist needing directions, I was told I would fit very well into the Amish community in America."

"Thou wouldst."

I studied his profile. His features were

beautiful, strong and chiseled, as though he had emerged from the marble of a Roman statue.

He turned his face to me. Eyes searched my soul, somehow knowing more about me than I knew about myself. "Lora." He leaned close and spoke my name as if he was asking a question.

His face was so near mine. Close enough to kiss. I felt breathless for a moment. I drew back. "It just occurred to me. Eben? I don't know anything about you. Not much anyway. I was a child when I first met you. You don't seem to have a life but this. You were there when we needed you, but . . ."

"No one listened. No one believed."

"How did you know? What was coming? We could not have imagined."

He shrugged. "The past gives us the clearest picture of the future. But this time the violence will surpass anything the world has ever seen."

"How can you know such a thing?" I remembered the fires of Kristallnacht and shuddered.

He did not reply, but I knew he could see what was ahead of us. "I have lived long enough to know. That is all."

"You are alone?"

"Do you mean, was I married?"

"Yes."

"I was. Once. A long time ago."

"What happened?"

"She flew away. Died."

"I'm sorry."

"Leaving this world for the next. She is alive. After life comes life."

"Did you live here?"

"Britannia." He used the ancient name of Great Britain as a scholar might move in and out of a discussion on western civilization.

"Have you lived alone, long?" I contemplated my own loneliness. As long as I had known Eben, he had never mentioned a wife.

"Too long." He stood abruptly as though the subject was too painful for him. "Centuries. Her name was Lily, and her hair was fair. The color of stalks of wheat glistening in the sun." Gently, he brushed my hair back from my cheek. "Her eyes, the color of . . . bluebells. Like your eyes, Lora." He blinked at me as though seeing me for the first time. "I thought I recognized you; knew you; the instant I saw you at your father's house. You were so young. So long ago."

"Switzerland," I said.

"Was it? I thought we were last together . . . somewhere else. So long ago." He gazed at me with such longing. Was he seeing Lily's face? I could not mistake his unspoken thought or the familiar touch that accompanied his words to me. I resembled Lily, his beloved.

I looked at the far shore of the Thames and imagined I could see Eben with his Lily sitting beside the river. Another time. "I am sorry for your loss."

"And I? I am sorry for yours, Lora."

"Does it grow easier with time, Eben? Missing her? Living without love?" I asked for my own sake.

His smile was bitter, his reply curt. "No."

His honesty stung me. I had somehow envisioned growing content with loneliness. "The cinema . . . such a love story. Have we missed it? Are we too late?"

Eben paused before he answered. "Too late? I truly hope not." I knew he was not answering the question I had asked, but another. Glancing at his wristwatch, he extended his hand to me. "The world as I once knew it, Lora . . . *Gone with the Wind*."

29

Eben and I were ushered to our seats in the crowded theatre as the musical prelude to *Gone with the Wind* played. The atmosphere was thick with the buzz of anticipation. House lights dimmed. The audience applauded and then fell silent. The music swelled as the red velvet curtain drew back.

Eben took my hand in his and slid his other arm around my shoulders. I did not resist. The love story began.

Vivien Leigh as Scarlett O'Hara looked remarkably like Eva, I thought. As Scarlett flirted with her southern beaus, I leaned closer against Eben. His jacket smelled of bay rum, cloves, and talcum. Strong fingers stroked my palm. The film flickered on the screen. Embers within me flickered, then sparked. I closed my eyes and inhaled the clean masculine aroma of Eben. Delicious warmth poured over me; electric desire coursed through me. I resisted the urge to bury my face against his neck. Scene by scene and line by line I imagined Eben as Rhett Butler, pulling me close against him in a passionate embrace. I only half heard the dialogue. I played out more intimate scenes in my mind.

The intermission lights came up.

"Well, what do you think?" Eben asked.

I did not dare look at him. Did what I was feeling show in my expression? "Wonderful."

"It is warm in here." He stood. "Your face is flushed."

"Is it?" My hand flew to my cheek. I felt my color deepen. There was nothing I could do about my cursed tendency to blush.

I was certain I would not, could not, breathe, unless Eben's lips touched mine before the night was over.

"I think Rhett will tame Scarlett," Eben said.

"I do hope so." I once more pictured Eben pulling me into his arms and kissing me hungrily.

I felt my face redden again and hoped Eben would not notice.

"So," he said cheerfully, "it's been a very long time for you, eh?"

I swallowed hard. Was he a mind reader? "Long time?"

"You said it had been a very long time since you had been to a cinema."

"Oh! That. Yes." I fanned myself with a program. "I should. Come. More often. Good for language skills."

He observed me with unconcealed amusement. "You should. Perhaps I will come. We will. If you like, more often."

Inane conversation passed between us. It was something like lighting a candle to read by while the house was on fire.

The music began again and, ready for Act 2, everyone took their seats.

Eben put his arm around me. The electric current in my core uncoiled slowly. I grew weak at his touch. Hopeless, I leaned away from his arm and clasped my hands together. He looked at me curiously. The corner of his mouth turned up slightly. Did he understand what his touch had done to me?

Atlanta burned. Rhett rescued Scarlett and Miss Millie from the Yankees. Something wonderful and powerful had reignited within me. I had known breathless, awkward love with the boy I had married, but only briefly. When I had learned of Varrick's death, I had decided it was enough to live the rest of my life, merely remembering what it had been like to lay in a man's arms and yield to his kisses. That night, as I sat beside Eben, I knew memory was not enough. I felt alive again. I wondered when Eben had last held his beloved in his arms.

No sooner had we emerged from the theatre than the air-raid sirens began to wail. Since it was exactly straight up on the hour of eleven, all London's clocks and bell towers appeared to also protest the disruption of the peaceful, romantic night.

If the blacked-out byways of London were a pit of gloom, then the plunge inside the closely curtained Oxford Street underground station was to enter the mouth of something like Dante's vision of hell. The steps were lined with reflective tape, but the procession of pedestrians tramping into the depths was so closely packed and so orderly that little guidance was needed. When we reached a landing and turned a corner, small electric lights again provided their dim glow. Even so I was grateful to have Eben in front of me, where the presence of his back beneath my hand was a comforting reassurance.

All talking was subdued, almost as if the Londoners feared their conversation would climb to the ears of the German pilots. Once we reached the level of the train platform the crowd spread out. Movement slowed, like a wave subsiding on a sandy shore.

"I'm scared, 'arry," said a woman who trod on my toe as she searched for her husband in the mob. "Ooh, I'm sorry, dearie. Beg yer pardon."

"Now don't fret, old girl," returned Harry. "Naught to be a'frighted of. This is what'yer call just a precaution."

"Not a raid, then?"

Eben reached up and patted my hand where I had let it remain on his shoulder.

"Them Nazees," Harry explained patiently. "Bombin' all them warehouses and ships down t'the river. But never you mind, Myrtle. We'll be out in the air again quick as Bob's yer uncle."

"I do hope yer right, 'arry."

"Me too," Eben whispered with a grin in his tone.

That was just before the distant thump of anti-aircraft fire reached our ears. Buried as we were, it was impossible to judge directions, but it was clear the sounds came from a great distance at first, then drew nearer and nearer. Soon smaller caliber fire added its rasping pop to the heavier *whomps* of artillery.

"Hang onter me, 'arry!"

"Must be close," Eben muttered. "They don't waste ammunition if they don't have targets."

I pictured the soldiers up the street from my house, the ones atop the knoll in Primrose Hill Park. Their searchlights must even now be stabbing the sky, trying to pin the invading bombers like moths to a velvet-lined box.

"What's 'at?" Myrtle demanded as an ominous drone penetrated even past the racket of bursting shells.

"Heinkels," Eben answered. Under his breath he added, "German bombers. Slow but . . . just keep close."

I needed no urging. Scenes from the burning of Atlanta played over and over in my head—fearful flames that reached above the level of the housetops.

The floor jumped beneath my feet as the first of the German bombs detonated. Like a thunderstorm heard rolling in from afar, the explosions gathered force and speed. With each succeeding thump the pavement under my feet bounced. The mob on the platform swayed drunkenly. The lights flickered.

Myrtle groaned. "Why'd we hafter come t'the West End, 'arry? Whyn't we stay where we belonged?"

I wondered where in London she thought was safe when bombs rained down so impersonally. A half-dozen detonations underscored my point, followed by three more in quick succession.

At last the raid seemed to be relenting. People

began to offer each other crooked smiles, registering, *See, that wasn't so bad, was it?*

That was when the biggest, closest blast rocked the tube station with the force of an earthquake. My skull bounced off the brick wall of the tunnel, and I saw stars that were never really visible beneath Oxford Street. Eben sank with me to the floor, cradling my head beneath him and sheltering me with his body.

Myrtle screamed as the lights flared and winked out, plunging us into absolute blackness. Plaster dust dribbled down from overhead, causing some to shout that the tunnel was collapsing.

But the tube station remained intact, and in a minute the lights came back on.

The all-clear sounded, but there was no immediate rush toward the exits. The hesitation betrayed by the crowd showed our desire to be absolutely certain the danger had passed.

"There you are, luv," Harry said. "Right as rain."

" 'arry," Myrtle returned, "don't never take me to a West End picture show never again."

So the burning of Atlanta had been in her thoughts too!

No one in the Oxford Street shelter was seriously hurt. Any scrapes and bruises, unlike the lump on my head, were more a result of being crammed into a narrow lair with a couple hundred other humans than from any action of the German bombs. The shared experience of living through a bombing raid caused a kind of camaraderie in the group emerging from the Underground.

There were jokes and a general air of good humor. This atmosphere continued until the head of the file exited the stairs. Then came an abrupt change in attitude: stifled exclamations of horror, accompanied by the wail of sirens.

No more than two blocks away, a house in the middle of a row of others had received a direct hit. The scene was illuminated by burning buildings on either side of the gap. The smoke billowing up to overhang the scene and the orange light peering out the windows combined to create the illusion of a skull: fiery eyes surmounted a gapping-jawed smile.

My hand flew to my mouth. I was shocked at the devastation. My sense of disbelief was heightened because only seconds before we had been laughing and joking.

Eben allowed me no time for self-recrimination. Grabbing me by the elbow, he dragged me north up Regent Street toward the fires. "They may need help," he shouted.

The building that had completely disappeared in the blast was no more than half a hundred yards from All Souls Church and the Langham Hotel across from it. Fire crews were already on scene, but they directed their hoses at the structures flanking the bombsite.

I tried to recall what had occupied the now vacant space: a three-story-high set of shops, offices, and flats had ceased to exist in the blink of an eye. What was left of it consisted of two piles of bricks: one partially blocking Little Portland Street, while the other spilled a trail of masonry guts across Mortimer Street like a slaughtered stone beast.

Eben ran ahead of me as I struggled in my dress shoes to climb over fragments of roof slates and chunks of cornice. He arrived in front of the surviving house just west of the bomb crater even as two men emerged from the building. An Air Raid Warden with the letters *A.R.P.* stenciled on his tin hat, and a passerby in shirtsleeves with a cut on his forehead, appeared on the steps, carrying an unconscious woman between them. Eben helped lift her over a heap of debris and lower her to a clear bit of sidewalk on the far side of the street. The firemen continued to play their streams of water on the upper floors of her building.

She lay very still.

"Is she . . . ?" I said.

The warden looked up at me. "Just knocked out, miss," he reassured me. "No wounds visible. Found her on the stairs."

I knelt beside the woman and the men relinquished her to my care. The warden handed me a folded blanket, which I placed under her

423

head. She appeared to be about thirty years of age. Her honey-blond hair was pushed back from her face as if she had just combed it with her fingers. A gold wedding band and gold cross on a chain around her neck were all her jewelry. Her white blouse was unwrinkled and her dark skirt unmussed. She was in her stocking feet. She might have been napping.

"Keep clear!" a fireman shouted. "There's a ruptured gas main the next street over."

As if entering the stage on cue, a sheet of bright yellow flame erupted from the ground floor of the woman's house. The firemen hastily backed away. They now concentrated their efforts on an adjoining undamaged house. "That one's a goner, that is," one of them said. "But we can save the rest of the block . . . maybe."

The woman's eyelids fluttered. Calling Eben to me, I noted, "She's coming 'round."

Unfocused eyes gazed upward for a space of a dozen blinks, then the victim asked, "Where am I? What happened?"

As I began to explain she abruptly sat upright. "Take it easy," I said. "You're safe. What's your name?"

"Name?" she repeated dully, looking about as if missing something but not sure what it was.

"Jenny," she answered, then, "Bill! Where's my boy, Bill? Have you seen him? He was in the kitchen when I went down to get the post."

The heads of the two rescue workers, as well as Eben's and mine, pivoted toward the burning building. As we stared at the blazing upper stories, Jenny's gaze was drawn to follow.

Then she screamed and struggled against my grip on her shoulders. "He's still in there! I know it! Bill! Bill!"

While the other two men sat paralyzed, Eben grabbed the blanket. Draping it over his head and shoulders, he sprinted toward the firefighters. "Wet me down," he said. "I'm going in."

"First floor up," the frantic mother called out. "At the back."

"You'll never make it," I heard one of the firemen reply.

Nevertheless, their hoses soaked him thoroughly even while I cried, "Eben! Eben!"

Jenny and I hugged each other as Eben dashed up the steps. I saw him hesitate only an instant as a tongue of fire licked the porch above him. Ducking his head, Eben darted inside and disappeared.

"Upstairs. At the back," Jenny repeated over and over, as if Eben could still hear her. Perhaps the power of her desperation added to my anxious prayers could guide him through the thick, black smoke and curling flames.

How long could he stay inside? Already the heat of the blaze was scorching the plaster next door. Little drips of lead fell sizzling from the rain gutters and roof seams as fire burst through above.

I felt the heat boiling out of the conflagration even from the other side of the street. My face prickled with it, while the distracted mother was reduced to hoarse cries and tearless sobs.

"Best come away, miss," the warden said. "Let me help you move back."

"No!" I replied fiercely. "Help him. Him!"

And then Eben was there, tottering at the top of the stairs. The blanket was steaming, and his clothes and face were streaked black. In his arms was a tow-headed five-year-old—very much alive and anxious to get to his mother. Eben delivered the child into the arms of the warden, then pitched forward into mine.

Suddenly our world was upside down. Eben dusted himself off and made ineffectual daubs with his handkerchief at his face. London was alight with fires from burning structures. Smoke rising over the city turned the moon blood red.

Eben grasped my hand and pulled me quickly along the burning street, out of the damaged shopping area and down toward the untouched dark reaches of the city.

Down past Piccadilly Circus and Leicester Square we went, and on beyond Trafalgar. "There's more to come," he said. "Hurry!"

In the distance we could hear the crump of bombs falling on the warehouses of the East End where so many refugees were interned.

Almost in the same instant the siren wailed again and men and women scrambled back into shelters. Eben did not turn to the right or the left but continued toward the Embankment and the Savoy Hotel, which was among London's few buildings fortified by steel. We charged into the unlit, deserted lobby. Flames from an inferno across the river lit up the interior that flickered softly. A doorman, looking strangely out of place in his livery, shouted over his shoulder as he ran that we must take shelter in the basement with the other guests.

Eben said, "Go, Lora. Get to the shelter. This will last all night."

I did not let go of his hand. "I want to stay with you, Eben."

"You're not afraid?"

"No."

"All right, then."

We walked calmly together into the dining room. The bandstand was deserted, instruments abandoned and sheet music strewn across the floor. Meals were left uneaten on dining tables overlooking the Thames and the blazing docks. The orange conflagration reflected in the water of the Thames was strangely beautiful and terrifying, like the images on the screen of the burning of Atlanta. In the distance the hollow, ringing thump of anti-aircraft blasted away at the empty German bombers.

More would certainly be headed our way before long.

Eben found a table beside the open doors leading to a balcony. There was roast beef, roast potatoes, and fresh dinner rolls set out before us. We were alone in the most elegant dining room in London.

"We should eat before the next wave arrives," Eben said, as if expecting nothing more consequential than a train. "They will use the fires along the Thames as a path to guide them here from France."

"What will happen?"

"They will drop more bombs."

"Eben?"

"Yes, Lora?"

"You are not afraid?"

"No."

"Never?"

"Never for my own sake. No."

"Why? How are you unafraid?"

"I am certain of what comes after this. What is beyond the horizon. So I am not afraid."

"How can you know?"

"I have seen it."

"Seen it? I am speaking of . . . Eben? I am not speaking of earthly things."

"Nor am I."

"Who are you?" I whispered. "Where do you come from?"

"Another place. Another time. You know, Lora. Don't you? Your heart knows me. I have seen it in your eyes. In your smile. You know."

Yes. He was right. I had known all along that he was a man, yet unlike other men. But I still could not comprehend that my suspicions could be more than imagination. "What am I to do with you?"

"Marry me."

"Marry?"

"I meant to ask you tonight. I believe there is so little time left for the world, Lora. I feel I must taste happiness . . . live for a while like other men live."

I tested my suspicions. "Like younger men?"

He laughed. "If you like."

"How long have you waited to love me?"

"A very long time. Centuries. What do you say?"

"It has felt like centuries since I first loved you. Yes, Eben. I will marry you."

We raised our glasses and toasted whatever future we might have together in this broken world.

And so we ate. Our meal was a banquet. I had not tasted such a fine meal since the summer at the White Rose Inn. By the light of burning buildings I could see the bench where Eben and I had shared our meager picnic only hours before. He poured two glasses of champagne. We toasted *L'Chaim*: "To Life."

Eben drew his chair close to mine and pulled me against his chest. He stroked my cheek and kissed me gently, as though my lips were wine to savor. Tracing my chin with his forefinger, he lifted my face to his. Warm eyes drank me in, devoured me. Then his mouth covered mine. He kissed me urgently, fiercely, tasting my mouth with his tongue. Embers of desire ignited within me. Desperate with long dormant desire, I returned his kisses.

His breath brushed my face and neck. "In the morning, my White Rose. We will marry, and I will make you mine at last."

"Yes. Oh, Eben!" I whispered. Yielding to his touch, my resistance melted in his fierce embrace. I longed for him to take me away; to find a quiet place where I could lie in his arms through the night. "Please." I sighed. "Now."

Suddenly a siren screamed as the next wave of German bombers swarmed up the Thames. He raised his head and took my hands, leading me out onto the balcony.

Searchlights bored into the black canopy of night like white pillars holding up the sky. Lights locked on the German bombers. Black swastikas on tails were plainly visible.

Bombs began to explode upriver. Anti-aircraft guns boomed. Eben held me and searched my face. "Lora, suddenly I am afraid . . . truly . . . I don't want to lose you. Do you understand? I want to spend the rest of my life with you."

Luftwaffe bombers came in relays.

British fighter planes soared almost vertically into battle, as bombs rained down throughout the long night. But in Eben's strong arms I was not afraid.

We rode the tube to Hampstead Village and climbed out of the deep tube station on High Street while it was still dark.

"Would you like to come to my flat?" For years Eben had kept a tiny, one-room, pied-à-terre on Church Row.

"No. Better not." My hand in his was electric. Knowing what was ahead, I felt weak from his touch.

"A cup of tea?"

"A cup of tea alone with you could be dangerous."

His laugh was husky, and I knew I was right. "Later, then. I'll fix you tea after we are properly married."

"I'll fix you tea and bring it to you in bed."

In that moment I remembered the nights Varrick and I had shared together. We had been so young—so eager and clumsy in our lovemaking.

I knew this time that experiencing passion in Eben's arms would be different.

Eben took me to a park bench on the edge of the heath. He held me close as we watched the red sun rise through the smoke to hover above the smoldering ruins of London.

He knew the elderly priest at St. Mary's Church, Hampstead, and had asked him to marry us first thing in the morning.

"Should I be offended?" I asked, as we slowly walked toward the church.

"Offended?"

"You arranged for the wedding before you asked me to marry you."

"I didn't want to waste any time."

"What if I had said no?"

"I would have taken Father Brocke to breakfast at the Hollybush, and he would have told me it was all for the best that you had refused me in these uncertain times."

"You thought it all out."

"No. I knew you would say yes. Fresh linens and cleaned the place. I bought a new brass bed. Delivered yesterday. It fills up my room."

"Not too big, I hope. I wouldn't want to have to look for you."

"It's a very small room. So you can always find me."

"You were certain of me."

"From the moment I saw you again in . . ." He

shook his head as if in amazement. "Not a child, Lora. But a beautiful, beautiful woman."

I did not have a watch. I did not have a change of clothes. Perhaps it did not matter. "What time is the wedding?"

"Before early service. Seven."

"So early. You're in a hurry," I teased.

He stood and looked over the smoke-filled basin of London beneath our vantage point. "Today will be our day. Tonight I suppose the bombers will come back."

"I don't think I'll notice, Eben." He tugged me to my feet and I pressed myself heavily against his chest.

One more kiss and then we walked back along the wooded path to the Georgian houses on Church Row. Eben pointed up to the open windows of his garret room.

We turned onto the steep narrow lane called Holly Place that sloped up past the iron gate of the graveyard to little St. Mary's. The entrance of the church could easily be missed. Its white façade was only as wide as one house, but inside it opened up into a plainly decorated space with high whitewashed walls and a dark-beamed ceiling. The crucifix above the altar was the focal point.

Father Brocke was dressed in his clerical robes and waiting when Eben and I arrived. He was a small, balding, cheerful man with sharp features and a broad smile. His Irish brogue was only slightly diminished by long years in England.

"Ah, Eben! I prayed for your success with the young lady all the long night through. I hope this is the one you were after, and you've not had to fall in love with another."

"This is Lora." Eben seemed proud to introduce me.

Father Brocke beamed. "Heaven is smilin'. I see you won her over! Took you all night, as I said. Lovely! Lovely! A brilliant mornin' to be wed, eh?"

Suddenly shy, I shook his hand. Pleasantries were exchanged, then Father looked at his wristwatch and declared that the exiled leader of the Free French, General Charles DeGaulle, would be arriving for morning worship and we had better hop to it. He called a janitor and the organist to serve as witnesses.

And so we were married. No music. No march down the aisle. No guests. No public celebration. Eben's vows were so muted with emotion I could barely hear him. And I could not speak above a whisper. Yet my heart was so filled with love for Eben that the covenant we made seemed so much higher and deeper than any promises ever made between a man and a woman. I felt the presence of angels; Papa and Mama at my side.

Father Brocke recited the words ". . . till death

do you part?" Eben shook his head slowly from side to side. "Not even death shall part us."

Only minutes passed before Father Brocke blessed us and said, "Before God and man I now pronounce you man and wife. Mr. and Mrs. Eben Golah. Glory be, it's a good thing I'm not hard of hearin'! That's the quietest weddin' I've ever presided over. Any questions? Well then, Eben, my boy! You may now kiss the bride."

Church Row was just waking up as Eben led me home to his garret flat. Workmen were already at work removing ornate iron railing outside the Georgian townhouse to be melted into bullets and tanks.

A narrow private stairway led to the tiny room tucked beneath the eaves. He turned the key in the old-fashioned lock. Hinges groaned as the door swung open to reveal a brass bed. Fresh white linens were neatly turned back over a white bedspread.

"What would you have done if I had said no?" I smiled.

He did not reply but kissed my mouth. I grew weak. He swept me into his arms and carried me across the threshold. It was a moment before I opened my eyes. He held me, my arms around his neck, as I took in the details of his flat.

I smelled a hint of new paint. The walls were the color of fresh cream. The open window was framed by cornflower blue curtains. A small table with two plain wooden chairs overlooked the Row. Two teacups and a centerpiece of white roses told me Eben had been expecting me.

A chest of drawers stood against the opposite wall beneath framed magazine engravings of scenes from Shakespeare. A pale green alarm clock ticked loudly in front of a neat row of books that lined the top of the dresser. Stacks of volumes formed a sort of multi-colored wainscot around the four walls of the space. A tall walnut wardrobe was beside the yellow door leading to the WC.

Eben carried me to the bed. He lay down beside me. I still clung to him. The pillows were crisp and smelled like fresh lavender.

His face was above me. I was lost in his eyes.

I admitted, "Eben, I don't know. . . ."

"Would you like a cup of tea?" He brushed his mouth over my lips. "First?"

My pulse quickened. "Eben, I love you," I whispered, as a rush of desire swept through me.

His words stroked my cheek. "Lora . . . I have waited. Waited for you so long. So long. It's all right, my darling. No hurry."

Eager, I fumbled with the buttons of his shirt. He kissed the palm of my hand. "Love is a slow dance on a warm night. Listen—you will feel it in my heartbeat. I will lead and you? You follow . . .

move with my touch." He traced the curve of my hip with his fingertip. "You see?"

I nodded, unable to speak.

Undressing me slowly, he savored each new revelation. His hands and lips explored the landscape of my body tenderly, awakening feelings I had never known.

The late summer day passed slowly, divided between passion, drowsy contentment, and desire reawakened by a sigh. Love was our music. Eben and I danced to a rhythm only we two could hear.

30

It was late afternoon when the workmen on Church Row tossed the last desecrated morsel of decorative iron onto the wagon. Cockney voices faded away toward Flask Walk, the pub, and a pint of Guinness. Silence, punctuated by footsteps on the pavement, fell like a curtain as the sun sank lower in the west.

Exhausted from ecstasy, I fell asleep with my face on Eben's chest. The steady beat of his heart in my ear was like a lullaby.

It was almost dark when I awoke. Reaching out for Eben, I opened my eyes with a jolt of panic. I was alone in the bed. Alone in the garret. Where was he?

Wrapping myself in the sheet, I stood in the center of the now gloomy room.

"Eben?" I listened for some movement in the WC or the hallway. His trousers and summer jacket were gone. How had he slipped out without me knowing? And why? Where had he gone?

I bathed and washed my hair in the cold water of the tin tub. All the while I grew more anxious.

What if the bombers came while Eben was away? What if he was hurt in a raid and could not make it back to me? How would I live without him now that he had aroused me from my long dormant sleep? How would I live through even one night without him?

The hour of blackout drew near. The last rays of sunlight tinted the clouds red above the heath. How incredibly my life had changed in these few short hours.

I dressed in yesterday's blue dress and went to the window to scan the Row for some sign of him.

And then I saw the note and a single red rose beside the vase of white roses.

Darling Lora, Didn't want to awaken you. Such a day. I have gone to fetch a few things you'll need. Took your ration book along. Forgive me. I fear we have forgotten to eat today. I know you must be hungry. Make tea. Kettle on the electric plate. Back soon. E.

I inhaled slowly with relief. The scent of roses filled my senses. I glanced down and saw a crisp white envelope with the words inscribed, A GIFT FOR LORA.

I opened the envelope and found a black and white photograph of myself, giddy and gangly, as I perched on the front steps of the White Rose Inn four years and a lifetime ago. Eben's image was also captured in the frame. Though he was exiting through the doorway behind me the moment the photo was snapped, he had not escaped being recorded there.

I gazed at the faded memory, struck by one thing more than any other: though I had bloomed into a woman, Eben had not changed at all. He had not aged one minute from the instant the shutter clicked. He had neither gained a pound nor lost an ounce. His perfect teeth gleamed in the photo as they did when he smiled at me this morning.

The envelope contained a slip of parchment decorated with a vertical rose trellis of thirty-six words without punctuation. The roses were intermingled red and white and trimmed with delicate Hebrew letters.

Sunset
Raspberry
Sky
Ripens
Delicious
Thoughts

Awaken
Long
Dormant
Seeking
Light
Desire
Stirs
Impatient
Shoots
Spiral
Upward
Penetrating
Warm
Yielded
Soil
I
Taste
Your
Summer
Mouth
Breathless
Sweet
Longing
Lingers
On
My
Tongue
You
Consume
Me

I pressed Eben's poem to my heart and glanced out the window as the last red-tinged beam of light faded from the sky.

Thirty-six words contained worlds and galaxies. They spun and collided and hummed and sang a hundred different messages to me.

Who was this man I had married? What sort of soul could capture my longing and our love in thirty-six words?

I turned at the sound of his footfall on the stairs. The key turned in the lock and the door swung wide.

He remained in shadow for a moment and I waited for him to come into the light.

"I see you found it."

"Eben?" I sighed. "What am I going to do with you? It is so high."

He entered and placed a bag of groceries on the table. Crushing me against his chest, he kissed me hard, his tongue probing my mouth.

When at last we breathed, he said, "I never knew it could be like this."

"I was desperate that you weren't next to me."

"And I. In the line at the bakery, I could think of nothing but you. You!"

We drew the blackout curtains and lit two candles. At eight o'clock the church bells rang the same instant the air-raid siren wailed.

I vaguely remember asking Eben if we should go to the High Street tube station. If he answered me, his words were lost beneath the alarm and the sound of hurrying feet running toward the public shelter.

Eben and I lay awake, the only souls in Hampstead still above ground, as the boom of artillery and the crump of bombs shattered the night.

I was not afraid when, later, Eben led me to the White Stone Pond at the top of the hill, and we watched with horror and fascination as London burned at our feet.

I held Eben's hand. His face was golden in the light of the flames. "Are you afraid, Eben?"

He hesitated a moment before he replied. "Not until now. And now I fear only one thing. Only one . . . living the rest of my life without you."

"It won't happen." I rested my head against his arm. "Not now. Not after so much."

"Well, then," he said quietly as we started toward home. "I'm not afraid of anything."

The next evening German bombers again ravaged London. That night Eben and I decided to stay outdoors.

"We are watchmen on the walls," he said as he guided me to a park bench at the top of Primrose Hill. There was not a glimmer of light from any window in the village behind us. Below, the face of London was veiled.

He sat beside me, so close I could feel his knee

against mine. Looking up, we drank in the innumerable stars above us. "So, in the darkness of war the heavens awaken with light. This is the sky as it was two thousand years ago."

He said those words with such conviction that I almost believed he had stood on this hill in ancient times and looked into a starlit sky.

I settled in. "Heaven is too far away. Something like that. Eva said it to me about when Poland fell, and no one came to help. She said, 'God is too high up, and England is too far away.' I said something like it myself when we fled from Brussels."

He did not reply for what seemed like a long time. He sighed and spoke quietly, as though our voices might stir a curtain and let a gleam of light out to guide an enemy. "God was never too high, but always waiting for England to take a stand for His kingdom."

"My father always hoped." I fixed my eye on the brightest star and imagined it was a window through which Papa could see me below. "But nothing came of it. Only talk while the devil made his plans to conquer the world."

Eben answered, "I was sorry to hear the news about your father."

"It was inevitable. The earth can't bear men who are so good, so filled with God's light."

"No. So it has always been. I have seen it again and again and no one learns. The next generation

443

all is forgotten and the cycle begins again. The godly are the first to fall."

"You speak as if you have lived it." I inhaled deeply and let my breath out slowly. "Varrick is dead. He was barely more than a boy when I last saw him. I loved him as a girl can love a boy. Not like you and me. But I don't know what he died for. Or why. So young. Only that he is dead."

Eben said, "I am sorry."

"You said so."

"I mean it. I am sorry."

"That makes two of us who care."

"You sound bitter." He seemed surprised.

"Not bitter. Just so weary, Eben. Before you loved me, I never really knew happiness. My whole life. And now . . . all the rest. Varrick barely had a chance to live. I don't know the details. Not how he died, or when. Nothing really. Just that I heard he was dead, then believed he was alive, and now he isn't." I turned my face to Eben. "Do you think they see us? Or is it too sad for them to look?"

"They are alive. I know this. They are a cloud of witnesses who cheer the living on toward the goal."

"And what is the goal?" I raised my hand toward the pinpoints of light.

"Heaven. Heaven is our goal. It is . . . quite different than we imagine."

Eben's certainty annoyed me. How could he say

such a thing? How could he know? "I suppose it is. It would have to be very different from earth or it would not be heaven. I have about decided that, except for you, earth is more a mirror of hell. If anything happened to you, I hope I would not live long if the Nazis invade England. That's all. I hope I will die at the barricades fighting the men who killed my father."

"Don't be in such a hurry."

"Why? What would I have to live for?"

He stood up abruptly. There was irritation in his tone. Unmistakable. "You must live to speak for those who have no voice. For people who have lost more than you, Lora."

"You make me sound selfish."

"Before this war is finished, the world will be filled with broken men and weeping women."

"It already is."

"We have only begun. And you are weary?"

"Who isn't?"

He took my hand and lifted me to my feet. "Come on. Let's walk. Tonight may be our last night. I think it will be the last for a very long time."

"What do you mean?"

Suddenly his voice was animated. "Do you hear that?"

I shook my head, and then I heard a nightingale singing.

"He sounds anxious," I said. "And nearby."

We traced the warbling to the limb of a plane tree encircled by a fringe of brush. "He's not afraid of us," I said.

"He's waiting," Eben noted, standing very still and listening. "Waiting for us to do something for him? I don't know."

A faint scrabbling reached me. It seemed to come from a pile of fallen leaves just at the base of the tree trunk. A mouse?

As soon as I moved toward the leaves the nightingale trilled even louder.

"Careful," Eben warned.

The muted flutter came again. "I think it's a . . ." And it was. Buried in leaves, covered in dust, was a female nightingale with a broken wing. Her weak cries were pitiful. "Can't we take her home, Eben?" I said. "Perhaps we can save her."

"Of course, but we'll have to hurry."

I recognized immediately what he meant: from out of the distance in the direction of the sea came the ominous rumble of approaching airplanes.

"The blackout will not stop them, Lora. Nor will the sea. Nor any barricade. They will keep coming, now. Stand and be strong." The last word fell from his lips as the air-raid siren began to wail.

Sheltering the injured bird beneath my jacket, so that I could feel the throbbing of her heart against my own, we carried her into the shelter. And when the all-clear sounded, we took her home with us.

31

There could not have been a gloomier day. Eben had been gone for eight days. The nights passed in the restlessness of longing. Why hadn't he written?

The postman slid the mail through the slot just as the teakettle came to a boil. I set the tea steeping and hurried downstairs.

Among the letters was a postcard from Jessica and a thin white envelope addressed to me in Eben's handwriting. Thin meant a poem. I laughed and held the envelope to my heart. Closing my eyes, I imagined him alone in a dim hotel room, thinking of me.

I scanned Jessica's brief note in tiny cramped handwriting:

Weather fine. Baby healthy. Met a very nice American airman from Texas at a community dance. Fellow lost his arm . . . had so much in common might go out with him again.

Jessica signed off with *"wish you were here!"*

I smiled to think of my sister grasping hold of her life again with both hands. It did not matter if the Texan only had one hand to hold her with, Jessica sounded so happy.

I propped Eben's unopened letter on the table

and prepared my tea. I savored the aroma of Darjeeling and the delicious anticipation of reading.

I only lasted through two sips of hot tea and a cookie before I opened the envelope with a butter knife and took out the lined sheet of legal paper.

"It is! It is another poem!" I whispered. Unfolding the sheet, I began to read, and summer nights filled the room.

My darling Lora, Remembering summer nights, I am thinking only of you . . .

lilac
breeze
white
sighs
linen
stirs
your
breath
silken
nuance
brushes
my
cheek
urgent
you
whisper
me

awake
Lips
part
one
kiss
suddenly
fierce
we
dance
soaring
swirling
swaying

I read it. I read it again. Each time I emphasized a different word or phrase until a hundred messages of Eben's longing took shape.

It was twilight before I set it aside.

I spoke his words aloud: *"You consume me . . ."*

How I wished that we could be together every minute. He understood my hunger for him and felt the same for me. Our delight in one another was a banquet.

My tea was cold when I replaced the poem. I heard the sound of an airplane passing overhead. It was one of ours, but I thought again about the bombing raids and burned-out hulks of buildings. What if a bomb fell on our little flat? What if Eben's poems were burned in a fire? What if . . . ?

Considering the loss of lives and the loss of

everything else, this seemed a strange, selfish terror. Nevertheless, I frowned and kissed the missive and searched for someplace safe to keep it.

I looked at the tall chest of drawers and remembered Eben kept receipts in a sturdy metal box in his top drawer.

Eagerly, before I drew the blackout curtains, I gathered all his letters and poems, removed the metal box, and opened it on the table.

The last rays of sunlight gleamed through the window and glinted on something bright beneath bits of paper and ration cards.

"What's this?" I asked as if he was there. Lifting a book of ration stickers, I gasped.

Beneath everything was a familiar envelope inscribed in red ink. The flap was open, revealing a man's silver cigarette case and a pressed poppy. Where had I seen this before? I removed it and held it up to the light.

The case that was so familiar to me, yet I could not remember where I had seen it last.

Curious, I opened it. A lock of hair and a photograph tumbled out. I read the inscription. I gasped and read it again.

My memory suddenly flooded with the vision of the man without a face who lived at a cemetery in Flanders. I remembered saying to Judah Blood as I read the inscription, *"I feel like I'm eavesdropping . . ."*

Could this be the same cigarette case? I knew, somehow, it had to be! How had Judah Blood managed to get it to Eben before Judah slipped beneath the waves at Dunkirk?

Impossible!

But how had Eben come by it?

I stood motionless as the last gleam of daylight faded.

Who was Judah Blood? Who was the man who lived behind the mask in Tyne Cott?

I remembered his hands; the hands of an artist; of a healer; a man dedicated to saving lives and mending broken hearts.

The memory of Judah Blood's hands on the desk were vivid. Familiar hands.

What had he said to me that day? "I could use your face as a model for the Madonna . . ."

I sank onto the chair and caressed the box. "Oh Jesus!" I cried. Then I noticed the bottom was false. Removing the contents, I plucked at a leather tab and lifted it.

A blue silk kerchief concealed something about the size and shape of a man's open palm. I slammed the lid and walked away. If Eben wanted me to know, he would have told me.

I drew the blackout curtains, as if by resisting temptation for a moment, I could overcome my desire to know what this thing was.

Switching on the table lamp beside the bed, I hung back. The light reflected on the cigarette case. The box with its contents, strewn on the table seemed to speak.

Judah Blood at his desk in Tyne Cott.

The bouquet of poppies in the artillery shell vase.

"Loralei Bittick—Kepler. Missus . . . Varrick Kepler. A happy ending after all . . ."

Somehow that evening, I resisted the temptation to pull back the blue silk scarf.

I did not yield to my curiosity to discover what, if anything, Eben had kept from me. I replaced the false bottom and then the cigarette case treasure from Tyne Cott, covering the mystery with ration books and receipts.

As the lid snapped shut and I returned it to its place and closed the drawer, I told myself it was nothing; just nothing. I believed that he would tell me what I needed to know about him, if it was important for me.

I fixed myself a fresh pot of tea, filling Mama's Meissen china teacup with comfort. I pressed my lips on the gold rim and sipped, remembering Mama smiling at me over a cuppa. I suddenly missed her. Terribly. And how I missed Jessica! I wanted to go north to Wales and meet her new beau. I longed to hold the baby. Shalom! Peace! How desperately I wanted to live an ordinary life. I knew that real living was made up of ordinary moments all strung together like the notes on a sheet of music. And in the end of life all those ordinary moments would make one eternal symphony of praise in heaven.

I closed my eyes, savoring the metaphor. I made a mental note to tell Eben all about it when I saw him.

An air-raid siren sounded moments later. I emptied Mama's teacup and wrapped it up, placing it in my purse. The hurried footsteps of our neighbors tramped down the stairs. The front door opened and slammed shut. Voices called to others as the people of Church Row made their way toward the deep shelter of Hampstead Tube Station.

Only I remained behind. In the far distance I heard the crump of falling bombs. I switched off the light and opened the drapes. Explosions erupted down by the river. The street below me was empty now. Stuffing Eben's letters and poems into my pockets, I retrieved his metal treasure box and my purse. Carrying these few precious things, I climbed up the steep stairs to the roof of our building.

All around the great metropolis of London, fingers of searchlights frantically combed the sky like the premiere of a Hollywood film. From this highest vantage point I looked down on the city and the river. The flotilla of barrage balloons were caught in the glow. Enemy aircraft moved through the strobe. Explosions of anti-aircraft artillery as the Nazis released their deadly cargo.

Fire and light seemed strangely beautiful, like fireworks at the New Year. Big Ben and the Houses of Parliament were bathed in a golden glow cast by the conflagration. Warehouses along the Thames as far as Greenwich burned. In the tarnished pewter smoke of the inferno I imagined glimmers of souls rising up to heaven. I began to pray the words of Psalm 91 as Mama had taught me: "A thousand shall fall at thy side, and ten thousand at thy right hand; but it shall not come nigh thee . . . Thou shalt not be afraid for the terror by night; nor for the arrow that flieth by day. . . ."[7]

I was perfectly calm; ready, no matter what befell me. Peace like a river flowed over me and into me. This peace extended far beyond the absence of fear. It was, rather, the reality of passing through the valley of the shadow of death without any fear of evil.

I set my heart on praying for those I knew were dying. A shellburst hit near the wing of a sleek silver Nazi plane. Engines sputtered flame. The craft shuddered violently as it passed above the Thames on its desperate route to the sea or perhaps with some hope of landing on the river. I followed its tortuous progress until somewhere beyond the Tower Bridge the sky erupted in a

---

[7] verses 7 and 5

starburst shower. I wondered about the pastor's son, a boy I had allowed to kiss me on a long ago summer night. Later he had betrayed his faith in Christ and betrayed his father to the Nazi tyrants. His face was clear in my thoughts. He had laughed the night we all sat up by the lake and talked about heaven. He had mocked his younger brother when he mentioned hell as the final destination for Hitler. I remembered his words: "You say this is the truth? What is truth? I say truth is only what you can experience."

Tonight the end of the world had come for so many. Was tonight the night the boy would experience truth?

Why could I not remember his name? Was the inferno I witnessed in the sky his inferno?

Suddenly I turned away, feeling deeply what a fine line every soul walks between eternal redemption and damnation. Eternity is always just a breath, a heartbeat, away.

The great battle for men's souls raged all around me. Holding tightly to Eben's treasure I returned to the stairs. The way down was illuminated momentarily by the dancing shadows of the conflagration. Closing the reinforced door, I was left in complete darkness. Groping for the wall to steady myself, I was two steps down when behind me an enormous blast sounded from the direction of the High Street. I felt a wave of energy and stumbled, holding onto my purse to keep Mama's precious cup from smashing. Eben's letterbox tumbled from my hands and clattered down the stairs.

Steadying myself, I paused a long moment before continuing. I was certain the lid had flown open, and the contents were strewn everywhere. I reached into my purse and found my flashlight, switching on the low beam. Amid the litter of receipts and ration cards I spotted the cigarette case at my feet. I retrieved it, scooping up the mess as I descended.

And then I found the blue silk scarf. Beside the scarf, Eben's secret gazed up at me from the last step.

When the "all-clear" sounded I replaced everything as it had been. I put the box back into its nest among neatly folded socks and underwear.

The kettle boiled, and I made fresh tea. My neighbors tramped back home to a fitful few hours' sleep.

I could not sleep. Though I knew somehow that I had become a part of a mystery kept for centuries, I sat down and spread Eben's letters and poems out before me on the table. The puzzle made perfect sense to me now, though I could not truly grasp it. Had my father known?

I reined in my thoughts. What was it the Lord had spoken to my heart this very night? *". . . ordinary things of life . . . notes strung together on sheet music . . . and in the end, in heaven . . . a beautiful symphony from every righteous act and every righteous life . . ."*

Perhaps I was Eben's attempt at living an ordinary life? Once again I resolved not to question Eben about his secrets unless he brought up the subject first. I read aloud his poem to me. It was the poem of an artist.

"Lora. I look out at the wide sea and can only think of the color of your eyes, my darling.

cerulean
blue
brush
stroke
me
embellished
hues
you
sigh
desire
lapping
parted
lips
tongues
of fire
sing
me

awake
waves
arousing
tranquil
sea
swelling
breaking
embracing
the shore

My darling girl, you are the one my soul has been searching for. I see your smile before me as I write down these words. Remember I told you once you are so beautiful that I would like to use your face as a model for the Madonna? I remember now where I saw the likeness: Very much like the face on an angel in the great rose window of Notre Dame. Beautiful you, my only love.
    Eternally yours,
    Eben"

32

I did not fear the bombs as long as I was in the presence of Eben. And when we were apart, each of us doing our bit in the war against Hitler, I never feared my own death. I feared only one thing in life: living without Eben.

He had traveled north to deliver a group of

Jewish children who had escaped the Nazis by hiding in the hold of a French fishing vessel. I finished a long day attempting to find foster homes for East End children outside of London.

There were four air-raid alarms that day. Smoke and death, brick and mortar dust hovered in the air along with the strong smell of cordite. I prayed that Eben would make it back to our little flat before the blackout.

I made my way home after three hours of detours. The sky seemed brighter and cleaner in Hampstead. I breathed easier. Turning on to Well Walk, I joined a long line of women at the bakery to pick up our rations at the grocer.

There were historical markers all over London and I had never paid much attention. But I glanced up at a marker on a neighboring brick house. For the first time, I noticed a blue plaque. *JOHN KEATS, POET, RESIDED HERE.*

I looked at the rippled antique glass set in the tall narrow window like a picture frame hung on aged red brick. For a moment I thought I saw the pale face of Keats gazing back at me.

There was a flash of movement on the tree limb beneath the sill. Another nightingale perched there among the branches. If he still lived, Keats could have reached out and touched the bird.

Unbidden I recalled the words to the nightingale that the poet had written, looking out the window of that house.

That I might drink, and leave the world
* unseen,*
And with thee fade away into the forest
* dim:*
Fade far away, dissolve and quite forget
What thou among the leaves hast never
* known,*
The weariness, the fever, and the fret,
Here, where men sit and hear each other
* groan . . .*

I remembered how Keats had left the woman he loved and never come back to her. The fear of losing Eben swept over me in that moment. I trembled as the women spoke of friends and family killed or wounded in the latest raids. "Keep their ration books, I tells 'er. Don't do no good for the dead. Keep their ration books and eat the rations what remain when they're gone. Why not?"

Wanting to run away, I inched forward in line, at last presenting my ration book along with Eben's. Receiving our meager portions, I hurried home to Church Row.

From the sidewalk I heard a radio playing. We did not have a radio, but looking up at our window I saw Eben's face smiling down at me. He waved.

"Eben!" I cried.

He thumped his palm against his heart and put a finger to his lips.

Running up the steep stairs I was breathless when I threw myself into his arms. He covered my face with kisses as if our time apart had been weeks instead of hours.

He whispered, "Our anniversary. Four weeks and I haven't longed for any heaven but the heaven I found in your arms."

"Oh, Eben! I was so afraid."

"Afraid?"

"That you wouldn't come home to me."

"I'll always come to you. What do you think? I bought us a radio . . . you didn't notice your anniversary present."

"No. I . . . only see you."

We closed the blackout curtains early and slow danced as Vera Lynn crooned my favorite song on the BBC.

> *"That certain night, the night we met,*
> *There was magic in the air,*
> *There were angels dining at the Ritz*
> *And a nightingale sang in Berkeley*
> *   Square . . ."*

The air-raid sirens sounded, awakening me from the contented sleep that followed after a long dance in Eben's embrace. I heard the slamming of doors and the rapid click of heels on the pavement as our neighbors ran for cover.

And then silence.

I turned to look at him, still sleeping. Beautiful dark lashes made his eyes smile even when they were closed.

"Shall we go?" I asked.

Eben's lips moved against my shoulder. "Let's stay."

"You're never afraid."

He opened his eyes. Liquid, shining, so beautiful. "Only when I am not with you."

"So perfect. Can anyone so perfect really be flesh and blood?"

He sat up and stretched. "Are you hungry? I'm hungry. Let's pack our rations and go out on the Heath. Our task tonight is to pray. We must pray like Moses prayed at the battle. We will see our boys knock the Huns out of the sky."

We dressed and packed our food in a basket and headed for our spot at the White Stone Pond. Eben spread a blanket and we lay down as the first rumble of German bombers was greeted by the sweep of searchlights and the crump of British artillery.

He watched calmly as the sky battles began. He prayed quietly in Hebrew for God to bless and send warrior angels to protect the British fighter pilots.

Fearless. His face showed no doubt that a greater, unseen battle was unfolding above our heads.

I held his hand. He did not flinch as great

explosions rocked the world and incendiaries rained like brimstone on the metropolis.

By the illumination of the fires I recognized Buckingham Palace; the Houses of Parliament; Westminster Abbey. I began to cry. Eben continued to pray. He paused, his eyes glinting green and gold in the terrible light. "Don't be afraid, Lora. England will not fall." Then he wiped my cheek with his thumb and placed my tears on his lips.

"Who are you?" I asked, speaking my questions aloud for the first time. "Eben?"

He smiled enigmatically. "Tomorrow you take the children to Harpenden?"

"Yes."

"I've never showed you where I used to live. Before . . ."

I asked, "Before Oxford? Before Hampstead?"

"I'll go with you tomorrow. Show you. If the trains from King's Cross are still running."

As he spoke there came an enormous explosion near St. Pancras and King's Cross rail stations. Overhead, to the east, a flaming German bomber exploded, its fuselage spiraling away like shooting stars.

Eben watched as the fragments dissolved. "Poor souls," he said. "Poor souls."

33

I breathed a little easier when the twelve refugee children were safely delivered to Highfield Oval in Harpenden. It was not that I expected any to disappear on the brief train journey from London to Hertfordshire, but there had been unfortunate cases. Some of the fostering families had inexplicably gotten cold feet and refused to accept evacuee children when we tried to deliver them. It was agonizing.

This tragedy was unlikely to happen at Highfield Oval, since it had been a National Children's Home since its founding in 1913. Still, it was a relief for me to see a dozen German-Jewish boys and girls comfortably settled into their dormitory rooms and hear Sister Louise exclaim over each one as if greeting long-lost relatives.

Eben Golah accompanied me on this Saturday journey. "Very impressive facility," he remarked.

"I'll keep my fingers crossed to see how well they get on with the other children," I said. "If it works I expect Highfield Oval to accept even more refugees."

"So you never stop worrying about the next placement and the next and the next?" Eben teased.

"Never!" I vowed solemnly. "I lived through

only a fraction of what these children have endured, but even so I cannot bear the thought of them being unloved and unwanted one moment longer than necessary."

Eben bowed. "I humbly acknowledge your devotion. But I have to ask: since it is too late today to place any more children, and since tomorrow afternoon will certainly be another painful experience . . . can you not perhaps give your motherly emotions the rest of the afternoon off?"

I thought he was going to suggest a cup of tea or perhaps even a film, but when I asked which he had in mind he replied, "Neither. You asked about my life. I used to live near St. Albans, a long time ago. One train stop away."

So at last Eben was going to give me a glimpse of his past. I had heard of the famous Abbey church of St. Albans. Once I had seen it as my train passed by. It loomed above the surrounding countryside from the mist. I asked the conductor the name of the place, then looked it up in my red *Baedeker's Guide*. But I had never visited it.

The church dedicated to the first British martyr was located at the top of a steep hike up from the station. As we trooped through the crowded market square, Eben did not entertain me with stories of local history, as I expected. When had he lived here? Had he been married at the time?

Along the road he paused to silently gaze upon

some building or wall as if it was an old familiar friend. He led me through an almost hidden pedestrian corridor between two buildings. We emerged in the back gardens of the ancient church.

More recent, Victorian-era pinnacles surrounded a lofty central tower of red brick. The church loomed above us. While I was impressed with the present vision, Eben's eyes grew misty with scenes of the past.

"Five hundred feet from end to end," Eben said in a reverent tone. "Second longest in England. The oldest part you can see—the tower there in the middle—was built from red brick rubble before 1100. Beneath that, a Saxon crypt. Below that . . ." He shrugged.

"It's beautiful," I said.

"It's a hodge-podge," Eben corrected. "Look: Square tower of red tile. Pointed Gothic windows. Flint-stone walls in the nave. Sold and almost scrapped in the time of Henry VIII. Restored with those elaborate Victorian stone decorations at the far ends just fifty years ago." He added, in a kinder tone, "This spot has been an object of devotion for close to 1800 years. And each succeeding generation expressed their love of this building in the way that was most meaningful to them. The entire history of Britain is woven into this building."

I looked at him curiously as he paused. Eben

stared at an enormous rose window as if it reminded him of something intensely personal.

"Was St. Albans your church?" I asked. "Your home?"

"I lived there." He gestured down the hill toward a broad expanse of open field. He began to walk, passing the entrance of the church.

I called after him, "Eben? Aren't we going in?"

He shook his head. "Later. What I have to show you can best be seen from out here."

An expanse of lawn extended down another steep slope to the south of the church. Above us a great hawk spread his wings and circled slowly. In the middle of this greensward was an ancient, gnarled oak. The hawk flew to perch in the branches nearby. It studied Eben with golden eyes. It was to this marker that Eben escorted me, placing me on a low horizontal branch as an impromptu bench.

"Look down the hill," he prompted.

I did so, taking in a creek, and a millrace, and beyond, a green pasture broken up by softly mounded stone walls. "I have the feeling like I used to have as a child when Papa told me a story."

"Yes."

I settled in. "All right then."

"My home—it was there," he said with that same faraway look. "Just there. The Romans named it Verulamium. A great city marching up

467

that hill and out of sight in the distance, all built of perfectly formed, shining red tile. A theatre. A market square. Temples. Horses and chariots. And . . . Albanus. He lived just . . . there." He pointed to a knoll.

I was certain I was being entertained with a view of the ancient world as an Oxford scholar might see it. "This is lovely. I ask the questions and you give the answers? Is that right?"

"Something like that."

It was a good game. "Tell me," I whispered, wanting to encourage this story and not interrupt it. He spoke as if telling his personal life story, and not as a historian giving a dusty lecture about the long-dead past.

"It was a major Roman town. Almost as big as Londinium. So important that it was a *municipum*, meaning, to be born here automatically made one a Roman citizen. My wife and I were born in a municipum. Both of us Jews."

"You and your wife. Roman citizens, then?"

"Yes."

"And Alban? A friend of yours."

"Yes."

"Of course."

"A Roman, of noble birth. He became a Christian when it was forbidden by Imperial decree. Penalty: death. Saved a Christian priest from being captured and killed by exchanging clothes with the man."

I knew part of the history. "The priest escaped?"

"Yes."

"Did you know him too?"

"Very well."

I laughed with delight. "Oh, Eben! You're so good at this. When the war is over you could be the world's greatest tour guide. All right. What was the priest's name?"

"He was called, when he was young, Cantor. Amphibalus was his Roman name."

"But Alban was caught."

Eben nodded. "Given a chance to recant. 'Worship Isis and all is forgiven,' Alban was told. He refused. So they took him out of the city and"—he pointed behind me at the church—"up to that very spot, where they beheaded him."

He shuddered as if his imagination was so vivid he saw himself standing in the crowd watching the execution. Once more he shook himself free of its grasp. "The Romans didn't just forbid the worship of Jesus. No, they wanted to crush it; to stamp it out utterly. They thought harsh repression could eliminate Christianity from these isles forever."

Eben pointed across the creek. "What do you see there?" he demanded.

"A field. Some ancient walls."

Eben agreed. "What remains of the Roman city. Within a hundred years after Alban, Roman rule in Britain was in trouble; in two hundred, finished. Celtic tribes forced the Romans out, burned the city; tore down the walls, and the theatre, and the temples. Now look there," he insisted, pointing again over my shoulder. "Look at the central tower of the church. What's it made of?"

"Red . . . tile?" I said, my eyes widening with comprehension.

"Alban's church is built from the rubble of Verulamium. The buildings where the pagan crowds jeered now form the church built to honor his martyrdom. Within that same two-hundred-year span there was a Christian church here. Dedicated to Alban's memory. . . . right there, where he died. And when it was time to rear a majestic tower, they built it from—"

"They reused the red tiles from the ruins of the Roman town!" I said with excitement.

"Exactly," Eben agreed. "Those who vowed to eliminate the worship of Jesus forever were themselves dispersed and forgotten within four generations. But Jesus . . ." He waved again toward the red tile pinnacle gleaming in the westering sun. "Jesus remains. And Alban's faithfulness inspires us still. And so it has been for two thousand years. That is why we cannot be afraid, Lora. Why we must not give up. Especially now with a new darkness threatening the people of the Lord."

Suddenly Eben looked sheepish. "I talk too much sometimes," he apologized. "Why don't you stop me?"

"I want to know what you know. I want to love what you love. History. It is a wonderful story."

"A true one."

I laughed. "And you were here."

"The miracle is that I am here now. With you."

"And the girl you loved."

"You are very much . . . like her."

"Your wife?"

He reached past me to touch the rugged bark of the ancient oak. "Buried here."

The hawk, startled by Eben's move, launched himself into the air with a flutter of wings.

I stood, suddenly chilled. Was this only a game? Or did Eben believe in fairy tales? "Buried here? Where?"

"Beneath this oak."

I stepped away from the massive tree. I did not ask him any more questions.

We did not enter St. Albans church that day. I thought as our train rattled back to London that perhaps the strain of events had driven Eben just a bit mad.

He asked me, "You are so quiet. What's wrong?"

I answered truthfully, "I'm disappointed. That's all."

"Disappointed?"

"I hoped you brought me here to share something about yourself. Your life. About her."

"Ah. It's just as well. Sorry." He lapsed into silence. He gazed out the window at the green fields and grazing sheep of the English countryside. I studied his clasped hands. Young. Beautiful. Strong. I imagined him in love with a girl who looked like me. I imagined his hands holding her. Did she rise to his touch like the crescendo of a symphony? And then, unbidden, the vision came of Eben's hands on me. I longed to lie in his arms and dance with him again. It was clear he must have loved her very much. I wondered if it was possible for Eben to love me as he had loved her? I knew I loved Eben with the passion of a woman.

34

I did not ask Eben the questions swirling in my brain after our visit to St. Albans. I was afraid of the answers, I suppose.

The guns of summer boomed into autumn, like near lightning strikes on the Heath. In Hampstead we called our two neighborhood anti-aircraft weapons, St. John and St. James, after the Sons of Thunder in the Gospels.

Eben told me he thought the two apostles would have been amused by the compliment. His casual smile at the remark sent my brain reeling.

"How would you know such a thing?" I challenged.

"They seem to have been fellows with a sense of humor." He kissed me good-bye as we each departed separate ways for work. His answer was not an answer.

At tea I studied the notes about the "Thirty-six" I had gleaned from the British Museum. It was good I had gotten the information. The Museum's Reading Room had finally closed, due to bomb damage.

Still, I was afraid to ask Eben directly what he knew about the Lamed Vav of legends.

Daytime in London was close to normal. It was a matter of pride for us to hold our chins up, square our shoulders, and return to work. The red buses continued to run through bomb-damaged neighborhoods. Winston and Clemmie toured neighborhoods. The king and queen, whose palace had been hit, made the rounds of demolished row houses and visited the wounded in hospital.

Eben and I continued to seek and find placement for evacuee children and refugees who were now homeless. His daily meetings and journeys were intense, and often he did not return to me until after blackout.

The sirens sent up the alarm about seven each evening when the German bombers reached the coastline. About a quarter of an hour after that, James and John began to bellow. Shells flew up miles into the air, then exploded at a certain altitude, setting off a great flash in the sky. The fragments were meant to hit the enemy bombers and hopefully knock them down. The laws of gravity proved dangerous. The shrapnel from our friendly shells tumbled from the sky, piercing roofs, shattering automobiles, and sometimes hitting people. Men in uniform were required to carry steel helmets. Those of us counted among the civilian population preferred our umbrellas. Not even a tin hat could stop a fragment of hot metal falling from a mile high.

Some evenings the Luftwaffe passed over London on their way to drop the deadly cargo on other English cities. Returning to Reich airfields late at night, the Nazis often dropped a spare bomb on a London neighborhood.

We called such single bombs "incidents." But when we passed the sites of such "incidents," it was likely that an entire block of houses had been taken out.

In spite of this, Eben and I did not take cover among the thousands of Londoners below ground in the tube stations. Each night we made our way to the White Stone Pond and watched and prayed as life and death for a nation and the world was played out above us and around us. We held one another and, when silence fell at last, we listened for the song of the nightingale from the tree beside the water.

"We should go," Eben said.

"Not yet. It is the nightingale and not the lark."

He did not pick up my cue from *Romeo and Juliet*. Instead, he focused his gaze on the blazes across London.

It had been an especially violent bombing that night in late September. Thousands of incendiaries were dropped on Central London. Beneath us the skyline bloomed like bright strawberries linked by a twisted vine of orange flame.

"Very bad tonight." I leaned my head against Eben. It was still dark when the all-clear sounded.

His dark eyes reflected the carnage. "We sat upon this very hill when the great fire. . . ."

"Where are you? Where did you go?" I held his arm tighter.

"Another time."

Did he mean he would tell me at another time? Or that he was envisioning another time?

I asked, "When?"

"It's nothing. Nothing. From this vantage point it seems as if I've seen it all before."

"Eben! What are you talking about? What do you see? Tell me."

He glanced down at me briefly. "You know."

"I don't know."

"Your father knew."

"Papa?" All the things my father had said about

Eben came back to me. The ancient voice. The nightingale.

"Lora." Eben spoke my name with a finality, as if he was speaking the name of someone who had already lived and died.

I drew back. "Eben, you frighten me."

Long minutes passed. In the distance explosions rocked Central London. The sound reverberated against the hills.

"I took you to St. Albans. You heard the story."

"The story—I understand the words, but not the nuance."

"Life is nuance."

"Then you must show me. I don't understand."

He squeezed my hand. "Your notebook. It fell from the table."

"The Thirty-six?"

He sighed with relief. "The legend."

"What is the truth?"

His skin seemed golden, ethereal, as if the light came from within him. "There were many more than Thirty-six in the beginning."

I managed to whisper, "Tell me."

"Haven't I tried?"

"No. Tell me plainly. In plain words. My future. The nuance is too high for me to grasp. I will grow old. If I live ten years? Twenty years? Forty years? Who . . . what . . . are you?"

"Plainly, then. After the Cross. After the great earthquake. After Yeshua's resurrection. Matthew wrote what he witnessed with his own eyes. How many were raised and seen alive in Jerusalem's streets? Only thirty-six?"

My mind leapt to Lazarus. Then to the son of the widow of Nain. The daughter of the official of Capernaum. All were raised by Jesus from death. Had they returned to life, only to die again?

"Who . . . are . . . you?" Suspicions and fantasy came into sudden focus. My words were a hoarse whisper. The nightingale began to sing from her perch.

Eben lowered his chin and gazed into the White Stone Pond. "A thousand years is as a day unto the Lord."

"And two thousand years?"

"Some who were healed by Yeshua and managed to escape martyrdom lived on."

"On?"

"Centuries."

"And you?"

"Eben means 'stone.' The Hebrew letters, read in reverse, mean 'prophesy.' I was given the name . . . some time ago. I use it now . . . hoping. As for my past, here sits one whose name is written in water."

I began to weep as I saw in a very few years that time would come between us. "Eben! What is to become of me? What is our future?"

He folded me in an embrace as if comforting a frightened child. "The hours grow short.

Everything we have looked for . . . every word of Scripture. This is the beginning. Birthpangs. Terrible pain, increasing. Israel must be reborn. Prophecy proven. Messiah will come in that generation. And so the devil grows more fierce against the people of the Covenant." He kissed my brow again. "Until then we few remain strong and faithful until the King of heaven and earth returns."

The pastel sky ripened as we walked slowly home. I heard the church bells call the faithful to prayer. The ringing declared life must go on. One more day for those who had survived the night.

Eben opened the blackout curtains. Dawn flooded the room. We lay together on our bed and made love as though it were the last sweet morning of the world.

We had named the injured nightingale Rosalind. It was an elegant name I had always admired. Papa called me Rosalind in jest sometimes, in my more dramatic adolescent years. I fancied the name as a pseudonym if ever I went on stage as an actress.

When Eben sang to the nightingale, Rosalind's wings flicked with delight, and her golden eyes gleamed when she looked at him. She was indifferent to me. As she healed, I was of no more emotional significance in her little brain than the wind. I merely moved her cage from one patch of sunlight to the other. I was her source of bread crumbs and fresh water. But the sweet crooning of Eben Golah made her want to live.

"You are the Bing Crosby of the bird kingdom," I teased.

Eben sang a comic Bing reply: "You are Paradise . . . her eyes afire with one desire . . ."

I laughed as our nightingale fluttered jealously in her cage.

"She's ready to go back to her one true love," I said.

"I know a little fella who's awaiting his gal on Primrose Hill."

"Let's hope he hasn't found a new love while she's been gone."

We covered the birdcage with a pillowcase lest Rosalind keel over from the shock of London traffic. Boarding the bus, we traveled to Primrose Village, returning to the place we had found her.

"Do you think he waited for her?" I scanned the trees.

Eben set the cage on the grass, unperturbed. "He's been waiting. You'll see. The path of true love and all that."

I opened the cage door and Eben offered his index finger as a perch. The bird stepped on his hand and remained in his palm for a long moment. With perfect mimicry, Eben whistled, summoning the lonely male from his perch. The leaves rustled nearby.

"Look! There he is, Lora!"

In an instant Rosalind spotted her beloved and flew to his side. The two groomed one another as if her time away had been nothing but a bad dream.

"I'll miss her," Eben said as we hurried back to the bus stop.

"Would you wait for me, Eben?" I asked.

"Forever." He clasped my hand and kissed my fingers. "My Rosalind."

"Tonight I expect you to sing to me too."

"Anything. As long as you promise never to fly away."

35

On the morning of December 22 I awakened to the tinkling of wind chimes outside our Hampstead window. During the worst of the bombing Eben had carefully picked through shards of stained glass from the shattered windows of a Christopher Wren church. For weeks he had laid the pieces out on our table. A nightingale. Roses: crimson and white. A flaming heart. An angel's fingers on a flute. Coral lips smiling. Patiently he drilled a hole in each fragment and strung them together into a wind chime and hung it outside the window. The sun shone through the glass, casting a bouquet of color on the floor.

Who is this man? I wondered in awe as I watched him work. From brokenness, he created a song for me.

That morning I opened my eyes and reached out for Eben. His side of the bed was empty. A fleeting instant of panic seized me, then I remembered his trip to Oxford. The last Jews in Berlin were deported to Polish ghettos. Nazi brutality against God's beloved people escalated beyond human imagination.

Eben was meeting with C. S. Lewis and a group who could rally public support to lift the immigration ban on Jewish refugees fleeing to the British Mandate of Palestine.

He had planned a great Christmas surprise for me, he told me. I was to follow him on the afternoon train. My valise was packed in preparation for a long, passionate weekend at an old Elizabethan-era inn that he knew well.

On the pillow beside me was a folded parchment, inscribed in Eben's elegant hand: *Happy Christmas, my dearest!* I opened the letter to find a poem.

WINDCHIMES

Forest
rush
wind
chimes

sing
me
awake
beside
you
breathe
my name
again
please
you
touch
my
lips
burning
whisper
familiar
sighs
kindle
fire
warming
my
Rugged
Heart

Every word, every thought, of him was incendiary. Even after four months of love, the embers were never fully quenched. Kindled by the thought of him, I lay in bed and read his words again and again in different combinations: *"breathe my name again, please . . ."* and: *"please you . . ." and: "sing me awake beside you . . ."*

There was magic in his poetry. I said his name, "Eben!" Throwing back the heavy curtains, I inhaled the winter morning and stood dripping in Eben's pool of color.

Though my train would not leave for hours, I hurried to bathe and wash my hair. I could not think of eating. I could only imagine him meeting me at the Oxford train station, sweeping me off my feet, and carrying me away to his secret hideaway.

The train to Oxford was slow, stopping at every village along the way. I brought a copy of *Sense and Sensibility* to read but never opened it. I gazed out the window at snow-covered pastures. Here and there was evidence of bombing. The rail lines and manufacturers had been a target of the Germans. Yet still my brave little adopted island homeland stood firm. I was in awe that England was still England after a year of brutal pummeling by the Nazis. Perhaps soon the Americans would come in as Churchill hoped and Eben predicted, and then we would win back the world. Eben and I would work together for a Jewish homeland in Israel.

The clatter of wheels on the tracks and the chatter of passengers did not penetrate my consciousness.

I prayed for Eben's success and for our future as the hours passed.

It was the golden hour when the spires of Oxford University appeared outside my window like a painting from a medieval fairytale. I strained to see Eben as the train finally reached the Oxford station.

He was there, waiting, his hat in his hands. His head was down. His usual smile was absent. I knew with a glance that something was terribly wrong. Had the meeting gone badly? Had his ideas been rejected?

I picked up my valise and was already standing when the locomotive lurched to a stop almost directly beside him.

I shouted his name, certain that no matter what was wrong, I could help him work through it.

He raised his gaze to me. Such sorrow. Such terrible grief.

I disembarked. He did not come toward me but only stood with his gaze riveted on me. My smile faded. I was filled with a sense of dread.

Kissing him lightly, I asked, "Eben? What is it?"

He took my bag, then linked his arm in mine. "Not here. We can't talk about it here."

On the walk from the train station Eben said nothing. I kept shooting glances at him, unsuccessfully trying to catch his eye. He stalked, wrapped in his overcoat, his head bowed almost to his chest, shoulders stiffly braced, striding into the icy breeze.

"Eben, what? Please tell me," I implored. The wintry air was nothing compared to the chill gripping my heart. "I can help, whatever it is."

He raised his gloved hand, palm outward, in a gesture of denial. It felt as if he were pushing me away. I felt something like a dagger pierce my innermost senses, especially when I saw his upraised fingers trembling violently.

His color was gray, ashen. His eyes, always so bright with life, darted everywhere, but focused on nothing. He walked ahead of me, almost lurching from step to step over the cobblestones.

What could it be? Some terrible news from abroad?

Since the fall of France precious few souls had escaped from Hitler's Fortress Europe; fewer still from the eastern reaches of the Nazi Empire. Still, some of those rare, brave individuals who managed to get free brought horror stories of what was happening in the camps for political prisoners. We had heard of slave laborers, living on meager rations and dying of pneumonia and typhus in unbelievably crowded conditions.

Could such news have reached Eben? Could bearing the burden of such tales be what was crushing him?

Or was it something to do with his work with the Jewish Agency? Some new tragedy unfolding in the British Mandate, dashing all our hopes for a Jewish homeland?

The station of the London and Northwestern Railway lay at the extreme west end of Oxford. After crossing the canal on Bridge Street we entered the university precincts. A clinging drizzle began to fall as we set our backs to the spires and quadrangles, passing Worcester College on our way up Walton.

And still Eben did not speak.

These past four months had been the happiest I had ever known. Nothing must be permitted to break that. Nothing would be permitted to!

As we turned onto Great Clarenden I recognized our destination from Eben's description. Tudor, from white-washed walls and exposed beams to sway-backed ridge line, the Burleigh Arms perched amid the bare trunks and naked thorns of last summer's roses.

Amid the skeletons a single white rose bush soldiered on, sheltered between a corner of the inn and a brick wall. Its few remaining leaves and fewer blooms sagged beneath the weight of rain dripping from the eaves.

"Oh!" I exclaimed, clasping Eben's arm. "The inn is beautiful. Wonderful!" I wanted desperately to sound cheerful; to rouse him from the depression that had claimed him.

Acting desperately cheerful does not help.

He did look at me then—a stare so bleak, so full of despair, that I shuddered.

Suddenly the inn was not pleasing, not remotely

appealing. The winter-blasted garden seemed fraught with decay, like a neglected churchyard.

We did not stop to admire the gabled entry, or respond to the cheerful greeting of the bald-headed innkeeper, but went straight up a crooked flight of steps. From a hallway just over the entrance we entered our room.

The chamber, with canopied bed and jutting bay window and cozy, flickering fire, was picture-perfect . . . it was the occupants who were dismal.

Flinging his overcoat onto the floor, Eben threw himself down in one of the chairs drawn up to a mother-of-pearl inlaid table. He pushed aside a bowl of freshly cut white roses. Somewhere, even in these near Christmas days, he had located and purchased flowers for me.

Then what was wrong? Why was my heart so apprehensive?

Eben removed the stopper from a crystal sherry decanter. Without offering me a glass he poured a goblet of pale amber fluid for himself, drank it off, and poured another. He looked grim, haggard, and something I had never observed in him before: he looked old.

"Eben, you must tell me! What is it? We're alone, now. Tell me."

Still without speaking he reached into the breast pocket of his suit coat.

Withdrawing a folded piece of light blue

stationery, he tossed it onto the table where it fell across the blossoms. "Read it," he said.

Fearful beyond imagining, my nervous fingers plucked at the letter, tearing a bit off a corner as I opened it. I scanned it, terrified at what I would find written there.

In response to your inquiry, it said, *here is what we have determined. The subject in question, Varrick Kepler, is confirmed to be alive and a Prisoner-of-War.*

There was more, but my eyes no longer made sense of the words; my fingers no longer retained enough strength to keep a grip on the message. It fluttered to the floor.

"Varrick," I said. "He's alive!" And then, "Varrick is . . . alive." My heart racing, my head spinning, I felt joy, amazement, and horror—each succeeding the other, racing through my emotions. One hand groped for the arm of a chair as I felt myself sinking, sinking.

Eben was on his feet then, guiding me as I sat, pouring a glass of wine and thrusting it into my hand.

When the chamber stopped spinning, and I could see again, Eben was on his knees in front of me. He also gripped my chair, as if needing the prop to hold himself upright.

"He's alive," I repeated. "Wonderful news, but . . . but Eben, I love you. I love . . . *you.*"

"And I you."

"We were kids, just kids, Varrick and I. I wasn't even the same; I'm a different person now. Varrick and I—that was a whole lifetime ago, after you . . . since you and I . . . ."

Fiercely he said, "I won't give you up. I won't! They say I must, but I won't. I can't live without you."

And then I was in his arms. His kisses were greedy, demanding. I returned them the same way. The news—the war—shattered lives on all sides. But in this room, warmed by the fire, surrounded by sheltering walls and enclosed by Eben's arms, what did anything else matter? What could take from us our happiness? What could take us from each other? *Nothing!* I demanded of myself and God. *I won't let anything part us!*

Sweeping me up in powerful arms he carried me to the bed.

"Don't stop," I urged. "I am yours. No one's but yours."

Though the rain turned to sleet and the storm slashed at the windows, all the world outside our sanctuary disappeared. Loving, dozing, awakening, and being awakened . . . everything I wanted was beside me.

I lay awake, my face on Eben's chest. His heartbeat, strong and steady, reassured me. I wanted nothing better, no greater happiness, than to live in this moment, always. Whatever was outside this room could not touch what we had. Whatever might happen, we would face it, together, and overcome it.

Eben's heart kept perfect rhythm with the mantel clock above the fireplace. Lifting my head ever so carefully so as not to rouse my love, I noted the time: not quite midnight; 11:46 exactly.

That vision, when the clock hands were so near to clasping each other, and to embracing the new day, is forever engraved in my thoughts. For at the instant the time registered with me a distant air-raid siren began its wavering cry.

How could there be a raid in such a storm? No pilots could locate a target beneath such a concealing cloak. "Eben," I said drowsily, "the alarm. Shall we go to a shelter?"

"Umm?" he murmured.

Like a string of signal fires, each igniting the next, another air-raid signal wailed, still closer, and then another. I remember thinking, *Why would anyone bomb Oxford?*

And then a shrill whistle overcame the angry wind, driving sleet, and insistent sirens.

Eben's eyes snapped open, locking on mine in startled disbelief. And then the war, the devastation, the heartache rushed in upon us.

I don't recall hearing the bomb explode or feeling the blast. The floor suddenly was compressed toward the ceiling and the outside wall toward the fireplace.

And then I was somewhere . . . else.

I felt no pain. I knew no fear. I saw with a clarity unequalled in my life. There was no sleet, no smoke, no dust, only a view down a tunnel toward what remained of a shattered four-poster bed and fragments of a mother-of-pearl table. Beside it, kneeling, I recognized Eben. He was holding something to him with a desperate, frantic clutch.

He held me—my body—in his arms.

He rocked and then stopped, staring into my open, unseeing eyes. I heard him cry out and hang on even tighter than before. His shoulders bobbed, and his body swayed, as though in prayer before the Temple. I saw his face, when he raised it towards heaven, streaked with my blood, mingled with his tears, and creased with anguish.

"Lora," I heard him cry. "Lora! Don't go. Don't leave me." He was begging, pleading. "Oh, God, don't take her from me."

"Lora?" I heard another voice echoing my name.

I don't recall turning away from Eben, yet I was looking down a hallway I knew faced the opposite direction. At the end I saw someone waving, silhouetted against a bright but pleasant glow. "Lora," Papa called. "I'm here. Here I am, Loralei." Mama was beside him.

The two cries, one grieving, one welcoming, mingled.

"Lora," Eben sobbed. "God, don't take her. Please, my Lord! You said if it was Your will that we live until You come, what is that to anyone? She is everything to me! My Lord, let her live. I'll do whatever You ask. I will give her up. Only let my Lora live again. Let her live again. Bring her back! I surrender to You, Lord! She is not mine; she is Yours. Lora, come back!"

Time was nothing. I felt a longing to go to Mama and Papa and others whom I sensed were near. Hovering above Eben for a time, I watched as he gathered my limp body in his arms and carried me to a sofa. He smoothed my hair. Kissing my lips, he lingered over me, saying my name again and again.

Darkness.

Something was compressing my chest. I could not see what. Bits of powder sifted onto my cheeks. Snow? Ashes? I could not move my arms to brush it away.

When at last I summoned the strength to open my eyes I looked up into the face of a man wearing a tin helmet bearing the initials *A.R.P.* "'ere," he called over his shoulder. "This 'uns alive, right enough. Bloomin' miracle, it is. Hey, mister, you was right. She's alive. Mister? Mister?"

Where was Eben?

I drifted for a time. I knew only that four men carried me on a stretcher. It seemed that hours of hauling and pulling, digging and backtracking, were needed to maneuver me out of the wreckage of the inn.

I came to when they transferred me to a hospital bed. Something fell out of the blanket and onto the floor.

The nurse picked it up and placed it on my pillow.

"Must've been your good-luck charm," she said.

It was a single white rose.

I remained in London through the war. I did not see Eben again.

After the war ended and the truth of the Holocaust was revealed, the nation of Israel was reborn in 1948, just as Eben predicted. A new war to annihilate the Jews began against Israel as the returning survivors of the death camps reached her shores. Or perhaps it was the same war against the Jews, continued in a new way.

It was six years after we had parted before I saw Varrick again. We were strangers when we embraced one another. He had grown into a man—handsome and hardened, eager to fight the new wars facing Israel.

Though I longed to remain in England, I made a new life with Varrick. I learned to love him again, and discovered the love of our youth had ripened into something rich. He needed me. I needed him. We were to one another like anchors, mooring two ships in stormy waters. Varrick was a warrior to his core and I lived the life of a soldier's wife. We had one child together, a son. Our baby was handsome and bright like his father. With the baby, the focus of my life changed. Eben receded further in my memory. Varrick was a wonderful father, and I was thankful, yes, thankful, the Lord had preserved Varrick and brought him back into my life.

My longing for Eben lay dormant during those happy years as Varrick's wife and the mother of our son.

In quiet moments, I quoted Keats: *"Was it a vision, or a waking dream?"* Only sometimes I remembered, unwillingly, our brief days of passion and love in Hampstead. When I was alone, there were nights when I thought I heard the nightingale, and I dreamed of Eben's face just above me.

Once, in Tel Aviv, I thought I saw him. He was on a passing bus as I was pushing a baby carriage and shopping. His profile, so cherished and distinct when we were together, seemed unmistakable to me. I shouted his name and raised my hand to hail him, but he did not hear my voice. It was probably better for both of us, I reasoned. What would I say to him? How could I thank him for sacrificing happiness to bring back my life? Heaven had been so beautiful. Better heaven than life without Eben, I had thought in Oxford, and later, alone in London. But I was wrong. Life, even without the love of my life, was sweet. There was heaven here on earth as I held my baby in my arms.

As the years passed, I wondered if Eben would recognize me if we ever met. Then I looked in the mirror and saw that my face had not changed in the years since he left me lying on the bed in the room in the Burleigh Inn that Christmas. My youth remained undimmed.

I lived on, content without him as uncounted women have lived with loss for untold centuries. Our love was written in water. I had so longed for it to be written in stone. Again the words of Keats reminded me, *"Fled is the music: do I wake or sleep?"*

My world was once again turned upside down in 1956. The Sinai Campaign was fought to put an end to terrorist incursions into Israel and to end the Egyptian blockade of Eilat. Varrick was among the Israeli field commanders who transformed the IDF into a professional army. He was at the heart of the planning. I did not see Varrick after the first of October 1956. He was involved in creating the battle plan for the operation.

October 29, Varrick was one of the soldiers who parachuted into the eastern approaches of the Mitla Pass near the Suez Canal. The French and British gave an ultimatum to Israel and Egypt, calling on both sides to withdraw from the canal area.

On October 30, in spite of the British and French ultimatum, heavy fighting between Egyptian and Israeli units raged. In an operation of a hundred hours, under the leadership of Moshe Dayan, the Sinai Peninsula fell into Israeli hands. The cost of our victory was the lives of 231 Israeli soldiers killed.

On October 31, 1956, there came a knock on my door in Tel Aviv. I was faced by IDF officers, dear friends of Varrick, who gave me the news that my husband had been killed in action. This time there was no question.

EPILOGUE

The embers on the grate glowed red and gold. I caressed the cover of the journal and closed my eyes for a long moment. *Could it be?* I wondered silently. A row of three Meissen teacups stood as honored sentries on a high shelf.

Moments passed. There was a footstep in the room behind me. The nightingale rustled her feathers in the cage beside the piano. It then began to sing.

I gasped and raised my eyes to meet Loralei's unwavering gaze. Beside the beautiful young woman stood a strong, dark-red-haired young man of about thirty, dressed in a brown tweed jacket and moleskin trousers.

Loralei's red lips curved in a gentle smile as she observed my expression of wonder. "The nightingale always begins to sing when Evan comes into the room, Bodie."

"Evan?" I closed my eyes again and covered my face with my hands.

Loralei answered, "My husband. Evan."

497

The man spoke. "Evan. A good English name, don't you think?"

"Oh," I cried. "Oh! When I saw your face at the door tonight, I thought of the photograph: Lora at the White Rose Inn. And Eben standing behind her. Look at you!"

He went to the bookshelf and removed a battered metal box. Opening it, he smiled down at the contents and passed it to Loralei. She carefully unfolded the blue silk scarf and showed me what she had seen that night when the bombs rained down on London.

An enameled tin mask of a man's face, perfect in every detail, lay within.

I gasped. "Judah?"

Evan nodded and answered my question with a quiet compassion. "One of many names over the years."

So it was out. I began to cry quietly and asked stupidly, "Did you ever find the woman . . . the one pictured in the cigarette case?"

Loralei smiled. "Yes. Eben found her many years later. She was glad to have it back. Glad to know." She knelt beside me and wiped my tear with her finger, placing it to her lips. "Don't cry, my dear friend. I've wanted to tell you everything for so long. But . . . you understand."

"Only letters. Never face to face." My thoughts tumbled through my mind faster than I could speak. "But I heard the voice of a woman upstairs. An old woman's voice."

Loralei replied, "My sister, Jessica, lives with us."

I stammered as understanding stole my breath. "It was you! You've not grown old! But . . . you are . . . you . . . both of you . . ."

Evan opened the birdcage door and extended his hand. The nightingale hopped onto his finger and remained as Evan held the songbird close to his cheek and stroked the tiny feathered head. "It is almost midnight for the world. These are the final moments of *The Book of Hours.* We who remain have been granted permission . . . live . . . until He returns."

The vivid memory of Jesus' words in Scripture exploded in my mind: *"And if I want him to live until I return, what is that to you?"*

Evan smiled. "We wanted you here with us tonight. Sixty-eight years since that night in Oxford. The blink of an eye. We thought of you when Lora found the injured bird in the garden."

Loralei said, "That generation almost all flown away now. So many old friends. Soon Jessica will leave us. But you—you must save the memories."

Evan completed the thought, "The sages say that the ink of the scribe is as precious in the eyes of the Lord as the blood of the martyr."

Loralei nodded. "You must write what we were in that generation. How the world turned away and what apathy and ignorance cost in the end."

Evan lowered his chin and held me fast with his green-gold eyes. "We have begun a new life now. A new generation. The names of those two lovers who lived in the garret room above this house are written in water. But their love and their stories must be recorded in stone."

Evan moved toward the French doors, throwing them wide to the garden. "The past must not be forgotten." Tucking the bird beneath his chin he motioned, beckoning us both out into the frigid night air.

The stars shone clear and bright like a diamond pathway above our heads. Light from the lamp beside the piano fell upon the trellis of a rose tree. A few brown-tinged leaves stirred as suddenly a second nightingale hopped out. The male bird cocked his head and eyed them expectantly.

Loralei whispered, "Look! There he is, Eben!"

Evan nodded. "He's been waiting there for her, Lora. Singing to her every night. Waiting until she was free."

Loralei put her arm around my shoulders. "So many songs yet to sing . . ."

Evan lifted his hand, releasing the nightingale. She hesitated only a moment, then, seeing her mate, fluttered away to his side.

"Adieu! Adieu! Thy plaintive anthem fades
Past the near meadows, over the still stream,
Up the hill-side, and now 'tis buried deep
In the next valley glades:
Was it a vision, or a waking dream?
Fled is that music: do I wake or sleep?"[8]

---

[8] John Keats, "Ode to a Nightingale."

TAKING IT DEEPER . . .
Questions for individuals and groups

1. For over ten years, Bodie the journalist has been intrigued by Loralei's life story. Whose life story intrigues you? What interests you specifically about that person? If you could interview him or her for ten minutes, what questions would you ask?

2. "I was both fascinated and terrified by the thought that Eben might be my nightingale" (p. 56). "He sacrificed himself to save the white rose. He gave his life for hers. By the shedding of his blood, the white rose was given life. A picture of Christ, some say" (p. 56). How did Eben truly become Lora's "nightingale" toward the end of the book? What price did he pay, in return, for loving his white rose? How does this help you understand Jesus' sacrifice for you?

3. "Knowing I'm right is not the same as *showing* I am, in front of people who might otherwise believe such stupidity . . . things will only get worse. If I . . . if *we* are not prepared for *everything* to come, this lunacy will continue until . . . I don't know what will happen. I just know that they're very bad

people, the ones who make these claims based on *science,* and they will use gullible people to do unspeakable things if we don't all know how to speak up." Do you agree with Varrick's statements (p. 66)? Why or why not? What examples can you give from history—and the lives of your loved ones? In what situation *now* can you make a difference if you take a stand?

4. Lora, an American, makes a stunning decision to marry her friend Varrick, in order to keep this member of the Kepler family safe from the Nazis (pp. 95-96). Would you have made the same decision? Why or why not? What life event(s) do you look back on now that caused you to suddenly grow up? To see things from a different light?

5. "It seemed incredibly unjust that Judah and the good sergeant, who had accomplished so much and brought us so far, should have died so near to safety . . . it left me feeling bitter and angry" (p. 258). If Lora could have known then that Judah didn't die but lived on, how would that have changed her perspective? If you could look down the road a few years and see "the good" that may come from a current situation in your life,

how might your perspective change to make you less bitter and angry?

6. "The world as we knew it was coming to an end, yet I could only think of myself," Lora says (p. 262). "It was as though there was no tragedy . . . no story but my own. There was me, selfish and self-absorbed . . . and then were those hundreds of thousands of refugees all lumped together into one tragedy." When life gets chaotic, do you tend to become more "me-centered" or "other-centered"? Why do you think that is? What patterns did you see modeled in your own family as you were growing up?

7. The young Belgian girl, Inga, has gone through such traumatic circumstances that she wishes she were dead (p. 373). Have you ever felt hopeless and depressed, like Inga? How did you respond during those times? Who helped you endure and fight through them? In what way(s) can those tough times strengthen you for the road ahead? How might you encourage others who are going through similar hard times?

8. Eben sits for hours with Lora in the Paddington tearoom as she recounts her story (p. 307). "His eyes, tender, were fixed on me,

drawing me out of myself. I talked more than I had intended. I wept without embarrassment. At the same time his gentle questions drew me into his soul. He wiped my tears like an old familiar friend." When you have felt "inside-out," as Lora did that day, whom do you turn to? Why is that person so comfortable for you?

9. Were you surprised that Lora found love with Eben, and that they married? Why or why not?

10. In a London park Lora meets a middle-aged woman with a pleasant smile. The woman asks Lora questions about Eben's photographs, then points out the Hebrew words embedded in the pattern of each rose in his poem. Lora is stunned, because she hadn't even seen them until her eyes were opened by the woman's words: "Everything means something" (p. 333). Have you ever encountered a person you thought might be "an angel," sent to help you? If so, tell the story.

11. Do you believe it could be possible that there are Thirty-six Righteous (witnesses of God's glory) walking the earth today, holding back God's judgment against the earth? (pp. 397-

400) Why or why not? How could the *possibility* of it being true influence the way you look at others? Respond to others? The way you relate to your Creator?

12. Would you want your name to be written in water (p. 495)—or stone? Explain.

13. Step into Lora's shoes for a moment. You're married to the love of your life when you discover that your first husband, whom you thought was dead, is actually alive (p. 488)! What would you think? Feel? How would you resolve the situation?

14. Do you believe that "We must speak for those who have no voice" (p. 287)? Why or why not? How are you actively "speaking" your beliefs? What are you doing for "the least of these"?

15. Every life has a story to tell. What about your life might be intriguing to "the next generation"? What events might give them hope in the midst of their own tumultuous journeys? Why not share your story? (Even better, write it down!)

ABOUT THE AUTHORS

BODIE and BROCK THOENE (pronounced *Tay-nee)* have written over fifty works of historical fiction. That these best sellers have sold more than twenty million copies and won eight ECPA Gold Medallion Awards affirms what millions of readers have already discovered—that the Thoenes are not only master stylists but experts at capturing readers' minds and hearts.

In their timeless classic series about Israel (The Zion Chronicles, The Zion Covenant, The Zion Legacy), the Thoenes' love for both story and research shines. With The Shiloh Legacy and *Shiloh Autumn* (poignant portrayals of the American Depression), The Galway Chronicles (dramatic stories of the 1840s famine in Ireland), and the Legends of the West (gripping tales of adventure and danger in a land without law), the Thoenes have made their mark in modern history. In the A.D. Chronicles they step seamlessly into the world of Jerusalem and Rome, in the days when Yeshua walked the earth. Now the Zion Diaries cover the time period between their best-selling Zion Covenant series (1936–1940) and Zion Chronicles series (1947–1948). "These timeless tales are the missing pieces of the lives of some of the most beloved characters from our

Zion Chronicles and Zion Covenant series," the Thoenes say. "Their compelling stories of courage and love chronicle the darkest of times, when good seemed lost, but God's Truth stood firm and shone as a beacon in the midst of Hitler's evil. Based on decades of interviews and divine encounters, the Zion Diaries are our most up-close and personal books ever."

Bodie, who has degrees in journalism and communications, began her writing career as a teen journalist for her local newspaper. Eventually her byline appeared in prestigious periodicals such as *U.S. News and World Report*, *The American West*, and *The Saturday Evening Post*. She also worked for John Wayne's Batjac Productions and ABC Circle Films as a writer and researcher. John Wayne described her as "a writer with talent that captures the people and the times!" Long intrigued by the personal accounts of history, and the romantic and often mysterious stories based in Hawaii, Bodie has also authored *Love Finds You in Lahaina, Hawaii.* "There, the past and the present overlap through the lives of elders sharing their memories," Bodie says. "When I met an old Hawaiian woman, who was making *leis* in the shade of Lahaina's banyan tree, I was entranced by her photos—and her personal remembrances of Princess Kaiulani. The rumors she shared shed new light on the old story, as if Romeo and Juliet had a happy ending. As she told me the legends and the romance, I knew I must write it one day."

Brock has often been described by Bodie as "an essential half of this writing team." With degrees in both history and education, Brock has, in his role as researcher and story-line consultant, added the vital dimension of historical accuracy. Due to such careful research, the Zion Covenant and Zion Chronicles series are recognized by the American Library Association, as well as Zionist libraries around the world, as classic historical novels and are used to teach history in college.

Bodie and her husband, Brock, have four grown children—Rachel, Jake, Luke, and Ellie—and seven grandchildren. Their children are carrying on the Thoene family talent as the next generation of writers, and Luke produces the Thoene audiobooks. Bodie and Brock divide their time between Hawaii, London, and Nevada.

www.thoenebooks.com
www.summersidepress.com
www.familyaudiolibrary

Center Point Publishing
600 Brooks Road ● PO Box 1
Thorndike ME 04986-0001 USA

(207) 568-3717

US & Canada:
1 800 929-9108
www.centerpointlargeprint.com